"VIRGIN, GIVE ME YOUR LOVE," THE DRAGON SIGHED.

"You're joking!" I yelped.

"Joking? I fully intend to explore the matter of mortal humor in the future. First, however, sex."

"Se—se—sex—? *You don't mean that!* With another dragon, surely, but not with—You can't—You know, if by some stretch of the—the imagination it were possible—which it isn't!—I wouldn't be a virgin anymore. Then what would you do if a unicorn came traipsing in here?"

"I have been lucky so far. I feel that the loss of my life to a unicorn would be a small price to pay for gaining firsthand knowledge of mortal love. Besides, I'm lonely." So saying, he tumbled over on his side and rubbed his beaky mouth against my legs. "So how about it?"

I squeaked and scampered to the summit of the tallest pile of gold in the cave, but bullion doesn't provide much traction. I came skidding down again and fetched up against the dragon's partially opened jaws.

"Foolish virgin," said the dragon, renewing the pussycat act with belligerent tenderness. "You know that I do not ask the impossible. I am cognizant of the laws of physics. I would not suggest anything to hurt you. You will thank me for it someday. I will be gentle. I will be considerate. I will respect you afterwards. I will not think solely of my own pleasure. I will devour you if you refuse."

Harlot's Ruse

by Esther M. Friesner

POPULAR LIBRARY

An Imprint of Warner Books, Inc.

A Warner Communications Company

POPULAR LIBRARY EDITION

Popular Library® and Questar® are registered trademarks
of Warner Books, Inc.

Cover art by Victoria Poyser

Popular Library books are published by
Warner Books, Inc.
666 Fifth Avenue
New York, N.Y. 10103

 A Warner Communications Company

Printed in the United States of America

First Popular Library Printing: March, 1986

10 9 8 7 6 5 4 3 2 1

For Cathy Shoup,
Dance Mistress of Dragonship Haven and Writer of Songs,
And
For Kate Muise,
Mistress of Arts of Dragonship Haven and Singer of Same.
To say nothing of all other
Gentles of that peerless Barony
Who know of the "other" Megan,
No Relation.

Prologue

Sex is like the pursuit of wild mushrooms: Both are fascinating hobbies, both can prove most addictive, and both for the most part yield tasty results.

And yet, for the novice, there exists always the chance of making that one fatal mistake. Ah, but if one lives, one learns!

Therefore, my loves, take counsel of me, for I am Megan, harlot extraordinary—also called trull, slut, whore, doxy, meretrix . . . you get the idea—and in my life I have had more than my fill of wild mushrooms. To be sure, when you earn your living on your back, it leaves you prone to thought, and now that I at last (and alas!) have time to spare, I would share what I've learned of this wicked world with you.

There is, of course, no substitute for learning by doing, but if I show you where I erred, perhaps you may be spared some of my more unfortunate interludes.

Education is a wonderful thing. Read on.

CHAPTER I
Strumpet Voluntary

My true love's name was Hyu. He was a shepherd's assistant, an orphan, and full fourteen years old before he saw his first bit of minted king's-gold. He thought it was something to eat.

A girl has to start somewhere.

My own mother was dead, dying of a late summer fever soon after my tenth birthday, but her second husband survived her and put me to work tending his sheep as soon as decent after the burial. By his reckoning, this was two days. I followed the shifting woolly crowd with the tears still streaming, and in my grief I managed to lose track of three lambs and their mothers, for which Stepda said I was to be beaten.

"I'm only doing this for your own good, Megan," he said as he searched the thickets behind our hut for a birch switch having exactly the right length and flexibility. Not just any bunch of twigs would do; the man was an artist, in his own cruel way. "You're too much the hoyden, and there's little place in this world for scatterbrains. This"—here he broke off his speech and the switch simultaneously—"will help you keep your mind on your business in future."

With that he slashed the air with such vicious strokes and cross-strokes that I grasped the business at hand instantly. I was a bright girl, and I didn't wait to learn from experience whether the branches would cut my flesh as wickedly as they cut the air. I could theorize.

I could also run.

Our village was small, but I made it smaller. Busy housewives looked out their doorways to see me spread hysteria among their poultry. Cur-dogs set off as a yapping, snapping guard of honor at my heels. The few old men who lounged outside Mistress Shana's house—our nearest excuse for a tavern—set down their mugs of autumn ale to wager sleepily whether I was pursuer or pursued. Not a soul dreamed to interfere.

It wasn't easy running; the way was breakneck steep. Sheep and goats were the main business of our village, and such beasts prefer the mountains. I scrambled up the single dusty track that tumbled from the grazing grounds above, down among the houses, and finally spilled into a poor neglected side-track of the King's Road. I ran barefoot, and I didn't stop until the dirt and pebbles were gone from underfoot and I only felt meadow grasses between my flying toes.

I stood there panting, peering down the way I'd come to see whether Stepda was after me. If I'd been any older than ten, I might have known that men of his stripe will gladly discipline their young ones—very strictly, of course, and always for the child's own sinful good—but they lose interest quickly if the object of their moral lesson has brains enough to beat it. Their zeal diminishes in direct proportion to the distance the child puts between the switch and her bottom. Stepda knew I'd have to return sometime—where else had I to go? And when I did come back, he'd resume where we'd left off. In the meantime, he was a widower, and as befitted his grief, he took a comforting swig from the old stone bottle behind my late Ma's butter churn.

I sank down in the grass, already crisping with the chills of early fall. As soon as I had my breath back, the tears returned. The naked mountain peak that loomed over the little alpine meadow cast a craggy shadow and brought memories of witch-tales my Ma had told me until my true father would stop her with a kiss.

"Don't fright the child," he'd say, and there would be kisses enough for me too, and promises of a golden crown for me when I'd grown up to be his princess.

I've had golden crowns since then, and dragon's treasure, and the favors of kings and greater than kings. And I would trade them all for that which there's no bargaining for in this life: to have that lost, best love again.

What did I know of golden crowns then, promised or prophesied? I was only a little girl, and I was all alone. I scrubbed the tears from my face as soon as I could and made a great, brave vow never to cry again so long as I lived. I broke it the next breath. It was darker by the time I'd had the last of my tears out, and the crag's shadow had engulfed me. It was growing colder, and I dreamed I felt the touch of witchy fingers in every stab of the icy evening wind.

Then I heard a sound behind me that froze me worse than any wind. It was an eerie sound, a wailing cry by some poor being lost and seeking, but it wasn't anything human. *Gods, keep it from finding what it seeks!* I thought.

I made to pull my cape closer around my body, then realized I'd left that thick, warm, comforting bit of my dead Ma's weaving hanging neatly from the wooden peg nearest the door in our hut, right where I'd put it before reporting the lost sheep to Stepda. Without the cape, I had only an ill-fitting old dress of Ma's on over my shift, both of them spun from linen and too light for the high meadows without the covering cape. If I didn't build a fire or go home soon, I'd freeze to death up there that night.

Freeze, unless the wailer found me first.

I could not go back home. I would not. I was very stubborn, but not very resourceful. I started bawling again, and the wailer echoed. It must have liked me, because its cries grew louder and longer. Full dark had almost fallen, and the weird ululation came closer and closer upon me out of the icy black.

Ah, gods, what shape could such a horror have? Wide leathery wings, and graspy claws, and smoking yellow eyes with steel-blue sparks spilling out of them, like a blacksmith's furnace? Or would it be all slimy and slick, a crawling, cowardly nightmare whose very breath was poison to stun its prey, the better to eat it alive but no longer struggling? So I sat there, working myself into a bottled frenzy with my imaginings and pulling every nerve in my body so harpstring tight that little wonder I shrieked and flailed out like a loony when Hyu's hand touched my shoulder.

"Here, what're y— OOOOOWWWW!" I caught him in the cheek with my knuckles on a lucky backhand blow. His shepherd's staff flew from his grip in surprise and tapped my other shoulder, which only made me whirl about and throw myself on him, still screaming like a live-plucked eagle. No fool, he defended himself, but it was dark entirely now, and the best way we both lit on for night-fighting was to latch on to your opponent and not let go, doing what you can with teeth and nails and feet.

It was a short fight, but bloody enough. Hyu had the advantage of age and size, and soon had me pinned with his knees clamping my arms to my sides. The moon began to show herself then, and our husky breaths left little puffs of silver mist on the air. All around I heard the mysterious wailing cry, this time mixed with the familiar reek of sheep. And I cursed myself for a cloth-head, because I'd spent the whole day hearing that same strange cry and never giving it a second thought: lambs. The trembling baby bleat of lambs.

"Demons' breath," swore Hyu. His own voice was a little like the lambs' bleating. "Who are you?"

Something tasted too salty inside my mouth and my ribs ached from bearing his weight atop me. "Megan." I had to say my name again, because at first it came out in a whisper. Few enough folk lived in our village for us all to get by with one name alone.

"Megan. . . ." He got off me double-quick and helped me to sit up. There was moonlight enough for him to see the marks of tears on my face, even with the extra coat of grime I'd picked up during our battle. I could see his face well enough too, and I knew who he was.

"Hello, Hyu. I'm—sorry I hurt you."

"Hurt *me*?" He had those godsgift blue eyes whose color is visible even by night, and they looked all bewildered. "You couldn't hurt— I mean—I'm sorry if I hurt you, too, but you hit first, and no warning. What'd I ever do to you?"

"I thought you were a witch. Or a monster; dragon, maybe."

"A dragon? *This* high up?" He laughed, his voice soaring high at the start, plunging in midpeal to a baritone that made me shiver, not with cold. "Don't you know anything about dragons, girl?"

And so it was that Hyu, the shepherd's apprentice, threw his own cloak over me and left his herd in care of his great black dog, Bix, and took me back down the mountain to my home, all the while telling me what he'd learned of the habits of dragons, demons, mages, and monsters. He spoke like a grown man whose wisdom—or foolishness—there's no contradicting.

"How do you know so much?" I asked, lifting my eyes in wonder. We had come to the lantern-lit border of the village, and the amber light made his blue eyes glow brighter. That same imagination of mine that had conjured up midnight basilisks out of an empty meadow now saw in Hyu's youthful face the looks he'd have when he became a man. It was a very tempting picture, and ten years old is not too young to dream of wise and handsome princes.

Hyu shrugged my worship off, but he did look pleased with

me. "I learn what I can where I can. I listen to the stories the old men tell outside Mistress Shana's and try to sift out bits of truth. Once Mistress Shana even kept me in her house, the time I was sick with fever, and she showed me a book she's got. She thought to cheer me with the pictures, but I asked her about the words. I think that struck her funny—a sheepboy wanting to know letters—but she taught me some. She'd have taught me all of them if I'd had the luck to stay sick longer."

"Maybe you'll get sick again," I said by way of comfort. "I hope you do. I mean—"

"I know what you mean, Megan," he said, smiling, and I felt the gentlest touch of his hand on my hair.

Stepda was drunk when we came home and what he said about how I'd come by my tousled hair and grass-stained clothes wasn't true; yet. Then Hyu broke in and spoke up for me, even though he was only twelve and Stepda twice that.

"I found your girl up in the crag meadows alone. There's laws against women being up there past sundown, especially when the moon's growing big."

"Sheepmen's law," my Stepda sneered. "What's behind it's what it's worth: nothing." He was sprawled by our hearth on a greasy leather sack stuffed with bracken, disdaining the clean-scrubbed benches and the little hobstool. A wise disdain, for a man with that much liquor in him doesn't do well on backless seats.

"If I tell the Council about it, you'll find what's behind the law." Hyu's jaw was stern, and all at once I felt the warm, safe knowledge that as long as he was with me, Stepda wouldn't dare raise hand or switch. "There's reason behind it besides. It's females hold most magic in 'em, and magic's called out by the moon. Sheep and magic don't mix, as any fool knows, so women don't tend herd by night. That's the law, and the reason, and the Council takes care of explaining it further to anyone who doubts it."

"Megan! Get over here!" Stepda's drunken roar turned my stomach sour. He was losing the match with Hyu and had to

save face at someone else's expense. I came nearer very reluctantly. To my horror I saw that the dreaded switch lay on
the floor between him and the fire, within easy reach of his
fingertips. "Aren't satisfied with losing precious beasts for me,
hey? No, you have to run off and bring the plague-mad Council
down on my neck! If you thought I'd be hard on you for the
sake of three ewes and lambs, you've got no notion of how
much *lighter* I'll make your punishment for bringing the Council onto me, my girl!"

I was shaking all over. I wasn't afraid anymore; no. Not
with my Hyu standing by me. Rage was shaking every bone
in me, and I had to grit my teeth to keep from howling out all
the curses I'd ever learned in my young life before seizing the
iron ladle hanging at hearthside and smashing it into Stepda's
face. I was too little to strike a killing blow, worse luck. I
don't care to think how Stepda would have paid me back for
it, even now. But I would have hit first and toted up consequences after if Hyu hadn't spoken up again.

"Three ewes, you say? With young? Then that's where the
strays come from that joined my herd this evening! You'll have
them in your keeping pens tonight, or put back to your flock
when Megan pastures them tomorrow morning if you like."

This good news calmed Stepda almost magically. He forgot
all about me, offered Hyu a pull at his faithful bottle, and when
the shepherd's boy refused he praised him for so much self-
restraint (and leaving one swig more behind for himself).

"That's the trouble with the young," he said, hugging his
bottle mournfully. "No idea of controlling themselves. Wild
and thoughtless creatures. Ungrateful. A man works hard and
might expect a hot meal when he comes home, clean clothes,
a house made fair and smelling sweet. But *that* one"—with a
gesture he consigned me to the Netherplane—"gives no thought
to all I've been through these past weeks. Her own Ma sick,
and me left to find burial clothes, bearers, diggers, all that
costs a man's good money when the woman wouldn't get well.
Yagh!" His spittle hissed on the hearthstones. "And her no help

at all, forever weeping and clinging to the bedside, like a
double-damned cat! And now the woman's gone, is she any
more help than before? A lazy bitch! Home last of all the other
girls that tend sheep, and loses 'em, and runs off from her just
punishment without stirring up so much as a spoonful of hot
soup to comfort my empty belly!"

He went on further in this same vein, and I started eyeing
the iron ladle again.

"I'll mend it," said Hyu. He looked very solemn, and my
Stepda's babyish ramblings made the two seem to have switched
skins, man for boy and boy for man. "I'll tend your sheep with
my own herd and leave Megan home to see to your comforts."

Stepda's bleary eyes blinked. He was a rheum-eyed ancient
dog that mistrusts every proffered bit of meat as hiding poison.
"Generous. And how much will you skin from me for it, hey?
The girl's no pampered silkskin. Let her earn her keep!"

"She will," said Hyu quietly. "She'll see to the house—the
cleaning, the cooking, the wool to card and spin and dye and
weave, the baking, the brewing, the—"

Another gob of spit hit the hearthstones. "Little enough to
pay me back for her keeping! She's not even mine."

"She's as much yours as the sheep."

Plain truth when it's not welcome has a snake's sting. Stepda
lurched upright in his filthy leather nest and brandished the
switch angrily. I nibbled at my knuckles, praying that he'd
take a swipe at Hyu. I had no doubts that the healthy lad could
tear it from the old soak's hand and lambaste him royally. Oh,
how I prayed!

"You know it's so," Hyu went on. "So does all the village.
It's the law says that anything live and growing goes from
mother to daughter, but all hard and handmade goes from father
to son. That's King's Law," he added when he saw Stepda's
mouth gape to reply, "not just sheepmen's."

Stepda subsided, grumbling. The switch fell from his hand
with a dry clatter. "Ungrateful, ungrateful all the pack of you.
The herd's hers, then, and why should I be the one to keep

watch over it while she stays snug in *my* house? For you're not going to jaw me out of knowing that the house is mine!"

"It's yours." Hyu was still calm as well-water, and I could see how that added to my Stepda's rage inside. "But fair's fair, and I've in mind a way that'll suit us all."

"Us?" Stepda had an ugly laugh, more like a phlegmy cough than honest merriment. "How do you cut a slab of this pie? You're nothing and you've got nothing, Hyu, and *that's* something the whole village knows, too. Your father was a tinker and your mother was his bitch. She died whelping you in Mistress Shana's own blessed bed while your worthless old man got himself into a drunkard's fight. He pulled a knife on an honest man and had it stuck back into his own scrawny side, damn him. Oh, what a day that was that wished you on this village!"

I didn't dare look at Hyu directly. What Stepda said was true—or as much of the truth as anyone could recall. For all I knew, the honest man whose name was never mentioned in the tale was not so honest. Perhaps blame for the brawl started elsewhere than with the tinker, on the honest man's side. Maybe it never touched Hyu's father at all, and he only tried to intervene and make peace. But the truth of it as the gods count truth was lost long ago, and who in this village could ever admit that the wandering tinker wasn't to blame? That would be accusing one of their own, you see. To stop a snake from stinging, cut off its head and bury it deep, my darlings.

Hyu's head was bowed. I couldn't see much of his expression, peeking at him sideways like I was, but his voice remained level. "What I offer is this: I'll tend your sheep with the herd already in my care. I'll come for them by dawn and return them by dusk or keep them grazing on the high meadows with the others until shearing time, just as you want it. In exchange, let Megan stay at home and cook and mend for us both. Hot meals and bread that doesn't taste of grit are pretty rare up there." He jerked his thumb at the mountainside wall of our hut. "I'll eat at your table when it's time to bring the herds to town, otherwise let her bring me dinner once a day."

"Is that all?" My Stepda looked sly.

"And a new cape once a year. I'll find the wool, but she'll do the rest. And that's all."

"Done!"

So they shook hands and I allowed myself a weary yawn at last. Since there was to be no battle after all, I climbed up into the loft and curled up in my blankets. Hyu's and Stepda's voices—now very man-to-man—lulled me to sleep.

That was the last of my sorrows, for a time. I kept to my end of the bargain, making the house almost as clean as Ma had done, seeing to what the village men all laughed at as "women's chores." (But let one of them live alone and try to do those scorned "women's chores" for himself!) I still hated my Stepda, but we were civil. He "looked after" the money my sheep brought in on their fleecy backs and earned some of his own by selling to Mistress Shana the harsh juniper liquor he brewed. We saw Hyu at our table once a month, and I took him his dinner every day no matter what the weather.

Strange, but I always knew where to find him. The grazing meadows weren't so large, but there were many of them and they were scattered all up and down the mountain flank. A wise shepherd never decided where he'd graze his sheep until he'd seen the weather and the beasts' tempers that day. The other women who trudged up the paths to give their men hot meals sometimes wandered for hours, and the meals got cold, but I always found Hyu in less than half an hour from the time I left our door.

Very strange. I just knew where to find him. Yes, very strange, and almost . . . magical.

Magic! Oh, I soon had reason to hate that word. Two happy years I had before the King's Man came, two more before he came again and ended all my little joys.

I was twelve years old the first time the King's Man came, and my breasts were beginning to show. They showed themselves to no one but me, and that only at bedtime or when I took my solitary bath. Otherwise they were well hidden under the folds of Ma's old dresses, all of them too long for me and bloused up baggily over sashes or taken up with great, awkward, heel-catching hems.

It was just after shearing time when news reached us of the wandering King's Man. The messenger who brought it came trudging up the path to our village, surveyed the huddle of houses, the dirt track, the knot of loafers outside Mistress Shana's, and sighed as if it wounded his soul to look at such a miserable spot.

His soul healed itself fast enough when Mistress Shana herself came out, her hips swaying, a tray of clay mugs balanced on nature's own generously padded shelf. In a moment he forgot the bone-wearying climb and the wear and tear it had made on his livery. His lips were dry; watching Mistress Shana they grew drier. He ambled over to see about quenching his thirst.

It didn't take the crowd already there long to learn his business. While pretending not to care, they scooped him clean as an oyster shell.

"Why, didn't you know? It's the Tenfold Search that my master, Lord Deveril, has undertaken in the King's name. You mean no one's ever come this way before?"

The villagers swore that no one half so finely dressed or of such noble bearing as their princely guest (meaning the messenger; they were saving the real ewe-balls for Lord Deveril) had ever favored their unworthy lives. Whereat the newly appointed prince bought everyone a round.

Mistress Shana's green eyes were warm on him as he took his second mug and leaned back at his ease against the stone wall of her house. "Well, my friends, I think it's shameful that this is the first Tenfold Search to reach your lovely little town. However, it's also the first one my Lord Deveril's ever headed. You can bet he'd never make the mistake of overlooking such a fine place as this in his travels!"

Everyone agreed that the lord wise enough to hire such a gracious and learned man as one of his servants would have to be brilliant indeed. They begged him to enlighten their poor, dense minds further. He did so, as soon as he paid for the next refilling of their mugs.

"The Tenfold Search is made every ten years—which is why the name, y'see—and its sole purpose is to find the hidden treasures of the kingdom. Oh, not gold or jewels, my friends. We have wizards who can summon up the demons of the Netherplane anytime the King desires a particularly showy bit of precious stone snagged up from under the earth."

(Loud cheers and a generally noisy drinking of the King's health, followed by replenishment all around, at the patriotic messenger's expense.)

"The treasures Lord Deveril seeks in the King's name are children." The messenger held up his hands to quell the wondering murmurs and garbled speculations of his audience. "Friends, talent is no doxy to follow only where gold jingles. Even in the poorest hovels artists can be born as often as cutpurses. In the cities of the kingdom, it is easier for a child with some inborn talent or another to come to notice. Our gracious King has provided scholarships and apprentice bonds for those who cannot pay but who have a genius that must be brought along. In the end, the kingdom's the richer for it.

"But what of the young born far from the city walls? Their precious skills might go unheard of and unused if not for the Tenfold Search. Why, do you know where they found Rupert of Keren—the man who built the tomb of our late lord King Thorit? Tending swine!"

By this time, the rumors of a loose-coined fool buying free drinks for anyone willing to gape had reached the length of the village. A sizable crowd gathered in a semicircle, hemming the messenger in. Housewives let their chores go hang up the chimney and came to share the fun. Babies on their mothers' hips gurgled and screeched and nursed and slept and were ignored for the moment. Because it was just past shearing time, the mob was fattened by the full complement of local shepherds, all down from the meadows to collect their yearly pay and spend it.

Hyu was there with his master, and I trailed close behind. I'd taken to keeping a wary eye on him lately, especially when he came to town. Every moment he wasn't in our house, at our table, I wondered where he was and what business he had being elsewhere. Whatever it was, I didn't like it. The two of us came just in time to hear the messenger mention the famous former swineherd.

(Also to hear old Simmon gasp dramatically, and fall into a choking fit that could only be cured by a fresh draught of Mistress Shana's best ale.)

"Rupert of Keren, did you say?" Hyu shouted the question into the lull that followed while Mistress Shana was tending to old Simmon. She had to bend over a lot to reach him, and it presented quite a striking tableau.

"Aha!" The messenger smiled happily at the bright young lad and beckoned him to step forward. "So even here you've heard of King Thorit's master architect! Tell me, boy"—he put his arm around Hyu's shoulder when the crowd parted to let the shepherd's assistant through—"would you have known his name if not for the Tenfold Search of Thorit's time?"

"No," Hyu admitted.

"And he'd never have been more than a swineherd. He'd never have become the King's own architect. He'd never have designed a tomb that has drawn men from distant lands to pay homage to its beauty—a beauty which can never be duplicated while the gods reign and the world spins!" The messenger made a sweeping gesture that would have looked ridiculous even if he hadn't managed to spill his beer too.

"And King Thorit would never have had his head lopped off to make sure Rupert of Keren never built such another masterpiece for someone else," said Hyu in his quiet, carrying way.

Someone made the mistake of laughing. The messenger

turned red to the ears, paid Mistress Shana her reckoning, and huffed off down the trail to the King's Road. Everyone except the latecomers took his departure philosophically.

"Aye, better a live swineherd than a dead artist!" became the village watchword for a time. No one thought more about it until, two weeks later, Lord Deveril himself arrived.

Master and man were as different as seawater from spring. None of the villagers' ruses worked on the spare, somber King's Man, and the wiser men didn't even try their luck. One look at those narrow gray eyes, the wolf's face, and the tall body sitting his black horse rigid as a killing lance, and they recognized the type. When Lord Deveril and his two attendants rode up to Mistress Shana's, the Council assembled itself hastily and paid for the ale.

The men flanking Lord Deveril were softer than their master, but not by much. All three wore the supple buckskin traveling gear of long riders, with only the richly gemmed pins holding their capes back at the right shoulder to mark them for men of rank. Deveril's pin glittered brightest, and since his companions hung back a few paces, it was fairly certain who was the chiefest among the three.

Wirol was our Council headman and no fool. He hurried forward to offer Lord Deveril a hand to help him dismount. The black-haired Lord fixed him with a scornful look and swung himself to the ground unaided on the other side of his horse.

"I am Lord Deveril, the King's Man," he said. "Bring the children."

That was all the explanation he'd have given too, if Wirol hadn't asked such niceties as: How old? Lads and lasses both? Only the sound and the sane? Should we wash 'em first?

Lord Deveril leaned against the side of Mistress Shana's house, stretching the hard-ridden kinks out of his long shanks, and said, "Let them be no younger than eight and no older than sixteen, unless there's any who are older or younger than that whom you've noticed as special. *Have* you remarked anything

extraordinary about your children? Any genius? Any talent?"
Wirol's face was blank as a clean plate. Lord Deveril's lip
curled. "Of course not. What would you ever notice that didn't
bleat at you first? Bring the children."

It didn't take long. As soon as word of the approaching
King's Man hit the village, the houses emptied as if bewitched.
All the village brats were on the spot and only had to be
separated according to age and bullied into a row. I was squeezed
in between fat Ollie, the tanner's son, and Lina, Mistress Shana's
godsgift daughter (Mistress Shana was well beloved of the
gods, who sent her four other miraculous babies—miraculous
being fatherless).

Lord Deveril accepted a tankard from Mistress Shana and
stared at us where we squirmed. His companions sipped their
beer slowly and whispered together, but he drank his at one
go before measuring the length of the line, his dagger eyes
stabbing at each of us. Three girls and a boy began to cry as
soon as their gazes met his. Their parents were quick to snatch
them out of the row and Deveril didn't stop them.

When he reached the end of the line, he motioned for one
of his men to accompany him: the brawny blond. This time
no one cried, but the pair paused many times in their stroll
and tapped child after child, a gentle tap that meant rejection.
Those singled out as unworthy seemed relieved. They scampered back to their parents, even the biggest.

Now there were only five children left, and I one of the
five. I dared to look away from the sinister Lord Deveril, trying
to read what my fellow villagers made of all that we young
ones were undergoing. Lina was still on one side of me, but
fat Ollie had been dismissed. Mistress Shana's eyes were full
of anxiety whenever they rested on her godsgift child. You'd
almost think she didn't want the King's Man to discover that
Lina possessed some precious hidden talent.

Accidentally I spied Stepda in the waiting throng. His eyes
gleamed the way they did when we brought a whole roasted
lamb to our table once a year to celebrate the feast of our

King's foremost god, Sarogran of the Spears. The sight of so much meat always made his mouth water with greed, as if he could choke down the whole roast himself or die trying. A whole lamb, that was wealth for him! And now I was on the point of being transformed into that same lamb, for who could tell what toothsome rewards the King's Man would heap on the parent of any child he chose?

Someone joggled me on the side where fat Ollie had so lately stood. I turned and saw Hyu's master shoving the lean-limbed fourteen-year-old into place. Lord Deveril's men sent the shepherd a questioning look, but he bowed himself away quickly and lost himself in the crowd.

"You almost missed the fun," I whispered. Hyu grinned.

"That would be a shame. If they try to make you the King's architect, Megan, run for your life. And if they catch you, build him the ugliest tomb you can dream up."

Lord Deveril beckoned to his men. The three of them conferred. His lordship peered closely at Hyu and nodded before plunging back into council with the others.

"It looks as if you can stay," I said.

"It's like culling lambs. I've got strong legs, but they'll come by another time to see if I've got foot-rot." He slipped his hand into mine and pressed it. "What a cold little paw! Are you so afraid?"

I shook my head, then nodded. He squeezed my hand more firmly. "Hush. I won't let his regal boneship scare you. He's big on giving that icy eye to babies and watching them bawl. Let's see how he likes getting the same cold stare right back!"

"I'm no baby!" I started to protest, but by then Lord Deveril and both his men were coming back for another inspection. This took less than a breath, for they waved aside Lina and the other three children as soon as they reached the line, leaving only Hyu and me. True to his promise, Hyu faced up to the swarthy Lord boldly, a heroic gesture that had no effect at all.

"Well, Master Gwyth?" Lord Deveril remarked to the third man, who up until then had had no part in the inspections. I heard Hyu draw in a sharp breath. *Master* Gwyth. There was only one class of men that the King's nobles called *Master:* the men of magic.

The wizard looked no different from an ordinary mortal. His skin wasn't pasty or pale from years of solitary study. His limbs weren't spidery weak or his back bent double. In fact, he looked the sort of man who could summon a demon to defend him and then draw his sword and chop his enemy to cutlets offhand if the demon took too long showing up. When he gave Hyu the same icy eye that was Lord Deveril's specialty, my poor defender quailed.

"Here is one," he said. A murmur of awe rose from the crowd. He kept his eyes on Hyu until it subsided.

"And the gift?" asked Deveril, coming up to peer at Hyu over Master Gwyth's shoulder.

The wizard had a smile colder than the lord's. "Magic."

At once Lord Deveril seized Hyu by the arm and tore him from my side. "What's your name and age, young man, and who are your people?" Hyu explained himself. "Ha! An orphan. And a lucky one to have such a master who'd put you forward today. He'll have his reward."

(I could hear my Stepda moan with barely restrained greed and tension, even with him buried in the mob. When would the blessed King's Man's touch turn little Megan into gold?)

"You are young yet," Lord Deveril went on. "Your talent will want training, but since it lies in a field where man can only train, and not compel, we will return in two years' time. Often the inclination to sorcery is strong in the young, but fades as they mature. Sometimes being a virgin is enough to make a weak dab of mana seem like more power than it really is. *Are* you a virgin, boy?"

Hyu mumbled something not even I could hear, but there were loud hoots of derision from the shepherds' contingent in the crowd, and so I safely assumed that Hyu's virginity was common knowledge and a common joke among his companions.

"Two years," said the King's Man. "By then, virgin or not, we'll gauge your powers better. If Master Gwyth's opinion remains the same, you'll be sent to study at Routreal. My congratulations, boy." He dug a gold coin from the pouch at his belt and tossed it to Hyu, who caught it and stowed it in his own pouch without thinking. Then Deveril languidly extended a gloved hand. Hyu raised it to his forehead and started to flee, but remembered me at the last moment. I felt his presence at my back and thanked him silently.

"Now, Master Gwyth, what do you make of this one?"

Wizards have eyes no different from any other mortals', but what on earth do they do to make them cut so deep? I have been stripped naked with a man's eyes more than once (oh, many times more! And with more than eyes, and by more than men!), but a natural man's most lustful looks are nothing next to the lightest glance of a wizard. I felt Master Gwyth's stare go right to the bones of me, and I crossed by arms over my bosom in a useless try to hide my infant breasts from scrutiny.

It seemed he looked at me an hour when it was less than a minute. At last he turned to his lordship and said, "This one . . . I don't know."

"What? *You* don't know?" Lord Deveril's black brows flew up.

"No, and neither did you when you left her in line!" The mage was snappish as a prodded turtle. "There's *something* in her, but by all the gods, I can't put a name to it."

"Sorcery?"

"Not that. Or at least I don't think so."

"Music, perhaps? Or art?"

Master Gwyth shook his head. "Neither one. And yet there is *something*. . . . My lord, I say we let time work on both of these cubs. In two years perhaps I shall be able to read her talent better, and she's younger than the boy. Even if it's a talent for something requiring long apprenticeship, she can spare two years."

"Done." That was all the word of parting we had from Lord

Deveril, who remounted his waiting horse and rode off down
the mountainside, his party following after.

No, that was not *quite* all. For just after Lord Deveril rode
away, while Master Gwyth was checking his girths before
pursuing his lordship, the nameless third man stole a moment's
flirtation with Mistress Shana. He held his steed by the bridle
while he tried his luck with my pretty neighbor, but in my
girlish opinion he was a fool to waste time with a common
woman when he had such a gorgeous roan gelding for company.

Gods, I'd dreamed of horses! How many young girls shared
those same dreams? Men imagine themselves mounted between
the burning wings of dragons, flying through the skies on a
living sword of scales and fire, but women know that true
flight's never measured by the heights to which you climb, but
by the beauty of your passing. And what overgrown lizard can
match the beauty of a sleek horse stretched to the gallop?

So while Mistress Shana returned the man's harmless winks
and flattery, I stole up and patted his horse. First I stroked its
flank, then worked my way forward to the neck, and finally
snaked my hand out to touch the unutterably soft velvet of the
creature's muzzle. This last pat made the gelding snort and
jerk up on the bridle, and in turn made its master catch me in
the act.

I looked as innocent as I could. He smiled. I returned it.
He pulled the horse's head down and with a nod and more
smiles showed that I could pat it some more. When I'd had
my fill of this, he said, "Maybe you're to be one o' those
women warriors, hey, pretty? Ridin' a fine horse like Battle
here. And I'll be old or dead when they're still singin' about
you. Is that the gift Gwyth didn't see?"

My voice came out mouse-sized. "I don't think I'd like to
be a fighter, my lord."

He knelt to my eye level. "No, I'd not think you would.
Here, gi' us your hand, pretty." He turned it palm up in his.
I could feel every callus left by sword and battle-axe and bridle.
"I can read the gods' gifts almost as well as Master Gwyth

and Lord Deveril, did y'see me? I'm only a knight, but his lordship calls on me to sort out the children before he summons Master Gwyth's sight. I could've told him what your talent'll be."

His eyes were gray like Deveril's, but a warm shade that made me feel unafraid, for all that he was near kin to the nobility. "Please . . . can you tell me?"

He clucked his tongue. "Without his lordship here to witness? Master Gwyth'd turn me into a toad for stealing his glory. Wait the two years, lass, and if the answer hasn't come to you by then, ask for me to speak to Lord Deveril. Now give us a kiss so it'll be a sealed promise between us."

I leaned in to meet his cheek and stumbled against him, planting my kiss strongly on his mouth. To my surprise, he responded in a way that filled me with fright and exultation at the same time—a guilty pleasure thrills deepest. He pulled his lips away with a hearty laugh.

"Now it's fixed, and a wager atop of it." He handed me the horse's bridle to hold while he undid the jeweled emblem at his shoulder. He pressed it into my hand, saying, "If you haven't guessed your own talent before I tell it—and gods, how I yearn to see Deveril's face when I do!—then give this back to me. But if you have, it's forfeit, and well lost for what we've shared, my little queen." I was still puzzling out what he could possibly mean when he snapped the bridle from my hands and was up in the saddle and racing off to catch the others.

I pinned the bright badge to the inside of my skirt. What nonsense had the man been talking? I tried to get Mistress Shana's advice, but then a ruckus upstreet distracted me. The shepherds were milling in wild panic, like their sheep during thunderstorms. The villagers were adding to the to-do with frantic questions and shouts. What had happened? Mistress Shana and I both waded into the mob trying to find out.

What had happened? Oh, my poor darling! Hyu had taken out Lord Deveril's golden gift privately, studied it, and tried it on his teeth. Too big a bite will choke a pig, they say, and more so if a well-meaning friend comes up behind at that very moment to slap your back and give you congratulations.

Hyu swallowed the coin.

I left him in the clutches of four jolly shepherds who were holding him by the heels and shaking him madly while everyone else cheered them on.

Lord Deveril's two years passed. My breasts were no longer small enough to pass unnoticed, my Ma's old dresses no longer baggy enough to conceal a thing. In our village they say that a girl becomes a woman when she *hears the moon sing*. I heard the first notes of that song just before my fourteenth year, and like all my friends I went to Mistress Shana to learn what I'd have to do for myself now that I was a woman.

Mistress Shana said, "Be clean and be careful."

"Is that all?"

"That, and don't believe everything you hear about the gods. Especially not if a man tells it."

I frowned. "That's not very much."

"That's always been enough for me. Now shoo. And remember, when you hear the moon sing to you next month, don't go up to where the herds graze or come in where I'm brewing my beer."

I would have pressed her for reasons, but suddenly I realized that if I wasn't to go near the herds sometimes, I'd have to find a way to send Hyu's dinner to him. Who could I trust to carry it? Not another girl! And all the boys our age had their own jobs to mind.

This problem ate at my brain so that poor Hyu went hungry for a few days and finally presented himself at our door to see whether I'd been taken sick. Two years had put muscle on his tall form; very attractive muscle. I would've bet that there were no more jokes made at his expense, whether or not he was still a virgin.

(And if you think I didn't know what a virgin was, you're

town-bred. There is a vast difference between innocence and stupidity.)

"Is that what kept you away from me, Megan?" he asked when I told him what had happened to me. His eyes danced over my body. I could swear I felt their passing, and it gave me the most pleasant, prickly feeling. "I should've known. Anyone can see you're not a little one anymore. Listen, I'll mend it. My master's got me training a boy to take my place when Lord Deveril comes back for me. I'll send him to fetch my dinner from you. We share it anyway."

"But Hyu, you won't send him every day? . . . "

It was very still in the house. If I close my eyes and send my mind back, I can almost touch the way every roving particle of time paused and waited, watching us two. Even after so many years, the memory is matchless. It lives forever in an endless Now all its own while other memories dwell in Thens. What a silly thing to detain Lord King Time: a girl's—a woman's—question that asks a shepherd's lad something in cipher. Only one person can hold the all-solving key, and if it's been misplaced—worse than that, if I only imagined I'd given it to him, to my Hyu— Horrible thought! And so horrible that I banish it from my mind.

Hyu has to know. He must read the hidden message I send. He must. If he doesn't, I will die.

Hyú's hand is a man's hand. What star do boys hear singing them welcome into manhood? Stepda is downstreet at Mistress Shana's, haggling for her to trust him the price of a pail full of beer until his latest batch of liquor's ready. We're all alone, just two, until his hand cups my chin and he kisses me. Then who's to say we're two anymore? The cipher's found.

"You come to me when you can, sweet Megan. Don't spare a day more than you must! Do you think I came here to seek out your cooking?"

After another kiss I shove him away playfully. I'm so relieved that I must find a way to throw all my old, now-foolish worries out of my mind. So I play the kitten, though I'll feel like an idiot for it later. "What's wrong with how I cook? It's suited you for four years. Don't tell me you waited all that time just to kiss me!"

"Most of that time I waited for you to stop boiling lamb to leather. When I saw you'd never learn, I figured I'd better see if you kissed better than you cooked."

This needed an answer without words, and we stood pressed against each other so long that I almost forgot what he'd said to me. Then it came back, and I replied, "Do I?"

"Do you what?"

"Kiss better than I cook."

Hyu rubbed his cheek. "That's a riddle fit for Master Gwyth. I suppose we could prove it against gold. First you can try earning your living as a cook, and then—"

I slapped his hand and the pair of us laughed, hugging, feeling a bright, glorious joy bounding with so much radiance that we couldn't understand why the whole village didn't come running to see whether Stepda's house was afire.

Fire . . . Ours had to be banked. Both of us knew what we wanted to do, neither one knew the proper way to bring the other to do it. Gray heads that look at the young and call them wild animals that rut both in and out of season don't know a damned thing.

When the gods created the world, they made three people. One was male, one female, and the third was a mule who stood aside and whined, "Will you two *do* something already? I can't do it *for* you! You know you *want* to! Look, why don't you try lying down, and now *you* come over here with *this* thing, and I swear by my absent balls, I'll keep an eye out for the gods and whap the first one who laughs at you. Now *go ahead*! I haven't got eternity, we're *all* bored out of our skins, and there's nothing else those immortal muddlers have given us to *do*!"

Laugh all you like. More babes are born from desperation than desire. We never grew too bored or tongue-tied in each other's company to make love for lack of conversation. Besides, Hyu and I had little chance to repeat our first comparatively mild experiments. Rapture soon went skittish. What if my Stepda came in and caught us? What if Hyu's assistant came searching for him? We saw a hundred uninvited callers in the doorway, and we had no obliging third party to keep watch for us.

We parted hungry for each other, and we never got more than a taste and a nibble to keep us content after that. When I couldn't take Hyu's dinner to him I pined, but when I went up the mountain to bring it, it was worse.

Shepherds don't live like the poets pretend, making up love-songs all winter, singing them to the nymphs all spring, tumbling the verse-deafened nymphs all summer, and committing suicide in the autumn when the nymphs get fed up and leave. Hyu's assistant was always there, and when he wasn't another shepherd would happen by, tired of talking (or whatever) with his flock. We couldn't risk so much as a kiss, let alone more. Even if we'd been given time enough to ourselves, we'd have wasted it in sighs, longing looks, and sweet words, all the time our thoughts were probably identical: *Why doesn't this silly nit do something?*

If Lord Deveril hadn't come back when he did, I don't know how much longer Hyu and I would have gone on like that. All I do know is that when the King's Man returned and sent a runner up the mountain to fetch Hyu, my unhappy love didn't look at all well. Under great inner pressure, one might say.

On that day Stepda burst into our house roaring that I was to drop everything and come to Mistress Shana's. I was up to my wrists in bread dough, but he yanked me away by the elbow. I did what I could to wipe the sticky dough onto my apron as he hustled me down the street. Every step I took I could feel the jeweled pin hit my thigh. I'd always worn it hidden inside my skirts ever since the day Lord Deveril's knight had given it to me (along with the first kiss I ever had from a man not my father). It wasn't easy hiding the bauble from Stepda. He raised so much fuss when he learned Lord Deveril

had given Hyu a gold coin and me nothing that I was nearly
tempted to toss the pin into his face. Wisely, I resisted. Now
I was going to see my knight again and learn the answer to a
two-years' riddle.

People were assembling outside Mistress Shana's. I saw
Lord Deveril's black horse first, then a glimpse of his lordship's
sour face. Stepda hollered, "Make way! Make way for my
daughter, Megan, who his lordship's chosen!" The people let
us through.

Hyu was already there, and Master Gwyth, but there was
no sign of my golden-haired knight or his lovely roan. The
wizard scowled to see me; men who can read the stars hate it
when something as simple as a girl refuses to be read.

"Where is—the third?" No one paid attention to my question. I wound my hands in my skirt and felt the bumps of his
wager-pledge, the gems of smooth-cut cabochon style very
sleek under my fingers.

Master Gwyth had Hyu step up first. This time he took little
time before announcing, "The finding is true. The power is
there and needs only study to be brought out."

A cheer went up from the shepherds in the crowd and was
echoed by the villagers. Lord Deveril looked as pleased as
possible without actually deigning to smile.

"Then we shall meet you at the Grubbing Bear tavern on
the King's Road within two days. That should give you time
enough to make your farewells here. When you reach the
bottom of the path down from this place, turn towards the
setting sun and you'll find it. We'll get you a mount there for
the ride to Routreal."

I looked at my Hyu. He was in a daze. We'd often spoken
about how it would be when Deveril returned. We'd painted
every possible outcome for each other, doing them in detail to
fill the uneasy times between kisses. Our favorite had Master
Gwyth pronouncing Hyu the greatest mage ever born, Lord
Deveril begging him kneeling to study at the King's expense
in the University City of Routreal, and Hyu accepting gra-

ciously, in the manner of a man who is only doing so as a personal favor to an inferior.

Instead, Hyu made fish-faces at his lordship until his pack of former sheepherding companions surged forward to bear him away in a gabble of good wishes.

Master Gwyth's mouth went small as he came back to my case. We locked eyes until I thought I'd faint or throw up in the wizard's lap. "Have two years made it better?" asked his lordship, looking over Master Gwyth's shoulder. The magician grumped. "I see not."

"It is still there, my lord. But *what* it is— Oh, I give up! She's like an iron treasure house, and iron's proof against magic's sight: No mage can ever know what she holds, but *suspect* it until he goes mad!"

Lord Deveril wasn't pleased, and he expressed his displeasure with a silence so heavy that the whole village stood holding their breaths, afraid to break it. Cautiously I worked my skirt up until I could undo the clasp of the precious badge.

"My lord—" His look implied that everything was all my deliberate doing and I had no business bothering him further. "My lord, when you came here two years back, there was another man with you. He said he could read—what my talent was." I showed the pin. "He gave me this as a pledge that he'd tell you what he could about me."

Lord Deveril took the badge. It shone like a small sun in spite of doughy smears clinging to it from my unwashed fingers. I visualized Stepda's shocked face, his immeasurable rage when he realized I'd kept such a prize from him for two years. Good. I hoped he burst a blood vessel just thinking about it.

"He gave you this?" A crest was outlined in rubies—two griffins embattled beneath a pine, their eyes topaz, the tree limned with emeralds. "Sir Juris's device. He was thrown from his horse and broke his neck last spring. A pity." Lord Deveril pocketed the badge.

That was all. Lord Deveril and Master Gwyth mounted up and started down the path to the King's Road. The villagers let them get out of earshot before breaking up into smaller groups to discuss Hyu's golden future. I was ignored and went back upstreet to finish my baking. That batch was heavy and didn't rise properly at all.

Hyu came to say good-bye the next dawn. I stole out to meet him without disturbing Stepda, who was deep in beery slumber by the hearth. The few flocks that spent their nights in pens behind their owners' houses were being driven up the sloping street to the pastures, their grass-sweet breaths trailing scarves of golden mist in the new light. We hid on the far side of my house and clung to each other until the streets were empty of sheep and the first householders were just stirring.

He promised he'd write to me through Mistress Shana, who could read his letters aloud to me. I promised I'd learn to read for myself, and Mistress Shana be damned.

He promised he'd find means to earn money above what the King's dole gave him so that he could send for me. I promised I'd do extra work at my loom and sell cloth to pay my own way to Routreal.

He promised he'd keep his eyes fixed on his books so that he'd be a great wizard sooner and conjure up a dragon to fetch me to be his bride. I promised I wouldn't wash, in order to keep the eyes of the village boys off me.

He promised he'd love me forever.

I cried all that morning and half the afternoon. The next day I only wept in the morning, and in the afternoon I went to Mistress Shana to arrange for her to teach me my letters. I spent six months with her youngest brat tied by a tending-string to my ankle while I carded and spun and wove in exchange for those lessons, and when Hyu's first letter came I was able to make out most of it.

Certainly I knew the word "love" when I saw it, and in the letter I saw it fifteen times.

Two months later there was a longer letter, but "love" only nine times. Two months more and the letter and "love" dwindled together: a tally of five. A year finished, and Hyu's fourth letter wished me an elegant happy birthday (belated), then went on to describe the marvels and pleasures of the University City. He wished I were there, in just so many words. "Love" came above his signature and no more.

Mistress Shana's brat bawled and tangled itself in its leash. I set the letter down and worked on releasing the creature. While I was so occupied, I didn't hear Stepda come in. A papery crackle alerted me, but by the time I turned, it was too late; he had the letter in his hands.

"That's a smart lad for you!" His hateful chuckle sounded louder and cruder than ever. "Live it up while you can, Hyu boy! Aye, and in the University City there's places enough for that, I should know."

I perched the baby on my knee, pretending I didn't hear him. When he insisted on reading the entire letter aloud, I had to speak up. "Put that down! It's my letter, not yours!"

"Ha! It's hard and handmade, isn't it? And that's a man's portion. King's Law, as your absent friend 'ud tell us. Besides, a man's got the right to guard his daughter from wicked doings. The right? The duty! I'll tell you, Megan, once I thought we could do worse than have you marry Hyu. He was a bright lad, and like to have his own flock someday. But now he's turning into a wizard—a city-bred wizard!—I think I'll look elsewhere to find you a mate."

"You'll find me nothing! I can take care of my own life."

"Can you?" His beady eyes strayed back to the letter. "You know the best pleasures of Routreal, girl? You know what swarms where students are? If you've taken such pains to learn your letters, tell me this: What word's spelled w-h-o-r-e?"

I pursed my lips. "Warhorse?"

Stepda bellowed. "Har! Can I bear to give such a gem as you to that one? You're a green sprig, a lamb, a market-day wonder! Yes, *warhorse,* sure, what else could it spell that you'd know?"

The baby had gone to sleep in my lap. I tucked it into the cradle its mother brought with her every day she left the mite in my care. "Even if I can't spell, I can choose my own mate. Put down my letter and go to the table. There's rabbit stew for your midday dinner."

Stepda still laughed very deep in his throat, but he did as I told him while I stirred the pot with the iron ladle. My face grew hot as I bent over the fire, but when I dipped out his portion and saw the look he was giving me, it grew hotter. Lately I'd had too many looks like that from him. It had been like that since shortly after Hyu had gone away, but I'd done my best to ignore Stepda's burning eyes.

"What are you staring at, Megan? I'm hungry. Bring it here." I set the bowl before him and retreated to the fireplace. He took one spoonful and smacked his lips, then pushed his bench away and came to stand behind me. I was ladling out my own share when his hands fell on my shoulders and whirled me around.

"And shall I waste something so tender on a boy?" His voice had a rough, strained quality that made my skin crawl. I got no time to wonder at it long before he clasped me hard against him and covered my mouth with a reeking, nibbling, slobbering, revolting—

Let us just say that in that moment I first theorized that my poor Ma might have died in self-defense.

"Megan, my sweet Megan," he murmured, nuzzling my neck like a great tame ox, all the while I did my best to wrench myself free of his embrace. I slammed my stew-bowl into his ribs, the iron ladle falling from my other hand, but the hot meat splattered to the ground without touching him and a wooden bowl makes a poor weapon.

"Why do you fight me?" His fingers dug deeper into my flesh. He was a big, shaggy man, and he gave me what he must have thought was a gentle, cautionary shake. My teeth clacked together in my head and the bowl went flying into a corner.

I screamed then, and I have always had good wind. But what good did it do? It was midday. The houses flanking ours belonged to men who were out in the fields or up with the flocks, and their wives would be bringing them their meal at that hour. Mistress Shana's house was too far downstreet for her or her customers to hear me. Her baby snuffled and turned over in its sleep, the only being disturbed by my yell. For all that, my uncooperative attitude displeased Stepda no end.

"Here! You quiet down!" This time there was nothing gentle intended in the shaking I got. My head snapped back and forth on my neck. "Don't play proud with me; I know you. What'd you get that pretty jewel for, hey? The one you hid from me, you little bitch, and lost to his tight-fist lordship? That served you right! But what were you paid for, girl, and you only twelve?"

I gasped, not understanding why Stepda had gone loony and was asking such weird questions. "What are you talking about? He never *gave* it to me. It was a wager-pledge—"

Stepda guffawed. "Milk a ram with that tale! Don't take me for a witling. I haven't any jewels to hire you, girl, but I've spent more than the value of that pin on your keep. Now if you won't give me fair-trade value for it, a man's got the right to take it!"

I screamed again when he lunged for me, and tried to run. He caught me around the waist, making me swim on dry land while he laughed at my attempts to wiggle away. Then he tired of play and threw me to the hearthstones. His greater weight pinned me down, and he only paused to tug the leather sack of bracken closer, then hoisted my rump onto it and pushed my skirts up to my shoulders.

"And no clawing, little cat," he hissed in my ear as he groped to undo his breeches. "I'm not a man who finds that rousing. Leave a mark on my face and you'll find I still know how to use a birch switch, no matter how big you've grown."

"Please . . . please, I promise I won't." I patted his whiskery cheek timorously with my left hand. "Don't hurt me." I put every atom of wide-eyed fear and helplessness into my plea.

He liked that. There are many men who do. "Sweetheart,

you be good to me and I won't hurt you. What's more, you'll thank me for this someday."

"Someday?" (Still just the right note of tremulous terror in my voice, the proper submissive gaze to keep his eyes on mine and nowhere else, the cajoling touch of my left hand on his face to make him forget I'd ever had a right hand.) "Why not . . . *now*?"

The iron ladle slammed into the back of his skull. My scrabbling fingers had found it while he'd been making his lustful preparations for the "favor" he'd do me. I'd even purchased time enough to fiddle it around into the cookfire and scoop up half a dipper of blazing embers. Stepda's hair went alight. He leaped up shrieking. I jumped to my feet a blink after and enjoyed the scene.

I didn't relish it long; that would have been cruel, and I never wanted to kill the man. We kept a filled water bucket near the hearth, so I grabbed it and sloshed the contents into his face.

Then I smashed the bucket over his head for good measure. He crumpled in a puddle of water nicely mixed with blood.

I only tarried to make sure he was still breathing, then set to packing my few things, humming all the time. I stowed a traveler's sack with rations for the road, but I'd need money if I were to sleep safe in good taverns by night. Routreal was four days' march from our village, as Mistress Shana had told me, and four nights are too many to pass out in the open.

Mistress Shana too was the one who bought the three fat sheep I extracted from my flock. The lad who'd been trained as Hyu's replacement asked no questions, since all the bleaters were mine. Mistress Shana did ask:

"Why are you selling them?" She had her baby in her arms, for I'd brought the brat back to her.

"I'm afraid my Stepda's sickening for something. He's in his bed and not stirring a peep. If he'll need an herbman's care, I thought I'd better get the coin together in advance. I'm sorry, but I can't mind your child while Stepda's like this, y'see."

Mistress Shana agreed and paid me a fair price. As I was about to leave she said, "Your Stepda's a bigger bastard than any I've ever known, and I'm an expert when it comes to bastards. Yet you're taking so much trouble over him. . . . Megan, you're too good to him and he doesn't deserve it."

"Thank you, Mistress Shana," I said, "but I'm sure he deserves everything I've ever done."

My passage to Routreal took shorter than I'd thought. I hadn't counted on the jolly fellowship of the King's Road when I calculated my journey. I was given free rides in farmers' wagons, I was invited to perch atop the jumble in peddlers' carts, and I was even encouraged to ride pillion on the mounts of solitary riders, although one of them had me ride astride before him. This went well until he said, "You know, it looks like rain."

"Does it?" That worried me. We could already see the University City as a blur on the horizon, and I'd hoped to reach it looking my best. A soaking in rainwater wouldn't help. "But the sky's clear."

"Ah, but my old nurse was a farmer's wife and she taught me ways of reading the weather. There's no surer gauge of coming rain than the heft of a cow's udder at noon."

I looked at the sun, directly overhead as it was, and recalled that we'd ridden past several herds of cattle, although now there were none nearby. "Well, it's noon, but I don't see any cows. . . ."

"Don't fret, love, a wise man makes do."

And he did. And I elbowed him hard in the ribs, slid off the horse, and chunked rocks at it and him regardless until it stampeded away with its master shielding his bruised face with both arms.

I walked the rest of the way to Routreal. It didn't rain. In the University City grounds I was quick to question the milkiest young man I could find as to where the newest students lived.

By luck he was a new student himself and knew Hyu by sight and reputation.

I decided to learn what he meant by "reputation" later. He was kind enough to guide me to the house where Hyu had his lodgings and left me outside my darling's door.

It was evening by then. I saw a slice of yellow light under the door. I knocked, and when Hyu opened it and saw me, he said nothing. Neither did I. He stood back to let me come in. His room was small, but all his own. There was a game-legged table covered with books and raggedy sheets of foolscap; a smaller shelf above it with more books, a glowing oil-lamp, and a cloudy crystal ball on a bronze stand; a spindle-backed chair, a small fireplace with a black iron pothook and tripod, and a rag rug.

There was also a bed big enough for one.

We made do.

CHAPTER II

What's Up, Doxy?

People who are in love should never be sent out shopping. Love lends a rosy glow to all we see. Unfortunately, this includes limp vegetables, graying meats, and wine that should have been poured out for vinegar long ago. But when you are in love—ah!

You can't tell the butcher he's a slime-sucking grave-robber because there is *something* about the way he says, "Take it or leave it," that reminds you of your beloved. And you can't tell the spotty farmer's lad just where he can stick that poor excuse for a turnip (and don't think he hasn't tried!), because his hair is the same color as your sweetheart's. And all the vintner needs to do is murmur, "A little something special . . . just for two?" and you shower silver coins into his outstretched palm in exchange for a bottle that's half sediment and half pond-scum.

Romance ought to be banned at mealtimes, or else our King should select a special board of Caretakers to see to the material needs of new lovers until they're ready to return to the real world.

The money I'd gotten from the sale of my sheep (less the expenses of my journey to Routreal) soon went frisking off in a series of bad bargains. When it was gone, Hyu and I had to live on the wretched stipend the King's bounty assigned him. It was scant enough to support a student on his own (no doubt some fat advisor to His Majesty assured him that students expect to suffer and starve, becoming huffy and resentful if they ever get a square meal) but when that student is entertaining a secret boarder, the royal allowance gave poverty a bad name.

Hyu and I didn't mind. Or rather, I didn't and assumed Hyu shared my sentiments as surely as we shared bed, board, and bodies. At first it was great fun. I would hide under the bed whenever there was a knock at our door. Hyu would throw a robe on and send the caller packing, then give me a secret whistle to signal that it was safe for me to emerge. I'd crawl out and complain that I'd picked up splinters in the most unfortunate places, and the rest of the day was happily lost as Hyu set to work extracting the slivers and kissing the hurts away. (Some required further therapy.)

Soon he no longer had to throw on his robe to answer the door because more and more of his time was spent fully dressed. So was mine. I no longer came out of hiding with so many splinters to be plucked and kissed, and often all I got was the splinter removed and a pat on the head. There wasn't time for more.

Hyu had gone back to his studies after those first wonderful months when we were new lovers.

"I can't neglect my work, Megan, don't you see?" He was very reasonable and very patient. "I'm sure you can find something to keep yourself busy while I study. You want me to be a success, don't you?"

A silly question, and with only one possible answer. "Whatever you want, Hyu, darling." I left him to his all-important studies of necromancy, sorcery, and the assorted dark arts, meanwhile casting about for something I could do to mark off the hours until he could spare some of his precious time for me.

Well, there was no wool to card, spin, dye, and weave (nor carding combs, spindle, dye-pots, or loom). There was scant food, and what we had took little time to prepare. All that I had was dust. I declared war to the death on it and set to scrubbing our single tiny room. It kept me busy while Hyu was in his classes or the library or bent over his books at home. If that was what he wanted, I was content.

He wasn't.

One day, while I was polishing the pothook (which curved up just like Hyu's lips when he smiled), I heard our door open. "Hyu!" I cried, and flung myself into the arms of a total stranger.

"Faith of the phantoms, what a welcome!" He was taller than Hyu and much thinner, but wiry enough to hold me fast. Only his lopsided smile told me that he meant no harm. "You must be Hyu's Megan. If you're not, I'll make a thank-offering and take you for my own, finders keepers."

"I am Megan." He let me go, all flustered. How did this stranger know my name? Had I been too incautious in my comings and goings? What would the University authorities do if they learned Hyu kept a woman in his rooms? Could this man be one of them, the dreaded Authorities? He seemed so young. . . .

"What a shame. But we can be friends, though I was hoping— Well, all things change. I'm Sandar, a classmate of your . . . attachment. Hyu asked me to bring you along to meet the rest of us tonight."

"The rest—"

"We've got young Thares through his resurrectionals today, after three tries, so he's buying. The secret"—here flame-haired Sandar dropped his voice most confidentially—"is to make sure Thares drinks two to our one for the first hour, then he'll be too slogged to notice that we're drinking three to his one for the rest of the night. Come on, they're all waiting to meet you!"

I was entirely confused. My hands fluttered from smutched face to wrinkled dress to tousled hair. "You mean, Hyu *told* you I was here?"

"And about time, if you ask me! Keeping you to himself all these months—tchah! We'll give him a penance for that sin later. Oh, you look *fine,* love, but have a wash and comb if you're such a purist. I'll be happy to wait."

As Sandar later escorted me through the evening streets of Routreal, he casually explained that there was no official penalty attached to a student keeping a "guest" in his rooms. "Provided that the guest is not demonic. No Succubi or Incubi until after you've passed your finals. You're not a Succubus, are you, sweetheart?" He wound a strand of my golden-brown hair through his fingers, nearly undoing the haphazardly tied ribbon holding it back from my face.

"I don't even know what that is."

"A female demon of sex, and an Incubus is her male counterpart. Voracious little devils. Never had much taste for Netherplane lovers myself." He let my hair fall with a reluctant sigh.

Hyu and the others were in a tavern called the Horseman's Bones. The trade sign showed a stark-visaged rider with scythe to hand sharing a friendly tankard of suds with his skeletal mount. The pair was arm-wrestling and the horse getting the better of the match even though he lacked an elbow.

Not one of Hyu's drinking companions had a similar handicap, which they proved by bending their elbows frequently during the course of the night. Hyu himself was seated next to a chinless blond who I guessed was the newly passed resurrectionist Thares. He had passed out with his head in a plate of ropy cheese, but his purse was safe in Hyu's keeping. Before I could demand an explanation, Hyu had yanked me onto his lap and was presenting me to the company. There was so much loving pride in his voice that I decided not to pick a quarrel.

Was it Hyu's fault he hadn't told me that my presence was legal?

Wouldn't my angel feel simply terrible if I accused him of deliberately keeping me confined in his room, scrubbing my heart out, when I might have gone out anytime I liked?

Who but I would be at fault if Hyu's remorse put him off his studies and he ended up a failure, forced to go back to sheepherding?

I found myself apologizing to everyone there — the barmaid included — for having been so antisocial. Hyu patted my hands and said he forgave me.

This was only the first of many such outings. The pattern remained the same. Hyu went directly to the Horseman's Bones after classes and sent one or another of his friends to fetch me. Once in a while he would also send me back to our room with an escort before the night was done.

"All the other girls are leaving, Megan, but I have important things to discuss with my friends; to do with our studies, you see."

His studies! Those mysterious, terrible, awesome studies in the forbidden! (Yet one man's forbidden art is another's required course.) I asked Hyu about them many times, always getting the same reply:

"It's very complicated, Megan. I couldn't begin to explain it to you, and you probably wouldn't understand it anyway. Besides, you haven't got a talent for sorcery. Master Gwyth himself said so. So why do you want to be filling your head with things you've no use for?"

I made myself agree with the logic behind this. Logic or not, I envied nearly all of the other women whom I met at those student sessions in the Horseman's Bones. Some were the lemen of Hyu's friends, others were themselves students who were preparing to become sorceresses, witches, and herb-wives. When I tried to chat with this latter bunch, it went like so:

"So you're Hyu's friend. My, my."

"Are you in one of his classes?" A weary nod. "Which one?"

"Portions and embrocations." A yawn.

"That sounds very interesting. Are you specializing?"

"Delayed-action poisons." An imploring look shot at her fellow students, a silent bid for rescue.

"Do they give you a separate course on antidotes?"

"Speaking of antidotes, I missed that session. Gavi, love, were you there when Master Yuri— Oh, you *will* excuse me, Megan, won't you, but this is *very* important. We must get together sometime and you can tell me all about sheep." And the seat beside mine would be empty until Sandar or Heliad would fill it.

Always Sandar or Heliad, mark you; no one else. Like Hyu, those two were also the products of the Tenfold Search. They'd come from the countryside. The rest of Hyu's companions were of Thares's mold—city-bred and sophisticated, the sorceresses-aspirant too. Their lemen were also from behind the walls, and not one of them was dependent on the King's miserly allowances. They dressed well, ate well, and lived high.

Hyu managed to fit in among them. I saw to it that his plain tunic was always lovingly laundered, then smoothed out to dry wrinkle-free on the sun-drenched rocks near Routreal River, at the bend just before it pours itself into the northern sea. Being a student, no one expected him to dress too well, and the richest lad at Hyu's table often showed up in a student's robe more raggedy than Heliad's (Heliad's poverty having passed the legendary mark and gone straight on to becoming a Seminal Myth).

It was another story among the women. The sorceresses-to-be and their leman sisters never came to drink unless their hair was elaborately braided and ornamented, their cosmetics and scents meticulously applied, and at least one item of their clothing made of shimmering silk. In my wool cape and linen gowns, with no cosmetics, no scent beyond what nature gave me, and my hair tied back in a single housewife's braid, I felt very small. The sidelong, assaying glances they gave me made me wish I were smaller.

Never mind, I consoled myself. *Hyu loves me.*

Forever, as he'd promised.

One day, as I was scouring the hearth of ashes, I sat back on my heels and did some finger-figuring. Could the answer be right? Had it been *that* long since—?

(No, no, my dears, it wasn't what you're thinking. One of the benefits of taking a student-mage for your lover is that he knows all sorts of uses for the most common herbs. I'd heard the moon singing my song just as regularly as ever, thanks to Hyu's . . . safety measures.)

What I was counting was the number of days since Hyu had sent anyone to fetch me to the Horseman's Bones. *Fifteen? That many?* I got up from the hearth and went to the window. The sun was going down; classes were over. I washed my hands and combed my hair. *Fifteen? Well, then it's all the more likely that he'll send for me tonight.*

("Darling, I'm so sorry, but you wouldn't have enjoyed it. It was strictly business, what with examinations coming up. I want you to be with me when we can have some fun.")

Examinations were over. Wouldn't there be some sort of celebration to attend?

("Sweetest one, you have no idea of how rowdy my friends get after exams. I don't think you ought to hear some of the language they use about the Masters, and as for the songs they sing and the jokes they tell—! You're too much of a lady, my precious, to have to listen to that.")

No one could keep up a post-exam orgy for more than three days running and still survive. Might there be a funeral or two to attend, with drinks afterwards?

("Megan, my angel, you hardly knew poor old Anshal, and we were all too depressed to be very good company for you.")

Fifteen days.

The knock at our door sounded like a thunderclap. I ran to answer it, happy to banish the goblins.

It was Hyu.

Why had he knocked? It was his room as well as mine.

Why was he looking at me like that?

Why didn't he say something as he came in, shut the door, made me sit on the bed while he pulled up the chair?

He made up for his silence soon enough. Leaning forward, he took my hands in his and said, "Dear heart, I have some wonderful news for you."

His looks had prepared me for anything but good news. My body slumped with relief, though when I felt something cool and hard passing from his hands to mine, I perked up amazingly fast.

Coins. A roulade of gold coins bound with blue silk.

Hyu tilted back his chair and watched my innocent joy with a self-satisfied smile. I was chirruping like a squirrel, and acting half as bright.

"But how—? Hyu, why did you—? Where—?"

For an answer he gave me a kiss that was mostly lip-brush and air. "When a man has loyal friends, they share their good fortunes with him, Megan. I'm helping Thares and that crowd with their lessons. The longer I stay here, the more everyone sees the talent in me that Master Gwyth first recognized. They know I'm meant for great things, and they'll never equal my powers, but I can tutor them; and they can help me."

"Help us, you mean," I responded, laughing as I unbound the coins and tossed them up in my skirt.

There was no answering laughter.

The coins scattered clinking on the floor. "There's something else, isn't there, Hyu?" When had his mouth grown so small and selfish? Once it had been ever-hungry for my kisses, ever-generous with words of love. When had his eyes stopped holding my image? I saw nothing in them but glints of fallen gold, and that was when I knew.

"I'm going to be busier than ever, Megan, tutoring my friends and all. We'll have less time than ever to ourselves. You know how much it costs to live in Routreal? Even with this extra coin, we'll have to scrape along badly." He had my hands again. "That isn't fair to you. You deserve better than that."

What I deserved, according to him, was a trip back to the bucolic joys of home, sheep, and Stepda. He would send for me when he finished his studies, as we'd originally planned. And hadn't I been the foolish little girl to upset those plans by showing up uninvited on his doorstep? And wasn't he being the benevolent, generous man to pay my way back home and say nothing further about the matter?

All of I sudden I realized just where Hyu had plucked that delicate little phrase he used on me: "You deserve better than that." It wasn't his own at all. Hyu was merely repeating what his fancy friends had told him, and three guesses what it was that they were talking about. *A country wench for your leman? You, who'll be the greatest wizard of this kingdom someday? Come now, Hyu! You deserve better than that.*

Hyu wasn't the only one who'd benefited from a University City education. I used every oath I'd ever overheard in the marketplace and near the dockside fishstalls, called him every foul name I'd picked up from nights in the Horseman's Bones, and finished with some good old upcountry curses. When he tried to urge the gold on me, I knocked it from his hands. Wild with rage, I tore my cloak from the wall and stormed from the room.

It was a drizzly evening. I splashed through the puddled streets for an hour before the first flame of my anger dampened down. I'd run off without much thought to where I was bound, and I hadn't a very good sense of direction. Apart from my trips to the markets and the Horseman's Bones, I didn't know the city streets.

Now I know that I must have wandered into one of the wealthier sections of town. Amber lamps hung like fat moon-fruits at every cross-street and before some of the finer homes. The mist gave each a hairy halo, but there was no one out of doors. The merchant-princes and high-ranked professors from the University were all cozy behind their iron-bound doors, sitting down to a hot dinner with their families. They wouldn't dream of sending even a servant out in such weather. If I meant to find shelter, there was none to be had in that quarter of the town, and no one to ask for directions to a more likely section.

Without my rage to keep me warm, I blundered wearily on. Tears mixed themselves with the rain, although I screwed up my eyes and commanded them to stop. The fine neighborhood dribbled away house by house until I was in a different section of Routreal where the only lamps were tiny white clay cups filled with oil and set in niches at the street corners. The smallest gust of wind would extinguish them, and in a rain they didn't fare well.

I went seven blocks before I found a corner where all four lamps still burned. There I sat down on a curbside mounting block to think over what I should do. I'd been roaming so long that even the light mizzle had seeped through my cape. The minor case of shivers I got didn't help me think any more clearly.

What *was* I to do?

Go home? And what would become of me there? I'd run off, and there were laws about gallivants, the worst of which decreed that any soul who ran away forfeited all property he or she might have left behind. As there was no other female heir, Stepda had inherited my flock by default as surely as if I were dead. If I went back, I'd have to live on his charity, and the gods knew what price he'd demand for it.

Go back to Hyu? At that moment, Stepda seemed like a court gentleman in comparison to him, which should give you some hint that the bloom was off my first passion.

I suppose I could have gone to Sandar's room, or Heliad's. They'd been the only friends I'd made in Routreal, but I didn't know where they lodged.

A breeze snaked around the corner, making three of the oil-cups flicker and one snuff out. It smelled of salt and iodine and dead fish, a breeze from off the northern sea. I followed it, if only because I'd heard the students say that they got inspiration for their finest work after contemplating something as vast and immortal as the sea.

It wasn't hard to find my way to the docks. What with the rain and the hour, they were deserted. I saw the hulks of many midsized merchant vessels at anchor in the harbor, with a flotilla of smaller fishing craft tied to the piers, but the moon remained hidden by the rain clouds and the sea held on to its secrets.

My feet hurt and my shoes squelched with every step. I sat on the edge of the wharf and leaned the weight of my woes against a pier.

"Hey! Move off there! This is my territory!"

At first I could see nothing but a lumpish figure outlined against the dull glow of a clouded night sky. A skirt and hooded cape like my own, a face concealed under that hood, a pair of white hands waving me off, and a querulous voice; those were the pieces of puzzle I had to put together into the girl looking down at me.

"G'wan, get along or I'll tip you in the drink, you catch-penny whore!" She nudged my rump with her foot, as if about to put teeth into her threat.

This was wrong.

I seized her ankle and upended her. She hit the wharf with a squawk of surprise and outrage. Since she was already mad, I sat on her stomach. It took the breath out of her and really didn't make her threats any worse. In for a lamb, in for a ram, as the sheep-stealers say just before we hang them.

"I didn't know this wharf was anyone's territory," I explained, making myself comfortable.

"Get off me, you pox-rot bitch!" the lady shrieked, hitting out with her fists. This inhospitable move only made me tie up her hands with my hair ribbon. Snakes of rain-wet hair stuck to my cheeks in damp squiggles, but it was better than being bruised.

I determined to be reasonable. I knew from Hyu how irritating that could be.

"Take back those names, friend, or you'll have a swimming lesson yourself," I said. "Catchpenny whore! Poxy bitch! What did I ever do to you?"

"Pox-*rot* bitch," mumbled my captive. I slapped her face, sharply but lightly.

"There are times when you shouldn't insist on your *very* words." She didn't take criticism well and spat at me. I gave her another slap, harder this time, then wiped the trickles of rain from my forehead. To do this I had to pull back my hood all the way.

I heard her suck in her breath. "A new 'un. Nor much smart, from the minted look of you. Here, you working alone? You could bring a top price, if it's well haggled for you."

"Why do you insist on thinking I'm a whore, for Esra's sake?" I exclaimed. I hadn't sworn by the Lady of Grain for months, sure that my beloved goddess of field-fruits wouldn't be much help to me behind city walls.

"Well . . . ain't you? Markets all closed, so no need for a serving girl to be out. No great temple festivals to see. You're dressed near poor as me, so don't come calling yourself noble! Anyway, rich lasses have their fun indoors on nights like this. Doorways're good enough for me. Have to be!"

She grinned. Her hood had fallen back too, and with my eyes used to the gloom I counted three gaps in her smile. Her skin was very fine, young but not fresh, and clumsily painted. Her hair was the color of winter wheat, with its shine obscured under a layer of grease. She wasn't much older than I—maybe younger—and everything about her said "Used! Used!" Her ancient, knowing eyes were Hyu's color. This had no effect on me now.

"Did you think I might be a student? There's that, y'know."

"You?" Her imperfect smile widened, revealing another missing tooth. "Do sommat magic then. Turn me honest!"

"Oh, shut up." I hugged my knees and sulked.

"Knew you weren't a witch-study." Her small triumph made the girl smug, even if she was still my cushion. "So you must be a whore. What else's left for you?"

What else's left . . . ?

How many folk waste good gold on the temple oracles when they could hear the future's hard truth from the lips of a—a catchpenny whore on the docks of Routreal? What else was left for me indeed?

I was about to admit as much, when the girl emitted a shrill whistle through what teeth she still had. Before I could react, I was lifted by the shoulders and dumped to one side. A steel blade flashed, but not for me. I saw it plunge at the little whore, and I screamed.

Silly me. The only fatality was my hair ribbon. The knife slashed it expertly in two, freeing her wrists.

"How'd you get diddled this time, Queenie?" said a broad-shouldered shadow that had sneaked up on the two of us and only waited for Queenie's signal before pouncing.

"Scrat that, Tol. She's makin' off. Get her!" Makin' off I was, but not for long. Queenie's command sent giant Tol after me, and it was never an even race. His stride covered four of mine, and I was tucked under his arm bedroll-fashion before I got off the dock.

Queenie nodded approval when Tol presented me for her inspection, balancing me on his right hip. She rubbed her wrists and winced. "Too tight. Sometimes you'll have call for tying one of 'em up—some like it—and then it won't do to make it that tight."

"Who is she?" Tol cocked his head to examine his catch. All the kicking and squirming I could do was only a passing inconvenience. He gave me a squeeze and I stopped thrashing.

"Dunno, Tol, but she's worth sommat to us, one way or 'nother. Think you and me can train her? How'd you like two girls workin' for you?"

Tol's smile was dreamy, empty, and frightening to see. "Yeah

. . . like the *real* bullymen. You'll still be my best 'un, though."
He ducked to give Queenie a peck on the forehead.

"I am *not* a whore!"

"Quiet, you." Tol's second squeeze set my ribs grinding
together. "You'll be what I say you are." Queenie giggled.

"Tol's good at talkin' sense into a lass." It was hard to focus
on her face with the way Tol kept resettling me on his hip, but
I think she winked at me. "Now me, I said I wasn't no whore
neither, but Tol took his time. 'Cause he loves me, y'see. He
won't have that much patience with you." To her bullyman
she added, "She'll train."

The rain had stopped and a stiff wind was beginning to
blow. It swept the moon's face clean, letting me see my captors
more distinctly. Shadows or night's own inborn terror may have
glamoured what I saw, but there was so much ruthlessness, so
little pity, such scantling traces of humanity left in them!

I couldn't help it. I didn't care if Tol broke my ribs on his
next try. I screamed.

Tol whipped me out from under his arm and slammed me
against the piling head, which came to just above my waist. I
bent backwards over it, my head hanging down the other side
so that I saw the wavelets lapping at the root of the wharf. He
and Queenie leaned in, their ghostly faces swimming upside
down. I felt their hands on me, but I hurt too much to do more
than gasp and let tears stream from the corners of my eyes.
Their laughter seemed to pour out of some place so deep and
terrible that the demons of the Netherplane feared to go there.

Then, as if it were true that thinking of demons summons
them, a third face appeared in my sight. It was a face of such
immeasurable ugliness that I summoned up an impossible extra
breath and yowled. My paltry shriek was lost, however, in the
racket Tol and Queenie set up when they took a good look at
the horror that had sprung up at their elbows. They released
me so abruptly that I started to slide off the piling head into
the water.

A firm hand pushed me the opposite way and I landed on the wharf timbers. I clung to the piling and sobbed my relief.

Relief, because the demon I'd summoned might have been repugnant, but he was on my side. He took a stand between me and the others so that they got the full impact of his face. All I had to bear was the sight of his back, silver hair streaming like a frost-star, stick-and-knob fingers sending balls of blue fire out to singe Tol and Queenie into yelping, cowering, trembling miseries.

"Begone!" my demon boomed. He sent a last stab of leven-light sizzling into the planking between them. They ran for their lives into the welter of dockside streets.

The demon turned to me.

Esra, save me. What does one pay a demon? I pressed my hands to my mouth. None of the demon-tales Mistress Shana told had any encouraging suggestions. Demons always demanded blood or flesh or worse for their wages. They are poor creditors too, or so the stories say: Pay now or pay sooner.

The stories never told me that demons were courteous, or that one so evil-favored as this one would kneel, touch my arm softly, and ask, "Are you unharmed, child?"

"I—I—"

"You're cold." It didn't take demon-sight to figure that out. The duck-bumps were big as warts on my skin. "Come with me. I don't live far from here. I haven't much to offer you since poor Graniva died, but I know well enough to lay a fire and boil water for myself. We must get the chill off you."

Ah, so this fiend liked his meals at room temperature! I knew better than to disobey. He offered me his arm and conducted me from the wharves back into the finer part of town. At one of those cream-walled houses with an amber lamp burning warmly above the gate, he spoke words of power and the twisted iron swung back.

I heard the gate clash shut behind us as we crossed a tiled courtyard and went up broad serpentine steps into the house. A swarm of rose-gold sparks came out to greet their master when we entered, casting a steady glow over our faces. The odd, charitable quality of that light made the demon's face look less awful. I could stand to look at him without turning my head away, which was fortunate since his next act was to call down a greater light from the ceiling.

It bloomed with the ivory radiance of a water lily and banished the shadows. I saw that we had come into an octagonal room with a firepit in the center. Four of the walls framed doorways leading the gods knew where; the other four were lined with bookshelves. Silk rugs and velvet pillows trimmed with gold were scattered on the floors. Braziers for incense stood sentry at each doorway, their bowls chased with silver, studded with ruby, tourmaline, diamond, and canary-yellow sapphires. Even the books were objects of great price, their spines stiffened with gemmed gold. I had never seen so much wealth.

I had never seen so much filth either.

What I'd taken for silver netting swagging the doorways turned out to be webs of a different sort, and the spiders merrily adding to them. Gray piles of ash spilled over the tops of the braziers to mix with the unscented dust flouring the floors and dimming the colors of the silk rugs. One of the floor-pillows stirred. A fat mouse popped out, having gnawed his way through. My demon growled, which made no impression on the little vermin.

"Nestra! Nestra!" The mouse sat up on its haunches. Did demons name mice and keep them for pets? No, as it turned out. *"Nestra!"* He starred his hands and a sheet of orange light slipped down one of the mysterious hallways like a living carpet, which returned bearing a fat, drowsy particolored cat: Nestra. She stirred when the light-rug landed, stared at the mouse, gave my demon a look that said, *Was that all?* and went back to sleep.

My demon swore and blasted the mouse to flying hair.

"You must excuse me, child," he said. He looked terribly embarrassed, which also helped make his looks more human.

"Things have been in such a state since I lost Graniva. She was my housekeeper."

Even I knew that demons don't hire housekeepers, so it came as no surprise when he went on to say, "I hope you won't think too ill of me. I am Master Urion."

"And I'm Megan." We shook hands formally. "*Master* Urion? Then . . . you're a wizard."

"What did you think I was?"

I didn't take as long as you'd think to find an acceptable answer. "My hero."

And I meant it, too.

He looked both pleased and shy at my words. "I was having my evening stroll when I heard your scream. Scaring off those creatures was the least I could do. I'm no hero."

"Yes, you are; you're mine." I wasn't speaking lightly. "Please don't deny it. I feel—that I need a hero now." Before he could ask too many questions, I picked up a rug and began shaking the dust out of it with great vigor and little sense. "And you—" I said between choking and sneezing and pounding Master Urion on the back while he did the same, "could use a good housecleaning. That's the least *I* can do, if you'll let me."

He consented. But it took me more than a night to cleanse that one room, and then there was the rest of the house to see to, and the pantry to restock, and the kitchen to set right, and even lazy Nestra to be retaught the fine art of mousing. By the time I'd done all that, I was as much an accepted part of the household as the wizard's cat and no longer in agony about where I would go or what I would do to live. A silver-haired magician with a face like a curse had saved me from despair, and what hero ever slew a more deadly monster?

Nestra, apprentice mouser, was not the only new student in Master Urion's house. Master Urion happened to be the most powerful of Routreal's wizards, and the University's most highly regarded instructor. He could not stop teaching even outside the classroom if there was a willing ear. One of the first lessons he taught me—his new housekeeper—was that power can command wealth but wealth can't always command power.

"Then why don't all sorcerers live as well as you?" I asked while I chopped vegetables for our dinner. We'd often have long chats in the kitchen, especially when Urion got so wrapped up in his studies that he missed one meal and wanted the next one before it was ready. Talking to him kept him out of the stewpots, the oven, and my hair.

"Not all adepts have the same amount of power. Or else they do, but some can't control their gifts as well as others. Some never learn where their source lies, and so it remains potential forever, never actual. Oh, we're not having *spinach* again?"

"It was a good buy and it's good for you. It makes your hair shine."

Urion sighed and made his ragged mane of silver hair form itself into a braid. It levitated and twined itself around his neck like a tame serpent. "Lovely. An ogre with shining hair. That should fetch the ladies."

I threatened him with the vegetable knife. "You're *not* an ogre!"

"No, why flatter myself. I should look that handsome!"

I rammed the knife-point into the cutting board. "How many months has it been that I've worked for you, Urion? Six? Seven? And for all your wisdom you still haven't learned how *tired* I am of hearing you call yourself ugly. Will you *stop*?" The blade snapped. "Now look at what you made me do!"

Urion wiggled a finger and the pieces of steel melted back together. Another wiggle honed the edge to blue-gray perfection. I wasn't placated.

"Why do you make me so angry?"

"Do I? If you don't want me in the kitchen . . ."

"That's not what I mean!" He slid off his favorite perch for Megan-watching, a high stool between the brick oven and my worktable. I grabbed a handful of his azure robes to halt him, tugging the fabric off his back.

Urion yanked it back up and gave me a sorrowful, accusing look. "Have a care, Megan. I'm foul enough to see when it's only my face. The face you're used to by now, but the rest—"

"The rest is you, and so's your face, and I don't care! If you're so great a wizard, why don't you change your looks?"

"Why don't I?" He fanned his hands over his face and when he took them away he was too handsome to be anything less than a god. "What woman wouldn't bed me now, eh?" He crossed his wrists one way, then the other, and his entire body gleamed naked and perfect. I gaped until mouth and tongue were dry. The apparition said, "Why, I could go to Madam Glister's House of Prayer right now, couldn't I, and have the finest harlots in Routreal fighting to share my favors. For free!"

"Harlots. . . ."

"Only the best work at the House of Prayer. I know, because this is the seeming I put on when I was younger, and newly come into my full powers. Without this disguise—and I know, because first I tried to go without it—there's a limit to what even a harlot will do. But with it, it was as I'd hoped. Those were the days when Madam Glister herself served the special clients. Do I look special enough, Megan?"

"Very." It was a croak.

"So Madam Glister herself took me on. Would you like to know what happened next?" I nodded, and the demigod's face became even more handsome when he smiled. "My price for a story's end is a kiss."

I walked through a dream to kiss him, and his lips were warmer and more knowing than Hyu's. I closed my eyes, letting myself melt into that one kiss, hoping to hold it forever. Urion's hunger matched my own, and when I thought I would topple from legs whose bones had gone to water, I opened my eyes.

Urion's unbelievably ugly face was back. "That's what happened," he said, and put me away from him at arm's length. "No power is absolute, Megan. Every talent claims its price."

"I know," I said bitterly. "Hyu's talent collected a beauty."

Urion touched the tear that had escaped without my consent. "I know your Hyu very well, Megan. He's one of my finest students, but it's his pride that made him treat you so poorly, not his talent's price. When he grows wiser, he'll see the mistake he made and then he'll ask for your forgiveness."

I shrugged his words aside and got back to my vegetables. "You still owe me the end of your story, not Hyu's, and I paid you for it."

"So you did, so you did. An old man thanks you, even if he did steal that kiss under false pretenses."

"That's another thing; you keep calling yourself *old*! And *ugly*! I'll have you know—"

"If you snap that knife blade again, not all the magic in the world will mend it." I grumbled at Urion's caution. "Very well, Megan, you and I don't agree, but your opinion changes nothing. I can wear a hero's looks, but the slightest stirring in my blood destroys the illusion. The gods are whimsical. Ordinary mortals find that desire gives things the seeming of magic; for me, it destroys magic's self. For that reason I abandoned all hope of love many years ago, or even what passes for love at Madam Glister's."

I heard him sigh, and when I looked up from my chopping board, I was alone in the kitchen. He did not come back to eat when the food was ready, and no amount of knocking at his tower-study door would make him answer.

That night I could not sleep. My thoughts kept returning to Master Urion. His melancholy eyes haunted me, though I had seen similar looks many times at our table at the Horseman's Bones. I'd clicked my tongue and made sympathetic noises; hollow ones. I hadn't lost sleep over their troubles. Why should it be different for Master Urion?

He had given me a fine room only half a story lower than his tower from whose wide window I could see moonlight on the northern waves. My bed was also wide—wider and more comfortable than any I'd known—and the sheets smelled of lilac conjured into bloom throughout the year by Urion's enchantments. A branch of that same sweet flower nodded in a silver vase on my bedside table.

I sat up in bed to finger the clustered trumpet-shaped blossoms. Urion and I had been talking of this and that and I had mentioned that lilacs were my favorite flower. Now he grew them for me.

Why did I see his ugly face in the heart of such a lovely flower? I thought about it, and I couldn't find the words. Then I knew that this was no matter where words would serve me.

I reached for my dressing-gown and got out of bed, a sheepskin rug and slippers waiting to protect my feet from the chill stone floor. Had I remarked once—only once—that I could bear anything but cold feet? The fleecy slippers and rug were in my room by that evening.

The house was silent as I padded through the halls. I surprised Nestra enjoying a midnight snack, the thin pink mouse tail dangling from her whiskered lips. There was no slit of light visible under the tower-room door. I went down a level and a half to the narrow room Urion kept for himself.

("I am a pocket-mouse, Megan. I like to sleep well tucked in, with walls as well as blankets. The room I've given you may be the largest in the house, but no matter where I sleep, it will still be the master's bedroom, now won't it?")

His door was unlocked. A star hung transfixed at the apex of the lone lancet window. The room itself was austere, clean even when the rest of the house had been cluttered. No books were here, no fine rugs or sparkling lamps. I folded my dressing-gown and laid it across the little bench at the foot of Urion's bed. I braced myself for the cold shock when my slipperless feet touched the bare floor before I pulled back the covers and slowly slid into bed by his side.

Urion stirred and rolled over. His eyes snapped open the moment he realized I was no dream.

"Great Sarogran! What are you doing h—?"

I rested my hands on his chest where the hair was silver shot with gray and strands of black. He was not so old as he

claimed, my Urion. My arms glided up to wreathe his neck
and bring his mouth down on mine. He thrust himself away.
"Are you insane, Megan?"

I wrinkled my brow. "I don't know. Mistress Shana used to
say that every soul's entitled to wear seven skins in a lifetime,
and sometimes insanity's one of them. Do you think I'm crazy
for kissing you?"

"Yes!"

"Why? I didn't think you were insane when you kissed me
this afternoon." I leaned up on one elbow, recalling the incident
fondly. "I liked it."

For some reason Master Urion readjusted the covers over
me. "Well, of *course* I wasn't crazy to kiss *you*! You're—
you're a wonderful girl; so sweet, so young, so very pretty.
But I am old, and ugly, and—"

"And stupid." I kissed him again, this time with no nonsense
allowed. "Mistress Shana said that if only pretty folk kissed,
where did all the plain folk come from?"

"I am worse than plain, as this all-knowing Mistress Shana
of yours would tell you the minute she saw me. Megan, Megan,
your heart was badly used when you came here, and I'd rescued
you from danger. I gave you work and a place to belong. Don't
mistake gratitude for love. Don't feel you must pay me back
for a debt that isn't there."

I cupped his dear, kind, hideous face in my hands. "I haven't
got a wizard's wisdom, Master Urion. But whatever my inborn
talent is, Lord Deveril's mage couldn't read it, so wizards don't
know everything. I can tell love from gratitude ... and from
revenge, if you're afraid I'm only doing this to spite Hyu. I'm
not here because of the things you've done for me, but because
it takes a certain kind of man to do such things in the first
place. I'm here—" and I moved closer until I could feel the
heat emanating from him and hear his quickened breathing
come louder than my words, "because I love that man. I only
just puzzled it through for myself an hour past, and I came
soon as I knew."

I spoke this last so near his face that our mouths brushed, then clung together.

Which seemed like such a good idea that our bodies soon copied it, improved on it, and took it to its logical conclusion.

Later I plucked tangles out of his silver hair and teased, "I can leave, if you like. No man should have to share his bed with a madwoman."

"Dearest Megan!" my Urion gasped. "If I'd have you leave me now, I'd be the one who's insane."

Little changed for me after that. Little, and everything. I still kept Urion's house in order, merely exchanging one bed for another when my workday was done. He still lectured me while I worked in the kitchen, only now he interrupted my work to do it.

"Today we had the most interesting discussion on the advantages of blood sacrifice when calling upon the powers of the fourth plane. Young Taleen insisted that a little blood always makes the spell-casting go better. Foolish cub!"

"Yes," I said, not really listening. Pie-crust tends to absorb almost as much attention as a rowdy two-year-old. "No results without blood sacrifice."

"Megan—" He forcibly separated me from my rolling pin. "Love, you know as well as any of my students that the powers of the *fourth* plane are *nurturing*, not *destructive*. They consider blood sacrifice an insult."

"Fourth plane, fifth plane, seventy-third plane!" I threw up my hands. "How should I know the difference?"

Urion was perfectly serious. "Because I told it to you once, and once is enough for an intelligent human being."

"Intelligent?"

"It's no insult."

"I never said it was, Urion. But *me*, intelligent?"

It was a revelation. No other person in my life had bothered to conjecture whether I had a brain capable of doing more than counting sheep, washing socks, making love, and baking pies, not necessarily in that order. Urion soon set me straight, for he'd seen enough students to know intelligence from flash (a far harder distinction to make than that between smarts and stupidity). Our kitchen chats took on a new dimension from that day. Now I listened, and listening, learned.

He tried to teach me some sorcery, but Master Gwyth was right: I had no talent there. I had occasional successes, but for the most part the spells I cast were never *quite* right.

"Your talent must lie elsewhere, my dear," Urion mused after my last try at levitating a bunch of grapes from our bedside table. They had risen, wobbled towards us, and exploded in a series of juicy *plops* as they cruised in over the bedsheets.

I swore a number of new oaths Urion had taught me. "And what is it, then? Getting juice stains out of linens?"

He laughed, and bathed the sheets with white light that left them spotless. "I can't say; nor do I care. I love you with or without your mysterious talent, which is only right. For when we warm each other, my magic deserts me. We are happiest as equals, you and I."

I agreed it was so, and did what I could to sate my democratic impulses then and there. But alas, sometimes the gods' whimsy hides great cruelty. My Urion lost all magic when in my arms, even the minor magic wards he'd placed over his health, never telling me. He was not so old as he claimed, but not so young as I thought either, or so hale.

He died in my arms that night. I slept deeply, and never knew when my lover's breath stopped.

His three apprentices found me weeping over his body the next morning when they came to fetch him for his first class. They shooed me from the room, but not quickly enough for me to miss the expressions of disgust they exchanged. I went to my quarters and dressed, assembling my possessions on the bed. It hadn't been used for more than a mattressed table in eight months. I knew what was coming.

The senior apprentice didn't bother to knock. "We have seen to Master Urion's body. There's nothing more for you here, wench."

I refused to look at him. I still nurse a childish aversion to slugs. He mistook my silence for complacency.

"I said you can be off! Master Urion left no will, if you're thinking of vulture-pickings. His estate reverts to the King."

"Even Nestra?"

"What? That crazy old man had *another* doxy tucked away?" The apprentice's expression made me think of a toad the minute a cartwheel passes over its squat body. "No wonder he dropped dead!"

"Nestra is—was his cat." Right on cue, Nestra presented herself in the doorway and leaped onto my bed, where she curled up purring and went to sleep.

"Oh." The slug looked cheated. He also looked over my assembled belongings closely. "At least you're an honest wench. I see nothing of the Master's here. You can pack up and go. Take the cat, if you like," he added in a burst of generosity.

He remained to make sure I packed only what was displayed on the bed. It made a compact bundle which I bound across the small of my back, then took Nestra in my arms. She mewed once for form's sake before resuming her nap. The slug backed himself against the doorjamb to avoid contamination as I passed.

I stopped at just the point where the two of us had only a hair's-breadth between us. It wouldn't be polite to go without saying a proper good-bye.

"Fellow, I am no more a doxy or a wench than Master Urion was a 'crazy old man.' A doxy trades sex for pay, a wench has no dreams beyond her scrub-bucket, your mother was a whore, and you're a drip of snot. Good day."

I contaminated him in the nuts with my knees for emphasis and was out the front door before he collapsed.

It was still very early. Servants clattered through the streets to do the first marketing of the day for their masters. They had better things to do than note a young girl carrying a plump calico cat. I hadn't far to walk; the house I sought lay comfortably near the best neighborhood of Routreal.

I hadn't the luxury of time to mull over what I should do

with my life now. The mediocre bits of jewelry Urion had
given me as gifts were tucked inside my sash where no apprentice slug had bothered to look, but I couldn't live on them
forever. Urion had awakened me to my own intelligence, and
my intelligence told me I'd be foolish to hope for a second
miracle to swoop down and take care of Nestra and me. I made
what I felt was the best choice for us; made it quickly, though
it wasn't an easy one. Perhaps I'd always known I'd come to
it. I could wander door to door, seeking a housekeeper's post
and settling for a drudge's grind, or . . .

The doorkeeper at the House of Prayer was grouchy, but he
let me in when I mentioned Master Urion's name. Madam
Glister herself was less than cordial, which was understandable
given the unholy hour, the sun still *ascending*, for the love of
heaven!

"You and Urion?" She squinted her hard blue eyes. "How
could you stand—? Pfff. No concern of mine, is it? If you
could do that, you'll do here. And you're pretty enough. We'll
try you for a week, then out."

"Yes, Madam Glister. I'll go whenever you say. But would
you mind"—she was suddenly awake, and alive with cold
suspicion—"if Nestra stayed on? She was Master Urion's, and
I'd like to know she's cared for."

Madam Glister's fat, pearly-skinned body shook with laughter that was astonishingly warm. "Bless you, girl, the kindness
of you! I think I see why you were able to take poor Urion to
your bed! But if you come into the House of Prayer with love
packed in your baggage, you won't last long."

In the small room she assigned me, I made my blanket into
a bed for Nestra. I laid out all my things, this time placing the
jewelry in plain sight as well, then drew up the only real
treasure I'd brought out of Urion's house, hanging from a
brown silk cord around my neck. The apprentice slug hadn't
noticed it, or thought it held some ignoramus's amulet.

It didn't. Three vials of gilded glass came up the cord one
by one, tied to it cunningly so they wouldn't clink together,

each tightly stoppered and ringed with brass. Master Urion had given me more than jewelry.

("For me? But you said I had no skills in sorcery."

"As little skill as I have in reading the future. Yet sometimes I still toy with the crystal. Take them."

"What did you see in our future, beloved? Am I going to have a rival?" I thought I would tease him. "Will I have to reawaken your desires with love-potions?"

Urion shook his head. He wasn't smiling and he refused to say any more. There were bans on recounting future visions that applied to any mage not a licensed oracle, bans Urion respected and feared.)

I held the three mysteries up to the light, pondering their contents. When my lover gave me the vials, he'd promised to teach me how to use them when he had the time to spare.

When he had the time. . . . I wept for Urion.

The week's trial run went by and I stayed on. My coworkers had the benefit of more experience and greater technical proficiency, but I had—something. "Born to the bedsheets," to quote Madam Glister. My name and reputation became more widely known with every night that passed. My employer was pleased. Amazing how easily she let seven days become seven months, then more.

"Megan, precious," she cooed, braiding my hair with her own hands and starring it with the emerald ornaments that were a gift from Lord Deveril's brother-in-law. "Have you ever wondered why I called this place the House of Prayer?" I shook my head, which made her chuckle. "Because our clientele spend so much time on their knees. Only, lately they spend it begging for you. I hate to see grown men beg. I prefer it when they grovel. I'm going to give you right of refusal. You can turn down any customer except the few we don't dare reject."

Nestra leaped onto my dressing-table and interposed herself between my face and the mirror. The furnishings and decor of my suite were a dramatic change from my originally assigned hole-and-corner. Such are the perquisites of success in the finer arts. I stroked the cat and murmured, "Who could those happy few be? The ones we don't dare turn away?"

Madam Glister tossed her short, artificially golden ringlets. "You'll find out when you need to. I'd think you'd be thanking me! Not every one of my girls gets to pick and choose so early on in her career. Don't you appreciate your refusal rights?"

Ho, didn't I! Especially when doe-eyed Jaroel spread the word that a party of wealthy University students were coming to the House of Prayer solely to bid for a night with me. They were waiting downstairs and had ordered the best wines in Madam Glister's well-watered cellar.

Jaroel, Sarita, and I all knelt giggling in a circle around the Eye of Heaven, a cunning peephole set in the floor of the second story which gave the girls clear sight of their waiting clients downstairs.

"Students!" Jaroel hissed. "But rich ones. I didn't think they existed. Oooh, here they come now. I know 'em by the tunics. I wonder what it's like, having a would-be mage for your lover?"

"Shut up, stupid!" Sarita gave her a nudge in the side that knocked her off her knees. She jerked her head in my direction. Sweet Sarita was the best friend I'd made in the House of Prayer, in spite of being city-bred. She knew about Hyu, and I shared her secret—a baby being brought up far from Routreal by a farmer's wife. Nearly all her earnings went for her baby's keep—and sometimes some of mine.

"What was that for?" Jaroel smoothed her gossamer robes, silvery and transparent as a waterspray. "Don't hog the Eye, Sarita. I want another look at the chinless one."

"Chinless one?" I was the one who elbowed Jaroel aside this time. One look confirmed what I'd suspected ever since the news of "rich students" filtered into the brothel: Thares and his crew. There they were, all the familiar faces from the Horseman's Bones; the moneyed ones only, to be sure. I didn't see Sandar or Heliad with them.

I did see Hyu. Tutoring half-heads like Thares was paying

well. He wore a gold chain whose every link would buy a night with Jaroel or any of the lower-ranked women.

One night with me would cost him a quarter of the chain. *If* I did not refuse him.

I straightened up and looked at myself in one of the many mirrors lining the corridors of the House of Prayer. Nights of love could wear away the most willing woman, but days spent being pampered, well-fed, and waited on when you've had a life of mostly hard work and little thanks worked a contradictory magic. I had bloomed into a well-contented flower of the night.

What a world of difference between this life and that pitiful little dockside whore's existence, I thought, whirling on my toes so that my gold-green gown billowed out and my tiny bronze sandals shot back rays of light from the candles.

What did I know of how thin the barriers are that lie between certain worlds?

"Ladies, let's not keep Routreal's most promising future wizards waiting." I offered Jaroel and Sarita my arms.

When we three entered Madam Glister's parlor, the gentlemen all rose. You may guess how they reacted when they saw my face. After the requisite moment of shock, the hurried gale of whispers—*Can it be? Is it really she? Not Hyu's Megan? Hyu's no longer, fool! Gods, and did we never see what she was? Our instructors often said we'd pay for our ignorance. Pay's the right word! Madam Glister commands her highest prices for a night with that one*—they fell back to talk matters over.

Hyu alone stood clear of the huddle. He stared at me, all the blood gone from his cheeks. I smiled demurely and poured wine for our other guests. Thares had to call him three times by name and loose a small fireball at his rump to make him turn around and pay attention. The students' conferral grew more heated once Hyu joined. He tried to break away, but his friends hauled him back. Madam Glister's unofficial "husband" stirred in his corner long enough to growl a threat of eviction if they didn't dumb up, show their money, and make their choices.

Thares won that worthy man's affection with an immediate show of gold, a roulade twin to the one Hyu'd pressed on me the day he wished me well and farewell.

"It's all settled, friend. Only one of your resident divinities will do: Megan."

I continued to pour, keeping my back to the students. Madam Glister's man would handle matters from this point. I saw no need to speak up . . . yet. Out of the corner of my eye I saw him heft Thares's gold and find it satisfactory.

"Well, this'll do . . . seein' as yer students." (Thares had merely paid twice my going price, poor sot.) He tossed the take in the air and Madam Glister's doughy paw snagged it at the apex. "Arrrrr . . ."

"Don't sulk, lovey, you'll have your share." She chucked him under one of his stubbly chins. "These young men are our guests. A band of brothers. Aren't you going to ask them to have a taste of something while they're waiting for their friend? The lucky lad who'll go with our Megan." She simpered at Thares. She tried chucking him under the chin too, but gave it up as hopeless.

"Oh, it's not for *me* to go with her, Madam Glister." Thares gave a signal, and four of the others converged on Hyu, wedging him forward. All were leering like depraved midden-dogs; all had their arms around Hyu's shoulders. That was a powerful burden of arms. Hyu staggered, then recovered nicely.

Thares purred into Madam Glister's delicate ear, "She's a gift. For him."

Madam Glister rolled the silk-bound gold coins back and forth in her hand from palm to knuckles to fingertips. "Such a thoughtful gesture. A pity your friend doesn't look more appreciative."

"Oh, he'll thank us for it tomorrow. He's—been having trouble getting over a lost love. You know how it is, Madam. Time adds such an aura of romance to what was just another woman. Sometimes it takes the hair of the dog to cure you of more than drink. Or the hair of some other pet." Thares all but patted himself on the back for that bit of wit.

"And one woman's so like another, is that it?" Madam Glister's eyebrows rose. Thares's head bobbed frantically. "A born horn-head. What a plum husband you'll make someday." Before Thares could ask for a repetition, she sailed to my side and asked, "Well, Megan? Will you have him?"

"Wh-why are you asking *her*? I paid in good faith!" Thares looked like a mortally insulted rabbit.

"And you shall be reimbursed in good faith if Megan refuses your friend. In view of her popularity and renown, I've given her that privilege."

"*Refusal?* Of a paying guest—in *advance*, no less!—by a common *whore?*"

Madam Glister's "husband" lifted Thares's collar half a span higher from behind, which gave Thares an entirely new perspective on things. When he let Thares's feet touch the floor once more, the young mage-to-be cleared his throat painfully and used more courteous terms.

Madam Glister waved his excuses aside. "It's up to Megan. Well, child?"

I set down the silver pitcher and sauntered over to where my four former drinking "friends" still held Hyu. I put everything I had into that saunter, and I'd acquired plenty during my stint at the House of Prayer. An oiled eel was stiff as a stick next to me, and not half so interestingly endowed. I let the silence get thick as I pleased before I shrugged and said, "Why not?"

Hyu's friends pounded him on the back and traded hearty congratulations, as if they somehow got to share my body vicariously that way. Hyu remained silent, following me at a distance as I led the way to my chambers. Thares and the rest were anteing the price of less expensive girls when we left them.

As I expected, Hyu found his tongue as soon as we were alone. "Megan! How *could* you?"

"Sheer good luck."

"Good luck? To be a whore?"

"Hush, Hyu, or I'll have to send for Madam Glister's friend. The one who gave Thares a lesson in levitation? Whores you find on the docks. Courtesans stay behind palace walls or keep their own households. Doxies cater to those whose coin's colored copper and silver, not gold. Harlots rank above doxies but below courtesans. Now do you have it right?"

Hyu sat on my bed and sank deep into the down mattress beneath the white and silver spread. He folded his arms across his chest, looking like a bottle-sprite newly uncorked and enthroned on his cloud of enchantments. "I have no use for that information, and neither will you. Get your things. We're leaving." *And no nonsense out of you, my girl!* his eyes added.

I curled up at his feet, my linked hands hugging his knees while I gave him the full force of my *Tell me more, you adorable, wise, and completely infallible man* look.

"Are we, dearest?" A nice catch came into my voice. "You mean—after all this time—you'll forgive me? You'll have me back?"

Hyu pursed his lips. If not, I suppose his brim-full self-righteousness might have spilled over and stained the rug. "You made a mistake, Megan. You ought to learn from it, as I learned from mine. I should have taken you home myself, before you got yourself so unfortunately involved here. I see now how badly you needed my guidance."

"Oh yes, dearest Hyu, I need you. I need your guidance. I need your wisdom. I need your firm hand . . . like a pig needs a purple pizzle!" I shot arrow-straight and -swift for the door. Flinging it open I shouted for Madam Glister, and when she came puffing up the stairs I told her that I'd changed my mind.

"As you like it, child," she said, trying to hide the good-bye–gold sadness in her greedy little heart.

"Sweet Madam Glister, cheer up. You'll keep the gold. Where's the chinless wonder?"

"In there." She pointed to Jaroel's room. "But he's already with—"

"Three isn't always a crowd. He won't mind." I knew whereof I spoke. Hyu got not so much as a backward glance as I floated blithely into Jaroel's room.

The next night, Hyu was back. I found him knotted up in a corner of the parlor when we all came down to begin our shift. His eyes lit on me for an instant, then he pounced on Madam Glister. "I want her; Megan."

Madam Glister was bemused. "She still has refusal rights."

"I only want to talk to her."

"I'm sure."

"I'm in earnest, Madam Glister. I can't afford to pay for more than a few minutes of her time. I know what a—what a mistress of this craft charges." A thick loop of gold traded hands; one link of the chain he'd worn the previous night.

Madam Glister dangled it thoughtfully by her earlobe. "Talk or not, it's still up to—"

"I'll talk to him, Madam."

This time Hyu was less demanding when we were alone in my rooms. "Please, Megan, you must come away."

I, in turn, was more direct. "Says bloody well who?"

Hyu paced the floor, hands behind his back, while I took the opportunity to freshen my paint and give Nestra an extra measure of milk. "I can't stand it, seeing you here. I hate knowing that it's all my fault! I must save you from this life."

"From regular meals, nice clothes, hot baths, and no *really* loathsome chores? From *these*?" I held up a strand of matched gray pearls. "Thares sent them by this morning." I rubbed them against my teeth and smiled. "They're real."

Hyu grabbed them and ground them into the rug. It didn't harm the pearls, but I got Madam Glister's "husband" and Hyu ended up in the alley, rump foremost.

From such romantic moments great traditions spring. He

came back the following night, and the next, and the next.
Always he paid for a few minutes of my time with a link of
his plundered gold chain. Always he spent his purchased minutes badgering, besieging, begging me to quit the House of
Prayer. As to what I would be leaving it *for* . . . Hyu waxed
vague. Sometimes he left on his own two feet when the time
was up, defeated. Sometimes he departed by air, courtesy of
Madam's "husband."

Don't think my stay at the House of Prayer consisted entirely
of these soul-satisfying interviews with Hyu; not at all. There
were other callers, many of them, and often enough these were
Hyu's wealthy student friends. Would you think I'd turn them
away as vengeance for how they'd turned Hyu from me?

Children, you have much to learn about revenge. It is an
art like any other, and has its master hands as well as its
dabblers. I like to think I rose from the amateurs' ranks with
my treatment of Hyu's friends. With one swoop I plucked them
of gold and gifts. With one judicious sigh I let each one dream
I loved only him. With one well-timed yawn I sapped them of
every drop of manly confidence and pride I'd falsely loaned
them. With one whispered lie I puffed their egos back up to
the point where they would nevermore find satisfaction with
another woman, then turned them away from my arms forever.

On days when Madam Glister gave us our short vacations,
I would often see Thares and the rest of my student handiwork
in the markets and shops. They fled to the far side of the street
when they saw me coming, or else stood shaking like wet dogs,
unable to flee until I turned my eyes elsewhere. Little children
in grown men's skins they were, every one of them, who want
the bright jewels they see glowing in the blacksmith's forge.
They grasp them, they're badly burned, they ought to have
learned from the experience, and yet . . . the beauty of the blazing coals still beckons and they will stretch out their hands for
them again.

Sometimes I would stop and accost one of them, link my
arm in his, and force him to squire me through the market. It

was gratifying to watch the changes run across his face: *Megan has chosen me! How lucky I am! ... Amn't I? Yes, of course I am, because Megan has ... chosen me for what? The last time I paid for her favors, didn't she say—? Gods above, tell me whether to rejoice or run away!*

If you are good girls and don't fall asleep too often during the duller festivals, you may hear the priests claim that revenge belongs to the gods and should never be the property of man.

Leave it to the gods to hog the best bits of life for themselves. When you have your enemies skewered, I think it would be wasteful not to stay and watch them writhe. I would even call it impolite. I value courtesy. With each of Hyu's darling friends I stayed, I watched, I improved upon the number and placement of the skewers.

It was fun.

The gods were not amused. They are past masters when it comes to exacting payment from mortals who have gone too far and displeased them by enjoying life too much, and I was among the guilty. Isn't it true that most temple sacrifices are made by those of us up to our necks in muck, or else are thank-offerings from those freshly hauled ashore? When all goes well, we tend to forget that the gods appreciate a cow or two slaughtered in their names now and then. It keeps things friendly.

If I'd known what the gods were preparing for me, I wouldn't have left an altar vacant or a cow alive within ten miles of Routreal.

CHAPTER III
The Lay of the Last Minstrel

Madam Glister and I knelt at the Eye of Heaven, although it cost my fat meretrix an effort to find her knees.

"No," I moaned. "Not him again!"

"Be still, child! He'll hear you. I did not make this peephole soundproof." To prove her point, she gave me a box on the ear that echoed the length of the upstairs hall. When my eyes uncrossed and I could focus them on the downstairs doings, I saw my swain's attendant decade of armed Guardsmen with their pikestaffs ready, searching everywhere for the source of that minor explosion.

His Serenity, Prince Zimrit, continued to play with his nose.

"You are the most contrary girl I've ever known," Madam Glister hissed. "Any of your sisters would be pouring out frankincense by the dipperful in thanks for a royal patron; the fifth son of our lord the King!"

"They'd need it. Prince Zimrit doesn't believe in baths."

"Do you want another smack?" She raised her hand. I'd learned to my sorrow that overall flab is no sure indication that your foe is a weakling. Madam Glister packed a substantial wallop, and the gold rings on her fingers were like iron bands on a cudgel.

"Don't you dare!" I cried, ducking. "You'll mark me, and then what will you tell His Serenity?"

Reluctantly the hand came down. "Hmph. I suppose *I* ought to be the grateful one: grateful that you're a pea-head. A lass with sense would have Prince Zimrit take her for a concubine, and then where would my cut be?"

Only because my cheek still tingled did I reply, "Maybe I've been too hasty. Smell isn't everything. Men who shower you with rubies are so much rarer than men who shower themselves. I wouldn't mind being Prince Zimrit's concubine. I'll just try the idea on him tonight." I got up and pinched the other cheek to have a matched set, both flaming red. "Too bad about your cut, Madam Glister."

"Still a pea-head," said the redoubtable bawd, not at all ruffled by my threatened defection. "Why do you think His Serenity insists on seeing you, hey? Jaroel's prettier, Sarita's more submissive, Barti's got so many surprises between her thighs that they ought to declare her *si'ir* a royal research library—"

"I'm more intelligent."

Madam Glister spat in a ladylike manner. "Prince Zimrit wouldn't recognize intelligence if it sat on his— Megan, the Prince has half a score of concubines already, and his father's forever buying him new ones because His Majesty has seven sons and *no* imagination when it comes to birthday gifts. Many of those harem girls have special training that would make even our Barti take notes. If you're so intelligent, tell me this: What can Prince Zimrit have from you here for pay that he can't have at home for free?"

I pondered her words. At last I admitted myself stumped. "Gods know what's so special he can have *from* me, Madam Glister, but I know that if he didn't pay and weren't one of those we daren't refuse, he certainly wouldn't have *me*!"

"Precisely." Madam Glister smirked. "Mortals always hanker after what they can't have. And Prince Zimrit also knows that while certain men may enjoy your body, no man can have your love. Which is why the dumb bastard insists on trying to prove he'll be the miraculous exception to the rule. You're his obsession. Do you know, I think he's actually trying to thaw that lump of ice you're cherishing between your titties?"

I crossed my hands over my heart. "Who ever said—?"

"Don't look so outraged, child. Rumors fly faster than dragons. Do you know what they say of you in the streets? Megan the Unapproachable. Megan the Distant Princess. Megan the Unattainable. Megan the Cruel Fair One whose heart has turned to stone, who ruins men for a whim, who has forsworn love forever!" She nibbled the tip of her finger. "You are a compendium of romantic possibilities. If only I knew my letters, what an epic I could write about you."

The disappointed authoress heaved herself to hands and knees, then used my outstretched arms as a ladder to get upright. She puffed like a walrus. "Shall we see to His Serenity's pleasure?"

Descending the stairs I said, "I don't ruin men for a *whim*, Madam Glister. I resent that! My reasons—"

"Your reasons concern yourself. I do not make up the gossip, Megan, though I'm not above profiting from it. We duskflowers are unique among women because if the man has our price, we go with him, and no balking allowed."

I thought of Stepda's demands and of Mistress Corinel back home, whose husband had a birchy way of making her agreeable to his embraces whenever he liked, but she didn't. Not too much room for balking there. Was Mistress Corinel to abandon her home and children? All she had to her name were six rachitic sheep; hardly the stuff of financial independence. In that family the wealth came from the inanimate side—the tools her husband forged and sold—making him master of the purse-strings. How could Mistress Corinel leave? How could she do other than consent to her man's demands if she stayed?

Prices aren't always paid out in gold coin, nor are dusk-flowers as unique as Madam Glister preached. Oh well, leave the lady her illusions.

"But you, Megan, are unique among duskflowers. You have the right to turn away any man."

"Not quite, or I wouldn't get within spitting distance of His Serenity."

Madam dug her burnished nails into my arm. "That will be our little secret. He *thinks* you can refuse him the same as any other man you don't fancy, but you never have. And never will. Yet the *possibility* of refusal remains, making you the one undependable pleasure in Prince Zimrit's life. I think the pampered highborn like the fantasy of equality. The idea that you might drain him to a husk and toss him aside to rot the way you treated that unfortunate former student of wizardry— What was his name? The one with those divine blue eyes who absolutely ruined himself . . . ? You know, the one who only came to chat with you? Not a bad-looking—"

"Hyu?" I pulled up short. This maneuver on a steep staircase is often dangerous, more so when you're being dragged along by a fat lady. Madam Glister's inertia would be legend if legends dwelt on physics.

"That one. Used to be a University student."

"*Used* to be?"

Madam Glister was overjoyed. Usually she was the last one to get the gossip from the girls, but this time she could do the telling. "Child, where have you *been*? Didn't you notice how long it's been since he's come around to speak with you? Well, our Jaroel noticed all right. When she crawls out of her bottle, she's got a sharp eye for the likelier men. I think she had hopes of his giving up on you and turning elsewhere. Being wise, she prepared herself. She had Nilsa—you know, our scullery wench—trail him, learn his comings and goings, find out his desires and delights."

Bitterly I asked, "And how did Nilsa like the crowd at the Horseman's Bones?"

"Hmph. No doubt she'd have preferred it to the crowd where that fellow *did* go. At least the Horseman's Bones is a tavern where the lice have the courtesy to stay upstairs. Not like the nameless hole he returned to the night she followed him. It's a greasy dive near the docks, very close to where the river pours into the northern sea. Upriver dockside taverns are rather nice, and the farther upriver you go, the nicer they get, but the ones on the salt—" She shuddered.

I remembered Tol and Queenie, whose purlieu was the salt-water docks. I shuddered too.

"But why—why was he there? Whatever else Hyu was, he was a brilliant student. He had the inborn gift of wizardry!"

Madam Glister tilted her head in speculation. "Well, well, it seems our Megan's not entirely stone. Those godsgift blue eyes found a mark."

"Hang his eyes and Hyu with them!" I stamped my foot. "We're from the same village, and that is *all* the tie between us. I was there when Lord Deveril, the King's Man, picked Hyu out for the University during the Tenfold Search. Magic's in him, and he had brains enough to tutor talentless winesacks like Thares and the rest. What happened to him?"

"Why, Megan . . . you did."

"*I?*"

"Close your mouth, lovey, it gives you a double chin. Why gape? Did your village boy come from wealthy stock? Did you fancy he had a bottomless supply of gold to spend on your little *chats*? Nilsa's a sharp wench and looks little more than a child. She pretended she'd lost her way, wept a bit, all the tricks, and snagged him with sympathy before pumping him dry. She found out that he'd spent all he had on seeing you— what for, the gods know—even to the meager stipend the King paid him. He needed more money, so he approached his fellow students."

"More tutoring?" I nodded knowingly. "Trying to fill Thares's skull with knowledge is like pounding sand in a rat-hole."

"The rat is sometimes home. Thares is rumored to have

offered Hyu a fabulous sum if he would attempt a spell of disguisement, assume Thares's looks, and take a nasty little oral exmination in his place."

"Hyu would never—"

"Oh Megan, you're too young to use 'never' with so much certainty! Your friend wanted money; doesn't that explain and excuse all? He took the risk, but the greatest dollop of native ability must be properly disciplined. He'd mastered *physical* disguisement only. When the examiners asked the first question of 'Thares,' Hyu's proper voice emerged in midsentence. They stripped him of the spell, then placed him on suspension for a term."

"Only a term? Four months. That's not so bad." I was surprised at how relieved I sounded when I should have been gloating.

"If you have ready cash to live on, a year's suspension is nothing either," said Madam Glister. "But your Hyu's a poor lad, and poorer, thanks to you. There's no King's stipend paid him during suspension, and so he's gone down to the salt-docks to peddle what scraps of magic he already has. At least I *hope* it's magic he'll sell down in that part of town."

I plucked at her thickly embroidered sleeve. "What do you mean?"

She stood on the sconce-lit stairway studying my face for some time before she answered. At first she said in a barely audible mumble, "The same village the only tie? Indeed." Then louder, "On the salt-docks there are some men who'll pay better rates for fine-looking lads than for student magics."

Oh, Hyu! Brighter lights made me blink. Madam Glister had led me the rest of the way down the stairs and into the parlor without my even noticing. Prince Zimrit patted the cushions beside him and I sat. He inserted one hand between my breasts, the other between my legs, and grinned at his Guardsmen as if awaiting applause for his artful way with women. I experienced his routine explorations in a daze.

My poor, poor Hyu!

"What's the matter with her?" Prince Zimrit whined for help from Madam Glister. Usually I'd wriggle nearer and make the appropriate sounds during our preliminary socializing. Now I just sat like a billet of cordwood.

"Nothing, Your Serenity; not a thing!" Madam Glister trilled reassurances in Prince Zimrit's hairy ears while giving me a surreptitious tweak. I snapped out of shock, but immediately lapsed into tears.

"*Now* what's wrong?" The Prince was offended. "Is she trying to tell me something? Is she going to refuse me?"

"Megan refuse *you*? Has she ever done so before?" I got another tweak, harder. My howl of pain blended right into a sob and Zimrit missed it.

"Women are . . . funny things." His Serenity chewed one end of his drooping black mustache. "You never know. . . ."

"Which is why a man of your wonderful instincts and sensitivity is so welcome in our happy House of Prayer. Only a real man can *understand* women. Megan's like the rest of us— such unstable emotions. The slightest thing affects her. Sweet child, she was reading a book of poems and accidentally stumbled across one in which a little crippled blind boy loses his only companion, a mongrel pup, when a cart full of winter squash runs it over. Written entirely in alexandrines, too. It's quite undone her. The sooner she reads another, *cheerier* poem"— I got a sharp thump in the back on *cheerier*—"I know she'll be her old self."

"We leave!" Prince Zimrit clapped his hands. The Guards formed up ranks and stamped their pikestaff butts smartly on the floor before all departed in a wedge of tramping boots. Madam Glister was beside herself.

Before the echoes of their departure died from the streets (and before Madam Glister could catch me in a wild sprint for survival from parlor to cellar to garret back to parlor and the ambushing arms of her "husband"), they returned. Madam Glister trod on her "husband's" toes as soon as she saw her bird of paradise safely in hand again.

"My *dear* Prince Zimrit—"

"Why does the big one hold a tattered piece of my Megan's robe in his grimy fingers?"

"Good luck charm."

This was drivel, a language the Prince spoke fluently. He accepted the explanation at face, then declaimed, "I am back!" The audience response was understated. Even Zimrit decided something more was needed, so he said, "I have brought the antidote."

"What anti—? I mean, who's been pois—? Uh . . . that is to say . . . how nice." Madam dredged up a watery smile.

The antidote smiled back. He was the scrawniest jack-a-dandy bit of dancing meat ever to enter the House of Prayer. Most minstrels wear a patchwork suit to cover the fact that their garments are all patches anyway, but this man's warp and woof threads were quickly parting company. His buttery hair was stringier than his clothes, though his black eyes darted all around the parlor, sucking up its fineries. He had the tallow-colored skin of a man whose living is earned by night, when it's earned at all. Only the full-bellied lute slung across his back had anything like a healthy glow to it.

"I could not buy her a cheery poem to read." Prince Zimrit sounded slightly sheepish. "All the booksellers were closed. My men found this in a wineshop. He says he knows poetry."

Prince Zimrit's chief Guardsman gave the fellow a buffet. "Earn the coin His Serenity's been gracious enough to pay you! Sing!"

The minstrel had his lute off his back and ready at once. A second buffet for dawdling would have snapped him in two. "I am at His Serenity's service." His voice was as rich as his life was poor. "What would these noble patrons hear?"

"Sing something cheerful or I'll have you gutted and strung to your own lute," said His Serenity. He drew me back into his arms. "You must make my lovely Megan smile."

The minstrel made a court bow with all the trimmings. "I

am Eliard, and I will coax a frown to a smile, a smile to laughter, tears to mirth and—"

"Sing."

I would have smiled anyway. Prince Zimrit always kept his word when he promised something sadistic, and I had a feeling we'd have to witness the whole sanguinary operation if Eliard failed. I grinned like a monkey as soon as he struck the first chord. Zimrit saw, and was pleased. He reinserted his hands, not before motioning the minstrel to carry on. I used all the old deceptions on the Prince, smiling the while, until I had to relax my facial muscles or have my cheeks fall off.

So I relaxed, and was astonished when the smile came back on its own. Eliard played and sang a comic song that made me laugh aloud, then drifted into another that made me recall when I'd had a true childhood and the world was new. Even Zimrit's leathery Guardsmen had looks of bittersweet nostalgia on their faces.

From that the minstrel broke into a bawdy song about the cuckolded scribe and the inkwell. All present joined in the rollicking chorus, and sprites possessed my feet. I just *had* to leap up and dance, dragging Zimrit with me. We capered like idiots in the center of the room, the Guardsmen clapping and stamping to the rhythm, Madam Glister passing goblets of wine to everyone (and asking no payment, as I later learned). Zimrit let go of my hands and staggered backwards, a country bumpkin in royal satins drunk at the fair, so I took hold of his hands again and led him, dancing, up to my chambers, where we fell onto the bed and coupled for the sheer joy of being alive to do it in a world where there is so much laughter and music.

By morning the spell was gone, but Eliard was still there. Prince Zimrit made a gift of him to Madam Glister's establishment the way any other satisfied patron would buy a case of wine for the girls. Madam in her turn passed the responsibility for Eliard's good conduct on to me.

"You know what these minstrels are, Megan. Poets are bad enough, musicians are worse, but mix the two—! He'll turn up dead in an alleyway with a knife in his belly if he's not cared for. You keep him out of trouble, there's a good girl."

I installed our new boarder in a disued wood-niche next to the cook-hearth. There really wasn't anywhere else warm we could keep him, and you must keep singers warm or they rasp. He declared it was large enough for himself, and proved it within a week when the potboy caught him tumbling Barti in a space where a cat couldn't turn herself. The potboy fetched me, and I sent Barti back to her room.

"Congratulations. You've foraged free on something men pay good money for." I did my best to scowl before his magpie's eye worked its charm. No one in the House of Prayer could stay mad at Eliard for long.

"Do you grudge a poor man a little entertainment? I can sing about as many beautiful, kind, highborn damsels as I please, but that won't put anything in my bed." He hugged himself and opened his eyes as wide as they would go, meaning to look pathetic. The attempt failed, so he turned it into a joke for the two of us to share and made me laugh with him instead.

"I just don't want you upsetting the potboy," I said between sputters.

"How many holy whorehouse potboys do you know?" His sigh made his ribs rattle. "Ah, lady, if you'll say nothing of this to Madam Glister, I'll be in your debt. I don't think the woman's as kindly disposed towards men being natural when there's nothing in it for her."

"Don't worry, I won't say a word. You wouldn't survive one of Madam Glister's love-pats."

"True, true." He slumped against the warm bricks. "I am a sad excuse for a man. If you wouldn't find it too odious, milady, I'd pay you back for your silence with a song."

Eliard's lute hung on a peg safely distant from the fire. He tuned it and retuned it with the painstaking attention of a mother fussing over a sickly child. When he had it to his liking he cocked his head at me. "What shall it be, gentle damozel? Another tune to make you smile? This time without my guts as forfeit. Or would you have a ballad? An adventure full of bold heroes and fearsome monsters, dark sorceresses with demons in their thrall, bloodthirsty pirates, palace intrigue, and the fiery wrath of gods?" He strummed a vigorous flourish, then stilled it with two fingers laid across the strings.

"Or shall it be of love?"

I scraped at the sooty bricks with my fingernail. I could feel him watching me. I etched a coppery U against the accumulated blackness; that was all. I left it alone because my finger could not decide whether I wanted to spell out a name from beginning to end or . . . end to beginning.

Eliard's lute made a hollow protest when he shifted it from his knees and its belly hit the hearth. He stood beside me, staring at my scratchings. "A smile. But why do you make it on these unscrubbed bricks when it would look so much nicer—" he touched first one corner of my mouth, then the other, "here?"

"Let me be." I turned my head aside.

"Oh yes. You are the one. In the city, when I heard the songs, I thought you were some rival poet's conceit; not a bad one, either: the lady without love! The myths claim that all duskflowers long to be loved, and many ruin themselves for it. But not Megan! She could make any man forget his sorrows in her arms, but she cherished her own unhappiness. Yet let any man speak of love—true love—and she sent them away, King's son and commoner alike."

"Is *that* what they say about me? Using my real name?"

Eliard liked to see me bridling. He clasped his hands in rapture. "*Say* it? Fairest one, they *sing* it! When I first heard the songs, I thought such a prime character was too perfect to be lifelike. Now I see that I was mistaken. You are everything the songs promised." The elation went out of his body. "I am not as happy to find you true-to-life as I anticipated." A hand at once soft and callused from years in thrall to music tilted my chin up. "What a waste," he breathed, a breath I felt on my lips an instant before he kissed me.

I meant to strike him; I swear I did. He was too quick for me is all, out of range in an instant, his lute up between us as a fragile shield, his fingers on the strings.

And he sang.

I heard the roots of my old mountains in his song, the clean air of the heights, the gentle music of sheep-bells. Was this a love-song? No, you could never call it that. It was a tale of sorrow, of a shepherd boy and girl kept apart first by their families, then by circumstances, and finally, when they won their way to each other and were united . . . love died. She woke to find a coarse stranger in her bed, he a shrewish scold. Nothing they tried—and they tried so much!—could ever conjure back what they had lost. She climbed the mountain where they had first met and fallen in love and heard another girl mourning the loss of her sweetheart.

Why weep? asked the unhappy woman. *Only your man has died, not your love. Love lasts beyond death if the ties be true. Mine is the greater misery. My man lives, but our love has perished. Who will bear the blame? He? Or I? Or both? I am sick of this living lie. I choose a better way.* Upon which she waltzed over the edge of a handy precipice and was dashed to death on the rocks below.

Rocks, incidentally, already littered with the disjointed body of her equally mopy spouse.

Children, at a certain age we are all highly susceptible to the subtle charms of music. We hear truth in every syllable a half-rate poet sets to song. We fancy that each amorous ballad was intended to immortalize our joys and our sorrows alone. I was of that certain age. Can you blame me for sympathizing so deeply with the unhappy lady of the song? To have love and lose love! And poor Hyu, who had landed on the saltwater docks through *my* doing!

Who will bear the blame?

Eliard plucked a random, wandering tune while I sobbed myself limp, then began another song in which a beautiful maiden who is sure she will never love again is seated on her balcony. It's a summer's night, and she hears the plaintive song of a nightingale. Of course she does. They always do. Nightingales are standard issue for lovelorn maidens; so are balconies and roses. She calls the bird to her (stupid bird; the loveless bitch might've wrung his neck!) and lo, he changes into a handsome youth who swears to love her forever and sing his songs for her ears alone. She clasps him to her bosom and—

Eliard and I ran away from the House of Prayer together and set up romantic housekeeping on one of the poorer streets of Routreal. There was no balcony. We were lucky to have a roof. At first we did all right, with Eliard going back to his pre-brothel round of taverns, but it was nothing like his first taste of glory as house-minstrel for Madam Glister.

Why *had* he done it? Why hadn't he left us both in the House of Prayer and contented himself with clandestine lovemaking? My question precisely, and I asked it good and loud on the morning he came home with an empty purse and a black eye.

"That's the thanks I get!" he shouted back. "I risked the wrath of Madam Glister *and* that lump of a bullyboy she keeps *and* Prince Zimrit, all for you, and *now* you turn on me!"

"I never turned on you, Eliard. I just wanted to know why we couldn't have stayed in the House of Prayer, had regular meals, clothing without holes, a solid roof—"

"And I suppose I dragged you, unconscious and unwilling, out of there in the dead of night? You ran after me voluntarily, and without sense enough to throw a few of those jewels Prince Nitwit gave you into a bag. Maybe then I wouldn't have to risk my neck every night earning us a living!"

"Who gave me time to pack? And you call this *living*? I know what the other minstrels rake in on just *one* market day, yet you go to ten taverns a night and bring back nothing but a hangover! If you were a halfway decent minstrel—"

"It's all your fault! You interfere with my inspiration! How can I create really moving, meaningful songs about love denied—which are always the most popular ones—when you deny me *nothing* in bed?" He pointed dramatically at the tattered curtain serving our hovel for a door. "Out! I am wedded to the Spirit of Song and I've played the adulterer too long. Be gone, vile temptress!"

After I finished laughing, I went. Madam Glister took me back, of course. My honeymoon with Eliard hadn't been long enough for the regular customers to notice. I even found most of my things just as I'd left them.

My jewels were all intact as well, but not thanks to Madam Glister. No sooner was I back, Nestra complaining around my ankles, than sweet Sarita stole into my chambers with a small, velvet-covered casket.

"I saw you run away, so I took your jewels, Megan."

"You a thief, Sarita? Then why give them back now?"

She lowered her eyes. "You know I'm no thief. I took them before any others could lay their hands on them. I thought that if you didn't come back, you'd send word of your whereabouts and then I could send these on to you."

I was overwhelmed, promptly opened the casket, and presented Sarita with a diamond spray. "For your baby to teethe on." I tried to be airy about my escapade, but the gratitude in Sarita's eyes melted me. I hugged her violently. "My dear, dear friend! I wish I could do more for you and your child, if only to repay you for this."

"Megan, please, I can hardly breathe!" She gently pushed me off. "What I did wasn't anything so grand or daring. It was nothing."

Slowly I shook my head. "You thought of me even when all the others considered me gone for good, and good riddance. You guarded what was mine. You *cared*, Sarita. It's been a long time since I had someone who cared."

Sarita's hair was a sheet of gold drawn back in silky wings from her face. Her huge eyes already showed the first signs of the hopeless drinker, as Jaroel's did, but her beauty was still strong enough to conceal most of the effects of the bottle. She was the most selfless woman I knew. Within two years' time she would be dead.

We did not speak any further of the jewels or my musical leave of absence. The other ladies of the House of Prayer were not so discreet. If I heard one more quip about "fingering" or "how the lute got a big belly," I was going to crack a few heads together.

One night, Eliard came back.

"Hark to that terrible row," groaned Madam Glister as she saw the last client of the night out the front door.

"What in the Netherplane is it?" wondered Nilsa, who had been promoted from scullery wench to understudy whore, in recognition of her many skills.

Jaroel yawned. "Nestra's got an admirer, 's all. Have Cook throw a pan of water out the window. Toms don't like having their serenades damped down."

"Nestra's past that or she'd have had callers before this. I'll have a look from the upstairs gallery." Nilsa clattered up and was down again with a delighted grin. "You'll never, never guess! It's the minstrel!"

"What minstrel?"

"You know. *Hers.*" All eyes were on me. Most were sparkling with merriment. Madam Glister's were not.

"I'll damp him down with more than water, damn his eyes! Hasn't he done enough to set this place on ear?" She ranted up and down the parlor, looking for something suitable to chuck at Eliard, something heavy enough to do real damage yet cheap enough to be expendable.

"I'll tell him to be off." I wanted to calm her so that we all could get to bed. I saw little likelihood of that until Eliard and his plaints were shown the road.

"Don't you DARE!" Madam gave me the beggar's farewell, one hand on my rump, one grasping the back of my robe, as she propelled me towards the staircase. "I'm not having you sneak off with that worthless triller a second time, not with Prince Zimrit coming to see you tomorrow! I took you back

out of the kindness of my heart once, but don't expect the same again if you play the fool!"

My protests were ineffectual. At the stairs Madam barked orders to Jaroel and Nilsa, who escorted me to my chambers and turned the key from the outside. I heard Eliard's song in the street outside reach an abrupt, unrehearsed conclusion and surmised that Madam's "husband" had stepped in.

Minstrels are fools, Eliard was a great fool, but he wasn't a damned great fool. He came back every night after that, yet saved his skin by becoming a wandering songster whose wandering pace accelerated as soon as he spied Madam's "husband" emerge from the House of Prayer, cudgel in hand. Once he made it four times around the block on "Kindly, Dying Lover" alone. Mostly we got to overhear snatches of several laments as he raced past our open windows.

He also learned to throw rocks while running. None of these missiles were intended as weapons against his pursuer, for they all had love-notes wrapped around them. I was twitted to the point of homicide when each of my sister duskflowers found one of Eliard's petitions in her room. Not knowing which was my window, he worked on the scattershot system. To the last, his notes were identical, begging me to reconsider, forgive, and remember the happiness we'd had together.

I remembered the roof.

The night came when Madame Glister's "husband" drew the line. He wasn't going to chase Eliard anymore. "Sniff-licker's too fast fer me. 'Sides, he comes back worse'n crabs. Any word outa you, woman, and you get what I'd 'a give him . . . 'fI coulda caught'm."

That was the night I first heard, from beginning to end, Eliard's melodic love-offering. He stationed himself smack in front of our door and sang every ballad ever written in which the Cruel Lady scorns the Humble Lover. The H.L. turns toes-up, the C.L. repents too late, likewise dies, and the survivors have a double funeral and a cautionary lesson for softening up the local virgins in future.

I was about to take up a chamberpot collection in appreciation of this uninvited concert when he began his final song: "Megan and the Unicorn."

It was Eliard's own composition, one I had never heard before. For all I knew, he'd written it after we parted ways. If so, there was much talent in the man and he was better off suffering in solitude, if that was what it took to create such eloquent music. By the rights of logic, I ought to have sprinkled him with nightsoil and banished him from my thoughts so that he might compose more masterpieces.

Instead, I packed those jewels dearest to me, slipped Nestra and the rest of the gems into Sarita's room while she slept, and shinnied down the frieze of obscene carvings that covered the facade of the House of Prayer. I flew to Eliard's arms with a glad cry, covering his face with happy tears and kisses. He returned the kisses, but he looked mightily astonished by his success, and a little dubious. I should have known.

Little ones, if any mortal under the age of ninety ever tells you, "I always learned my lessons the first time, before it was too late," mark that person well. He lies.

CHAPTER IV
I Cover the Waterfront

It didn't take Eliard long to revert from swain to swine. Our renewed idyll died the death after a fortnight. The jewels I'd taken were pawned the following week, all but the few shabby specimens given me by Master Urion, and we shambled on trying to pretend we were still as in love as ever. Ready money aids in maintaining the illusion of romance, but true love does not need to underwrite deceit. When the cash from my gems was spent and Eliard returned to the tavern rounds—with the same lack of success as before—he commenced nagging me to pawn Urion's keepsakes too.

"I'm sorry, but these mean something to me."

"Do they?" His sharp pink nose twitched when he sniffed, trying to look disdainful. "Why, might I ask?"

"None of your business."

"Very well, keep your petty secrets. I don't mind. And keep those knickknacks too. Pity you couldn't keep the *miraculous* lover who went with 'em!"

I narrowed my eyes. "He died."

That little gaffe kept Eliard quiet for a week longer, until Time charitably allowed him to forget that every time he opened his mouth he imitated a jackass.

"Megan, we must have more money!"

"Don't I know it! I'm making stew of turnips and air."

Eliard looked sly. "I hate seeing you go hungry, my love. Your rosy cheeks have faded, your hair has lost its sheen, your eyes have lost their sparkle and wax full dull, I ween."

"Is that the sort of stuff you've been setting to music these days?" He nodded. "No wonder we're in trouble."

Eliard had no use for constructive criticism. "Instead of telling me what's wrong with my songs—which happens to be nothing—you might do your part to bring some coppers into the house. You're not the pampered pet of the House of Prayer now."

"Thanks to you and your leprous unicorn song! Who asked you to come back and bother me with dreams? I lost my last dream ages ago!"

"Megan. . . ." He took me into his arms. I was shaking with rage. He tried soothing me like a highstrung horse, with strokings and whispered nonsense. I was just beginning to calm down and cuddle up when the bonebrain said, "You could always go back to work, my love."

I broke away from him with an almost inhuman shout. "*What* work?"

"Oh, you know; what you do best. Then you wouldn't feel so guilty about me slaving away to support two."

"So that's why you lured me back." I was circling him alley-cat fashion, ready to leap and claw. He circled too, on guard and skittish. "Scratch a minstrel, find a pimp!"

"Megan, I never intended that."

"Then why *did* you come back? I interfered with your inspiration, remember? Are all the males in this world fools? Will I have to look for brains in the Netherplane, for common sense among the gods?"

"Hey! That's not a bad notion," said Eliard, dropping his

protective stance. "'The Harlot's Quest'! Mind if I write it down? There may be a roundelay in it." He went for his stylus and wax-board. I went for his eyes.

A few minutes later, I was securing Urion's jewels in my sash while Eliard pressed a wet rag to the blood streaming from his split lip. My aim had been off.

"It was a mistake to have you back," he said thickly. "The first halfway decent idea you give me, and you knock it out of my head before I can jot it down. I'll be glad to see your backside."

"You always were."

"Sex isn't everything," he muttered.

"With you, it was nothing." I didn't wait for him to show me the nonexistent door, but departed unassisted.

One of life's greatest pleasures is having the last word. It's also one of the few self-indulgences never used as a means of forgetting sorrow. Alas, the euphoric effects of verbal stabs and death-thrusts don't last; drunken stupor does. I was on my own again, accompanied only by the knowledge that Madam Glister meant what she'd said: The House of Prayer was closed to me. Common chatter told me that I'd never find another brothel half so fine or another Madam so easygoing, clouts and all, as Madam Glister. And kindly though she was, for a Madam, she wasn't above revenge. She might have spread word to her guild-sisters already that I was an unreliable quantity. No doubt the anchored world of organized harlotry was closed to me. I would have to work on my own hook.

I would have to do what Eliard had suggested, but I wasn't about to strike out as a freelance duskflower without some fortification. The familiar, tarry, tangy, fish-rot stench of the salt-docks beckoned. I had a few coppers tucked into my pouch; enough to buy a round or two where the drinks were cheapest. Everything came cheapest near the northern sea.

It was late afternoon. The real business of the night hadn't gotten under way properly yet. The tavern I chose had no trade-sign over its door, few tables, no chairs that didn't wobble. I fancied myself the sole customer, for besides the grim, one-eyed sharkbait leaning against the row of kegs, we were alone.

"Off wi' ye! Whores comes round after nine by t' Universerry clock an' not before!"

I strutted in, took his horny hand from his hip, and stuck my last coins in. "The strongest that will buy, twice, my man. And mind who you call a whore."

He looked at the coins and his thick lips quirked. "'Tud buy ye four o' my best draft brew, handsome, an' that's its own punishment. But if ye've a mind t' stronger waters, 'twill serve ye a double cup o' northern *shayn*." His single eye rolled whitely in its reddened socket. "What them sea-scavengers does drink theyself before they takes a town, or what t' jobber told me."

"It will do."

With a magnanimous gesture he gave me pick of place in the grogshop. "Put it where ye pleases, handsome. Ye'll draw business, for all ye're no whore. Only keep yer lip tucked, else it's drink an' begone. I earn coin selling drink, and men as chat wi' hopes o' beddin' drink less."

"I'll send them packing. Now bring me my drink and tuck your own damned lip!"

The tapster showed his broken teeth. "Hoity-toity. Think I'm the one t' serve ye? Not likely, in my own place! Or what do I pay t' help fer, hey?" He whistled shrilly—not easy with those crumbling teeth of his—then hollered, "Hoi! Double *shayn*, an' mind ye spill none on t' towels!"

The double cup of northern murk appeared anon, presented on a tray that floated out of the back room on its own and drifted in to land on my table. Magic to amuse the customers *here*? I was tickled by this bit of elegant showmanship in such a hole; not so the tapster.

"Arrrh! That's done it! Who said ye could muck at practicin' wi' *my* liquor?" Roaring, he vanished into the back room and emerged holding a ragged young man by the scruff of the neck. "An' what if ye'd spilled any on t' cloths er furn'chur, hey?

Who's t' darn up t' burns an' fill t' holes it eats out?" (I eyed my drink with rising apprehension.)

My one-eyed host shook his erring servant soundly, then threw him against a narrow trestle bearing a row of bottles. The flying body swept the table clean in a crash of glass and a much more disastrous spillage of good liquor. Apparently it all depended on who was doing the spilling.

The young man stood up gingerly, picking shards of glass from his wretched clothes. Only when he turned to glare hatred at the tapster did I see and recognize who he was.

"Hyu." Not a whisper, not a shout, only his name. He heard it. He tried to run away, but the tapster barred his way to the back room and I was quick enough to cut him off from the front door.

"Here! No talkin' wi' t' potboy neither, handsome!"

I made a certain fingerplay.

Both Hyu and I might have ended up in the gutter for my sauce, but just then the entrance spewed in a stream of merchant sailors fresh off their ships and eager to spend their pay. The tapster's wench bounced out of her cubbyhole to help her master serve them and Hyu and I were forgotten in the crowd.

I made him sit down with me and try a sip of the *shayn*. Disgusting stuff. If the northern rovers did drink it, no wonder they became such fiends. The hangovers *shayn* begot didn't bear thinking about, but it did loosen tongues.

"You don't look surprised to find me here," said Hyu, making a face and pushing the cup back to me. "Why should you? The ballad-singers come even here. I make a nicely pitiful footnote to your list of conquests. Did you have to come and see for yourself what I've become?"

I thought of what Madam Glister had said of likely lads selling more than magic on the salt-docks and I had to smile. "A tavern potboy's not so bad, Hyu. Your suspension will end before you know it, and then—"

"By then I'll have forgotten most of what I knew!" He seized the cup and took a full jolt of *shayn*. The man was distraught or suicidal. "You saw how my *so* tenderhearted master reacted when I tried exercising the most basic levitation spell. Do you think he gives me the time I need to rehearse the rest of my lore? Megan, it's not enough to wait out the suspension and keep alive until then; I must practice what I've already learned. If I don't, I'll have to go back and relearn it all, and that will show on my examination records. Poor showing means dismissal!"

"Not you, Hyu. You have the gift! Won't Lord Deveril speak up for you? You're all his doing."

Hyu gave me a wry smile. "I wouldn't say I'm all Lord Deveril's doing, but let that pass. If I'm dismissed from the University, what shall I do? Knowing too much to be a shepherd again, too little to be a wizard . . . thinking of the future frightens me. Sometimes I think that anything's better than facing it; especially when I'll be facing it alone." He gripped my upper arms until they throbbed and his voice dwindled. "Don't let me be alone, Megan; I'm so afraid."

Curse music and all the spells it weaves, all the young girls it deceives! Once led into error for the sake of a song, we swear we won't be played for fools a second time. I had gone with Eliard not once, but twice—both times because he'd played on my sympathies as easily as playing on his lute—and my pride was still smarting. I wouldn't be a man's cat's-paw again just because his plight touched me. I would be hard, *hard*, and nobody's fool. Therefore I stiffened my shoulders and determined the most sensible thing to do.

Not the best, the most sensible. There is a difference.

"Here." I stuck my fingers in my sash and plunked the last of Urion's jewels into Hyu's hands. "Those ought to take care of your needs until your suspension's run out, provided you live frugally. Now you can practice. Please, don't mention it!" I forestalled his words with a facile lie: "You know I have plenty more where that came from."

I washed the taste of falsehood from my mouth with the rest of the *shayn* taken at one swallow and floated from the grogshop in a giggly fog. I never looked back. My *shayn*-winged flight lost momentum a block later, when the stomach pains started. I threw up and felt better.

Now I really had done it, and no mistake. Not even Master Urion's modest hoard to fall back on. I looked up and down the moon-washed street, then out to where the ships were anchored. This would have to be my new territory, until something better came up. I'd have to earn enough to pay for food and a roof and some prettying up if I wanted to move upriver and eventually back into one of the better cribs when the stories of Megan's Minstrel died away.

Little idiot! Go to Prince Zimrit! Wasn't he always mad for you? What's to keep you from being his concubine now?

Oh yes, and Madam Glister had explained what lay behind His Serenity's infatuation: my inaccessible nature. Only, how inaccessible was a lass who ran off *twice* with the same gangly minstrel? Not even Zimrit was that big a puddinghead.

Me for the docks.

I heard the sound of many oars in the water. Although it was full dark by this time, I figured that more richly laden ships had come into port and their crews refused to wait for morning before coming ashore in their longboats. It was that season of the year when trade boomed in Routreal and the wealth of this kingdom and many others bobbed in the estuary waters. Walking to the edge of the pier, I could see one ghostly hulk in particular, a ship of shallower draft and more graceful design than the others, from which a host of tiny barks swarmed shorewards like dragonflies.

Had I been fully sober, I might've wondered why not one boat among them showed a lantern.

It was as good a time to inaugurate a new business venture as any. I saw the first of the lightless longboats reach the pier, then hid myself in a nearby doorway and waited until footsteps approached before I stepped out boldly.

"Hello, sailor. New in town?"

"Tvarun's *tits*!" the client bellowed. His naked broadsword arced high, and the moon silvered a score of identical blades in the hands of the northern pirate horde that poured into the streets of Routreal.

He slung me over his shoulder without any further mention of his foreign goddess or her tits. My view of the ensuing pillage was upside-down, bouncy, and disjointed. I smelled smoke, I heard screams and the more terrifying, gurgling sounds of the dying. There was an awful amount of shouting for a *shayn* convalescent to endure, so I breathed easier when the pirate dropped me into the booty-laden bottom of his longboat, bawled for his crew, and made back for their ship with all oars. When we reached her, over the shoulder I went again, up the side, down a hatch, and flying headfirst into the carved headboard of a broad bunk so that fireworks exploded inside my eyelids before darkness.

I came to my senses with the sensation that I was being watched. The jabs of pain in my skull distracted me from feeling too bothered about it. *Watch and be damned* was my attitude. My brain sloshed clockwise in my head, my stomach counterclockwise in my body, and my guts rose and fell in charming three-way counterpoint until I leaned over the side of the bunk and emptied them. Then I sank back, wiping my mouth on my skirt.

There was a growl of satisfaction from a shadowed corner of the cabin. A yellow spark struck from a tinderbox flared, caught, and was applied to the wick of a thick candle set in a gimballed holder on the wall over my head. A befurred face eyed me, and it took no University City education to tell me what thoughts were slithering through the tiny mind behind those equally tiny eyes.

Rape.

I didn't like it. Stepda had tried it on me once and I'd developed a peculiar antipathy towards the whole matter ever since on principle alone. There are men who may argue that it's not real rape if the lady's no lady. Some add that husbands can't rape their wives. Some even append the proviso that if a virgin has been giving some poor, innocent man the unmistakable come-on that she really does want him and only squeals and struggles so in order to preserve appearances.

No doubt my hairy friend was also one of those philosophical types. Ravish first, justify later. I decided that I'd dispense a few lessons of my own in advanced philosophy.

"Thank all the gods, you've come to me at last!" I cried, and flung myself into his arms before he got one knee on the bed. Imitating the sounds of a cat with bellyache, I scrabbled with the rawhide laces holding his bearskin vest together. My hands slipped beneath the smelly pelts as I raked his back as deeply as my chipped nails could go, always mrowling and gasping enough to make bloody assault come on as an erotic compliment. (You can beat a man black and blue, bite him and scrape him skinless, and he'll limp away to show the wounds proudly to his friends if you use the right sound effects during the massacre.)

Tvarun's devout worshiper shook. His eyes bugged out and his jaw slacked open as my hands dropped lower, to fumble with his loincloth. The northern pirates dressed for easy action during their raids, some even plunging stark naked into battle, so it didn't take me long to shuck him like an oyster. I fell back momentarily to tear my bodice open before ramming his head between my tits, still sending up a litany of groans and breathy encouragements.

"I want you! Oh, I *want* you!" I wailed, doing my damnedest to smother the witless geek with the two best cushions nature ever fluffed. I toppled backwards onto the bunk and hauled him on top of me, my legs clamped around his waist. "Yes, yes, yes, now, don't wait, come on, hurry up, what's the *matter* with you, I must *have* you, yes, now, please, aaaaaaaaahhhhhh. . . ."

Etcetera.

Took the wind out of his sails faster than a jab in the johnies, and without the painful reprisals that must come when the victim's bigger and stronger than you and has recuperated.

The pirate leaped from his bunk, cursed fluently in several tongues, and scuttled out the door, which he slammed behind him. I sat up with my ruined bodice draped around my waist, harking for the sound of retreating feet, but it didn't come. I'd frightened him within limits; northern rovers are a heroic lot. The cabin door creaked open and he slunk back inside. He studied me suspiciously from beneath brows like two black caterpillars, keeping his back to the wall. I made kissing sounds and tried to lick my eyebrows at him, but the shock of my first sortie had faded.

"Woman," he said, his accent heavy when he spoke my language. "What do you want?"

I made my voice so husky as to be nigh inaudible: *"You."*

The pirate hawked and spat. "Speak the truth. We slit liars' tongues."

"What a loss that would be." I batted my eyelashes and tore my bodice an inch lower, leaning forward to give him a better view. "Of course I want you. What woman wouldn't? So handsome. So bold. So . . . big. *Every* woman in Routreal knows that northmen are . . . blessed by the gods in certain areas." (Or would that be "blessed in certain areas by the gods"? Oh, well!)

My captor looked ill at ease. "We are men like other men. Routreal women are like other women. My men have to fight the ones they take, make them stop screaming, hit them before they can enjoy them. Why don't you scream?"

I did a modified shoulder-shimmy. "I'm sure I will scream . . . later. I just can't *wait* to see you live up to all the legends. Mmmm-*mmh!* Tell me, is it true that northmen can take seven women three times apiece in one night because they eat snowrabbit? Or is it something to do with the climate? Oh, never mind. Come here and *show* me!" I fell back on the mattress and bounced.

"No. You are mad. Man who couples with madwoman is devoured by demons. I will sell you with the others, as a slave." He reached for the door.

Slavery is no career for a woman. I was at the door first. "Please, don't go. I'm not mad."

"Then why do you act it?" He was wounded, my sensitive pillager. "Why don't you behave like a real woman with Vrogar?"

I did some fast talking, putting my shameless, unwomanly behavior down to nervousness on meeting the mighty Vrogar, terror of the northern sea. Simply *everyone* had heard of Vrogar, didn't he know? But to have the privilege of meeting him firsthand, of nearly being *raped* by him, no less, had overwhelmed me. I tendered apologies, begged his pardon, introduced myself, and seduced him. It was like taking on a bear, but at least it was over quickly. So much for snow-rabbit. On second thought, he smelled marginally better than Prince Zimrit too.

Vrogar and I remained in his cabin for three days. When we emerged the ship was far from Routreal and I was dressed in the doeskin breeches and calico shirt of an ill-fated slave cabin-boy who had worn out on the previous voyage. Barefoot, with my hair in a braid wrapped around my head and stowed under a kerchief, I stood in the prow of the skip and watched the foam break green and white under our keel. Urion's three vials still hung around my neck, their slender glass vessels tinkling sweetly together as I drank the wash of wind.

"You are Vrogar's woman now." I saw no point in arguing. If you don't get seasick, don't mind fish, and aren't a prude about sacking cities, there are worse lives than that of a sea-rover. The raid on Routreal had turned up a few chests of uncut gems from the hold of an anchored merchant ship that Vrogar's men burned in the harbor. I got first pick of the pretties, hung twin emeralds from my ears, and decided that a sea-voyage would be good for my health.

That was before I remembered the other slaves.

They were trotted out on deck for fresh air and inspection the day after we divvied the gems and dry goods. The junior members of Vrogar's crew were muttering darkly among themselves (a bad habit common among sea-rovers) that the booty hadn't been apportioned fairly. Vrogar was feeling charitable and smug—the results of my attentions—and so, instead of quashing the unrest with the flat of his sword, he proposed that the human cargo be split up before they made a slave-market port.

"A captive for each of you to sell on your own!" He lounged on a bale of silks and held me on his knee while handing down his decision. "What you get for 'em will be your own doing. No more grumbling to me about it! Kivnar, bring 'em up now."

There were a dozen slaves, four of them women. If they were the ones Vrogar's men had been enjoying, it wouldn't be long until they paid for it; they were salt-dock whores, and poxy. If they'd screamed and struggled at all it was probably at the thought of giving it away for free. The men were also the pickings of Routreal's lowest quarter: five bullyboys, an effeminate dock-strutter who ogled the crew without shame or success, one scrawny minstrel, and one suspended student-mage.

I slipped discreetly from Vrogar's lap and hurried aft under the pretense of answering nature's most basic call.

Dear Esra! Hyu and Eliard!

Neither one had seen me. I wanted to keep it that way, at least until night fell. The slaves were all assigned keepers who would later sell them and pocket the price, then returned below. When the sun dipped into the sea, I stole from Vrogar's cabin.

The helmsman was the only man awake on deck. No guards stood watch, nor were any needed. Where would a man go if he did manage to escape from the slaves' hold? Over the side, to be the fishes' dinner? It was a far swim to any shore, even if you did strike out in the proper direction. Besides, the crew did not share the captain's privilege of cabin and bunk. They slept, snoring noisily, like a herd of beached walruses, their bodies littering the deck. I had to weave a path from one hatchway to another, with all stealth.

Stealth. Ha. My first step woke the lot of them, for sea-rovers sleep with one ear always perked for the sound of an enemy's dagger snickering from its sheath. The crew sprang up battle-ready to a man as soon as I set foot in their midst.

"Stand ho! What is it?" Vrogar's men were younger, grouchier, smellier versions of himself. Their swords wavered in a rippling sheet of steel by starlight while they sniffed at me like cur-dogs.

"'Sall right. It's Vrogar's woman," said one.

"What's she doing here? Wants ta piss, it's aft." Gallantly one of the gentlemen adventurers indicated aft with a sword-slash that just missed my throat.

"I'm—going forward, if you please," I said.

"What for? Nothing's forward but t'other hold. Full of our slaves." A fuzzy cheer for good Captain Vrogar, the Bilge-Sodding Bastard, went up from a dozen throats.

"All I wanted was to visit the prisoners," I explained. "I wanted to—comfort them, as one former citizen of Routreal to another. You see, now that you kind gentlemen are each in charge of one, they'll have better treatment, and I hoped to lighten their captivity by—"

"She wants t'antler Vrogar's head, she does," said a foxy soul. "Hot, this one, or else why'd Vrogar lie abed three days, ha?"

"What? Vrogar's not enough for her? Come here, woman! I'll stand the Captain's watch tonight!"

I was seized only briefly. The rest of the crew was loyal to their leader and one of them gave the man who held me a solid thwack in the temple with the pommel of his sword.

"Fool! If Vrogar learns she's bedding elsewhere, let it be a slave who's pitched to the sharks for it! Stand aside. Let her pass."

"Easy for you to say, Kivnar! Your slave's a woman and won't be the one Vrogar guts for jiggin' 'er, that's sure!"

"Shut up and let her pass, I say! Maybe she's telling truth about why she's going below. For her sake, she'd better. A slave won't be the only one Vrogar feeds the sharks if he grows horns." Without further ado, they went back to their smutty dreams and left me to my devices.

I took no light with me into the slave hold, though I'd dearly have loved a lantern. I made sure that not a wisp of hair had slipped out of my kerchief before I ventured after Hyu and Eliard; let me play cabin-boy when I found them, until I saw how the land lay. I was free, they were chained, and they might not react with unqualified joy to see me under such circumstances. Cautiously I alternated calling their names in a soft voice. I could see next to nothing in the dark, but I smelled unwashed human bodies nearby. One of the salt-dock whores woke from sweaty slumber and cursed me. At last I had an answering cry.

"Who's there? Who's calling me?" It was Eliard. I felt my way along the creaking timbers where water oozed in between the planks until I reached him. "Who are you, boy?"

I enjoyed that. Everything was shadow on shadow in the slaves' hold, and if I had the outline of a youth, all the better. I graveled my voice deep and replied, "A captive from Routreal like yourself."

"Woodworms and dry rot—*Megan*!" he gasped.

"Nice guess." I was piqued.

"No guessing to it. A musician's ear never forgets a voice, no matter how well it's disguised. In your case it wasn't disguised well at all," he added unnecessarily.

"Lovely. Your prime ear's going to bring one of these rovers a good price on the auction block when we land. How did they catch you? You hewed to the upriver taverns."

Eliard's head dropped in the dark. A horrid suspicion filled me. Suddenly I knew why the pirates had found Eliard so far from his normal haunts, as well as why he had lured me from the House of Prayer a second time. Why hadn't I realized it before?

"Oh, Eliard! Not 'Lord Carlac's Daughter'!"

He nodded, freely acknowledging his shame.

Maidens, take what comfort you can the next time a song

leads you down Hollowskull Highway: Minstrels are human too. The poison they dispense often infects them as well. In Eliard's case the bane was an old ballad—'Lord Carlac's Daughter'—which I thought I'd heard him singing more than any other in his repertoire. It seemed odd to me, for there was little call for that sort of sentimental goop in the tavern trade.

The story is of a poor-but-lovely lass who turns all heads and hearts but wants no man's love. Sound familiar? Along comes the poor-but-honest hero who must win her not once, but several times. Perils and setbacks beset their love—always good ploys for keeping the audience with you—until the day he saves her life and it is revealed that she is really the daughter of a fabulously wealthy and powerful lord who managed to misplace his cherished only child somewhere around stanza VIII. He welcomes her back, stuffs gold into every available orifice of the hero, and gets it all back as the chit's dowry when the lovers wed.

"Lord Carlac's Daughter," otherwise known as "Eliard's Doom." "You were following me, weren't you, Eliard? To bring me back a *third* time?"

"I couldn't let anything happen to you, Megan!" The shackles holding him to the planking rattled in agitation. "I couldn't have you escape me! I adore you! Our love was fated! Our song was ever meant to be!"

"Eliard, hush, I beg you. The others will hear."

Eliard laughed dryly. "We've privacy enough for a tryst down here, sweeting. The slaves' hold is divided into two sections, thanks to today's split of the spoils. Our new masters held council and decided that the troublemaking slaves should be kept apart from the herd. I'm one of the troublemakers. I *will* sing. That gracious damsel you tripped on's another; foul-mouthed even for a salt-dock whore and picks fights."

"Don't forget me, sweet song-sparrow!" came a piping. It was the dock-strutter. He wiggled his fingers at me and tittered.

"Yes, and him."

"Oohhhh, so grim he sounds, doesn't he, milady?" The dock-strutter clicked his tongue. "You have to rouse his spirits."

"If I can, I'll rouse everyone's. I mean to have you all set free."

The dock-strutter emitted a stifled yawp. "La! She sounds so set on it! I adore strong women. What's your plan, love? I'm not so eager for the auction block as these limps think. I like setting my own prices."

"You'll find out," I said. "I've become the Captain's woman, and I'll use my influence with him for your release, believe me."

"The Captain's woman? That barbarian!" Eliard's chains rattled again. This time they had a martial ring. "Megan, I forbid it!"

"You can't forbid what's done. Now tell me how I can reach the rest of the slaves. I want them to know what I'm planning as well."

"I refuse! Dearest lady, you can't sacrifice yourself for me. That's not the way it goes! You're distressed, not thinking right, but I'll be the one to—"

"Forward along the keel and you'll reach the door they put up between us," said the dock-strutter. He was a baritone when he liked. "It's got a horn-and-thong latch that's easy to open if you're not chained."

I was disturbed by Eliard's outburst. Hyu was no fan of "Lord Carlac's Daughter," but he was another sort of fool. Hadn't he stood up to my Stepda, and he only a stripling? If he learned I'd become Vrogar's woman, he might react twice as stupidly as Eliard. Remember, he was an educated man.

Therefore I prayed that his ear was duller than Eliard's when I spoke in a lad's voice, and my prayer was answered. At night all cats are gray, all slim shadows cabin-boys.

My prayers were heard, with interest. Hyu was chained nearest the door. He slept with his arms chained high, his head nestled into his own shoulder. Was it imagination, or was it lighter in this part of the hold so that I was able to see every curve and line of his face as plainly as if we were in full sunlight? He looked haggard, his skin sickly, but when he became aware of my presence and woke, I saw that nothing could dim his godsgift blue eyes.

"What is it? Who are you, lad?" He passed his tongue over his lips with a rasping sound. "Have you brought water? Please . . .?"

I scanned the hold and saw a leather bucket swinging from a nail. We were lucky; it held water and a wooden dipper which I set to Hyu's lips. He guzzled, coughed, and thanked me.

"For a while I thought our owners forgot that slaves need an occasional drink too, if they're to thrive. Thank them as well for sending you."

"No one sent me."

"Ah?" Hyu blinked and tried to ferret out a better view of my face, but the dark cheated him. "Well, you look young enough to still keep a kind heart. Don't grow out of it like your masters did, lad. We don't treasure kind hearts enough in this world."

I affected a coarse laugh. "What'd kind hearts ever do to fill a pocket, sar? You're city-bred, from the sound of ye, an' wi' an education." (Gods, what a mishmash I spoke, trying to sound the authentic sea-rover!) "Ye be slaves all, an' coin on legs fer that. I'm wise enough t' guard the crew's fortunes, else I'm who's the butt o' their tempers an ye shows belly!"

"*Huh?*"

I translated: "You die, I'm blamed. Don't think I've come calling down here out of kindness."

Hyu sighed mightily. "No, why should you? It's rare, and growing rarer. Fools never know when they've found true kindness until it's eluded them. Sometimes they're the ones who drive it away. What price do you think they pay for fools in the slave ports, lad? If it's high, my owner's fortune will be made. I'm the greatest fool that ever lived."

"You? You don't look half great t' my eyes."

"I looked great enough in my own opinion not so long ago.

I was a student of magic, a wizard-to-be. Even in my first year at Routreal I mastered some of the harder spells: the summoning of Succubi, the finding of hidden treasures, the wearing of many skins. Everyone told me how wonderful I was, and I believed it all. And because of the slop they poured in my ears, I lost the most precious hidden treasure of all."

My heart beat faster, but I evoked Eliard's face to slow it. Too soon for me to be snared again! "Treasure? You?" My voice cracked, but young boys often have that problem. Hyu let it go by.

"A lady who loved me better than I deserved. A kind heart, a fair face, a second skin to house my soul if I had been wise enough to see. There are greater mysteries to master than wizardry, lad, and richer treasures."

I leaned nearer, my mouth already framing his name.

"Guards! Guards!" Bare feet slapped out thunder on the deck above our heads. Down in the dark the barbaric battle-cries of the northmen rumbled and reechoed like the sky-gods' war. I sprinted from Hyu's side to see what had sounded the alarm, fearing as I ran that one of the crewmen had told Vrogar of my midnight slinkings and he'd chosen to believe the worst. If he was about to invite the sharks to dinner. I wanted to defend myself first.

It was over by the time I peeped out of the hatchway. In the moonlight I saw all the crew battle-ready, save one. That luckless man lay soaking in a puddle of blood and brains, newly spilled from a wide-cracked skull. Vrogar stood over him, naked except for the pelt that grew naturally on his body, a sword in his hand.

There was no blood on that sword. Vrogar hadn't killed him. Creeping nearer I recognized the corpse as the man who'd tried to "stand the Captain's watch" with me. Was my bearish lover the jealous type?

Wrong again. There was one more man on deck than before, though cut of leaner meat than the pirates. Eliard hung between two crewmen, his chains swinging free. The brackets that had held them to the bulkhead were a mat of splinters and gore.

Eliard was still alive, even with sword-cuts crosshatching his face and body and both legs broken beyond hope of healing. I drew nearer to Vrogar's bulk, not wanting to watch what would happen next, knowing I would watch anyway.

He saw me. He forced his head up and looked at me. They'd left little of his face, but he did manage to move his lips. What he said came as a wet, horrible mumble, unintelligible to the pirates. I understood every word.

"Had to 'scape, Meg'n. Save you. Shackles easy f' me t' pull when I knew wha' he'd . . . One tried t' stop me, but I swung th' chains. . . . M'lady . . ."

Kivnar smashed his fist into Eliard's face, silencing him. Another man doused him with seawater so that he would be fully aware of what they did to him. Before I could think, Vrogar strode forward and jabbed his sword into the minstrel's guts, slicing upwards to the breastbone, then wrenched the sad body from his men and heaved it over the side.

I rushed to the railing. The sea-rovers were gathered around the body of their fallen comrade, arguing loudly about whose turn it was to swab brains off the deck. They noticed neither my departure nor my tears. Eliard's body did not sink at once, but floated briefly on the side-wake water before vanishing aft of our ship. Call me fool—I have been called worse—but for as long as I could see my lost minstrel's body bobbing on the waves I sang very softly, just under my breath, a verse or two of "Lord Carlac's Daughter." And I like to think that the sweet-singing ladies of the deep, with their silver fishtails and trailing blue hair, are even now crowning Eliard's ghost with pearls while he teaches them new songs.

So I lost the lover whose only fault was believing in the songs he himself used to sing. He would have played the hero, and who shall say that he failed? Not all heroes live to have songs made for them, and those that do must sometimes hear their lives made into lies.

"Slaves!" Vrogar spat into the sea. "More damned trouble than they're worth. Whose was he?" A crewman raised his hand. "You take Luftag's slave in trade, then. At least it comes even." He paced the deck, grumbling and growling about the mad ways of city folk.

"My lord?" I had recovered myself and fought down sorrow for poor Eliard. The moment was ideal for the scheme that had just come to me. "My lord Vrogar, I could have told you this would happen. This Routreal trash will eat your stores bare and then die a day's sail from the slave port, mark my words. Moon-touched, most of them. I know, because they're all Routreal born and bred; not like me, who's from the healthier upcountry."

"Moon-touched?"

"Mad." I was gratified to see Vrogar's men react with dread, fearing insanity more than plague. Be assured, they thought one was caught from an infected person the same as the other. They began to mutter darkly among themselves (what did I tell you about sea-rovers' bad habits?).

"A fine stew!" boomed Vrogar. The crew began to argue what to do with a cargo of loonies, willing to take the loss and throw them overboard, but the big barbarian Captain was a merchant at heart. He could not abide waste. "We must make port faster, sell 'em off before anyone knows they're mad, and demons take 'em all!"

Here the crew got rowdier, half of them with Vrogar, half declaring they'd go below and slaughter the slaves before they'd sail a spit farther. My time had come.

"My lord Vrogar . . . gentles . . ." I climbed onto a water cask to be seen and heard better. Luck held. Vrogar wasn't the first to see his woman engaged in the unwomanly art of public speaking or else he would have been the man who yelled:

"Shut your mouth and get below, woman!"

Vrogar swatted him flat. "She is *my* woman! She speaks because *I* allow it!"

"Thank you, dear." I was tall enough on the cask to pat

Vrogar's head. "Men, all of you are witnesses that I was down in the slaves' hold tonight. I call on the demons of madness to possess my body this minute if I went there for any other reason than to raise the spirits of my fellow townsmen." I let a beat go by, and when the horde saw no demons accept my offer, I proceeded.

"While below, I saw that your slaves are—alas!—hopelessly insane. Devils on devils dance through their brains. I thank my own gods who protected me from—from the one who escaped his bonds and murdered our beloved comrade . . ."

"Luftag."

"Luftag. Yes. We'll all miss him. But men, if Luftag were alive now, he'd side with his captain in the matter of the slaves. Waste is a sin. You risked your lives to get these slaves, yet if they're all zany, you can't get full worth for 'em. That much is obvious. But while I was below, I learned something about one of them that will earn at least double what they'd bring on the block!"

Excited banter ran through the crew. I let it reach a high before I said, "One of the slaves is . . . a wizard."

Pandemonium. "A mad wizard? What good's that?"

"He'll bring demons down to devour us all!"

"Kill 'em now!"

"Lay a hand on my slave and I'll do some killing!"

"Peace! Peace for the Captain's woman!"

The ruckus subsided. Under their beards and battle-scars they were children, waiting for a word of guidance. I was enjoying myself.

"Men, would a full wizard still languish in your hold? He is merely a student-mage. But a student who has mastered the great spell of *treasure-finding*! Think! Think of the hidden hoards laid up on these coasts by the rovers of old! Their ships sank and all men who shared the secret of the treasure caves drowned, but the treasures are still there, waiting. We can't sell the slaves well. Let's make them a deal, then: Freedom for the treasure-finding spell! We'll put them all ashore on a deserted beach if the student-mage will turn over his incantation."

"Then we kill 'em, right?" I almost hated to disappoint Vrogar, he looked that hopeful.

"We do no such thing. We'll have to take off as soon as possible after we land 'em so—so that the spell won't get stale." Improvising further I added, "Besides, kill a loony and his demons fly into the nearest skull for a new home. How'd you like that?" Vrogar didn't. As an added touch I removed the emeralds from my ears and pledged the crew that they could sell them along with me and split the proceeds if Hyu's spell turned out to be a dud.

The next daybreak, Vrogar put my plan into action. I hid myself in the hatchway leading to the captain's cabin so that I could hear everything, but not be seen by Hyu. As I'd hoped, the mention of freedom for himself and his fellow captives made Hyu give up the treasure-finding spell without a qualm. The ship turned south and soon I heard the lapping of surf. A swift peep over the lip of the hatch gave me a last glimpse of Hyu and the others being helped over the side to flounder, paddle, and wade their way ashore as best they might.

"Now," said Vrogar to his men as I climbed on deck, "we sail for treasure!"

CHAPTER V
Doxy and Cream Cheese to Go

The cliffs rose up in ocher ranks, a tumble of black rocks in the churning waters at their feet. Caves gashed the cliffsides and gaunt birds rode the currents of air over our heads. All of us aboard Vrogar's ship were filled with the awe and majesty of those nameless peaks and wondered what purpose men could share in a world of such marvels.

"Ugh," said Kivnar, scraping a white blob off his shoulder. The sea-birds had a primitive but effective way of answering the Great Questions of Philosophy.

Vrogar leaned far over the side while his men cast anchor and lowered one of the longboats. The diamond pendant in our Captain's hands glowed with a bloody red light that pulsed blue at its center. Flashes of greater brilliance were also seen, and these began to throb with the regularity of a heartbeat.

"Ha! Just as the magician said!" Vrogar thumped the rail happily. "The finding-spell is strong, it works, it calls us there!" He thrust the pendant towards the seaside cliffs and roared for joy when the blue and white center lights beat even stronger and brighter.

I was in the longboat with Vrogar and the seven men he'd chosen to make up the treasure party. They were there to lend their powerful arms to toting away the treasure chests Vrogar was sure to find with Hyu's ensorceled diamond. I was there to have my throat cut if they turned up dry holes, or so Vrogar had told me the night before. It was some of the poorest pillow-talk I'd shared. Would he really allow his men to take out their disappointment on my hide if Hyu's finding-spell found nothing?

I was going to find out pretty soon. Vrogar had turned over and started snoring after dumping that cheery good-night in my lap. The diamond swung from a silver chain as the longboat cleaved the breakwater, all eyes on its mystic signs, mine most of all. No one had more riding on the whims of that gem than I.

"Up there! See how she pulls?" Vrogar's teeth flashed white in the bleak sunlight, and his men bared their fangs in response. The diamond swung in an irregular pattern, an ellipse with a distinctly pointed end, said end pointing the way up the nearest slope. We followed the diamond's call, scrambling up the brown and yellow scree, and saw a cave open its black throat to greet us.

By now the diamond was solid white, so radiant that it didn't bear looking at directly. It devoured the darkness of the cave better than any lantern, its light pulsating faster and faster until we all appeared to be moving in a series of awkward jerks. When the light could flutter no faster, it burst in one last crystalline flare and left us whimpering blind.

Vrogar groped for his trusty tinderbox and struck a light. The homely glow of a waxy candle-stub clamped in his paw was comforting. More comforting was the coruscation of flame reflected from a sea of gold coins, chains, crowns, gems, baubles, king-toys, and the preciously appointed images of unknown gods. Hyu's spell had come through.

"Tvarun kiss a goat, we're *rich*!" howled Vrogar. The men loosed similar irreverent cries of joy. I yipped with delight myself, both at the sight of so much wealth and the thought of having saved my neck, and dove into a cauldron brimming with unstrung pearls of every hue. The silky oyster-berries poured through my fingers, nested in my hair, cascaded down my breasts, tickled my nipples, and lodged in my ears. I cursed and grubbed out the one in my right ear, but the one in my left was an obstinate bastard.

"Vrogar, come here! Something's caught in my ear." My barbarian was busy elsewhere, throwing handfuls of rubies in the air and letting them raise welts when they landed on his upturned face. "Vrogar, I said I need *help*! Stop acting like an infant! You've seen gold before!" (Fine talk from a lady wallowing in pearls and greed.)

I tried once more to remove the pearl on my own. Failing, I lost my temper completely and shouted, "Vrogar, if you don't help me *this minute*, I'll make you sorry you were ever—"

A sheet of blue fire surged from the far reaches of the cavern and wrapped Vrogar and all his men in flaming agony. Flesh melted from their bones, their eyes turned to steam, and still the charring bones of their skulls seemed to hold on to a human look of anguish before flaking to black ashes.

$DETAILS, DETAILS,$ said the dragon, hustling past me, sending up a spray of man-dust and gold in his wake. The recalcitrant pearl popped out of my left ear unheeded. What looked like four King's Miles of gold and scarlet plate armor were whishing along at a deer's clip before my eyes, the monotony broken by a set of ebony wings folded high on the hill that was the monster's back. The tail slithered through as an anticlimax. By the time it came by, the law of diminishing returns had set in and I was used to dragons.

I climbed out of my bath of pearls and ran after the dragon, meaning to slip from the cave and get as far away as possible. At the lip, where blue sky and sunshine were framed in sandstone, I saw the beast take off. It was a short flight, its purpose accomplished before I could get more than two body-lengths up the cliff. Holding myself to the stone I watched the dragon circle Vrogar's ship once, leisurely, before blasting it to a steaming set of ripples.

Then he headed directly home, with one short stop en route. I felt his scythelike claws glide with preposterous delicacy under and over my shoulders, forming a steely harness. I was lifted into the sky, had the screams snatched from my mouth on a backwards roll, and fainted away when the monster plummeted back into his lair.

I never expected to wake up. I would be either devoured or incinerated and have my next interview with the Great Judge, if the priests were to be believed. Instead of the Great Judge, I opened my eyes and saw the dragon.

$WHY ARE YOU HERE?$

"Ah— it wasn't my fault. Those men—they were pirates. They captured me. They had a treasure-finding spell from a great magician—"

The monster's heavy head lay on his crossed forepaws. The thick eyelids opened farther, letting me see my reflection in the Worm's oily black pupils. I was a wretched, ragged, shaking, quivering bit of pink meat and unworthy of contempt, and didn't he just let me know it, mind to mind. Dragonthoughts rolled over me in scornful waves, smashing me down with the full weight of my host's disdain before he addressed me a second time:

$WHY ARE YOU HERE? KNOW MY DESIRES AND ANSWER WISELY.$

Silly me, I'd forgotten. All dragons have a reputation for great wisdom and ask no question without the deepest philosophic implications. They look down on ordinary conversation and suffer violent reactions to small talk. Question a Worm about his health or the weather and prepare to die.

I bowed my head. "Wisest One, as to why—for what purpose—I or any of my race are here on this earth, I have not the experience to answer. Be merciful and enlighten me."

This pleased the old lizard. His eyelids lowered, giving him an affected look of perpetual boredom. $WISDOM HAS ITS ROOTS IN IGNORANCE. YOU HAVE GOOD ROOTS. YOU ARE WISE. NOT SO WISE AS I, BUT ENOUGH TO LIVE. THOSE WITH YOU WERE NOT. WHAT ARE YOU?$

"I am human. I am unworthy. One is the same as the other, Wise One." (A load of sheepdung, naturally, but Master Urion had let me read about dragons and Hyu had told me about his more pompous professors. Both breeds fancy themselves all-knowing. Both require large amounts of sheepdung, well spread around. The only difference is that dragons do not need tenure.)

The dragon's barbelled chin bobbed majestically. $GOOD. I WILL KEEP YOU. NOW SAY, IN THE PETTY MANNER OF YOUR KIND, WHETHER YOU ARE A VIRGIN.$

My stomach dropped down around my ankles. "A—virgin? Wise One, if I may be so bold, why should that—that insignificant detail matter to one of your kind?" The treasure cave whirled while I spoke as Urion's lessons knotted themselves into nonsense in my memories. *A virgin? A virgin! Holy Esra, I thought it only bothered unicorns!*

The Worm's mouth was rimmed with smaller horny plates colored white as a well-polished grin. He seemed to be forever amused. $VIRGINITY IS A MATTER FOR UNICORNS. EVEN ONE OF YOUR INFERIOR BREED KNOWS AS MUCH. KNOW ALSO—HARK, HEED, LEARN, DRINK FREELY OF MY BOTTOMLESS KNOWLEDGE—THAT UNICORNS ARE THE ONE THING A DRAGON MUST FEAR.$

"Aha! Aha!" I jumped up and down when the light struck. I never had been one to pretend it was all old hat when a new idea came to me, though those who do are always accounted very sage (and very insufferable). "A unicorn can slay a dragon by virtue of his horn, but if you have a *virgin* around the house, the unicorn will be distracted long enough to lay his head in her lap while you save your skin, right?"

Steam gusted from the dragon's nostrils in the dank cavern

air. $MY PRESENCE HAS ALREADY IMPROVED YOUR
WORTHLESS MORTAL MIND. IF YOU ARE A VIRGIN,
YOU SHALL BEAR ME COMPANY AND GROW WISE.
IF NOT . . . $

I had grown wise before this. What I would tell the Worm
would be in the nature of an experiment. I knew the Cardinal
Rule of Experiments from Master Urion's house: *The wise
mage never tampers with the order of things unless his circumstances are such that the worst possible result of the experiment will be no more disastrous than not performing the
experiment at all.*

My experiment? A fib.

If dragons were as all-knowing as they liked to fancy themselves, this Worm would swallow lie and liar in one gulp.
However, if I told him the truth I'd likewise end up as a casual
snack. Therefore . . .

"Yes, Wise One, I will live with you and learn, if you will
deign to teach me. I am a virgin."

$I KNEW THAT,$ said the dragon. $MAKE YOURSELF
COMFORTABLE, VIRGIN. LESSONS BEGIN AT DAWN.$
He tucked his snout under his forepaws and rocked the cave
with his snores.

We got along fairly well. I was used to dealing with educated
morons, even oversized ones. Add six parts flattery to five of
playacting and you're home free. This is not to say that my
time spent with Dragon (so I named him privately, although I
always referred to him as Wise One, and he named me Virgin.
Idiot.) was entirely without profit. Like others of his stripe,
reptile and mortal, he could tell me the answer to anything . . .
provided that someone else had written it down in a book
previously.

"Wise One, although I am as a dab of suet melting under
the radiant sun of your learning, could you help me with a
problem?"

$IT'S NOT ONE OF THOSE MESSY VIRGIN PROB-
LEMS, IS IT?$ I indicated not. $GOOD. ASK.$

"When I was young, a great wizard said I had a talent within me, but he could not tell me what it was. Out of your infinite knowledge, tell me what my talent is!"

Dragon's massive head tilted one way, then another. His eyelids drooped and his sharply beaked snout nudged my skirts. (He had given me free rein among the cavern treasures, and now I was dressed in the sumptuously jeweled and embroidered gown of a dead princess.) A claw like a fallen sliver of moon poked me gingerly. The huge eyes closed and obscure rumblings issued from his snout. These ceased.

$NO,$ said Dragon.

"You mean you don't know what it is either?"

$NOT *KNOW*?$ He sprang up, wings unfurled in wrath. His roar dislodged a minor earthfall towards the seaward end of the cavern and knocked me flat. $DO YOU DARE VOICE SO ENORMOUS A CONTRAVENTION?$

"Who, me?" I shook my head, more to remove three fallen bats who were having a communal case of the heebie-jeebies. "Perish the thought."

$THE THOUGHT,$ said Dragon meaningly, $WILL NEVER PERISH. THOUGHT SHARES THE IMMORTALITY OF DRAGONS. YOU, ON THE OTHER HAND . . . $

"Wise One, forgive me. You expect too much from a mere virgin."

That calmed him. His wings ceased beating and folded back on themselves. $THAT MAY BE. EVEN I HAVE NOT LEARNED ALL THERE IS TO KNOW ABOUT YOUR SPECIES. IT IS NOT WORTH MY WHILE. HUMANKIND WILL NOT LAST LONG ENOUGH FOR SUCH STUDY TO BE FRUITFUL. WHAT I MEANT WAS THAT I WON'T TELL YOU.$

I decided to take a chance and ask, "Why not?"

$BECAUSE SOME THINGS ARE NOT MEANT FOR MAN TO KNOW. THAT GOES DOUBLE FOR VIRGINS, IF I RECALL MY MASTER'S TEACHINGS ARIGHT. AND I RECALL EVERYTHING ARIGHT.$

"Without a doubt. Sorry to have bothered you." So he didn't have an inkling either, the big lizard. I never mourned Sir Juris's death more.

Perhaps that is an exaggeration, for Sir Juris was a knight, a fighting man, and a day came when I realized that I was going to have need of someone familiar with the business end of a sword.

It began when Dragon remarked in an offhanded way, $A LITTLE LEARNING IS A DANGEROUS THING. DON'T YOU AGREE, VIRGIN?$

I looked up from my work, which at the moment consisted of seeing how many necklaces I could put on without breaking my neck, the ever-present string of Urion's vials, and the rules of good taste. "Always, Wise One." The agreeable live longer.

$I HAVE TAUGHT YOU MUCH, HAVE I NOT? I HAVE SHARED MY UNIVERSAL WISDOM WITH YOU FREELY. NOW IS THE TIME OF REPAYMENT.$

I shuddered. *Repayment* could so easily sound like *lunch* when uttered by Dragon. "How can I, a lowly mortal, ever repay you for all you have done for me, Wise One?"

Dragon chuckled. $YOUR MORTALITY ITSELF WILL BE PAYMENT. NO, DO NOT FEAR. I DO NOT MEAN YOUR PIDDLING LIFE. I WISH ONLY TO LEARN FROM YOU AS YOU HAVE LEARNED FROM ME.$

"I live to serve you, Wise One."

$YOU OUGHT TO. I WISH TO LEARN THE PHILO-SOPHICAL RAMIFICATIONS OF ALL THINGS HUMAN, AND YOU SHALL BE MY HELP. FIRST, AESTHETICS. I DO NOT HAVE ANY BASIS FOR UNDERSTANDING WHAT YOU HUMANS CONSIDER BEAUTIFUL.$

"Well . . . these are beautiful," I said, holding up a handful of jewelry. "Flowers are beautiful, and sunshine, and spring-time, and—"

$ARE *YOU* BEAUTIFUL, VIRGIN?$ For the first time ever, Dragon's eyes had opened all the way. $YES. I THINK YOU ARE.$ Before I could reply, Dragon harumphed several times and said, $THAT TAKES CARE OF AESTHETICS. NOW TO DUALISM. DO HUMANS BELIEVE IN GOOD AND EVIL? AH, YOU DO. FINE. AND I ASSUME, WITHOUT FEAR OF CONTRADICTION, THAT *YOU* ARE GOOD? VIRGINS SUFFER THAT REPUTATION.$

"I—I hope I'm good, Wise One."

$CERTAINLY. I SAID SO. DUALISM DOWN, ON TO ETHICS, OR THE STUDY OF RIGHT AND WRONG. DO HUMANS KNOW THE DIFFERENCE BETWEEN RIGHT AND WRONG, VIRGIN?$

I was growing more and more fidgety. "We hope we do, but sometimes it's hard to say. If you could give me specific examples, Wise One—?"

Dragon looked very pleased. $IS IT RIGHT TO IGNORE THE SUFFERING OF ANOTHER?$

"Of course not!"

$IF IT WERE WITHIN YOUR POWER TO HELP ONE IN NEED, WOULD YOU DO SO?$

"If I could, I don't see why I wouldn't."

$IN A WORLD WHERE SOLITUDE IS THE WORST OF PRISONS, WOULD YOU SET A CAPTIVE FREE IF THE KEY WERE IN YOUR HAND?$

"I— Just a minute. What are you saying?"

Dragon's sigh was a geyser that sent parboiled bats pelting down on the two of us. He sheltered me with his wings until the rain of cooked chiroptera stopped falling.

$VIRGIN, GIVE ME YOUR LOVE.$

My jaw bobbled up and down like a cork in a whirlpool. When I regained the ability to speak I yelped, "You're joking!"

$JOKING? I FULLY INTEND TO EXPLORE THE MATTER OF MORTAL HUMOR IN FUTURE. FIRST, HOWEVER, SEX.$

"Se—se—sex? *You don't mean that!* With—with another dragon, surely, but not with— You can't— I'm only— You know, if by some stretch of the—the imagination it were possible—*which it isn't*—I wouldn't be a virgin anymore. Then what would you do if a unicorn comes traipsing in here?"

$I HAVE BEEN LUCKY SO FAR. I FEEL THAT THE LOSS OF MY LIFE TO A UNICORN WOULD BE A SMALL PRICE TO PAY FOR GAINING FIRSTHAND KNOWL-EDGE OF MORTAL LOVE. BESIDES, I'M LONELY.$ So saying, he tumbled over on his side and rubbed his beaky mouth against my legs. $SO HOW ABOUT IT?$

I squeaked and scampered to the summit of the tallest pile of gold in the cave, but bullion doesn't provide much traction. I came skidding down again and fetched up against Dragon's partially opened jaws, not a heartening sight at all.

(Did you know dragons have uvulas? Very ugly ones, too.)

$FOOLISH VIRGIN,$ said Dragon, renewing the pussycat act with belligerent tenderness. $YOU KNOW THAT I DO NOT ASK THE IMPOSSIBLE. I AM COGNIZANT OF THE LAWS OF PHYSICS. I WOULD NOT SUGGEST ANY-THING TO HURT YOU. YOU WILL THANK ME FOR IT SOMEDAY. I WILL BE GENTLE. I WILL BE CONSID-ERATE. I WILL RESPECT YOU AFTERWARDS. I WILL NOT THINK SOLELY OF MY OWN PLEASURE. I WILL DEVOUR YOU IF YOU REFUSE.$

In that moment, children, I was so frightened that I forgot *how* to break into a cold sweat. Let any woman who claims she has come up against large-scale difficulties on her wedding night apply to me for some small consolation.

"This is—so sudden. Wise One, I must have time to think it over."

$TO THINK IT OVER? I OFFER YOU AN HONOR. YOU OUGHT TO BE GRATEFUL. VERY WELL. YOU HAVE UNTIL CHILDMORN.$

"Until when?"

Dragon hoisted himself onto his paws and sighed. $IG-NORANCE! IGNORANCE! IT HANGS ABOUT YOU LIKE A STENCH. I WONDER WHY I BOTHER WITH YOU. FOLLOW ME, VIRGIN.$

I didn't follow him, for one of his strides would have left me far behind. Instead I hopped a ride between the smaller upright plates that ran in a jagged spine down his tail. Dragon shambled through the cavern, going ever farther and farther from the entrance that gave on the sea.

I wondered what he was up to. The farther we went from the seaward mouth, the more I wondered. I never knew the cavern stretched out so far, nor that every foot of it was as richly carpeted with treasure as the king's ransom poor Vrogar and his men had romped in before they died.

It was terribly dark, darker the farther we went from the cave mouth. Dragon's own fiery glow was all the light we had, although it was multiplied by all the tiny golden and silver mirrors of the strewn treasure hoard. At last I saw a blot of daylight and realized that the cave had two mouths. He stopped and waited for me to dismount and jog up to conversation position at his shoulder.

$ENJOY THE VIEW, VIRGIN?$

"Oh, how pretty!" I cried, gazing down into the green valleys and forests that spread themselves in a verdant blanket at our feet. A trim village of whitewashed houses and neatly squared-off fields looked so fair and fine that it might have been the work of a master toymaker, not ordinary men. "I never knew we were so near to other people."

$YES.$ Dragon stifled a yawn. $VERY WELL-BRED PEOPLE, TOO. THEIR CHILDREN ARE DELICIOUS.$ My shock turned quickly to sick horror as Dragon elaborated: $ONCE A YEAR THE FOLK OF THAT VILLAGE BRING ME FOURTEEN CHILDREN, SEVEN BOYS AND SEVEN GIRLS, NONE OLDER THAN SEVEN. I HATE TO SOUND PICKY, BUT THAT'S THE MOST DIGESTIBLE AGE FOR A DRAGON OF MY YEARS. AND AS I DO MANAGE TO LEAVE THE TOWN IN PEACE FOR THE REST OF THE YEAR, I HARDLY THINK THEY HAVE CAUSE TO QUIB-BLE OVER MY ONE BIT OF SELF-INDULGENCE. THE DAY THEY BRING ME THE BRATS IS CALLED CHILD-

MORN, FOR REASONS THAT SHOULD BE OBVIOUS EVEN TO YOU. IT FALLS SEVEN DAYS FROM TODAY. ISN'T THAT A DELIGHTFUL NUMERICAL COINCIDENCE?$

"Delightful."

$THAT IS WHEN I SHALL EXPECT YOUR DECISION. CHILDMORN. HOP ABOARD AND WE'LL GO BACK NOW.$

For six dolorous days and nights I paced the seaward end of the cavern, wringing my hands and kicking aside uncounted loot as if it were trash. It was not my own fate that ate away at sleep and appetite, but the thought of those poor village children. The decision I made was for them. Love softens mortal men in more ways than one, and I hoped that Dragon might grant me the children's lives in exchange for my attentions. To be frank, I made my decision the first night. The additional days and nights of aggravation were spent on wrestling with the question: *With a* dragon? *Dear gods, HOW?*

The night before Childmorn I sidled up to Dragon and began to scratch him behind the left ear while he drowsed. It was the only part of his body I could reach that lent itself to something like an intimate caress. "Wise One, I have chosen. All I ask of you is that when you speak of this afterwards . . . you will be kind."

Dragon's head whipped up out of a half-doze so quickly that I was left tickling air. $WHAT DID YOU SAY?$

"I said I've decided that it's all right with me if you won't mind the place swarming with unicorns. Don't say I didn't warn you. There's still time to reconsider the—"

$STRIP.$

He was serious. My head began to throb, but I wasn't about to plead a headache. His yellow and black eyes shone as he watched me disrobe. Layer by layer I put aside the brocaded robes and pearled girdle, the tapestried undertunic and the pure white silk chemise. I was parting with my evening's selection of jewelry when Dragon made me stop.

$WHAT IS THAT?$ The tip of a claw hovered just above my breasts, where Urion's vials were my last adornment. Dragon sniffed at them twice, leaving me coated with a warm, wet spray. $I SMELL MAGIC.$

"Wise One, as my father—a great mage—lay on his deathbed, he bequeathed these three vials of potion to me. They contain nothing harmful to dragons, I swear it!"

$I KNOW THAT, I KNOW THAT.$ Dragon made impatient noises. $KEEP YOUR VIALS ON, THEY'RE NOTHING TO ME. PUT ON A FEW MORE GEWGAWS WHILE YOU'RE AT IT. THEY MAKE YOU LOOK RATHER NICE, FOR WHAT WE'VE GOT TO WORK WITH.$

"You're sure they don't bother you?"

$I FEAR NO SORCERY. DRAGONS ARE IMMUNE TO ALL MORTAL ENCHANTMENTS. IF YOU MUST KNOW, I WAS HAPPY TO SEE THAT YOU'RE NOT THE SORT OF GIRL WHO'S AFRAID TO COME NEAR A BIT OF HARMLESS GRAMARYE. IT WILL MAKE THIS ALL THE EASIER.$

As I decked my naked self out in a judicious assortment of anklets, chains, earrings, a modest sapphire diadem and matching chatelaine, Dragon sank back onto his haunches like a monstrous, scaly squirrel and spread the talons of his forepaws in midair. A swirl of wispy red light emanated from the right one, a hard spear of golden luminence piercing it from the left. The muzzy red light solidified into a shower of twinkling grains the moment it was transfixed, and these swept down like a crimson blizzard, drifting into hillocks and ridges among the treasures of the cave.

I prodded a small mound of the crystallized light with my toe. A flash of heat like the rush of strong wine raced up my leg and centered in my belly, leaving me trembling. Dragon saw and smiled.

$SO EAGER? I WOULD ADVISE YOU TO WAIT A BIT. IT WILL BE EVEN BETTER ONCE IT HAS BEEN PROPERLY PREPARED.$

I took several deep breaths to make my pulses slow down. "Wise One, what is this stuff? The feeling that it gives—I don't know whether to call it wonderful or terrible!"

Dragon's forepaws were busily describing a circle in the air, like a juggler who has lost his props but still keeps up the motions. Faster the huge paws went, and faster. Dragon's perpetual grin grew broader to show the smallest of his daggered teeth. Had my eyes been affected by what I'd touched of Dragon's making? Now thin air was thicker, and his ever-circling paws seemed to be feeding out a hoop of congealing blackness. The circle became substance, a massy, dark halo, a hoop of pyre-smoke now no longer spinning but held steady in a Worm's talons.

$PRETTY, ISN'T IT, VIRGIN?$ He returned to all fours, the better to let me see his handiwork. Up close the ring of darkness was even more wondrous, a braid of many-colored black. Oh, yes, there are shades of black just as there are shades of all the other colors in this world! Murky black, purplish black, watery black, glossy black . . . no end to them, and new ones ever breeding in Dragon's mystic ring.

He tilted the ring until it was parallel to the floor, its shades still whirling. Like watching the work of a potter's wheel, I saw the ring elongate as it spun, but here was a vessel that grew from rim to base instead of the right way of things. The blackness stretched downwards, made itself into a beaked vessel, sprouted whorls and bulges that were the forms of men and beasts and winged creatures, and gradually came to rest on its footed base between us.

$OUR LOVING CUP,$ said Dragon. $A MORTAL CONCEIT NOT WITHOUT ITS CHARM. I PLEDGE YOU, VIRGIN.$ A flick of his talons and the scattered red grains mounted skywards in a shimmering comet's tail, then swerved and cascaded into the midnight cup. Not a particle of frozen light was left anywhere outside.

I ventured nearer to the cup. It came breast-high on my body and was seductively smooth and cool to the touch. Inside, the red grains looked like a miniature desert. The bony shelves above Dragon's eyes rose. $YOU ASK YOURSELF HOW WE SHALL PARTAKE OF THIS MARVELOUS LOVERS' NECTAR? OR MERELY WHY? AH, MORTAL MAIDEN, THE IMPRINT OF YOUR LIPS ALONE WILL MELT THIS TO A LIQUID BREW WHICH BOTH OF US MAY DRINK. DO SO.$

"Like . . . this?" I pressed my lips lightly to the rim of the black beaker. Eddies of pleasure traveled from my lips through all the nerves of my bare skin. It was as if the first kiss I'd ever tasted had come back to me with all of its startling, frightening, tempting sensations. I closed my eyes and Hyu was there, his arms around me. . . .

Megan, I've sent those halfwits packing, them and their gold! If they scorn you, no wonder they're the bonebrains of the class. Who ever heard of a wizard blind to love?

$THAT WILL BE QUITE ENOUGH, VIRGIN. YOU MAY STEP AWAY NOW.$ I blinked, coming out of the spell. Dragon looked annoyed. $IF YOU FOUND THE TASTE OF THE VESSEL SO FASCINATING, I CANNOT WAIT TO SEE WHAT THE CONTENTS SHALL DO TO YOU. DRINK.$

Inside the black beaker the red grains had melted, just as Dragon promised. The liquid was too bright for blood, and not as wholesome. Its scent was very sharp and clean, the smell of early springtime rain that kills as many young shoots as it feeds. "Wise One . . ."

$DOES IT SCARE YOU, VIRGIN? PERHAPS IT SHOULD. TO MY KNOWLEDGE YOU ARE THE FIRST WITHOUT SCALES TO TASTE THE ELIXIR. MIND TO MIND DO WE WORMS MATE, OPENING THE INNER DOORS THAT SEND SELF POURING INTO AN ALIEN SKIN. THE TOUCH OF FLESH TO FLESH IS NEEDLESS AGAINST THE GREATER INTIMACIES OF THE BRAIN. THE BOND YOU MORTALS VALUE SO HIGHLY TURNS TO DUST, BUT ONCE TRUTH BREEDS TO TRUTH, IDEA TO IDEA, THE PAIRING IS ETERNAL.$

All of which gave me a whole new view on the concept "brainchild" and a fierce determination not to drink Dragon's odd elixir, come what might.

"Wise One, if you wish it, I will not be afraid." I bent my lips to the rippling surface.

$DRINK, THEN. BUT NOT TOO DEEP. THREE DRAUGHTS ARE ENOUGH FOR A DRAGON, AND MORE MIGHT CAUSE UNWANTED EFFECTS.$

"I obey," said I, and with the art of long nights spent play-acting in the House of Prayer, I made it look as if I had indeed swallowed three substantial mouthfuls from the cup. My performance did not receive the praise it deserved, for Dragon was in a hurry to plunge his muzzle into the brew and slurp up his ration. The beaker was dry when his huge snout came up. A shrill bellow blared from his jaws and he toppled over, his eyes transformed to a spray of stars.

The star-shower engulfed me, an experience too uncanny even to allow for the luxury of a scream. And why should I scream? I felt no pain, and as the stars swept me up in a dizzying dance I knew that here was nothing for me to fear.

$VIRGIN, IS IT YOU?$

I was in a place of dull bronze light, a sphere where phantoms trickled down the endless interior curve. I saw nothing beyond the sphere, but I heard Dragon's voice more clearly than ever before.

"Yes, Wise One, it's me. Where are you?"

A moan of betrayal worked its way out of my bones, if I still had bones in this place. $TREACHEROUS VIRGIN! PERFIDIOUS MORTAL! BEAUTY THAT HIDES THE SEALED HEART, THE CLOSED MIND, YOU HAVE LIED TO ME!$

Something scrabbled all around the sphere, an invisible mouse seeking escape. $WHY? WHY? WHY? I HAVE OPENED MYSELF TO YOU, BUT YOU HAVE SET BARS AGAINST ME! LET ME IN, LET ME IN! AH, THE COLD! THE COLD AND LONELY PLACES! OPEN TO ME, MY LOVE, MY CHOSEN ONE! BUT NO. . . . $ The voice ebbed away in misery. $YOU CANNOT. WHAT IS THERE LEFT TO DRINK OF THE ELIXIR? I HAVE HAD IT ALL, AND NOW I LOVE ALONE.$

So I knew where I was then, without being able to put a name to it. And I knew that Dragon's self was there too when he would have been inside my self if I'd really swallowed the scarlet brew. Children, you have not known the full tragedy of unrequited love until you have spurned a dragon. The rejected lover who waits out in the snow by your shuttered window with his modest bunch of violets is not half so pathetic as the Worm in his glory brought low because a mortal girl refused him entrance to her mind.

I felt sorry for Dragon then.

They will have to come up with seven kinds of new word for fool when they speak of me.

"Wise One ... Dragon ... I'm sorry. I was afraid to drink, and you're right; there's nothing left for me in the beaker. Oh, Dragon! It hurts me to see you like this—though I can't exactly *see* you, you know. Please, dear Dragon, is there anything I can do?"

The moaning seeped out of my bones again. Dragon's self was everywhere in the sphere, and in everything contained by it. $DO? WHAT CAN *YOU* DO? I HAVE MADE THE ULTIMATE OFFERING. I HAVE LAID MY ESSENCE OPEN TO YOU. THERE IS NO SECRET, NO SHAME, NO PART OF MY PAST I HAD RATHER FORGET, NO SILLY, SECRET DREAM OF MINE THAT YOU CANNOT KNOW. WHAT CAN *YOU* DO TO EQUAL THAT?$

He spoke the truth. If you stared hard enough at the ghostly projections all around the inner sphere, they became the solid images of the past and the brighter images of a desired future. Where I was, I didn't even have to concentrate to know the story those images told. They were as much a part of me as Dragon. He had indeed given me a matchless gift.

I considered my reply while the sorrows and shames and

brief joys of his life soaked into me. In the end I said, "Dragon . . . I could *tell* you things."

$THINGS? WHAT SORT OF THINGS?$

"Things about me. About my life. Secrets like yours, and dreams too."

Dragon's self thrummed with suspicion. $YOU WOULD *TELL* ME THESE THINGS, VIRGIN? WILLINGLY? I DON'T BELIEVE IT! NO DRAGON EVER WOULD, UNLESS COMPELLED TO OPEN BY THE CUP'S SPELL. WHY WOULD YOU?$

"I'm not a dragon; I'm mortal, and we have our little ways. I think you'll learn more of me if I *want* you to know it than you would have learned even if I'd drunk that cup. For one thing, I'll tell you that the only reason I agreed to this whole nasty experiment was to keep you from eating those poor children tomorrow. For another, I'm not a virgin."

$THE EGG YOU SAY!$

I crossed my heart and found I still had enough of a body to complete the gesture. "'Struth. Do what you like to me when the spell's worn off. Eat me, burn me, crush me, I don't care. Only let the babies be. You don't really need to eat them. I never saw you munch human flesh for as long as I've lived with you; only fish."

The presence in my bones released a sigh. $AND I GET DAMNED TIRED OF MACKEREL, IF TRUTH BE TOLD. BUT SAY ON, VIR— HMM. NOT A VIRGIN? I THOUGHT MORTAL WOMEN WOULD SOONER DIE THAN ADMIT SUCH A THING. YOU MUST BE TELLING THE TRUTH. AND WITHOUT POTION? A WONDERFUL THING. THERE MAY BE A MONOGRAPH IN THIS FOR ME WHEN WE'RE THROUGH. TELL ME MORE OF YOURSELF, LADY.$

"My name is Megan, Wise One. I'll tell you all my life's story, if you like. But the children—?"

$SPARED. SAY ON. ONE EXTRA DAY OF MACKEREL IS A SMALL PRICE TO PAY FOR THE TRUTH.$

I said on. I told him everything I could, my voice never tiring so long as we were both enclosed in the bronze sphere of Dragon's self. The images on the curving wall reflected Dragon's reactions to my tale, and there was never such an immediately sympathetic listener in the world. When I was done, the sphere flamed with a momentary clear light that wiped its walls clean.

$MEGAN...DEAR MEGAN...I THINK THAT NOW I DO KNOW WHERE YOUR TALENT LIES....MY SWEETEST LADY, I—$

Dragon's scream was a fearsome brilliance that blinded me, painting streaks of livid blue and green against the inner sphere. His presence inside me was siphoned out harshly, violently, leaving me alone in my own skin, wailing for him to return. A crack ran up the wall, another shade of black more awful than any contained in the ring: the final black of death. The surface under me shattered and I fell into night.

Blood was on my breast when I awoke. I was lying in blood, dark and warm, that matted my hair and stained my gold chains copper. I sat up and saw the black beaker in pieces, and a brawny man in a chain-mail tunic plunging his sword again and again into poor Dragon's heart.

CHAPTER VI
Doxy Walloper

I wailed and sobbed in my new captivity, tears streaming down my face until the corps of village matrons who had been assigned to tend me thought I had gone out of my mind.

"Poor lady, and wouldn't I run mad meself, cooped up with that horrid great serpent all those years," one confided to her neighbor as they washed the blood from my hair.

"Years? *Centuries* is what I hear he kept her prisoner, using all manner of hideous spells and enchantments to keep her from her rightful kingdom." The women all nodded in concert. Popular opinion had made me a princess from some exotic land and maybe some distant time. The town that has hired itself a hero and commissioned the slaying of a dragon is entitled to build the finest fairy tale it can upon the ruins.

The hero in question—the one who had boldly slain a drugged and helpless dragon with less fight in him than a new-whelped puppy—was named Iadel the Strong. He was strong enough to carry me, kicking and clawing, out of Dragon's lair. He was strong enough to give me a backhanded slap ("You're hysterical, your Royal Highness") that stunned me into a proper, maidenly faint in his arms. He was likewise strong enough to carry out load after load of Dragon's treasure before some unknown force within the mountain called up a quake that gave the poor Worm and all the rest of his riches a decent burial under several tons of stone.

The village women treated me as if I were a porcelain doll, and I let them, too miserable to bother with objections until one of them tried to remove all my jewelry before helping me into the copper bath.

"Not these." I crossed my hands over Urion's three vials.

Who would think two words could cause such a to-do? "She speaks our tongue, Kalissa!"

"Go on, you old jimcrack, you're hearing things! Asleep all those centuries, *and* her mother the Queen of the Mermaids, and you think she speaks as we?"

"I tell you I heard what I heard!"

"And I heard what Tecia heard too, Kalissa! She said, 'Not these,' plain as plain."

Kalissa touched the side of her nose. "But what did she *mean* by them sounds? 'Not these.' For all you two pulltoys know, she's laid the Curse of the Mermaids on us all because we've offended her."

"Oh, sheepdung," I said, stepping into the bath and letting the warm waters lave away all trace of Dragon's dried blood. "In the first place, the Curse of the Mermaids would be much more impressive. In the second place, I wouldn't know, not being one." I drew up my knees and slid down into the lemon-scented water until my shoulders were submerged, then let out an utterly satisfied sigh. "After all this time, a real bath."

"See?" Kalissa whispered. *"Centuries!"*

I splashed her. "You wouldn't be standing so near me if I'd gone that long without a wash-up. Is there any soap? I managed to keep clean by dabbling in a little rainwater pool we had at the back of our favorite niche, but if it dried up I had to have Dragon fetch me seawater in a jug. You should have heard him grumble!" I accepted the washball handed to me by the one called Tecia, youngest among my suddenly acquired ladies-in-waiting.

"You—spoke with the monster, Your Royal Highness?"

"Of course she did!" Stocky Kalissa fetched Tecia a friendly clout on the ear. "Now we've got the nub of it. See them pretties she won't be parted from? They're all full of horrible magic such as turns cows dry and takes all the good out of your husband. See, she was cursed in her cradle by a wicked sorceress to be a dragon's slave for fifty years. But then there came her guardian sprite and filled *that* bottle with a potion that kept her young for all the fifty years, and *that* bottle with sommat to keep the fiendish serpent from doing her any harm."

Even I couldn't wait to hear how it all came out. "And what've I got in my third vial, Kalissa?"

The matron clasped her wrists and struck a pose that said, *You shan't stump me!* "The third's full of a most unspeakable poison that'll kill the wretch who tastes so much as a drop! And *that* was given you in case the dragon tried anything a lady shouldn't have to stand for."

"Quite right." I bowed to Kalissa's omniscience. While I was bowed, I also had her scrub my back.

After the bath, I was wrapped in warm towels and blankets and conducted to another room. The house that the women had taken over in my name was Kalissa's, and she was the village magistrate's wife. I'd have expected no less from such a majestic woman. I later learned it was the only house in town to boast three stories, with the children's room up under the eaves, the parents' suite below, and rooms in common use on the ground floor. Kalissa had bullied her husband and his lieutenants into hauling all of Iadel's plundered chests up to the second story, "for safekeeping," and not even Iadel himself had the balls to make a countersuggestion.

Now Kalissa jerked her head at the assembled ranks of sealed treasure chests and invited me to inspect their contents first. "Some of it's yours, no doubt, and you won't lie about how much. Royal ladies are bred to truth-telling."

"This one's hers, certain," said Tecia, whose curiosity had driven her to open one. It contained no gold, but was packed full of the rich raiment I'd grown used to wearing while I dwelled with Dragon. The other women swarmed around Tecia and chittered with delight as one regal garment after another was whipped out for all to see.

They decked me in finery and watched with legend-hungry eyes as I went from one chest to the next, flinging back the lids and passing on. There were seven chests in all, one full of clothing, four of coin, two of jewelry. I think what bedazzled the ladies more than the heaps of riches was my indifference to them. I didn't mean to act so apathetic as I strolled through the glitter, but I was accustomed to it. In the cavern I'd slept and sat and sprawled on gold, with Dragon's blessing. I'd even made myself a comfortable seat out of mud studded all over with coins and gems—a seat with a hole in the center ringing a bottomless shaft that became the direct line to the bowels of the earth from my own. Do you wonder that I had lost all respect for riches?

"Hssst! The men want to come up!" cried a little woman who Kalissa had posted on the stairs.

"They can wait awhile longer," Kalissa decreed, but she was overruled by a rumble of boots in the hall and the gentlemen were among us. They were mostly of an age with the women attending me—past youth but far from old—and the perils of living in dragon-country combined with the regular aggravations of crops and taxes and dependents had conspired to relieve most of them of their hair. I gazed out over a sea of sweaty bald pates and my eyes fixed on the one good head of hair among them: Iadel's.

Handsome? It takes more than hair for that, and he had it. Broad at the shoulders, slender at the waist, virtually hipless, he let lesser beings merely *enter* rooms; he conquered them. Above the neck he was better than below, and below the belt he was divine. You speak with an expert in such matters, and I tell you from vast experience—even making my preliminary observations with the handicap of intervening chain-mail byrnie, leather tunic, linen underwrap, and heroic supporter (a must if you're going to hoist a broadsword all day)—there was a treat in store for the maiden who interested Iadel. Especially if she was fond of horses.

But I err. Such matters are not for your tender ears, or so your mothers would assure you. Your mothers would've fought each other barehanded for a glimpse of Iadel the Strong. And for more than a glimpse—? You'd all be orphans.

Iadel was, of course, in the front rank of the men. We found each other's eyes at once—two firebirds mistakenly shuffled in among the hens and capons. Smoothly he glided to one knee and took my hand. A sigh of vicarious fulfillment rose from every soul watching us.

"Your Royal Highness: I, Iadel the Strong, conqueror of demons, slayer of dragons, vanquisher of evil wizards, and our Lord Duke Nuraglion's undefeated mainstay swordsman, do humbly lay my blade at your feet. May you see fit to trample on this good steel which saved your life just as you have trampled upon my captive heart."

I looked at the women. They were all clutching their bosoms, which rose and fell at an accelerating tempo until I grew giddy and had to look away. I looked at the men. They were licking their lips, a unified effort that filled the room with a faint rasping sound. I looked at Iadel. It was difficult to view that granite chin, those steel-gray eyes, that adorably dimpled boyish grin, and equate him with the clod who'd smacked me senseless in Dragon's lair. *Maybe I* was *hysterical*, I told myself.

Last of all I looked down at the sword. Everyone was waiting for me to do something with it, to it, or about it. Iadel had suggested trampling on it as upon his heart, but I just couldn't. For one thing, I didn't want to trample on his heart. For another, when you wear nothing but silk slippers, it isn't wise to go stamping on sharpened steel.

I picked up the sword and presented it to him instead. "Accept my thanks for rescuing me and all my treasure as you accept this sword from my hands. May you win even greater fame with this blade in future, brave Iadel."

Not bad for spur-of-the-moment. Living with Eliard had left its mark on me. My remarks were a palpable hit with the crowd, but with none more than Iadel himself, who accepted the sword in such a way that my hands were still clasped to the metal under his.

"Let all the citizens of this good town be our witnesses then, fairest lady. For as much as you have not spurned my sword, but have graciously returned it to me again, so I vow that no harm shall befall you so long as I wield this blade in your peerless name!"

In the wild cheering that ensued, Iadel whispered, "By the bye, what *is* your peerless name?"

"Megan." The two of us were bowled aside by Kalissa and her crew, who were shoving the men this way and that as they charged downstairs to the kitchens. The men tumbled after, their goal the wine cellars. Iadel and I steadied ourselves at the window and watched the entire village turn topsy-turvy as benches and trestles were wrestled into the fountain square, tablecloths and crockery were deployed, kegs and barrels of drink were rolled out and broached, and mentally deficient livestock were lured to the butcher's knife and the roasting spit with soft, affectionate cries.

"Heavens. What are they doing?" I asked.

Iadel had a rowdy laugh. "Gods preserve that pretty head of yours, sweetheart, what do you think? It's not every day a dunghill village like this gets to host a double celebration: the death of a ferocious dragon by a hero's sword and that same hero's troth-plight to a princess."

My guardian sprite decided it would be too much to have me say: *A real princess? Congratulations! Who's the lucky girl?* For once my wits didn't run like spooked chickens, but I fear I loosed a very unprincesslike squeal anyhow.

"*Troth-plight? To me?*"

Iadel looked mildly put out with me. "You returned my sword, didn't you?"

"Yes, but—"

"Then we're trothed. If you didn't want me, you should have trampled on it. It's not as if you didn't have the chance."

"But— Good Iadel, I am unfamiliar with the customs of this land. You're forgetting I come from a distant kingdom where—"

"Which one?"

"What?"

"Which kingdom? It must have a name." So it did, and I told him what it was. The worst that could happen would be that he'd escort me home and upon delivery our King would point out that I wasn't one of his daughters. Or for all I knew, he'd assume that I *was* one of his girls, having lost track of some of them in the royal harem's Bookkeeping Department.

"So you see, we can't be trothed, Iadel. My royal father trothed me to a prince as soon as the midwife cut the cord. I've already got an intended spouse, and one simply doesn't go about mucking up royal wedding arrangements, even if you did rescue me from poor old Dragon."

Iadel's eyes took on a hard shine. "Had you claimed to come from a land I'd never heard of, milady, your argument would wash. But a true princess would know that the royal trothing rites are the same for all kingdoms participating in the Uniform Rites and Practices Act of the Fifth Wizards' Council. Whether you like it or not, you are my trothed bride." He seized my face then, and it was still tender on the side where he'd slapped me. He ignored my whimper of pain to add, "And whether I like it or not, it seems I'm trothed to a fraud. But a sly fraud who's laid claim to these treasure chests before witnesses."

I tried to remove his hand, but he tightened his grip and added a cruel twist that grated my teeth together. "You can have the chests, and I hope the dresses fit you!" I said as best I could with my mouth all squeezed up like that.

Iadel released me with a push that slammed me into the wall. "I don't think you understand. As my trothed bride, your chests *will* be mine when we're wed. Whoever you are— whatever you were doing in that monster's lair—I'm not having you destroy the tale of Iadel the Strong, slayer of dragons, savior of princesses." The grin returned. It wasn't as adorably boyish as before. It was downright malevolent. "For better or for worse, milady, we shall have each other."

"In a pig's eye! I don't want you, and all you want from me is this plunder. Take it and be damned. I'll run so far from this hogwallow kingdom that you can spread the word that I was whisked off by—by my mother, the Queen of the Mermaids!"

"That won't do." Iadel drew a stiletto from his belt and made a great business of pricking his thumb bloody with the point. "You see, I need you, Megan, not just your chests. When these bumpkins sent their petition to my Lord Duke Nuraglion, I was somewhat out of the ducal favor. Something to do with His Grace's daughter. You are twice as fair as that mush-faced chit, and a princess besides—or princess enough for the local nitwits to believe in you. If I return wed to a royal lady, there's nothing His Grace can do against me for fear of upsetting your father, the King, let Nuraglion's daughter howl loud as she likes!"

"I'm not marrying you so you can hide in my skirts, Iadel. I'm going down and telling these good folk the truth—all of it! Including how their mighty hero slew a sleeping dragon."

He actually let me get past him and halfway down the stairs, but I was simple enough to believe he was afraid of what I'd threatened. I heard a sound like stage-thunder and wheeled just as the copper bath came hurtling down behind me. It swept me from my feet, leaving me a heap of bruises, aches, and blood at the foot of the stairs. Kalissa and the other women came running in to see what was happening. My spinning head could hardly bear their uproar.

Iadel was there to scoop me up in his arms and shoo the women away. "Dragons die, but their curses linger," he said. "Her Royal Highness is lucky to be alive. With these eyes I saw the tub spring up and sail after her like a live thing. If I hadn't drawn my enchanted blade and uttered a countercharm, she would be dead now."

"The poor, sweet lady! She looks close to dead as it is!" Tecia exclaimed. "A deathcurse, you say? From the dragon?"

"From where else?" Iadel shrugged his magnificent shoulders. "I cannot watch over her constantly, yet the gods witness that she won't be truly safe until my spirit is bound to hers and can keep the dragon's vengeful ghost always at bay. Alas! If there were only some way...."

Of course there was. Kalissa thought of it, and her husband took care of details such as what the law said regarding half-conscious brides. They tell me I had a lovely wedding.

Iadel had collected a fat fee from the grateful villagers for his artless murder. He spent it all on a sturdy train of wagons to haul off the seven treasure chests and me. He also hired Tecia's younger sister, Alicorn, to tend to my hurts en route to Duke Nuraglion's castle, but judging from the sounds I heard coming from the woods when we camped, she also looked after Iadel.

"Tomorrow we reach the castle," my lord informed me. My bruises had healed enough for me to ride a horse, and Alicorn was relegated to the rear. "If you think to say a word against me, I wouldn't advise it. There are two sorts of women who live with dragons: One is the captive princess, the other the black sorceress. I can do a most convincing scene in which I recover from the glamour you laid on me and reveal that you have come into Nuraglion's court as an evil enchantress and assassin."

"It would take a bonebrain to believe that!" I snarled.

Iadel smiled. "I wasn't aware that you'd already met our Lord Duke."

I kept silent. At Nuraglion's keep I was made welcome by all the ducal court, but the hero of the hour was Iadel. Even the Duke's daughter forgot her swelling belly long enough to waste calf-eyes on him. Nuraglion himself set me at his right hand during the welcoming banquet and plied me with questions about my recent ordeal.

Iadel and I were given new rooms in the castle, as befitted a hero and his regal bride. That night he banished Alicorn to the servants' quarters and had me. I knew better than to try any slipperies with him. He wasn't the type to have patience with excuses, delays, or stratagems meant to keep him from what he wanted when he wanted it. He'd meet them all with the flat of his hand or worse, and no one would chide him for it. A man's wife is his own business, and so is how he makes her mind. If she's a princess, let her send word to her father when Husband's too heavy-handed. What? No word to the distant King? Then she must enjoy a beating now and then. Sure, she does. All women do. They just *pretend* they don't to egg you on, as every real man knows!

So he had me, but I saw to it that he didn't have much fun. He went back to Alicorn the next day.

Unfortunately for all concerned, Iadel could not leave well enough alone. He overheard too many men remark on his good luck—a hero's reputation, a fortune won, and a beautiful wife who looked as if she must be fire and honey in bed. *Must* be? Iadel began to have the sinking suspicion that he'd been shortchanged of a hero's proper due. The legends all said that dragon-bound princesses remained icy to the monster's slimy overtures, but presumably the ladies thawed once saved from the dragon's clutches. Why was *his* princess so cold—nay, petrified?

"It's not as if you're a virgin," he said. He sounded petulant. "Why do you just *lie* there? Alicorn doesn't do that."

I pulled the hem of my woolen nightdress back down around

my feet and crossed my ankles. "You must tell me what she does do. It sounds fascinating."

"She—wriggles. Sort of. And she makes—noises. Happy noises, like she's having a good time."

He didn't think it was funny when I flopped around like a beached trout and dutifully yelled *Yippeeee!* the next time he touched me. I got a sound slapping for it, but it was worth it. I went back to imitating a sack of barley in bed and Iadel grew testier.

"You're worn out, that's your trouble! You've been sneaking around behind my back, and don't think I don't know who's getting what's mine! It's Jepson, isn't it? With those mewly brown eyes of his and that bugger-me-darling voice and those lady's hands!"

"Don't be silly, Iadel. You've been doubling the servant girls regularly and you're still not too tired to come around pestering me." I thrust my needle through the fancywork hoop in my hands and viewed my stitchery with pride. "One is never too weary to do what one enjoys."

Iadel leaned over my shoulder to see what I was making. "That's my device. If you're making me a shirt, Megan, you've four times too much silk."

"Oh, it's just right for what I'm making, dear heart; perfect." And so it was, for your finer shrouds are measured out at four times the wearer's shirt-length precisely.

"Well . . . I've got my eye on you now, Megan, don't you forget it! If I so much as see you looking sideways at another man . . ."

See me looking at another man? Never. Imagine he saw it? Frequently, and for these offenses I was beaten: slaps first, then harder blows, then fists. The first time he gave me one of the serious beatings, I began to cry for Hyu. Maybe I thought that wizards-to-be obtained a sixth sense that let them know when one they loved was in trouble. If so, I soon learned how wrong I was, and capped the mess by giving Iadel another weapon. He took to taunting me with Hyu's name while he beat me.

Children, if you think I endured this situation long, you underestimate me. I only let it go on as long as it did because I had a few details to settle before acting. The bastard had to die—that much was self-evident—but murder is not as simple for a lady to accomplish as for a gentleman, especially an armed hero. There is the trifling affair of King's Justice to think of, and the executioner's block to follow. If not for these bagatelles I could have plunged my fancywork needle into Iadel's brainstem with a gladsome heart and gone on to eat a hearty dinner afterwards.

I was mulling over ways and means of domestic slaughter when the Duke's daughter herself innocently supplied me with the solution. She was very heavy with Iadel's child at the time and kept to a little herb garden against the south wall which was also a favorite haunt of mine. We met there often and sat working on the baby's clothes together in the warm spring sunshine.

We were struggling with the intricacies of infant underarm seams when Perdita said, "There are times, Your Royal Highness, that I wish the two of us might trade places."

"Do you mean being wed to Iadel, Your Grace? Then I share your wish." I jabbed my needle through the cloth and stabbed myself in the thumb. The spew of obscenities I used was beyond the education of most princesses and made Perdita laugh.

"Not that, Your Royal Highness! The gods defend me! I may be carrying his child, but I'm not the witling I was when I first went to the straw with him. When Iadel returned from the dragon's quest with a wife, I made an offering of thanks to Boriela, the Celestial Midwife, for having given me all the benefits of a husband without the burdens."

I sucked the blood from my finger in a foul humor. "I wish you might've told Iadel you didn't want to marry him, baby or no baby. I'd be free of him too, then."

Perdita held up a tiny coat the color of buttercups and admired it complacently. "But I'd be bound to him. Father would've seen to it. Now if he wants to marry me off, he'll have to sweeten my dowry with additional acres so my suitor will accept used goods. In the meantime, I'll have my child, and if I'm lucky I won't have *any* suitors until Father dies. Then I can inherit the whole estate and do as I please."

That was surprising. "Your Grace can inherit? But you're not male."

"If I am, *this* is a mistake." She patted her belly with love. "By our laws a female can rule if she's managing the holdings for a male heir. I will bear a son and Father will leave all he has to him."

"You seem very sure of your child's sex. It *might* be a daughter. Such catastrophes have been known to happen." We exchanged overly solemn looks at the horrendous possibility of girl-babies, then exploded into snorts and titters.

"No, no, Your Royal Highness, I *will* bear a boy. I know, because when Iadel rode off to slay your dragon, a wandering herbwife came to the castle. For a fee she scried my future and told me I carried a son."

"And then she left, and no refunds if she's guessed wrongly. If I were not a royal princess, I'd earn a pretty penny as that kind of fortune-teller."

"And we all know that you are truly a royal princess, don't we, Megan?" Nothing in her expression betrayed the fact that she alone was privy to my secret, which was why she was so punctilious about calling me by my full title whenever there was the slightest chance of eavesdroppers nearby. Dear Perdita! Oh children, never be without a friend!

"I have no doubts about the scryer's honesty," she went on. "She foresaw the success of Iadel's mission too, and had a certificate of study from Routreal besides. Even this far from your home we know and value the Doctorate of Demonology the University bestows."

"Then why would you like to trade places with me, unless

it's to do me a favor? I'd enjoy playing Lady Regent to a puppy-Duke, and no one to tell me what to do. Even though it means having to go through childbirth, I think I could—Why, Perdita!"

The Duke's daughter had burst into tears.

I set aside my needlework and embraced her, although her belly made it awkward. She sobbed and sobbed with her face against my shoulder while my eyes darted all about the small herb garden, fearful of what an interloper would say if he saw us. At length Perdita sat back and wiped her face with a remnant of cut cloth from the baby's clothes.

"You will laugh at me, Megan. Here I sit, so full of brave plans for ruling my father's duchy in my son's name, and yet I am terrified of the one thing that must occur before any of my schemes can come true: childbirth. I was so thrilled with the herbwife's prediction that I forgot to have her see whether I'd survive the birth. By the time I thought of it, she was gone. Oh, Megan, all through Father's court they say that you were able to hold off the dragon's foul attentions because you have some magic charm that a great sorceress gave you in your cradle! If only you could bear this baby for me, I know that Death would stay as far from you as that dragon did, for fear of your enchanted amulet. But I—when the time comes, I must face my dragon alone."

I gave Perdita's fingers a comforting squeeze. "My dear friend, I had nothing but my wits to save me from that dragon—no spells or charms or amulets. The only magic about what I wear around my neck is that none of the vials has broken yet. For all I know, they're colored water." I touched the strand tenderly. "But they do hold sweet memories. Otherwise, I'd give them to you gladly." Seeing the terror in her face, I added, "I'll be with you when the time comes. You won't be alone, and I have experience overcoming dragons. All will be well, you'll see, and when your son is in your arms—"

"You sound sure of yourself, Megan Herbwife!" Perdita's

biting tone sprang from fear. "Where shall I apply for a refund
if you're wrong and I die? Or the baby—"

"Don't say that! You and your son will live!" I closed my
fingers on Urion's vials. "By the mage who loved and taught
me, I swear it!"

"A mage?" Perdita goggled. "You had a magician lover?"

"*And* teacher! You'll be glad of it when you see how well
I remember what he taught me about distilling potions that blur
pain."

Perdita was restored to cheerfulness by that news. She gave
me a swift, fond hug and took up her sewing again. We stitched
on as if nothing had been said. When the light failed and we
rose to return to the castle, she made a casual remark

"A magician lover. Fancy that. What a pity he couldn't
teach you how to make Iadel disappear."

I don't think she even knew she'd said it aloud. Nightshade
and deadly hellebore too spring from the smallest of seeds.

Magic.

Could anyone blame me if Iadel vanished from the earth
through sorcerous means? A fortunate blast of lightning? A
convenient fissure opening at his feet? An obliging resident of
the Netherplane dropping by to rend him to gobbets of meat?
Yes, that would be the nicest: a demon.

Perdita was delivered of a boy. Mother and child came
through well, and Iadel gave me the beating of our married
life for participating in the birth. "You're supposed to be a
princess, you stupid trull! Royal girls don't soil themselves
with births! They leave that mess to the midwives, and if they
should *happen* to see a blink of what's going on in that room,
they faint."

"And when it's their turn in 'that room'? When they're in
there among strangers and the great hero who fathered their
child locks himself in the wine cellar so he won't have to hear
the screams?"

"Ignorant bitch. I should know better than to waste time

teaching you anything but what you understand." He reached for the broad leather belt that held his scabbard.

Later, while he snored in our bed, I drank the leftovers of the pain-blurring potion I'd brewed for Perdita. I had recalled Urion's lessons better than I'd hoped. The potion was a wonder. Vitality filled my veins as the pain of Iadel's beating faded. If I could dredge up a magical recipe so well when Urion had shown it to me only once, calling up a demon would be child's play. I got busy with chalk and oil on the bedroom floor while Iadel dozed on.

My lord and master awoke with a pair of warty claws at his throat and a mile-wide leer of canine teeth hovering near his nose. "Whu—?" he said.

The demon snapped his nose off.

Iadel shrieked and thrashed, but my Netherplane helper was seated on the hero's chest, all two hundred sulfurous pounds of him. His olive-green skin contrasted prettily with the splashes of pigeon's blood I'd poured out as an offering to fetch him. (I *think* Urion said it was all right to offer pigeon's blood to a Render when you can't get any fresh boar's blood for the spell.)

"Down, Tyroth," I directed. A moist, bubbly sound like a simmering pudding seeped between the demon's rubbery lips. He slid from Iadel's chest, leaving a swath of stink and stain behind him. Iadel's hands were clapped over his missing feature, blood welling up between the fingers, but that didn't stop him from trying to escape.

Tyroth did.

"I assume you're wondering about this," I said to my husband, squatting down to his level. The demon was sitting on him again to prevent any further breaks, at my command. "Call it an object lesson. Women are taught forbearance, but every person has her limits. You reached mine. Now you die."

"I was right about you, you filthy whore!" (Seeing no hope of mercy in my face, Iadel decided to go out badmouthing. I only wish I had the skill to reproduce his noseless pronunciation.) "You *are* a black witch! Cowardly hag, only let me reach my sword and I'll teach you manners!"

"Sword against demon? Wouldn't that be an uneven match?" I thought it over. "If you insist. Tyroth, off."

The demon rose and even fetched Iadel's sword from its place above the bed. The three of us faced off in the center of the floor. On guard, Iadel said, "This is the thanks I get for saving your poxy skin from a dragon! This is the gratitude one can expect from a woman after I made you a princess, married you, installed you in these luxurious apartments, permitted you the fame of being called the wife of Iadel the Strong!"

"Iadel the Noseless." Tyroth gluggled with raw merriment over my sally. He also dropped his battle-stance while holding his sides and laughing. Iadel was a seasoned warrior. He saw his advantage and seized it.

"Hyyyyaaaaahhhhh!" He raised his sword-arm high and charged.

"Tyroth, look out!" I shouted. Too late. Iadel had run like a rabbit out the bedroom door. Looking guilty, my demon picked up Iadel's abandoned blade. Wishing to lose the evidence of his incompetence, he hummed a careless tune and nonchalantly tossed it out the window. A chilling shriek echoed up from the courtyard. Tyroth and I wedged ourselves over the sill for a look. On the cobbles Iadel lay pinned like a butterfly, his own steel sticking out of his back.

"Lucky throw, Tyroth."

The demon blew on his nails. "Oh, we Incubi always do have pretty good luck. Except at cards."

"Incubi?" I stepped away from the window. Gray-green, ungainly, his glutinous skin covered with an assortment of unappetizing blemishes, Tyroth didn't strike me as the prototype of male sex-demons. "I summoned a Render."

"Nope. You summoned me." He smacked his lips. "*Love* that pigeon blood! So, now that No-Nose is outa the way, what can I do for you?"

"Do? You've done it already. You killed Iadel."

Tyroth's smoky eyes screwed up. "Yeah, but—that was an accident. I mean, I'm an Incubus; y'know, a lover, not a fighter."

I shook his paw. "Then you can chalk it up to new experiences. Perhaps there'll be a promotion in it for you. Does an Incubus rank higher or lower than a Render? How do you arrange these things in the Netherplane?"

The paw tightened. "That's something you're gonna find out firsthand, lady." Tyroth's paw swelled, engulfing my hand. My arm disappeared into the cloudy fist, followed by my shoulder, until soon I was entirely swallowed by a hand the color of gravestone mold and together we dove out of the bounds of the living world.

CHAPTER VII

Demon-strations of Affection

"I want Hyu!" I howled.

"Hey, baby, I want you, too," said Tyroth. "That's why I brought ya here, y'know? Like it?"

"What's not to like?" a feminine voice horned in from nowhere. "Ain't it the Netherplane?"

It couldn't be anyplace else. We'd landed on a windswept crag, the clothing torn from my body by our descent, and all around us the landscape seethed and bubbled. Stone cauldrons of boiling mud ringed our rocky tower, gouts of flaming gases leaping up to singe our feet. Sharing our aerie was a blatantly female demon whose ample charms were somewhat hampered by the addition of cow's horns springing from her brow, with ears and tail to match.

"Welcome back, Tyroth, honey. Whatcha bring me?" The Succubus threw her arms around my demon's neck and gave me a succinct kick off the cliff into the churning muck below. Nothing human could survive such a scalding.

I surfaced to the sound of Tyroth severely berating the

careless Succubus and to the comprehension that I was no longer human. When I shook my head to get the hot mud out of my hair and found I had a braid of golden serpents instead, realization was complete.

"What have you done to me, fiend?"

"What say?" Tyroth cupped an ear. "You'd better flap up here, baby. Can't hear you over the mudpots."

"Flap?" Another surprise; I had wings. They were midway between a bird's and a dragon's, covered all over with minute strips of curling flesh that gave them the look of wormy fleece. I oared the right wing around for closer inspection. Hundreds of tiny black eyes inspected me right back. Disgusting or not, the vermicular wings worked. I fanned my way out of the mudpot, up to the top of the crag, and accosted Tyroth.

"I asked you what you've done to me!"

"Hey, hey, not so hot and bothered, babe. A'right? You don't like the model, I can fix it. What'samatter? Don't gofer the wings? Or is it the hair, huh? Yeah, I bet that's it. Not too many gals gofer snakes, but I figured you wouldn't mind if they were *gold* snakes. Something you don't see every day, but still a classic look. Fine, you just let me know what goes, what stays, and I'll remodel to suit. Deal?"

My roar of rage wasn't specific, but I think it gave him the message. I underlined my arguments by throwing first the Succubus and then Tyroth into the boiling mud. He cleared the surface and looked up at me. I tore off a chunk of rock and pitched it at his head.

"Uh-huh. Yup. Doesn't like *anything*," he said. Next thing I knew, the naked rocks and burning sludge were gone. The three of us stood in the middle of a simply furnished room. A large looking-glass stood against the wall. I rushed to it and found that I was still nude, but otherwise myself. All I wore was a gape and a familiar necklace.

Tyroth and the Succubus had also suffered a change. They looked completely human, and more attractive than many humans I'd known. "Happy now, baby?"

I sank onto a padded footstool and let my head hang down. "I'm so confused. . . . Where did all those awful things go? Where are we now?"

Tyroth sat tailor-fashion before me. He still had a wide, white grin, but no longer carnivorous. "Honeycake, *you* know where we are. It's the Netherplane."

"Otherwise known as 'home, sweet home' to the in-crowd," said the Succubus. She sat at the dressing-table and gave her platinum blonde hair one hundred strokes. "The name's Mufki. Glad to have you aboard. We can use all the sub-Succubi we can get." Little lightnings crackled around her head as she brushed away.

"*I* don't belong here! I'm mortal!"

Tyroth shook his head and patted my knee. "Sorry, sweetie. You did a no-no, and now you're here to stay."

"What? Killing Iadel? *You* did that! Besides—I didn't even get a fair trial! Where's the Great Judge? I demand to see the Great Judge!"

"Oh, wow, do you believe her?" Mufki applied three separate pairs of false eyelashes. "To see the Great Judge you gotta be dead, sugar. And Tyroth just isn't into necromance. Like 'em with a little life in 'em, doncha?"

He whacked her behind amiably. "Get stuffed, Mufki, you're jealous. But she is right, Megan. You aren't dead. You aren't mortal either. You've become one of us."

I had. I had! I listened numbly as Tyroth explained the rules governing all summoning-spells. A spell is in the nature of a contract, fiend and wizard tacitly agreeing to abide by the unwritten rules. The wizard will call up the breed of demon best qualified for the job at hand and the demon summoned will do as he's bid provided that the appropriate sacrifices were made in payment. Failure by either party to comply with the above terms would result in forfeit.

"Of what?"

"Of whatever, snooks. Life, if the mage looks like he's got some meat on his bones. Liberty, if the demon balks and the wiz pops him into a brass bottle. In your case, for the improper application of an Incubus to perform a Render's duties, you can kiss the pursuit of mortal happiness ta-ta. We need more sub-Succubi, like Mufki said, and you're drafted."

Mufki was satisfied with her eyelashes and was now lacquering her nails vermilion. "Oh, it is just aw-ful, Megan, just *aw*-ful, I tell ya! Biggest rash of exorcisms you ever did see in the Kingdom of Alba. Some of my best friends got cast into the outer darkness quicker'n a doorway do-dah. Couple that with the big Pure-Body-Pure-Magic movement over in Carolandia and you've got these dink wizards calling up my girls just to try talking them into repenting their sins and quitting the sex-fiend service."

"None of them quit," Tyroth reassured me, shifting his hand from knee to thigh. "Not Mufki's girls. But that let the wizards pull 'em into bottles on a technicality because they didn't do their callers' bidding. We sure are shorthanded, honey."

"You're going to be short one more if yours goes any farther, Tyroth."

He removed his hand without fuss. "No problem, baby. I don't go where I'm not summoned. But I like you lots, and before you know it, you're gonna like me."

"Am I."

"Whoa! I'm an Incubus, doll. What no mortal woman can resist. Fact is, I'm the senior Incubus of this Time-Space cultural quadrant of the Netherplane. So make yourself to home. *Mi casa es su casa.* No rush, toots, and I swear I won't lay a hand on you until you want. And you *will* want. You'll come around; I got time."

The son-of-a-Succubus was right. He had time. Time was all we had in the Netherplane, and all the boredom you needed to fill it.

Mufki took me under her wing, which she could grow to suit her fancy. "See, Megan, now that you're a demon, you can do anything you want, just like the rest of us. Change your body easy as you change your mind. Don't like this room?

Dream up another. Want fire?" She waved, and the walls were turquoise flames. "Want flowers?" The flames erupted into perfumed petals. "Want four hundred iron-thewed slave-boys? You got it."

This time I waved, banishing the iron-thewed horde. "I want Hyu!" Nothing happened.

"A mortal, huh?" asked Mufki. "Sorry. That's the one thing we don't get, unless we're summoned by one. Only you can't be summoned 'cause you're only a sub. If a regular Succubus poops out on a call, you can have a chance then." I looked hangdog. Mufki did her best to jolly me up. "Heeeyyy, c'mon, get happy. There's lots to *do* down here while you're waiting for the first call."

"Like what?"

"Like snagging you an Incubus and— Oh. Right. You don't want Tyroth, huh? And he's the best. All right, how about we hit the Party circuit?"

"Parties? With Incubi, I presume," I said dryly.

"No Incubi; lamia's honor." She traced a pentagram on her chest.

When I returned to Tyroth's nest after the Parties, I had a desperate gleam in my eyes. Tyroth later told me they looked glazed and burning, and my tongue protruded like a dog's. He backed away—some spectacles give even Incubi pause—but recovered his aplomb when I grabbed him and dragged him straight off to bed. The workout we had would have given old Glister enough to retire on if I'd still been a House of Prayer acolyte. In a place where time has little meaning and space is a joke, Tyroth and I managed to gnaw a good chunk out of eternity before we fell out of each other's arms.

Tyroth lay spent in the monstrous bed I'd created for the occasion, watching me reabsorb the various additional limbs and appurtenances I had also grown as inspiration seized me. "Hail Columbia, Megan, that was something *else*! What changed your mind about having me?"

"The Parties."

Tyroth made a sign to ward off nameless horrors. "I've—I've heard stories about the Parties. We Incubi heard that—that at the Parties you Succubi—*do* things. You—you went?" He pulled the blankets closer, fighting chills. "What was it like?"

I fitted myself against him, taking comfort from his reality in a world where everything and anything could change according to anyone's will or whim. Only in his own nest was a Netherplane resident safe from the perception-fluxes wrought constantly by his neighbors.

"I—find it hard to describe, Tyroth, but I'll try. The first Party seemed so—normal. Only Succubi were there. They chatted, they snacked, they compared mortal lovers. Then . . . they brought out the box."

"I have heard of the box." Tyroth's teeth chattered.

"The Party was in Una's nest. She opened the box. We had to look inside. We *had* to! It was part of the foul spell holding us. The box contained pots of cosmetics that she passed around, and while we did that she asked how many we wanted to buy. I really didn't like them, but you know—after I'd enjoyed her hospitality and all—I said I'd take two of the lip pomades."

"Megan, how will you pay?"

"I gave her a work-pledge. I'll sub for her the next time she's summoned by a student-mage with complexion problems. I didn't think that was too bad. Then Una shouted, 'Everyone over to Mirga's! Time for *her* Party!' We all grew wings and took off for another Succubus's nest. When we got there, it was the same story: the chat, the snacks, the box—full of tatty jewelry this time—and the purchases. Tyroth, Tyroth, I went to *seven different Parties*! I bought dishes, nightwear, unguents, *garbage* that I didn't really need! I gave work-pledges—!"

"There, there, baby. I'll settle the pledge bit for you." Tyroth cradled my head affectionately. "You couldn't have known. I'll pay Mufki back for getting you into the Parties!"

"Oh Tyroth, don't blame Mufki. I went because I was bored

and—because I was avoiding you. But after going to those Parties—"

"Even old Tyroth's a better deal, huh? No sweat, cute stuff. You got wise. Not much fun always having things your own way, is it? Yeah, I miss the mortal world between sets too: solid scenery and a lotta surprises. The only part of the Nether-plane that won't cave in so easy when you poke at it with your mind is good old Inky-Sooky, y'know? S-e-x? It pokes ya right back. Come to papa, honey, and let's go back and try that underwater maneuver one mo' time. You know, where you grew tentacles . . . ?"

"Not now. I have a headache."

"A headache? Oh, *baby*! Now that's what I call mortal like Mama usedta make!"

In spite of our auspicious beginning, I tired of Tyroth's attentions before he tired of mine. Mortal women who go about wailing for their demon lovers may crave more, but if they were *given* the eternal embraces they whine after, they'd see their error. Sex: As above, so below. You run out of variations long before you run out of time. If Tyroth had paid half as much heed to the multiplex arts of conversation as he had to the acrobatics of fornication, we might have been happy.

I craved someone I could talk to.

Mufki understood, and she was right on the spot with a suggestion. Mufki was always there. She lived with us. At the one Party I hosted (to work off a work-debt incurred at a previous Party), Una took me aside and asked, "So how's Mufki taking it?"

"Taking what where?"

"Go-*wannnn*! *You* know! I mean, she usedta be Tyroth's Number One Sooky. Gave up her own nest to move in on him an' everything. Then he comes back from Up There with you. What's a Succubus to think? She's been on the Seventh Circle Diet ever since, but looks like Tyroth's smitten bad. Hasn't come near ol' Mufki in *ages*!" Una smirked. "If it was me, I'd rip your lungs out."

My lungs stayed where they were, Mufki made no un-
friendly moves. In fact, she was the one who introduced me
to the pleasures of Tyroth's *ujir*.

It was a day when every resident of the Netherplane had
decided that gloomy rain would be a nice touch. I felt like an
ass, sitting all by myself in an isolated puddle of sunshine, so
I retracted it and stayed indoors. Tyroth had some rainy-day
plans, but I stiff-armed him off and he stormed out of the nest.
Mufki waited until he was gone before approaching me.

"Bored, huh, Megan? Me, too. Y'know what I usedta do
when things got dull around here and Tyroth wasn't watching?"
She placed her lips against my ear and whispered: *"Ujir."* I
gave her a blank stare. "Wait, lemme show ya. I know right
where he keeps it." Mufki folded up into two dimensions and
came back bearing a purple triangular board which she lay
down flat on the rug.

I traced the pattern of silver dots on the board and made no
sense of them. My bemusement got worse when she added a
large ivory cone with a base big as a chamberpot. It was large
and heavy, but nonetheless it balanced readily on its apex when
she set it point-down on one of the silver dots.

"If you don't get motion-sick, an *ujir* can be fun," she said.
"These dots are the stars that govern mortal dreams. Pick one,
sit in the cone and rotate, and *ecco!*—you can pay a night-
call. You know how mortals react to finding an uninvited Succubus in their dreams? Bugs the living *badger* outa mosta them,
and what it can do to their bedlinens—? Hoo!" She tilted the
cone at me. "Have a seat?"

I wasn't about to leap aboard after what Una had told me.
The Netherplane never struck me as the place where fair play
flourished, nor did Mufki seem the typical good loser. "Can
anything happen to me in a mortal's dream? What if he's having
a nightmare? How can I turn it off when I've had enough?"

"Sugar, with you in it, how can it be a nightmare? And no
mortal sleeps forever. Anyway"—her smile was sticky-sweet—

"you can choose the mortal you like, long as you know his birth-star."

Need I say more? I was sitting and spinning on the *ujir* cone before you could say Wyvern's Eye (for every soul in our village knew the star ascendant when Hyu's poor mother bore him).

The sensation was like riding a riverwhirl the wrong way. I soon saw what Mufki meant about motion sickness. The *ujir* cone dumped me out just when I was sure I'd die if I didn't jump off.

I recognized the room. It was the one Hyu and I had shared in better times. He was at his table poring over a grimoire. I tiptoed up behind him and stole a look. In flawless calligraphy was the arcane and occult lore: *FOR A GOOD TIME SUMMON MUFKI.*

"*That's* not right!" I exclaimed.

Hyu turned. "Megan?" He looked inexplicably young. (But in dreams we brush the Netherplane and a worthy mage can harness the capricious forces that reign there to make himself look while sleeping whatever age he likes.) "Is it you?" He touched me and I felt like singing. Next thing I knew, I *was* singing; singing a jarring tunelet about the virtues of Bogram's Essence of Basilisk as opposed to any other wizard's brew. Hyu was crestfallen. "Oh. I'm only dreaming about you again."

"Have you dreamed of me?" I held his hands and gazed hungrily at him. I wanted to do more, but dreams are nearly as treacherous as the Netherplane from which they spring. They can sheer away from one reality into another as the fancy takes them; witness Bogram's all-pervading jingle, which was still tinkling in the air between us.

"Dreamed of you? Awake and asleep. Ever since I last saw you in that dismal dockside tavern, I've wanted to follow you, to find you, to beg your forgiveness for what I did to you. I did go after you that night, but as I was searching the salt-docks I was captured by—"

"Pirates. I know."

"How could you—?" Hyu's self-image went from beardless youth to whiskered, all-knowing maturity as comprehension came. "Of course. You're my dream. You know everything I do."

"Not everything." I sat on his lap and played with the handsomely trimmed beard he'd grown. "I'm a special sort of dream. Tell me anyway."

"Tell you what you know? It's painful for me, Megan. However—" He heaved a sigh and did what he could to staunch his pain by fondling my bare breasts. "The pirates freed their prisoners in exchange for a treasure-finding spell I gave them. In gratitude, when we returned home my fellow captives petitioned the University Authorities to reinstate me as a reward for liberating Routreal taxpayers. I completed my studies with honors and now hold a dual post as Assistant Lecturer at the University and Third Thaumaturge in the suite of His Serenity, Prince Zimrit." Fangs curved over Hyu's lower lip and a lycanthrope's hairy face added, "He says he knows you."

"If you make ugly faces, Hyu, you'll freeze that way someday!" The lupine look vanished. "That's better. I hoped you'd gotten over your jealous nature. What's past is past." I scanned the well-remembered room. "I can't say I think much of what Nitwit pays you; or the University. Couldn't they find you finer quarters?"

"These? I haven't lived in this closet for years. These are just the trappings of the dream. Would you like to see where I dwell now?" He gestured, and we lay on a velvet-covered bed set atop tiers of malachite stairs. Curtains of copper-colored gauze starred with seed-pearls moved amorously in the warm breeze from the open terrace. The terrace ringed Hyu's tower and gave a full view of the lamp-lit city. At the foot of the malachite steps the scented waters of a bathing pool rippled in the light of a dozen crystal candelarias.

A second twitch of Hyu's hand snapped us back to our squalid garret. "I prefer my dreams." He covered his eyes wearily. "I was happier here; with you."

"Oh my dearest, but I'm here now!"

Hyu detached my arms from his neck. "In a dream, the same as always. What good is that? I awaken to all my regrets. Megan, why didn't I appreciate you when I had you? Why did I listen to Thares and his toadies?"

I kissed regret from his lips. "Because they were so wealthy that it dazzled you, my Hyu. I admit they dazzled me as well, to begin with. Monkeys and mortals are attracted to sparkly things. What makes us different from the apes is that we sometimes crack the shiny shell and see there's nothing inside."

"I was a fool, Megan."

"I was another. We've both learned. It's all right between us now, my love. It will never be wrong again."

I thought his face had wrinkled up in laughter. Then I saw the tears. His shoulders shook with them and I gathered him against me like a child. "Oh, Megan, Megan, after all the dreams I've dreamed of you, this is the first time you've said you've forgiven me! And what if I can't remember it when I wake up?"

"Hyu, this is no dream. Or—not fully." I told him what had become of me, ending my tale by saying, "Since you're a fully enpowered mage now, free me from the Netherplane!"

"Free you! Ah, if I could. . . ." Hyu bit his lip. "You still believe in me so much, Megan. You think I'm capable of miracles, but miracles don't come to assistant lecturers. Not even the Prince's First Thaumaturge can break the barriers between worlds. Perhaps the Royal Family's High Priest might accomplish it; not I."

"It isn't fair, Hyu! To find you again and have to go back to Ty—to the Netherplane!" Hyu twitched and snuffled. "Why did you do that?"

"I always do that when I'm about to wake up, don't you remember? Megan, love, we haven't much time. At least I know you're alive, and I know what you've become. That's a start. Now I have something to work for, something to encourage my further studies in the Hidden Arts. I'll free you from the Netherplane someday, I promise. In the meantime, since you're a Succubus—" He gave another twitch and grunted loudly, then capped it with a third twitch so violent that the dream-garret began to spin. I spun with it, torn from Hyu's embrace, and as I spiraled down I called his name.

The *ujir* cone tipped me out onto Tyroth's floor. "Have a nice dream?" asked Mufki.

"Very. How soon can I go back?"

She rolled up the board and stuffed it into the cone. "Not too soon or we get mucho complaints from the P.T.B: Powers That Be, sugar. You'll hafta wait at least— *Sweet lovin' skinflicks!*"

Tyroth's nest lurched. Mufki dropped the *ujir* and flung her arms over her head. I somersaulted into the wall and landed with one of Urion's vials in my mouth. A deep rumbling reverberated through the Netherplane, shocking half the tenants out of their foul-weather maintenance. I regained my feet and saw the outdoors as a patchwork of rain, sun, snow, and every atmospheric condition in between.

"Mufki, what is it?" The rumble rose to a roar. I grew claws and dug them into the windowsill for support.

Mufki stopped nibbling her knuckles and latched on to my hand. "It's a three-blood summons! Come *on*, we gotta cover ground!"

Mufki dragged me out the window before I could get my wings fully deployed. I flashed them into existence just in time to avoid having us crash. All around us the air was full of Succubi. On the ground the Incubi were massing and moving in the same general direction, but they were keeping clear of the air.

"Because the three-blood summons isn't for any of them, and they know it," said Mufki. "Someone wants one of my girls, and he's using the big, bad, boogeyman granddaddy rite of all rites to do it!"

The vaulted heights of the Netherplane were now so thick with Succubi that we had to hover on updrafts to stay aloft.

There wasn't room to beat a wing. A few ingenious spirits had grown a double set of paddles on a stem off the top of their heads, paddles whose quick rotation kept them hanging in midair without the disadvantage of wings. I saw and greeted many Succubi I knew from the infamous Party circuit, but they ignored me.

"No one wants to miss it when it comes," said Mufki, herself speaking in a reverent hush. The seismic rumblings from below ceased as she spoke. "Ho boy, honey, it's gonna break any sec!"

"What is?"

"The *name*, toodles; the *name*!"

"What name?" The Sooky on my left jabbed me with her elbow and shushed me. I jabbed back, and a fight might've started under ordinary circumstances, but Mufki called for order.

"She's only a *sub*, gals. She don't know from nothing about a three-blood summons." For my ears alone she rattled off, "There's no more powerful way to summon Succubi, and it drains the mage who uses it f'days."

"Then why use it if there are other spells, lighter ones?"

"'Cause with others, you take what we send Up There; any Sooky who's on hand or on call goes. But with the three-blood, you get the one you ask for by name. It's a big feather in your snakes to get a three-blood summons. Now shut up. I think this ... is ..."

MEGAN!

"... it."

A hole like the bell of a black trumpet opened overhead and sucked me up into the chaos of the Midplane. Spirits, gods, demons, and all manner of interplane travelers who are neither Above nor Below are always found there, hastening to and from their ill-assorted errands. The journey was short, but unpleasant. I fountained up in the center of a pentagram that some spendthrift soul had carved into pure malachite.

"So it was a true dream after all." Hyu helped me step from

the star and presented me with a jacinth bowl of blood. I surprised myself by draining it ravenously before bothering to greet him. He watched me at my feast with melancholy eyes. "And it also seems true that you've become a Succubus. You accept the sacrifice."

I gave him back the empty vessel and wiped my mouth with the back of my hand, trying to look as if I hadn't enjoyed it. "But you summoned me, Hyu, and I had to drink it, didn't I? To make it legal? Now we're together!"

"Together, but for how long? Only the spell's length, and that ends with daylight. Like any other Succubus, you must return to the Netherplane at cock-crow."

I was having none of his gloom. His arms were firm and live around me, more so than when I'd visited him in the dream. We were in his palatial apartments and they were even more magnificent when seen without the intermediary measure of a spell. Hyu himself had improved with the years—for years had passed in the waking world while I lived Below. All of his baby-fat was gone, or else hardened to wiry muscle. He had grown somewhat gaunt, somewhat darker and more sinister, but in a way wholly flattering and appropriate to a wizard. I especially liked the malefic effect he'd achieved by cultivating upcurved brows like ravens' wings.

"What does cock-crow matter? You can summon me again."

"Megan, the weird I worked is a strong one. I haven't the stamina to use it as often as I want to have you with me. If I could invoke a lesser enchantment—"

"No. You'd have to take whichever Succubus you got then. Let's not worry about how we'll meet next time; let's use the time we've got."

We used it very well. I could have slipped into Hyu's mind and read his fantasies, making myself over to fulfill them to the letter, but I didn't. We didn't couple as demon and demonmaster; we set no lightnings dancing around the bed. We made love as Hyu and Megan, as we remembered love and as we hoped for it. There was no need to fill every minute with wild cries or bizarre contortions in the name of pleasure. The deepest joy we experienced was between times, being.

When day came and the black tunnel opened for me, I flew back to Tyroth's nest and broke everything breakable. Tyroth objected and I did my best to break him. Mufki sat at the dressing-table, her expression inscrutable. When I ran out of momentum and missiles, she spoke up.

"That was her childhood sweetie, y'know, Tyroth. No good talking sense to her about it. Why doncha just let her off the hook and ship her back to him, huh? She won't be good for anything else until you do."

"You keep outa this, Mufki!" A lance of sparks shot from Tyroth's index finger and goosed Mufki whooping off the boudoir chair. "You've been working to get her out so you could get back in, but you can just two-plus-two *for*get it! I caught her fair and square and she's a keeper."

Mufki rubbed her rear. "Why doncha ask her what she thinks of you, O Mighty Hunter? Only reason she went with you inna first place was 'causa the Parties. By her, you're one step up from self-seal dishes, Tyroth. How d'ya like them apples? But me, I *love* you, you big jerk!"

"Yeah, you big jerk, Mufki loves you!" I piped up. "I can't stand your greasy guts, but she loves you!"

Tyroth's skin crinkled and shimmied. He ran through fourteen different forms of escalating repulsiveness before he lost his temper. "*You!*" He gave Mufki a finger-shot jolt of power that made the poor Succubus sizzle. "If you love me so damn much, how come you don't lemme have a hobby? Snagging mortals for the Netherplane; who's it bother? I may be onto the wave of the future, but do I get any encouragement? And as for *you*—!" I tensed myself for a blast, but nothing happened. Tyroth had shot it all on chastising Mufki. He stared at his impotent finger in disgust, metamorphosed into a giant toad with sawtooth wings, and left home.

Our luck, he came back.

He never spoke of our family quarrel, but he never let me

out of his sight either. He took me wherever he went whenever he was obliged to supervise or direct his subordinate Incubi. The rest of the time he spent snugged up with Mufki and me in the nest. It would take an acute, impartial judge to say which half of Netherplane togetherness I found more tedious. The tedium was relieved—mildly and briefly—anytime a nonspecific request for a Succubus came in. That was enough to make Tyroth slap me in irons and transform himself into a slavering three-headed guard dog until another of Mufki's girls was dispatched Up There. Tyroth's constant vigilance likewise prevented Mufki from giving me any further experiments with the *ujir*.

This is not to say that she didn't use it herself.

One day the nest rocked with the power of a great weirding. I squeezed my hands together and prayed that it might be Hyu coming to call me back with another three-blood summons. Tyroth's glib grin cut short my devotions.

"Got high hopes, doncha, babe? Well, let 'em die. Your mortal sweetie can ask for you by name, accept no substitutes, and blend blood until he drains the kingdom dry. He's not getting you back."

"You can't countermand a three-blood spell!" I spat. "That's grounds for a millennium with a brass bottle-stopper rammed up your—"

"*Sweet*heart! Please, such language! Did I say I'd keep you home if you got summoned by name? No way. But there's no law says you have to go Up There *alone*." He enjoyed my silent outrage for a bit, then proceeded. "Hey, save that fish-eye for another time, Megan. What we're having right now ain't a call for Succubi."

"It's a double-goat incantation," said Mufki, who was filing her nails at the window. "Like the three-blood, only for Incubi. Those ugly suckers of yours are already swarming near the Midplane passage like nits on a beggar's balls, but don't *you* hurry, Tyroth. Last time someone asked for you by name it was a mistake. Wasn't it, Megan?"

"Shut up, Mufki. Megan, let's wing it."

"Taking her?" Mufki's violet eyes slewed around lazily. "She's no Incubus."

"I'm not leaving her alone with you just in case a Sooky call comes in while I'm gone."

"And what if, by some miracle, you're the Incubus tapped to answer the double-goat incantation? You won't have her with you then."

"Says who? If I'm picked, I'm going; *and so is she!*"

Mufki gasped. "Why . . . that *is* legal. La, Tyroth, it takes more smarts than I've got to put one over on you."

He gave her a backbreaking kiss and lifted her onto the bed. "Glad you finally figured that one out, baby doll. You wait right there and when Megan and I come back maybe the three of us can have some fun; now that you quit trying to be smarter than me, y'know?"

"Bye-bye. I'll be waiting." I heard her say that in the most docile, demure, un-Mufkilike voice imaginable just before Tyroth swept me out the window. I *had* to look back, and when I did, I caught the tail end of a wink.

TYROTH!

The voice behind the double-goat incantation was female, as was right. Incubi were created for a knowledgeable woman's pleasure. I wasn't at all surprised to see a tall, imperial lady awaiting my demon and me when we emerged from the black vortex of the Midplane. The corpses of two white goats prone on an obsidian altar dribbled blood into a granite basin at her feet. She watched indulgently as Tyroth thrust his face into the gore and guzzled.

Chin dripping, Tyroth intoned, "What form will you have me wear for your delight, O Mistress?"

The lady replied, "A thief's form for my pleasure, Tyroth, since a thief is what you are. And I have summoned you here to put an end to your thievery!"

Her hands shot from the sleeves of her indigo robe and a rope of rainbow glass arced from palm to palm. She cracked it in midair, driving a rain of bright slivers into Tyroth's flesh. He caterwauled and cowered behind the altar, but the elf-spears homed in on him against all laws of trajectory. A second glass whip snapped into being in the sorceress's hands, and another, and another, each one shattering and piercing Tyroth, no matter where he tried to hide.

He finally hid behind me.

"So bold, Incubus? Come out! You know who I am! You know how I treat cowards! But I am willing to bargain, thief. Return what you have stolen and we'll be quits. Will you? Or will you remain stubborn and see what other pretty tricks I'll play on your hide?"

Tyroth was gibbering, a dozen malformed mouths making and unmaking themselves on his face as he struggled to control his shape-shifting abilities. Poor thing, to be so terrorized! No one should be treated so cruelly; not even a demon. I pressed his paw to remind him that he wasn't alone with the witch, though I marveled at all the trouble she'd gone to in order to brutalize one specific Incubus. Why Tyroth?

I was going to ask that when Tyroth grew steady enough to make himself a workable mouth and shout, "Take back whatever you like, Nimora, only release me from your weird!"

The sorceress cackled and her whip of glass rolled itself into a hoop that rimmed the Midplane gate. Tyroth dove through it and I never saw him again. The hyaline ring fell to iridescent dust, the gate slammed shut behind him. He had left me; I faced the sorceress.

Her cool, pale eyes summed me up as I stood in the midst of the carnage her incantation required. Then she smiled, and it warmed the austere bones of her face.

"Welcome back, dear Megan, to your proper world and form." She took my hand and helped me pick my way through the scattered glass shards. "When I had my prophetic dream in which a Succubus told me of a mortal girl held captive in the Netherplane, I never expected such a pretty one."

A robe like hers, but green, materialized. She assisted me

to dress, her fingers lingering on the tangles in my hair. I was
still dumbfounded by Mufki's ingenuity when I heard the lady
say, "And to be honest, I never expected such a pregnant one
either."

I sat down hard on a dead goat.

CHAPTER VIII

Heterodoxy

> *How long must I live with you*
> *Ere you show your colors true?*
> *How long shall you dwell with me*
> *'Til your motives I can see?*
> —from "Wickersham's Lament" by Eliard of Routreal

The sacred Scrolls of Boriela's priesthood teach that the serenity of an expectant mother shall be a direct indication of how easily she goes through labor and delivery. The calmer the better, is what the Celestial Midwife's advocates preach. So let it be no wonder that my first childbirth was nearly my last.

Time crumples on the Netherplane, which can be most confusing when you are counting months backwards and forwards in order to fix upon the correct father for your child. The sorceress Nimora who had rescued me from Tyroth was little help in this vital matter.

"One sire is much like another. If the baby's healthy, why should you care who stuck you with it and ran?"

"I care because I really would rather not be carrying a demi-demon. I don't know the first thing about swaddling such, and if his teeth are anything like his father's, nursing him won't be very pleasant."

Nimora gave her high, artificial laugh. She was a beautiful woman—golden eyes like a cat and hair a chestnut river that nearly brushed the floor when she walked—but not once did I hear her laugh as if she meant it or wanted to; only as if it were the socially expected response.

"Dear Megan, you seem convinced that the demon planted male seed in you. Could you possibly be wrong on both un-happy counts?"

"I don't know. I'm afraid to find out. The alternative isn't much better."

"What's the alternative?"

The alternative, as I told Nimora, was Iadel. While in Rou-treal with Hyu and Urion, Madam Glister's patrons and Eliard, there had always been enterprising wizards available to sell a girl potions that prevented . . . certain inconvenient situations. I'd seen the last of those helpful draughts as soon as Vrogar bore me away in his ship, but I'd been lucky. The moon still sang for me while I was in Dragon's care, so it couldn't be Vrogar's cub. And it *certainly* couldn't be Dragon's.

Which left Iadel.

"Previous cases of mortals descending to the Netherplane may help us," said Nimora, getting down a monstrous tome of gramarye bound in worked cockatrice skin. She paged through it rapidly until she found the section we wanted. "Yes, here we are: '*Ye passage of Time Below followeth not ye same course as it doth Above. Mortals who have had ye misfortune to abide in Faery do remark upon return that all their elsewise quotidian functions were as if suspended. Even as ye bear doth enter his winter dreams and scorn ye acts necessary to sustain life there-at, so doth ye mortal man or woman who trespasseth upon ye*

Netherplane evince ye selfsame symptoms of ye interruption of his mortality. Thus, ye man on ye point of sneezing when whisked Below shall not discharge his nasal essence until he might return Above. Likewise ye mortal soul brought Below when upon ye instant of Death shall neither die nor even age so long as he abide in ye Netherplane.'"

Nimora shut the book. "Not a single mention of pregnancy, the garrulous thickwit. Isn't that just like a man?"

"Ye," I remarked. For all its verbiage, the passage was clear. My mortality had gone into hibernation while I was with Tyroth, including Iadel's seed. According to what Nimora had read to me, a child conceived in the mortal world would only make its presence known when I returned Above. A demonsown baby would also show up now. Iadel's child or Tyroth's, and thanks to the way the Netherplane wrenched Time, I couldn't even rely on counting the months to pinpoint whose baby I bore. Can you marvel at my panic now?

For all the apprehension I felt at the coming birth, the serene atmosphere of Nimora's home was at least a partial balm. The sorceress dwelled in a solitary tower far up in the hills surrounding Stanesinn, the Royal City. We were a day's journey from all the amenities of the capital but far enough off the King's Road for us to enjoy countryside tranquility. God knows I needed all the tranquility I could muster.

Nimora was ever mindful of my condition. "Don't worry your pretty head about a thing, Megan. I'll attend you myself when the time comes. But since we can't tell how far along you are, who knows exactly when you'll give birth? You'd better stay close to the tower, just to be sure."

I saw the wisdom in this. It was hard to have Stanesinn so close and yet so far, but for the baby's sake I would be a homebody. Tyroth's seed or Iadel's, the child wasn't at fault. If we could all pick our fathers there might be ten men on earth who'd have families. Nimora was being so kind, putting herself and her home so totally at my disposal, that I hated to do anything to put her out. Still, I had one request:

"Stanesinn's not that far from Routreal, is it?" We were making baby clothes together, as I'd done with Perdita somewhere in the Netherplane-crumpled past.

"Not very. And for one of my sisterhood, not at all." Nimora concentrated on her needle, which made her grumpy. "I don't know why you won't let me magic up clothes for your child, Megan. It would be so much easier."

"Nimora . . . when mages communicate with each other, can they forward messages from people who aren't empowered?"

The sorceress severed a thread with her perfect teeth. "All the time."

"Well, then . . . would you mind sending a message for me? It's to go to Prince Zimrit's Third Thaumaturge, a wizard named Hyu. I'd like to let him know where I am, that I've become mortal again, that I've escaped from the Netherplane, and that as soon as the baby's born I'll be going to— Or wait, he could come to me here, right away! So could you please tell him—"

"No," said Nimora. She swept from the room, leaving me to tag after. I caught up with her at the great solar window that looked out over the peaceful hills towards Stanesinn.

"But . . . why not?"

Nimora rounded on me fiercely. "Who is this mage called Hyu that I should expend my powers fetching him? Do you think I have nothing better to do than play courier? Where was he when you languished in the Netherplane? Who freed you, he or I? If he were worth anything, he'd send a searching-spell of his own to find you now. But has he? No, and he won't!"

"He won't because he thinks he already knows where I am. That's why I want to let him know I'm not Below anymore, before he wastes his time with another three-blood summons."

I could have saved my protests. Nimora was all worked up on the subject, going on and on about how undependable and selfish certain people were. Just when I thought she was going to bite herself, her wrath melted and she was all smiles for me.

"Sweet child, a thousand pardons. I didn't mean to shout at you. What was I thinking of? Doing handwork makes me ever so touchy. I'll send your message to Hyu for you as soon as I can. If he means so much to you, he shan't have a better friend in the world than I. But are you sure you want me to contact him right away? There *is* the little matter of your baby. Why don't we get you all safely delivered first and *then* we'll talk to Hyu. That way we can let him know where you are and what sort of child you've borne: boy, girl, or whatever."

"That *does* seem sensible."

"Very sensible. At such delicate, womanly times as childbirth, it doesn't do to have too many mages present, especially not males. Each practitioner of the Hidden Arts carries a strongly personal aura of power. These sometimes clash in moments of high tension, the weirds of one conflicting with the other's. A surfeit of magicians at a childbed is worse than none. Differing magics can meld with unforeseen consequences, whether we intend them or not. When you are giving birth, it would be best if only I were there to help you. I couldn't be accountable for the results otherwise." Her laugh clicked on and off, intended to set me at ease. "And you know how men get when babies are being born. Even wizards."

I remembered Iadel hiding in the wine cellar. If Hyu was going to behave the same way, I didn't want to know.

"You'll speak to him after the baby's born?"

"As soon as possible." She pressed her cheek against mine. "Forgive me for losing my temper before, Megan. I'm used to living all by myself and sometimes I don't recall how to handle people. It would break my heart if you were angry with me. I've forgotten how nice it is to have companionship."

I forgave her, swore to be her friend forever, and wound up apologizing for my unthinking, self-centered, thankless behavior. I gave my word that I wouldn't mention Hyu again until after the baby was born. Nimora was satisfied.

My daughter chose to be born an hour past midnight, making her intentions known fifteen minutes before that same hour. If this strikes you as remarkably considerate behavior for a first-born, allow me to point out that quarter-to-midnight beginning of labor took place two days before the hour-past-midnight delivery.

When the first pains came, Nimora directed me to go about my usual business for as long as possible, for the Scrolls of Boriela teach that babies arrive when least expected. If you hum a little tune and go on with your sweeping, the child will be tricked into thinking that your mind is a thousand miles away from his birth. He will get born as quickly as he can then, in order to remind you of his presence.

If someone can arrange to have the unborn babies read the Scroll too, perhaps the trick will work someday.

The little tune I hummed didn't sound so melodic when broken up by gasps and groans. And who got up to do sweeping in the middle of the night? Nimora clucked her tongue and shook her head, moderately disgruntled by my failure to abide by the books. "You are *supposed* to keep walking."

I was hunched over a table, sure that if I let it go I'd slide under it. I grunted at her.

"I see." She folded her arms. "Well, then I suppose you should get undressed and into bed. I'll see to brewing the pain-blurring potion. You won't mind waiting for it, will you?" I hadn't any choice.

While Nimora was helping me out of my clothes, she took her first real notice of the vials around my neck and asked what they were. The baby wanted to hear the story too, for she gave me enough of a respite to speak of Master Urion without interruption.

"*Another* mage? You've kept busy." She laid the string of flacons on the bedside table.

"Nimora, wait. Do you think one of them might be a specific against pain? Something to tide me over until you've brewed your own?"

Nimora was looking less and less pleased. "If this Master Urion was half as wise as you paint him—which I doubt—

he'd know better than to give you a pain-blur potion for any-thing but immediate consumption. They don't do a smidgen of good when they're stale, which is why I haven't any on hand. And why store so small a measure of a philter that even nonadepts can brew? If I know *his* kind, he gave you a sample of his aphrodisiac decoctions. They're always *so* proud of slop like that."

She pulled the stopper from one flacon and sniffed the contents, wrinkling her ladylike nose. "Not an aphrodisiac, but close. It's a seeing-draught whose vapors bring visions of your loved one when breathed in. Beyond question he thought you'd see *his* face when you inhaled the fumes, the vain creature." She plugged it up and threaded it back on the silken cord. "The others must be similar dishwash. I have the most adorable diamond collar—Prince D'zent himself gave it to me as a thank-offering—that would look stunning on you. Why don't you wear it instead of these and I'll just dispose of—"

A heartfelt scream from the bed froze her hand a span away from Urion's vials. I added another bloodcurdling bellow which whisked Nimora's mind back to the here and now. "The pain-blur! I'll start it straightaway!" She raced to her brewing and forgot about everything else.

The potion she made for me helped for a time, but not for the full two days. There was a limit to how much she could give me safely and still keep me from slipping into that state where there is no pain—or any other sensation. I was not fully awake or aware of much that happened in that time. At some point I know that the great sorceress called on the help of commoner souls, for I saw an old woman in the room with us. She mopped my face with cool water and said she was the nearest village's midwife.

"Seven of my own I've borne, and no counting how many other women had their babes from my hands. There, chuck, you're worn to dust! You should've sent for me earlier on."

A sip of water moistened my lips. Tired as I was, I felt it would be ungrateful not to defend my protectress. "The lady

Nimora—is a powerful sorceress. Her brews—can destroy all pains that—that—" Another twisting of my innards and another shriek gave me the lie.

The midwife's rosy face softened. "There, there, my little one. The gods didn't give all the answers to magicians either, else what use would we simple folk have in the world? When there's a stubborn womb and a hard labor, my hands work more wonders than any wand. You'll see."

She spoke the truth, although I very nearly wasn't conscious to witness the proof of her words. The pains continued, worsened, then flicked out of being. In the delicious haze of relief I heard a thin cry that swelled to a demanding wail.

"Bless the girl, how fair she looks!" the midwife declared. She had hustled off into a corner with the newborn and there was the sound of splashing before she returned to lay a securely wrapped, sweet-smelling bundle in my arms. "Suckle her, my dear, it's your milk she wants, and I know no better way to heal a new mother's hurts than her baby at the breast."

I peeled back the blanket from my daughter's face. She was not the red, wrinkled monkey I'd expected, but a furled rosebud. She nuzzled for my breast and tugged it while the midwife tended to tidying up. Nimora was nowhere to be seen.

I named my daughter Nara as she suckled. When the nipple fell from her lips she looked at me for the first time.

She looked at me with eyes of godsgift blue. Hyu's eyes. I had taken his seed on that one night when I was still trapped as a Succubus, and here was the result. The joy of it filled me too full to bear and left no room for doubts.

"Poor lady, I'll see to your little one." The midwife took Nara from me. "You sleep now. She'll be here when you've rested. Such a pretty babe. . . ."

I slept, but when I woke up, Nara was gone.

"She's with a wetnurse, a qualified woman who was highly recommended to me," said Nimora. "You needed sleep after such a long labor, and the baby wouldn't have allowed for that. This way you both benefit."

"Could the nurse bring her to me now? I feel ready to tend her myself."

There was a measured spurt of laughter. "Ready, yes; but able? Megan, the baby isn't *here*. Her crying would have broken your sleep. She's staying with the wetnurse, as is best for you. Why are you looking at me like that? As if I'd done something awful! Sweeting, just look at your breasts. They're dry as dragon's tears. You haven't a drop of milk for the infant, so would you have her taken from the woman who *is* capable of feeding her?"

"Then let's have the wetnurse stay here with her!"

"In a sorceress's tower. *My* tower is to be transformed into a nursery. I see. Where you feel free to extend invitations, give commands, and perhaps endanger your own child should one of my enchantments take an unexpected turn. It's been known to happen. For instance, I thought that this was *my* home, but it seems I was in error."

A flood of penitent declarations soon had Nimora mollified. She was restored to full affability as soon as I agreed that she was right, Nara was better off in the nurse's care, at least until she was older. But no matter how vehemently Nimora preached the common sense of farming out infants, I still yearned for my child. I also wanted to summon Hyu so that he could meet his daughter.

Nimora was too busy.

Nimora was in the middle of a sensitive conjuration.

Nimora was fulfilling an assignment for one of her many mysterious clients.

Nimora was not feeling up to it.

Nimora had prior commitments.

Nimora declared that the aetheric conditions were not right for sending messages to Routreal.

Nimora did not have the right supplies on hand that were needful for casting the spell.

Nimora was sure she had made the call already and there was no such magician as Hyu in Routreal.

Nimora had sent my message to Hyu and he had refused to answer.

Nimora had a headache.

Nimora wondered aloud why I didn't find some other interests to occupy me instead of this constant harping on some talentless hedge-wizard who had probably forgotten what I looked like.

"You're wasting yourself, Megan. Day after day I find you puttering around the tower doing work fit for a servant. You've plucked clean every berry-bush in sight and made enough preserves to last us for twenty years." We were standing in the pantry, where endless rows of newly capped blackberry jam vouched for her words.

"If I had Nara here, I'd have plenty to do!"

"We have been through that. The baby has colic and can't possibly be disturbed until her digestion regulates itself."

"Then what *shall* I do here if not housework? Sorcery? I haven't the talent, and I'm not going to fool with it again after what happened with Tyroth."

Nimora's smile always looked as if she were telling herself a joke that no one else would understand. "I'd think that a woman as fortunate as you—rescued from the Netherplane and all—would stop thinking of frivolities and turn her thoughts to the gods. Religion is a mighty comfort. Our own King has devoted his family to Sarogran of the Spears—and he needs comfort these days. There's been a terrible rash of unexpected deaths among the royal Princes."

It astonished me how well Nimora kept on top of the doings in Stanesinn when she never left the tower. Obviously the aetheric conditions were just fine when it came to sending and receiving her own messages.

"I hope Prince Zimrit's not dead," I said. "If he is, Hyu will have to find another—"

"His Serenity"—Nimora frowned—"lives mostly in Routreal and has not yet accepted a dinner invitation from his elder brother, Prince D'zent, the heir apparent. His less fortunate brethren did dine with D'zent and soon after succumbed. In Stanesinn they are saying that Prince D'zent really ought to find a better cook. However, if you'd like to thank the gods for all they've done for you—and put in a good word for Prince Zimrit at the same time—"

"I don't want the gods to find me ungrateful."

"Then you *will* want to join the Daughters."

Nimora opened her robe to show me a strange medallion. On a square of heavy gold was a low relief of vines so cunningly cast that they appeared to grow and intertwine as I watched. Amid the vines sat a girl holding a harp like Eliard's.

"This is Andraniu, a mortal whose gift of song was never equaled. Even without it they say that she would have been a wonder, if only for her beauty." Nimora tilted the medallion so it caught the light. "The gods themselves often notice extraordinary mortals. Liuma rules the earth's fertility, aided by the rain her brother Sarogran sends. She saw Andraniu, she heard her song, and she loved her. Liuma made a bower for her beloved—this bower you see now. She thought to keep Andraniu's self and her songs safe from all others."

A somber look crossed Nimora's face. "But it was all in vain. Sarogran of the Spears discovered Andraniu's bower. With falsehood and with force he stole his sister's beloved away and threatened to withhold his rain from the earth if she tried to regain what was hers. Isn't that just like a man?"

"What did Andraniu have to say about it?"

"What would you say, to a god?" Nimora snapped. "What is important is that Liuma spends a part of every year searching for Andraniu."

"Ah, yes! The seasons! Mistress Shana used to tell us that tale when we were little."

"*What is important* is that someday Liuma shall find Andraniu, and then winter shall cease and we shall have a golden age. Eternal summer, dear Megan! Isn't that something more worth your efforts than blackberry jam?"

It was a question begging only one answer. "Yes, but at

least I know how to make blackberry jam. What can I do that
will make any difference to the gods?"

Nimora knew. "You can do as much as I when you have
put on this medallion. I am a devotee of Liuma's Daughters,
my life a search that parallels the goddess's quest. It is written
that when each of Liuma's Daughters has found her chosen
lady, then the goddess herself shall find Andraniu again, save
her from the attentions of perfidious Sarogran, and then winter
shall cease and we shall have—"

"—a golden age. Aha." There are moments when the scattered bits of a puzzle come together and make sense. "No,
thank you, Nimora. The gods know I appreciate all they've
done for me, but they'll have to take my word for it. I can't
be one of Liuma's Daughters."

The sorceress shouted, "You *can't*? You dare to trifle with
me? I saved your life, I broke your bonds, I sheltered and
succored you!" Shock waves of rage emanated from her, making the jam-jars tinkle against each other on the shelves.

"And so WHAT?" I shouted right back, slapping the pantry
wall for emphasis. "Is this the moment *you* decide I must repay
you? Repayment! Gods, I am sick of that word! That, and
gratitude. Tell me—look into your crystal and tell me, great
sorceress—tell me why the same folk who sneer at the doxy
and the harlot and the whore see nothing wrong with telling a
woman she must sleep with them in exchange for a meal or a
roof or a ring? Or to erase a debt? Or out of any obligation
but love?"

One of my precious pots of preserves skittered off the edge
of the shelf and smashed. I picked up a second and hurled it
across the room in a passion. "Sweet Lady Esra, either let us
dicker over our own prices openly or call us all duskflowers
and be damned!" Five more pots gave up their lives before I
was calm again.

"Are you through?" Nimora toed the sticky mess prudently.
"After you've cleaned this up, you can think over what I said
about joining Liuma's Daughters. The initiation rites in Sta-

nesinn are really very artistic. If you consent, you will make
me happy and I will do my best to please you. If you don't,
I will never tell you where your puny brat is being kept, and
she can grow up as the wetnurse's child. Or perhaps I'll keep
her for myself. Or not keep her at all. There. Was that honest
enough to suit you?" The heavy preserve-pot I heaved after
her rebounded from Nimora's shieldspell as she left the pantry.

I leaned my back against the wall and moaned, but no tears
would come. I'd suspected Nimora of giving me some dose
that had dried my milk, but now it seemed she'd drained me
of all other natural juice. "Oh, Urion," I said aloud in my
despair, "how I wish you'd taught me to brew poisons as well
as pain-blurs. I'd give her a double shot and cheer as she—
Ouch!"

I had cut my sandaled foot on a shard of broken pottery.
For a while I toyed with the idea of breaking up one of those
pieces into smaller bits and swallowing them. It was a fool's
notion that only showed how hopeless I felt. Deep down I
knew that if I did have the subtlest of poisons handy, I'd stop
short of murdering Nimora, and how much farther than that
I'd run from the thought of killing myself! Children, the gods
call us when they choose, but not even the priests are eager
to answer.

However, pathos and heartgrief are very dramatic emotions,
and what soul can resist the temptation to star in his own grand
tragedy, for just a while? I wasn't about to end my life, but
contemplating self-destruction was more consoling than standing there helpless. Formulating fantasies of suicide gave me
the illusion of *doing* something concrete, if impractical. And
if I would soon be dead, I would have to see my love's face
one last time before I died. They always did it that way in
plays.

I took the vials from my neck, trying to remember which
one contained the seeing-draught. The first one I sniffed pro-
duced nothing, but the second was more rewarding. The pungent fumes sent my vision rippling, strands of amber mist rising

in threads across my vision. These consolidated and solidified and there was Hyu—wavery and ghostlike, but there. I prepared to drink in this one last sight of his well-beloved features before ending it all. Or not ending it all, which was far likelier, though not half so romantic.

"Ah, Hyu, my love, farewell!" I sighed.

"Farewell?" said the vision. "Then my theory was right! All things Below are a mirror-image of Above! Farewell, when you mean greetings! Say something else, Megan, dear. I'll get my tablets and take notes." The phantom Hyu dithered off a few steps, then looked back at me and asked, "By the way, I know I'm not asleep right now, and I didn't summon you. So how are you managing this?"

I shut my mouth, which had fallen open for all the usual reasons. "You . . . see me, too?"

"Foggily, but you're there. Is this your first seeing? The better ones include limited sensual interchange. Too limited for what I'd like, Megan." His horned brows rose roguishly. "I'll have a three-blood summons in the works as soon as I—"

"Hyu, I'm not calling from the Netherplane." His brows came together. "And I'm not a Succubus anymore."

"Then how—?"

I held up Urion's vial. Hyu's phantom presence reached out and took it. I was surprised that the fragile glass ampule didn't fall through his fingers as through smoke. He sloshed the contents around and took a sniff of the fumes himself, which made his presence become more clearly delineated. "A Master's work. A seeing-draught allowing two-way communication between true lovers. It would take a Master like that to free you from the realm of demons." His face fell. "I understand. You love me—or else we'd not be seeing each other now—but he released you, and out of gratitude—"

I roared. "RrrraaaaAAARRRRGH!" is what I said, if memory serves. "If ever I do what you're implying out of *gratitude,* may I get the austral pox! Does *all* the world think there's no other way of saying thanks than leaping into bed? The mage who brewed this draught is dead, Hyu, and the one who freed me from the Netherplane only placed me in a new captivity. I am the prisoner of the sorceress Nimora."

"Nimora!" Hyu whistled. "I'd not like to have her for my enemy. But I'll dare it, my love, and send you all the powers I command to release you from her holding-spells."

"No spells hold me here, Hyu." His look questioned me, and I told him that he was father to the sweetest daughter in the world. "Hyu, if you could send a finding-spell after Nara, if you could get her to safety, then I'd be free to join you. Find our baby, Hyu! Please find her!"

"Our baby." The wonder of it left him dumbstruck. "Yes, and so fast that Nimora won't know she's gone. Give me the image, my angel, and I'll begin."

"What image?"

"The child's image. For a mage to find a person he must either have an image at hand or else know the subject's looks by heart. Sometimes there are charms of disguisement laid over the subject. To pierce these requires the finder to know exactly what he's looking for." He smiled. "I'd need no image to find you, but I've yet to see our daughter."

"Oh no, oh no, I have no image of Nara! I could describe her—"

"No good; not good enough."

"Can't you read her image from my heart or mind?" He shook his head. "Esra's blight, then why amn't *I* the wizard? I could find my baby through a thousand spells!" I smashed another innocent jam-jar. Pieces flew everywhere before clattering down.

One piece did not. It hovered in the air like a hummingbird, turning slowly on an imagined axis, and kissed Hyu's fingertips. A radiant glow the color of deep garnets or ripe blackberries diffused itself along the shard's surface, and in its center was a pinpoint throb of blue. It lingered on Hyu's palm a heartbeat more, then glided into my hand.

"A treasure-finding spell can find many sorts of treasure. It doesn't always require a precious stone to fix it. Now you have the means to find our child yourself, Megan, if you can dream up a way out of Nimora's tower."

I pressed the charmed shard to my heart. "And it will work like the one you made for Vro— for the pirates? The light within will brighten the nearer I get to Nara?"

Hyu nodded. "I know where Nimora dens up. She's not far from Stanesinn, with good reason. The gods are favoring us, my love. Prince Zimrit goes to Stanesinn tomorrow and takes all his court. I will be with him. Find our daughter and I'll find you."

"Don't let him eat dinner with his brother D'zent."

My darling's mouth turned up at one corner. "How did you know—? But that's old news, Megan. His Serenity, Prince D'zent, has given up on removing his siblings, mostly since Prince Zimrit's younger and doesn't stand between him and the throne. In fact, I must stop referring to His Majesty by his former title."

"*Majesty?* D'zent is King?"

"Recently, from what news we've had in Routreal. It was a great sorrow."

"Don't tell me our Lord King was dumb enough to dine with his venom-happy son? Is stupidity inherent or just inherited in the Royal Family?"

Hyu raised his hands. "Who knows? A certain measure of brotherly murder is expected, so long as it doesn't get out of hand. The people appreciate a King who *worked* for his crown. His Majesty King D'zent was a very willing worker, but not a parricide. He deposed his father on grounds of mental incompetence."

"I'd love to know how he made that charge stick."

"Thus: D'zent bribed the old King's guard, raised his own troops, and suborned his father's most influential eunuchs and courtesans. Any king who lets all that go on behind his back and gets caught with his breeches down is obviously a mental incompetent."

"Then Zimrit comes to Stanesinn to pay homage to his brother?"

"Zimrit wouldn't stir a pace to piss in D'zent's beer. My royal lord is coming for the Games. King D'zent is initiating his reign with a week-long consecration festival beginning tomorrow; a sop to the gods as well as the people."

The threads of mist forming Hyu's image began to unravel. I took another deep breath from Urion's vial, but it was futile. No spell lasts forever. I called my farewells, holding the ensorceled shard for dear life.

Oh Hyu, oh my dearest Nara, soon! Soon!

That evening I was very contrite and humble with Nimora. "I've been thinking over your words. What will my daughter say about me when she's old enough to know wisdom? 'My mother was an ingrate'? 'My mother could have been the one soul needed to bring on the golden age, but she refused'?"

"You wouldn't want that," said Nimora.

"Certainly not. And endless summer would be so nice. No more nose-colds. So I have decided to join Liuma's Daughters. Is there something I have to sign?"

"My *dear* Megan!" I submitted to Nimora's ecstatic burblings and hugs. "You won't regret this." Her embraces became more lingering.

I stepped lightly away. "Nimora, please . . . this hasn't been the easiest decision of my life. I'd feel better if I had time to get used to it. After I'm an initiate and it's all official, it won't seem quite so—quite so—" I searched the air for words. "Quite so unofficial."

"Whatever you like, child. Didn't I say so? We can journey to Liuma's temple in Stanesinn and have you presented to the priestesses. When would you like to go?"

"The sooner the better. Tomorrow?" I almost felt sorry for Nimora, she received my wish for haste so joyously. "And . . .

might we go into the city early? I want to go before the goddess in a new gown."

"You shall have the finest gown in all Stanesinn, my sweet friend! And after the ceremony I'll take you to see the Royal Games."

Hide-and-seek is not a Royal Game. It calls for the quarry to know his tracker very well, especially if the tracker is a powerful mage and mistress of finding-spells. But for a finding-spell to work, the mage must fix all his or her concentration on an unchanging image of the quarry or else the spell disintegrates into an overlapping fan of masks. Finding-spells presuppose that the quarry will not change her looks the moment she's given her keeper the slip. Few wise quarries are so sporting.

I know this, for once I saw Master Urion himself baffled by a wayward merchant's daughter who evaded him and all his seekings for a week on the basis of a quick application of walnut juice to the skin. The image that her father gave Urion of his child was fair, not swarthy, and so it took even that mage among mages seven precious extra days before the conflicting visions resolved themselves. By that time the girl had gotten herself pregnant by her penniless lover. Urion was not invited to the wedding.

I would not need so much time as a week for my intents.

Nimora's tower, as I've said, lay a day's journey from Stanesinn, but that was the distance as reckoned for unmagicals. For us to reach the Royal City took considerably less time. She spread a silk carpet atop the tower's flat roof, graciously invited me aboard, spoke a low word, and the early spring sunshine spun itself into the walls of an aristocrats' inn within the walls of Stanesinn.

"I shall go below and inform our host that we've arrived," said Nimora, stepping off the carpet. "He doesn't mind catering to the sorcerous trade so long as we check in immediately, pay before vanishing, and don't perform any rites involving the vital organs of his other guests. Will you come with me, Megan, dear? Tapster Palo keeps an excellent cellar."

"No, thank you, Nimora. Our trip here— I'm not used to such whiskings. I think I'd like to lie down for a while and recuperate."

Nimora made sympathetic sounds and patted my forehead while I stretched full-length on the bed and feigned a lolloping case of the vapors. In a quiet voice I meekly asked her if Tapster Palo might have some combination of spirits that would calm a carpet-queasy stomach.

"I'll mix you something with my very own hands," said the sorceress, and bustled downstairs.

I could hardly restrain myself until her footsteps faded. I was up and rummaging through her bag of personal effects like a common housebreaker, seized her ceremonial dagger, and sawed off my hair to just below the ears. Next I cast my robe into the fireplace and turned its almond green to smutty gray and gave it a few dagger-slashes for good measure, tucking the loose ends up between my legs.

My legs. Yes. They were still a human color, but not for long. A further application of soot helped, but I wanted to make sure of baffling Nimora's spells with something more than dirt. A splash of red caught my eye from the window. There was a long box of geraniums flourishing outside. They did not flourish long. I rubbed the pillaged petals all over my skin until I looked like an escapee from a fever ward. If the Royal Games were anything like other major festivals, the unfortunate inhabitants of the city madhouses would be given a day of freedom, for the amusement of the people. No one would interfere with or detain a lady of my wild looks, or else he'd get some amusement he hadn't counted on.

And if the Royal Games were true to the type, they'd draw in every simple soul from all the countryside round. The villages for three days' traveling distance on all roads would be deserted. Who can resist the lure of free public festival, with

Games and sacrifices, mummers, mountebanks, and wandering madmen?

Who could resist such? No one. And certainly not, I prayed, a certain nameless wetnurse. A babe in swaddlings is no real hindrance on the road, and easier to take with you to the Royal Games than to leave behind.

Sweet Lady Esra, let it be so!

I looked back out the window, the view now clear of flowers. We were on the second floor of the inn, and I had done my share of stairless descents. Perhaps the facade of the Hawk and Harrier did not offer the sculptured toeholds of the House of Prayer's friezes, but a gnarl of grape vines had been coaxed up its fieldstone walls and that was even better for me.

Hyu's charmed shard came out of my bosom. It shone dully, and the blue glint within the red was small, but as I rushed through the fete-mad streets I saw the blue glint grow. Like a birding dog in a field of tall grass, I quested up one street and down the next, always seeking the thick of the crowds, stumbling over piles of refuse as I kept my eyes on the enchanted fragment. At corners I swung it to the four points, taking the road which blew light into the blue spark.

The charm's bright heart began to flicker more rapidly, the flame of it beating stronger, to a more regular rhythm. I knew what that meant. I had seen a diamond in a pirate-chief's hand react that way the closer we came to a treasure-rich, dragon-haunted shore.

I looked around. I had left the wider avenues of the Royal City and been led into one of the spiderweb byways that the nobler patrons of the Games would avoid. The street I had just entered was one where food vendors congregated to sell their wares. A few performers—jugglers, minstrels, acrobats, and rope-dancers—also had staked out their spots near the vendors' awning-hung stands, hoping to pick up a coin or two of the change patrons got for their money. There was nothing here to tempt the sophisticated palate or the refined tastes of the gentry when it came to entertainment, but plenty of good, cheap food and fun for countryfolk.

The finding-charm pulsed brighter, the blue paling to the white light of full discovery.

I found the wetnurse at a sausage stand, haggling with the seller to drop his price because he offered no mustard. A husky four-year-old clung to her skirts, his face a study of sausage grease and bliss. Strapped to her back, peacefully asleep in the midst of uproar, was my rose.

The vendor and the wetnurse both were taken aback by the approach of a grimy madwoman, but I was swift to produce a handful of gold (and would Nimora miss it?), which promoted me from dangerous lunatic to eccentric noblewoman.

"Excuse my appearance, my dear young lady," I said, clasping the nurse's hands. "I am part of the royal entertainments, and it's such a bother to don this costume and makeup that I tend to leave it on for the whole day."

"Very nice it is too, I'm sure, mum," said the nurse, eyes rolling. She groped for the toddler's fist and pulled him nearer. Until she knew my reasons for singling her out, she wasn't going to take chances.

I smiled to reassure her. It didn't work. "What's nicer by far, dear, is running into you like this. *Just* the person I've been wanting to see. Why, I've heard you described so many times—and in such flattering terms—that I knew you the moment I saw you."

"Oh?" You could scarcely hear her. "But—but I don't know your ladyship, I'm sure, not being citified. Is—is your ladyship sure she means me? I'm not Stanesinn."

"Neither am I. Neither was the blessed midwife who delivered my daughter and said that Nara should be tended by no one if not you."

"You mean Mother Reasa?" I meant no one else. The nurse puffed herself up proudly. "None's better than she when it comes to birthing babes in all these parts, I'm sure, and none wiser. That's why she sent your little love to me. She knows

my milk, does Mother Reasa. *This* one thrived on it." She
dropped a kiss on the toddler's head, then reached around to
undo the straps holding Nara. "Shall you want to hold her,
milady?"

"Yes, if you shall hold this." I gave her four gold coins and
had Nara in my arms all the sooner.

"Oh, but milady—" The wetnurse was stupefied by my
generosity. "Milady, when Mother Reasa brought me the girl
she likewise brought payment enough for two years' board and
keep."

"Which you *shall* keep, and my gift too. It's customary to
reward good service when it's no longer needed. I have recovered completely, as you can see, and I'll be taking care of
my child myself now. Her father and I . . . must leave Stanesinn
for Routreal very soon, which is why finding you here is such
a happy chance. If I'm going to make a gold thank-offering
to the gods for guiding you to me, shouldn't I also thank you
for obeying them? It doesn't do to displease the gods or their
obedient servants."

"No, it doesn't," said Nimora. The street-sounds died at a
wave of her hand. The rope-dancer froze on his silken perch,
the juggler let his copper hoops fall unheeded. Nara's nurse
didn't move as the sorceress took back the gold coins. I saw
the death-glow of the finding-spell she'd laid on her missing
money, not on me. The heads of fifteen iron spears stood in a
stiff rank behind her like a river-wight's teeth. Gilt-helmed
Guardsmen wearing the royal badge waited for the sorceress's
bidding.

Nimora's laughter rang true for the first time; true and cold
as steel. "Didn't I tell your royal master that I'd help your
hunt, Captain? There is nothing like a High Priestess's hidden
eye when it comes to spying out sinners. These two will make
up the score of harlots you need."

One of the men-at-arms stepped forward, rubbing his chin.
"I dunno. . . . Don't look like t'others we got. One's too clean
and t'other's too dirty. An' what about the kids they got wi'—?"

Nimora touched his helm. Something popped and the Captain crumpled to the pavement. A sluggish flow of red oozed from under the helmet's edge. The sorceress stooped to remove his mark of office and passed it to a trembling second.

"You can clean up one or dirty up the other as you please, once they're in safekeeping, Captain," she said sweetly. "Suit yourself, but cleanliness is no prerequisite for what's awaiting them. Is it?"

The newly made Captain shook enough to make his spear-shaft clatter against his chain-mail shirt. "Whatever your lady-ship says. But—but—"

Nimora raised one eyebrow. "Yes, Captain?"

"But—what *about* the children?" He took a step back, spear up to guard his helm. (It would have made no difference if Nimora were in a killing mood.)

She smiled. "It is cruel to separate mothers and children, even if the mothers are whores. Take the children along, Captain. When their time in the arena comes, the gods won't mind."

With armed men all around, the wetnurse and the babes and I were marched away.

CHAPTER IX
Slut Racing

"Men," said Barti, "are owldung." It wasn't the level of conversation I'd expected, seeing my old House of Prayer colleague after so many years, but in view of the circumstances attending our reunion it was mild stuff.

"Men are slugdrool," said another of the pent-up harlots sharing dungeon space with us.

"Men are wormnuts," said a third.

The competition had been going on for a full day and part of the night and the ladies were running out of epithets suitably vile enough for skewering the opposite sex. While the insults and imprecations flew, I had managed to finagle a basin of water from our guards, wash myself clean, and cajole my shorn hair into a cloud of ringlets. The dankness of the dungeon made it frizz, which was becoming at that length.

Barti watched my toilette with scorn. "If you're hoping to wriggle out of here on your back, Megan, you can forget it. It took these lumpsuckers long enough to round up twenty genuine harlots for the Games and it's their balls on a spear-point if they don't deliver twenty to the arena tomorrow."

Nara began to cry. She was hard put to bawl loudly enough for Cybelle, the wetnurse, to hear her over her own yowling. The country wench had done nothing but groan and bellow and leak water since the prison gate slammed on us.

"Put a clout in your mouth and feed the baby, Peachbloom." If Barti had any fellow-feeling for Cybelle, she hid it skillfully. "And wipe the sour off your face or all you'll spurt is curds."

"The shame!" wailed Cybelle, unslinging her left dug and helping Nara find the nipple. "I can't bear it, I'm sure. To think that tomorrow I must die with the name of whore!"

"And none of the fun. Cry for something that's worth your while, lady. Cry for these poor innocents who'll die with us." Barti ruffled the sleeping toddler's hair. "Poor Sarita. At least you died before you had to see your kid trampled to muck and bones."

Sarita's boy snuffled and rolled over on his pile of fouled straw. One of the few things I'd heard Barti utter that weren't anti-male curses or sneers directed at Cybelle was the infor-mation that Sarita had died of a fever nearly two years back, a mild fever that wouldn't have harmed a girl whose blood wasn't half alcohol.

"None of us knew where she'd farmed out that babe of hers, Megan. She never told a soul. But I'd seen the boy's face once, when Sarita had the kid brought into Routreal to visit, as a treat. That's when I met Stoneface here too, hey, Cybelle? Thought she was going to drop dead soon as she set foot in the House of Prayer—she sure howled loud enough about the *shame*, the *shame*! No emotions to her at all; a natural demon when it comes to playing cards."

Cybelle dried her eyes and said it was bad enough she was going to die with the stigma of whoredom on her, but a rep-utation for gambling as well was more than enough, she was sure.

"My little Minar's mother may be dead—the gods ward

her!—and no one to pay me for his keep since, but he's never been in want." Cybelle pulled back her shoulders and switched Nara to the other tit, leaning over the sleeping boy as if ready to bite any of us who came near him with ill intent. She looked just like a wolfhound guarding her pups to the death. "He's my boy now, bless him, nearly of an age with the babe I lost. He's had my milk and now he's too big for that, he's got my love. If there's half a chance of my saving his dear life tomorrow, I'll take it. That I will, I'm sure, even if it means calling myself seven kinds of whore to do it!"

I went on cleansing my skin and brushing my hair.

The Royal Games that His Majesty, King D'zent, had decreed were a combination of secular and holy events. There were ordinary athletic contests which were straight competitions in foot- and horse-racing, archery, wrestling, and spear-hurling. These had nothing to do with us.

The Gods' Games were something else again.

I left my cellmates to their curses and stood on a stone bench near the single window. If I stretched up on my toes I could just get my eyes over the barred sill. I had a fairly complete worm's-eye view of the arena where I was supposed to die next day. The sand was circled by tiers of wooden seats, only the royal viewing box and the gateways being carved of stone. Workmen had been busy earlier that day, erecting gold-banded poles at the four corners of the royal box and attaching a blue and silver silk shade to protect King D'zent and his favored companions from tomorrow's midday sun. The cloth looked flat black now, and flapped in the night wind like a giant batwing.

Stone too, and batwing black as well, was the focal point of the whole Games' grounds, the shrine of Sarogran.

Sarogran of the Spears, Liuma's irrepressible brother and our beloved full-time rain-god; Sarogran, the chosen god of our Kings since anyone could recall. (There was the brief affair of D'zent's great-great-great-grandfather, King Wadred, who tried to replace Sarogran with Netine, patroness of young gentlemen who earned their worldly wage as simply charming artists, perfectly delightful lyric poets, and astonishingly well-favored mummers. Netine is also credited with the invention of cosmetics. This defection from the robust rites of Sarogran did not last. King Wadred's queen's fourth lover stabbed him through his best dress.) A white marble image of the god stood atop his shrine, which was a stepped tower built of basalt blocks.

Tomorrow, at a prearranged point in the festivities, Sarogran's Course would be run. Twenty harlots would be lined up outside the shrine and told to start running. Ten mounted King's Guards would count to twenty and gallop after them. If the duskflowers were swifter than full-fed battle stallions and managed to circle Sarogran's shrine five times without being trampled to death under the horses' hooves, they were allowed their freedom.

If they were not so swift...

The ritual of running down the harlots in the god's name was supposed to wipe out communal sins, one major sin for each dead harlot at race's end. The fact that most of the sins had been committed by the audience and the Guards rather than the harlots did not trouble anyone unduly. Not anyone important. It was said that the origins of this quaint, traditional, unequal contest were lost in the mists of antiquity. All of which meant that it had probably been the inspiration of a disaffected court eunuch with an anti-duskflower axe to grind.

(In elder times it was common practice to use duskflowers as bait when the palace suppliers ran low on eunuchs. Many a candidate was "persuaded" to change the course of his life while held at dual knife-point in a harlot's bed. You may therefore surmise the shape of that ancient, anonymous eunuch's axe.)

"Casing the course? It won't do you any good. There's nowhere to hide." Barti was on the bench beside me, an arm hooked through the bars. She was nearly as tall as some of King D'zent's personal Guardsmen, and in excellent condition.

If anyone thought to place side-bets on survivors, Barti would have drawn even money.

"I did the same damned thing when they shoved me into this hole," she continued. "I was the first one they caught, y'know that? First I cried louder than Cybelle—and if you ever tell her I said so, I'll take a chunk off your cashbox. When I got a grip on, I started thinking about ways to cheat Sarogran's Spearlickers without dropping dead on the sand."

She undid the clasp of her cloak and wiggled it off her shoulders, the better to slide her arm farther through the bars and point out each feature of the course as she mentioned it. "See the shrine itself? Sarogran's priests lock the doors before the race, but what's to keep a nimble girl from climbing up the side and pissing on the riders?"

"A bad bladder?" I suggested.

Barti gave me a look. "Those stepped levels are terraces, smarty; terraces where Sarogran's priests squat down out of sight during the race *hoping* some poor working girl will try climbing out of the arena. When she does, she's theirs. They grab her, bind her, and take her to the topmost turret. *Not*," she emphasized, "for the view. They pitch her off right under the horsemen the next time they come around."

"Aha. Scratch climbing up the shrine."

"Now the *next* thing I figured to do was make a run for the wall and jump over, into the audience. I'd aim for a likely man and play on his sympathies."

Barti had been a formidable sympathy-player while a lady of the House of Prayer, and would be until her dying day if arthritis did not intrude. They claim that flautists paid for her digital attentions just to view her fingering technique at close quarters. So did trumpeteers, for related reasons.

"That sounds like a very good ploy for you, Barti," I said. "But why do I have the feeling you're about to tell me the reason it won't work?"

"Because you're a mind-reader when you're not being a whore. I overheard one of our pig-sticking Guards talking over other days of glory with a friend. The rules of Sarogran's Course are plain, and the priests repeat 'em every year before the race: Anyone helping a runner—anyone *touching* a runner for longer than three breaths—gets hoisted back over the barricades along with her." Barti's full lips curled. "Guilt by association. The people who take the ringside seats for this race carry cudgels to make sure we don't try making 'em share the honor of serving Sarogran."

The two of us stood side by side at the window for a while thereafter, each guarding her own thoughts. Behind us the other eighteen women fell asleep one by one. I let Nara rest undisturbed in Cybelle's lap. I had a plan, and if it worked, I would have all the time I desired to hold my precious one.

Barti yawned, reminding me of her presence. "Aren't you going to go to sleep?" I asked.

"What for? You can't expect to outrun horsemen. No amount of sleep will grow you two extra legs. The best you can hope for is to get trampled lightly, roll yourself out of the main track, and play dead. They tell me cripples can beg a good living in Stanesinn, and more if you manage to drag your bones back to Routreal. Students are softer touches."

"That reminds me, Barti; why Stanesinn? How did you end up here? You weren't the fool I was, to leave a good post like Madam Glister's."

"No, but I was fool enough to diddle the potboy once too often. The little pock-face was one of those butterfly-worms who grow up sudden and change. *He* changed into something tasty enough for Madam Glister's table, and the old bitch didn't like me nibbling her scraps." My old business associate worked a kink out of her neck. "Maybe I will have some rest after all."

I let her wrap her cloak around herself and waited until her breathing became regular. I didn't want any witnesses for what I intended doing. By the light of the iron-barred moon I took Urion's seeing-draught from my neck and uncorked it. That was why I'd taken pains with my looks: I wanted Hyu to see me looking my best, even in a dungeon. Once he knew where Nara and I were, he'd rescue us by magic.

I held the vial under my nose and took a deep inhalation. As before, a mesh of smoke curled across my sight. A figure formed against a background of serpentine haze. Wherever I had contacted Hyu, there surely was a lot of vegetation. How odd that the borders of the seeing seemed to solidify before the all-important central subject.

A gently strummed chord of music blended into softer laughter. The fringe of vines swayed to the sounds played by a hooded figure enthroned amid flowers. Hands too slim and white to be Hyu's played across the strings of a minstrel's harp. They stopped, and the ghostly harper turned.

I recalled the medallion where I had seen this tableau before. Although it could not be, I still called softly, "Andraniu?"

More laughter, and the sorceress pulled back her hood to put an end to her little joke.

"If I were Andraniu the Well-Beloved, do you think *you* would be worthy of my notice? A hedge-wizard's harlot is all you are, and all you deserve, falseheart. I was foolish to think you merited the perfect love of Liuma's Daughters, but you won't live to tell anyone how great a fool I was."

Nimora laid aside her harp, and the swaying greenery of Andraniu's bower knotted itself into bundles of hissing serpents. She teased them into wreathing her shoulders, their flickering tongues a cold caress on her cheeks.

"So now you think to escape by summoning your lover? Did you think I was so careless, Megan?" Nimora asked. "There is a shieldspell cast all around the Games' grounds, forbidding the passage of magic." She plucked a flower and twirled its stem between her fingers. "Now I suppose you will flatter yourself into thinking that I worked the witchery on your account. On the contrary, it is a routine precaution for any Gods' Games. Do you think you are the only whore who ever took a sorcerous lover? Sarogran's priests don't want the god shortchanged because some overly gallant wizardling plucked his doxy from prison before the race."

"If there's no magic coming or going from the arena, how are you here?"

The flower was a limp rag, twirled away to yellow smears of pollen in the sorceress's hand. "I am *within* the shieldspell's range, sweet traitor; in Sarogran's very shrine. Where else should the High Priestess of the Royal Household pass the vigil-night before the Holy Games? Run well, Megan. You might even save your own life if you don't run carrying your daughter." She let her serpents lick the golden dust from her fingers.

"Nimora . . . if you are King D'zent's High Priestess—could you stop the Games?"

The witch's mouth curved, savoring a secret. "I could. Nothing would be simpler. A last-minute message from the gods, perhaps, saying that the time or site was not propitious. Or merely that Sarogran himself was not in the mood for blood." She showed her teeth. "Why, Megan?"

"If you . . . will do that—if you'll stop the Games—I swear by Sarogran's holy spear that I'll come to you willingly. I'll enter Liuma's service with all my heart, take whatever vows I must, and do your bidding until the day I die."

"And your lover? And your daughter?"

"I will never see either one of them ever again, if you wish it so, Nimora. I swear that by Sarogran's holy spear too."

"So many oaths! Tempting, Megan. And all I have to do is postpone the Games?"

"Call them off; call them off and give these poor creatures their freedom."

"And for such a small price, you will love me?"

"Nimora, the hand that breaks a captive's chain deserves the love of every soul. Free them and . . . I'll love you."

"How interesting. . . ." Nimora tapped her chin thoughtfully. The serpents glided up and down her arms, eyes aglow. "I could not have your love when I freed *you* from the Nether-

plane, but if I release a clutch of poxy whores and a brace of
fatherless brats, you *will* love me? This is a mystery requiring
further study. I shall have to ponder it well . . . after the Games."
Her enigmatic smile burned itself into my eyes and kept me
awake until dawn.

Barti was the first up. "What? Didn't *you* sleep any? Gods
protect us, Megan, you're shaking!" She wrapped her arms
around me and squeezed hard. "It's the little ones, isn't it?
Listen, I can run pretty fast when I have to. I'm just going to
lay down and run like a red-rumped deer today—no half measures, no playing dead, nothing but riding the breeze. Trust
me with your babe. Let me carry her and run. I can't promise
you I'll make it, but it's the best chance she'll have. And if
you—don't—I'll be mother to her after. *Not* as a whore, either.
I'll do something else. I can—I can—" Barti made some empty
motions with her hands, then frowned. "Well, I'll figure something out after we win this race."

I stopped shaking and returned Barti's hug at double value.
"The gods bless you, Barti; better a live whore than a dead
virgin! Live through today and go on to be the best-known
duskflower in all the kingdoms! Yes, with your name and
specialties known even in the halls of the gods, and when you
die may they set your *si'ir* among the stars!"

"That'd give the sailors something to steer by, wouldn't it?"
Barti and I laughed until the other wakers thought we'd gone
loony with fear. Recovering, Barti said, "No wonder you ran
off with a half-staffed minstrel. *Twice!* You're crazy as a desert
dog, Megan."

A shaft of sunlight like a spear fell between us and the first
rumors of the arena workers' arrival seeped into our prison.
Honest men had so much work to do before the public could
enjoy their Games. A few of the women awoke, remembered
where they were, and began to cry. One started shrieking curses
at the world and the gods and herself until a friend smacked
her across the face. She collapsed, her sobs too raw to be
human.

Cybelle was not crying. She was giving my Nara milk and at the same time speaking gently to Sarita's boy, Minar. The toddler was staring with owl-eyes at the wild women surrounding him and asking Cybelle why they couldn't leave this nasty-smelling place and go home.

"Soon, my lovey, soon we'll be going home, I'm sure. And if we're lucky we shall meet a goodman farmer on the road, leading a fine horse. I'll chat him up so that he'll let you ride like a King's Man, all the way home in splendor. Will that please you, my dearest?"

"Oh yes, Mumma, yes. I do like horsies."

"Then I shall say a little prayer right now to Lady Esra, and she'll see to sending you a fine horse to take you home."

"Horses," gritted Barti. "Fine horses. I'd carry Sarita's kid too, if that weren't death for us all. Gods! If it'd save the babies I'd take all the riders to my bed this very morning, under the King's eye and with all the people watching. Yes, the riders *and* their stallions besides!"

"Barti," I said, suddenly thoughtful. "Barti, would you mind lending me your cloak?"

They came for the harlots when the sun was halfway up the sky. The first round of secular contests had ended and the time was right for one of the gods' events. Barti and a few of the more optimistic women ripped most of their clothing off and tucked up what was left to free their legs. Cybelle refused to touch her skirts or even get them out of the way. Moreover, she nearly bit Barti when the duskflower reached for Nara.

"I don't care what you say, I'm sure. I'm the one charged with minding these children and I've been paid to do it. No one shall take them from me. The gods know I've done nothing wrong and they'll stand by us, skirts up or skirts down. Hmph! Like to see what *you'd* say if some meddler tried to take over the job *you'd* been paid to do!"

"Let her be, Barti," I said, holding the borrowed cloak close. It was heavy crimson wool of a fashionable length on Barti's willowy body, but on a short bit like me it dragged in the dirt.

We went down a tunnel, up a shallow flight of steps, and huddled on the sands, blinking at daylight. "She may be right. The gods are supposed to protect the innocent."

"The gods can nibble my—"

The rest of Barti's theology was drowned out in a peal of trumpets from the royal box. I saw Nimora seated there in the black and argent robes of the Royal High Priestess, the electrum diadem on her hair. Next to her D'zent looked like a bumpkin who had filched himself a kingly crown. I recognized His Serenity, Prince Zimrit, seated on the other side of his brother, but he didn't see me. He was playing with his nose again.

A priest of Sarogran yodeled the rules of the competition from the top of the shrine. A wide gate opened opposite the royal box to admit the ten mounted King's Guards. Their half-armor made a glittering spectacle as they rode in five abreast. Little Minar saw them and began jumping up and down excitedly, tugging at Cybelle's hand. He wanted to go closer and pat the horsies. One rank of horsemen trotted aside in perfect formation, allowing the second line to join theirs. When they were all assembled in a single row, they formed a line that would sweep the entire track we were to run.

Twenty spearmen marched towards us, their job being to hustle us into our starting places before the King himself gave the signal to begin. When I saw them coming I took Nara from Cybelle over her protests and strapped my baby onto Barti's back with some strips of cloth whipped out from under my cloak.

"Here! I can bear the little one!" I struck away Cybelle's interfering hands and picked up Minar, who kicked and whined.

"Bend over and take the boy on your back, Cybelle. And you, Minar, shut up and hold on! Your Mumma's going to give her baby a horsie-ride. Won't that be fun?"

"I'm not a baby!" said Minar, clinging to Cybelle's braids. He struck a proud equestrian pose and lost his grip. Cybelle and I whirled to break his fall.

The nurse's eyes were wide as the northern sea with what

she saw when my cloak flew open. Minar saw too, and asked his Mumma an embarrassing question as I helped him remount. This time I tied him into the saddle too, while Cybelle turned scarlet.

The spearmen were prodding us into line when her color subsided and she hissed, "Milady, what *can* you be thinking of? Won't you leastways die dignified?"

I made a rude noise. "That for dignity. And hoist your skirts, Cybelle. You've got to run if you want your boy to live. Worry about him, not me." Cybelle looked dubious, but she bundled up her skirt after a fashion.

All was ready. The spearmen left the arena to get good seats for the race. The horsemen kept their steeds on a tight bridle, the high-blooded stallions already pawing up clouds of dust, eager for the battle-cry and charge. Those harlots not digging in their feet for a quick breakaway at the King's signal were rubbing shoulders and milling about like sheep, their faces empty of any will.

I had some sharp words for them, and a slap for as many as I could reach. "*Run* when the King says run, you bonebrains! If there's a chance to live, take it! Use it! And keep your ears open too, else you won't hear 'em give the twenty-count that starts off the horsemen; *or* the shout that ends the race!"

"That's one shout we won't hear," said someone. I was glad she was within smacking range. The audience cheered for the small set-to in the harlots' ranks and seemed disappointed that it went no farther.

King D'zent stood up and raised his arms. "May Sarogran of the Spears bless this Course, run in his name. Let the race begin!"

Nineteen women sprinted away; one loped after in a heavy wool cape, incapable of more than a trot. The public joined His Majesty in counting off twenty, each number marked by a drop of water falling from the clepsydra balanced on the stone lip of the royal box. The stallions were growing more and more restive, tossing their heads and snorting with frustration, their

ceremonial harness jangling. Their riders tightened the reins
still more as the count continued and all of the runners save
me dashed for their lives.

When the count reached seventeen, I stopped.

At eighteen, I turned.

At nineteen I reached for the clasp of Barti's cloak and at
twenty it dropped in the dust.

Naked but for a necklace, I performed Glister's Shimmy
for the dumbstruck horsemen, bawling the chorus of "The
Horned Scribe" as accompaniment. It was a popular tune. A
large bloc of spectators joined in:

> *"And so he said, 'My darling wife,*
> *I know my nib is thin,*
> *But if you hold the inkwell still,*
> *I* think *I'll get it in!'"*

And before I lost the interest of my mounted audience, I
yanked the vial of seeing-draught from my neck, emptied it
into my mouth, and sprayed it full in the faces of the stallions.

It is a prime spectacle to see a herd of phantom mares in
heat appear between yourself and death.

There was no controlling the stallions then. They jerked the
reins from their riders, or failing that, they bucked and kicked
until the Guards were off. The mares whickered and flaunted
themselves without shame, egging on their suitors. Fights broke
out in earnest, the huge battle-steeds rearing up to slash at one
another with teeth and hooves, and the gods help any Guard
still fool enough to cling to his saddle. Battling stallions bite
first and ask later whether they got a mouthful of horse-flesh
or human. Pandemonium raged in the arena.

The same held for the stands. Even the priests of Sarogran
who lurched on the shrine's lower terraces stood up and leaned
over to gape at the shambles below. I did a little war-dance of
triumph and gave a shrill shepherd's whistle for attention.

Of course the only beings in the arena capable of paying attention to me were the runners.

"To the shrine! To the shrine!"

The door might have resisted one desperate whore, but not a score of us. It cracked inwards and we swarmed inside. We tossed the lone acolyte porter onto the sands and locked him out with the siege-bolt he hadn't thought needful to lug across the door-braces.

He wasn't lonesome for long. Barti thrust Nara into my arms and leaped for Sarogran's altar, a fane bedecked with heavy stone and metal images of the god, to say nothing of ritual spears. Armed with these makeshift weapons, Barti led a cohort of women in a tier-by-tier purge of the shrine. Priests taken face-to-face as well from behind made lovely midair tumblesaults as Barti's fighters gave them invisible wings.

My Nara began to cry while all this was going on. "Babies don't give a fig for nonsense, I'm sure," said Cybelle. "Wants her milk, is all. Give her here."

With my hands free, I was able to mount the shrine in Barti's wake until I emerged at the topmost ring.

"Not a bad view," said Barti, hands on hips. The other ladies rested their improvised weapons on the parapet and surveyed the stadium. The phantom mares were gone, leaving a bunch of wounded, blowing, baffled stallions behind. Those of the forcibly dismounted Guard who were able to walk were carrying their not so lucky brethren off the field. The dispossessed priests too were taking care of their own.

In the stands, the reactions were everything from shock to puzzlement to blasphemous laughter. Prince Zimrit was holding his belly and roaring. His royal brother had the look of a puppy who has done the unmentionable on the carpet and wonders whether he'll be blamed. Nimora was surrounded by Sarogran's priests and a smattering of the other gods' representatives. It was impossible to see her face in the middle of the impromptu ecclesiastic conference.

"Well, Megan," said Barti. "Now what?"

"Now?" I had been relishing our victory too well to think about postscripts. "Now what? Why . . . we're safe now, that's what."

"For the moment. But do you think King D'zent will do nothing?"

"We survived the race. He has to give us our freedom." I spoke as one who has set her mind on a single acceptable outcome and won't entertain the suggestion that life is full of *other* outcomes. "He will. You'll see. He'll give a little speech about the will of Sarogran and divine intervention and all that, then he'll let us go. Otherwise he looks like a dog's ass. The people don't like being ruled by a dog's ass. A king must be strong!"

"Ummmm," said Barti. "Too bad D'zent agrees with you about strong kings. Look what's coming."

The gate through which the horsemen had pranced in and more recently retreated opened again, this time to admit a double stream of bowmen with the King's Colors marching at their head. There were at least forty of them, all armed with two-hundred-pound longbows. A grizzled priest of Sarogran came hobbling alongside, to lend blessing to their cause.

"Go below, all of you, and keep away from the windows. Block them off. There are plenty of sacred movables inside big and heavy enough to seal every mouse hole! Use the painted panels of the god and brace them up with his images. If they fire a shot, let them skewer Sarogran."

The women at the parapet didn't need telling twice. The roof-side trapdoor gulped them all down, all except Barti, who lingered.

"Megan, what about you?"

"I'm going to try treating with King D'zent. If we seal off the windows, the archers won't be able to do much against us, and he won't like being made to look dumb a second time."

"He won't look dumb unless the archers actually waste their arrows shooting at a sealed stone tower. I don't think that's his plan. The bowmen aren't supposed to attack us; only keep us from escaping. D'zent's got us under siege."

I set my lips together firmly. A siege was most definitely *not* part of my plans. Hunger would drive us out fast enough, thirst faster, and the children fastest of all.

"Then the thing to do is make D'zent look the fool in spite of himself, Barti, and I am an expert on fools."

Barti shrugged and slammed the trapdoor. (I like to pretend I did not hear her mumble, "Takes one to know one," as she bounded down the steps.)

That left the topmost tier of Sarogran's shrine to me—and Sarogran. His snowy statue, spear poised to strike, observed my actions with painted eyes the color of rain clouds. Like me, he disdained clothing, even up so high. If the sculptor who carved that masterwork received a direct, divine vision of the deity before beginning work—if what he carved was at all accurate—then Liuma's mortal friend Andraniu wasn't being kept against her will, she was holding on to a good thing while she had one.

I made use of several highly improper handholds to scale the god's image.

The populace held their breath. Sarogran's statue was the highest point in the stadium, and I didn't stop climbing until I was atop his head. This was not so perilous as you might imagine, for Sarogran wore a cloudy crown that served me as a low safety railing, coming halfway up my shins. Secure inside my marble nest, I executed an encore performance of the Glister Shimmy, ending with a reverse bow in King D'zent's direction.

A gasp of outrage came from the royal box. The priests around Nimora hummed like bees when a bear tears up their honeycomb. From far, far below I heard Prince Zimrit exclaim, "Bugger me to the Netherplane and back, it's *Megan*!"

He never was one to forget a face.

I continued to strut and wiggle, making faces, cocking snooks, and in general behaving beyond the pale of obnoxiousness. I wanted to bait the King into losing his temper and giving the order for his archers to fire. If I were lucky, they'd miss—the odds in my favor were good at that range, with the sun in their eyes too. If not, I'd still have accomplished something for the others, since an open attack on the shrine would make D'zent appear ridiculous before his people when it failed.

I'd leave it to Barti to negotiate a settlement with His Majesty later, in order to save his face. I had faith in Barti's methods, and if she managed to conduct the truce-talks in person with D'zent, Stanesinn might end up with a brand-new queen.

My ruse worked. You could hear the grinding of King D'zent's molars all the way to heaven. He barked an order and one of the archers took three steps forward. The man's upper arms were like young logs, the massive bow bending to his will as if made of wax. I gulped and prepared to duck. Sarogran's crown wouldn't shield me from this.

The bow bent, the arrow flew upwards. It arched over the god's left shoulder and fell harmlessly to earth. I let out a derisive whoop and made remarks about King D'zent's mother. His Majesty's face grew purple, a good color for royalty, and he gave the archer another command. This arrow would have gotten me if I hadn't jigged right. It missed, but my feet skidded on Sarogran's frictionless head. I grabbed for the deity's crown to steady myself and sat down hard, my heart lobbing double time. It took me awhile before I gathered my courage to stand up and resume my King-baiting dance.

King D'zent was beyond speech. His fingers twitched, unraveling the gold threads used to tack down the thousand pearls sewn into his cuffs. The precious sea-gems pattered and rolled all around the royal box. The luckless archer looked up, waiting for his lord's desire.

Nimora spoke for the King. Or rather, she said nothing eloquently, in his name. She shook herself free from the lesser priests and shouldered D'zent himself aside to glower at the bowman. A chute of tawny light poured from the royal box to the sand, transporting the sorceress down to where the bowman watched and trembled.

I knelt on Sarogran's head and peered over the crown of clouds to see what she would do. It was nothing I hadn't seen before, when the victim was an unlucky Captain not quick enough to do Nimora's bidding. This time it was worse because the archer wore no helmet. There was nothing to soften the sight of what Nimora's touch could do. The man's head split up the back as his soul fled. The sand drank his blood.

Nimora motioned for another archer to step forward and try his luck. This time he would not have two chances.

He was very, very young. I saw the fear of death in him even from so high up. One chance was all he had, and what was there to stop me from remaining hunched down behind Sarogran's crown? What law said I had to stand up and start dancing again, giving him a halfway fair target?

But he was young to die, and I'd accomplished what I intended. King D'zent had raised the siege by declaring open war, and that meant we could start negotiating peace.

Even if I weren't alive to enjoy it. I rather thought Nimora would have no truck with peace-talks while I still lived. She would kill every one of the King's archers until one of them brought me down, and if they failed, she'd call up something worse to hurl against the tower and all inside. I didn't need to buy that knowledge with another innocent man's death.

He nocked the arrow to the string and pulled it back. That was when I stood up to my full height and stretched out my arms to embrace whatever might come. The arrow flew. I marked its flight the way a bird marks the snake's eye just before becoming dinner. His arm was strong, his aim was good. This arrow would not fall short or fly wide. I closed my eyes and waited for the barb to find my heart.

A slap of cold air struck me first, head to toe, making my skin burn and tingle as if someone had picked me up and dumped me into a snowbank, naked as I was. I opened my eyes to the cheering of the crowd and also to a silver bell of brightness streaming from the sky. It ran like milky water in a protective dome that enclosed the shrine and left the bowman's arrow impaled in opal light an arm's length from my breast.

Nimora was so flabbergasted she neglected to kill the archer. He and his fellows took advantage of this lapse to hightail it out of the arena.

Sarogran's decrepit priest was frothing. He shook his fists at me and howled, "Sacrilege! Blasphemy! Unholy whore, may it please the gods to turn thy stinking dungheap body into a laidly toad!"

Then he turned small, green, warty, and hopped in circles until Nimora squished him. I guess one never knows what will please the gods.

Nimora wiped off the sole of her shoe. The spectators were going mad, half of them with fear, half with glee. Prince Zimrit had to be carried out of the royal box to have his ribs taped. He'd pulled a muscle laughing. King D'zent's expression would have physicked a woodpecker.

Being caught up in the middle of an unsolicited miracle is rattling. Try it sometime. I was just as helpless to act as King D'zent, with no more idea of how to get *out* of the missile-and-curse-repelling dome than he had of how to get *in*to it. But even if we both felt like boobies, he was the one left *looking* lumpish, and appearances mean so much.

"Niiiiimooooorraaaaaa!"

You'd think a King wouldn't whine.

He didn't have to. Nimora took one look at me and got blood in her eye. Gone was the calm with which she'd murdered that poor bowman. The sands under her feet crackled and fried, their crystals blackening into a pool of liquid glass. Her hands described the contours of a forming-spell, setting the glazed disk to turning. It rotated slowly, rising as it turned, lifting the sorceress higher and higher into the air.

The glass disk flew faster, circling the milky dome over Sarogran's shrine. Nimora threw off her cape and diadem, her hair snapping on a wind she whistled up to serve her. She was silver-clad, in sandals and a huntress's tunic, and two black spines burgeoned from her flying platform's rim. She snapped them off like weeds.

The disk spiraled up to bring its mistress level with me. We saw each other clearly through the dome, though the pearly essence of the shield made us look like ghosts. She threw one of the glass spears at me and it shattered.

Why did that make her smile?

I saw why. It was a test, a gauge of the magic protecting me. Nimora held her reserved spear in one hand and with the other tore the fabric of the sky. A tiny rent was all she made, but enough for me to glimpse the blackness of the Midplane. The witch dipped her spear into that ultimate dark, withdrew it, and gloated as its tip hardened with a substance that would penetrate any spell forged in this world.

She raised her hand to heal the sky, then took aim. A spear flashed in flight.

Nimora shrieked, pierced through with a shining bolt that sent her flying from her witch's disk. Impact hurled her against the shielding dome, which vanished as soon as she touched it. Her body sprawled on the trapdoor near Sarogran's pedestal.

I clambered down the god's statue to see whether she still lived. Somehow I knew it was an empty thought, but I had to be sure. And I had to know who had been the one to dare the wrath of D'zent's High Priestess—arch-mage of all the kingdom—to save me.

Hyu, could you—? Another empty thought. A Third Thaumaturge, no matter how skilled, would be no match for Nimora. But who else would want to? Who else would have the power and the desire to rescue me?

I knelt beside Nimora. She was dead. The spear that had taken her life was white, burning, and when I touched it, it melted into rain. Rain was falling from a cloudless sky, drenching the arena.

™Greet thee, Fair and Chosen.™

The dome was gone, its brilliance solidified into a slightly more than man-sized twin of the statue atop the shrine. Sarogran of the Spears scooped me into his arms, a blaze of lightning and rain enveloping us both. Through the tempest he scrutinized his titanic marble image.

™Not a bad piece of work,™ the deity allowed. Then he looked at me. ™Neither are you, Fair and Chosen. Ah, by Father Sky, how I *do* like a girl with spunk!™

"Oh, my god!" I cried.

™Exactly.™

CHAPTER X
Orthodoxy

It's not easy being the beloved of a god.

For one thing, he's never too tired. For another, he's a know-it-all. The topper comes the first time you try backtalk with a deity who is used to praise-songs, pleas for mercy, and promises of good behavior if only he will make it rain before the cows keel over.

Our first (and last) tiff occurred when I asked him to stop calling me Fair and Chosen because it made me sound like twins.

Sarogran went into a sulk that ruined the barley crop in seven duchies. I was besieged by every farmer's wife who could drag herself to Stanesinn, every last one of them bearing baked goods and shedding tears enough to have watered all the barley they wanted. The Sprinters of Sarogran insisted that I had to receive all the suppliants and sample their offerings in the god's name, smiling the while, or else it would be taken as a bad omen and cause widespread panic. Moreover—as the

Sprinters pointed out—Sarogran the All-Merciful and Good wasn't at fault for the drought. If I'd only been nicer to him . . .

By the seventeenth oatmeal cookie I was ready to surrender. I apologized to Sarogran and he brought back the rain. He also said that my comment about twins had gotten him to thinking.

That's another thing about gods: When they want to start a family, you start one, and if they want twins . . .

The Holy Twins were born on the very spot where their father first appeared to me in tangible form. Cybelle and Barti stood by me while a veiled woman performed the delivery. Down below in the shrine proper, the Sprinters of Sarogran were making up a four-part-harmony chant about how Boriela the Celestial Midwife herself was upstairs with the rain-god's beloved. They were only waiting to hear whether they would have to find a rhyme for *boy* or *girl* so that they might finish the song and start inflicting it on the people of Stanesinn.

My second delivery was miraculously painless, even though I did bear twins. There are some perks attached to bedding a divinity. The children, a girl and a boy, were named Fair and Chosen by their father, who had been away "on business" during the birth itself. They hated the bloody names worse than I did and grew up rowdy.

™Fair and Chosen?™ said my divine sister-in-law, Liuma. ™Sarogran's got water on the brain. I hope Chosen gets his very own myth when he's grown up. One where he castrates his father.™ The fertility goddess giggled and had some more wine.

Liuma's company was another of the benefits of serving Sarogran. When she first came calling, I was afraid she'd bear me ill will for my refusal to join her Daughters. And hadn't I been responsible for the death of one of her most powerful advocates, Nimora? Indirectly responsible, yes, but I learned fast that the gods don't deal with quibbles.

™Who? Oh, Nimora?™ Liuma clicked her tongue. ™She was the last one I dreamtouched, and the silly twit did nothing. I am going to have to smite the land with famine and pestilence if someone doesn't tidy up that Andraniu myth for me. I have appeared and *appeared* in the dreams of my highest-ranking Daughters, telling them the truth, but why won't they listen?™

"They won't listen because the myth suits them just the way it is. It gives them . . . an excuse: the immortal Liuma doing just what her mortal Daughters would do anyway, bower and all. The advantage your Daughters have this way is that if anyone objects to the way they carry on, they can say a goddess did it too, so it's either all right, or all *your* fault. Associate with mortals long enough, Liuma, and you'll find most of them blaming their peccadilloes on their gods, never on themselves. Gods are handy that way. By the bye, what's the truth about the myth of Andraniu?"

Liuma's sigh was the richest perfume. Breasts, hips, and thighs like hers would have fetched top price in the House of Prayer, and several of the young male acolytes who now served with the Sprinters of Sarogran wore curiously sated smiles every time she came to visit.

™Mortal, look at me! Without my webs that bind male to female, Boriela would go begging. Flower to flower, thigh to thigh, moan to moan, sigh to sigh, and *that's* where babies come from; not from girl-talk in a bower that never existed!™

"You and Andraniu . . . didn't . . . ?"

™Singing lessons,™ said the goddess. ™I was in my formative phase at the time and working my wiles upon a recalcitrant shepherd. Took a vow of *virginity*, did you ever? All those sheep around, too. I adored a challenge, and I heard shepherds love music, so I asked Andraniu if she'd teach me some songs. The girl had a divine voice, for a mortal.™

"No bower, then?"

Sarogran's sister spat. ™Bower my ass. The little slut took one look at the shepherd, sang him a chorus of "Under My Tunic It's Tight," and ran away with him. I hope she got anthrax. But you know how these rumors start: Mortal girl last seen in company of goddess is never seen again. Nothing else will do but to claim the goddess yanked her into a bower.

That's a nasty place to stow someone you care about, a *bower*! If that's where you're stuck waiting between trysts, you could go crazy. I can't think of a duller place.™

I could. I was in it.

Ever since the miraculous happenings at the Royal Games, there had been some changes made in Stanesinn's best stadium. Sarogran's priesthood conferred and announced that the place where their god had manifested himself must now be consecrated on a big scale. The whole stadium had to be converted into a full-fledged temple that would dwarf Sarogran's previous home on the Royal Boulevard. Thus the arena was roofed over to become a temple, the shrine promoted to altar, and the altar within the erstwhile shrine became the holy-of-holies, to be tended only by the Sprinters of Sarogran and their direct issue, if any.

The Sprinters of Sarogran. Ah, yes. When my immortal lover took human form, he carried me down into the shrine and politely greeted the children, Cybelle, Barti, and the seventeen harlots before asking directions to the nearest available bed. It was a religious experience for all. By the time Sarogran had made my acquaintance in the former High Priest's alcove, the whores were forswearing their old ways and loudly dedicating their lives to the rain-god. Barti thought they were touched in the head and said so, whereat they appointed her their leader.

"Why me, damn it? Do I look ready to play herdsman to a gaggle of pious puddingheads?"

Aliska Mothtongue—a duskflower whose reputation rivaled even Barti's—explained their decision calmly. "The hand of the god saved us from death, even though our deaths would have been his sacrifice. Therefore, Sarogran of the Spears has saved us to serve his aweful presence in some other way. But what?"

Sarogran and I jostled each other for the best listening post at the alcove wall just in time to hear Barti suggest, "Go back to work and donate a tenth of your take to the god. It's about time bullyboys and pimps had a divine patron."

Aliska Mothtongue took umbrage. The wispy working clothes she'd worn during the race were hidden under a high-necked vestment she'd appropriated from the priests' closet. It blared Solemnity, Dignity, and No More Fun.

"Sarogran has acted to save us from our former lives of sin. We must give thanks and make expiation. From this day forward, we shall sing praise-songs of our own composition in his honor. We shall be called the Sprinters of Sarogran so that all the kingdom may remember the circumstances of our god's holy incarnation."

"Good. I hope you can find some fancy rhymes for what Sarogran's doing with Megan right this minute."

"And you must lead us," Aliska plowed on unruffled, "because you are the only doubter. The lightning of your tongue shall always be there to sting us into greater efforts on the god's behalf, an ever-present reminder of the skeptics we must convert to the full knowledge of Sarogran's mercy."

"Hallelujah and just call me Sarogran's Saddle-Burr. I won't do it," said Barti.

"Then we'll kill you," replied Aliska, who had grasped the fundamentals of religious debate pretty quickly.

"Bless you, my daughter, and let's start penning those praise-songs!" Barti yipped, while the rain-god wet himself laughing.

Barti got used to being Sarogran's Saddle-Burr and even found it a palatable career when the first male acolytes started trickling back to the shrine-turned-temple. Soon she became so involved with interviewing aspiring candidates that I hardly saw her. ("You must show your comprehension of Sarogran's Greatest Mystery by reenacting exactly what happened during the Miracle of the Holy Games. You be Sarogran, I'll be Megan.")

So I didn't see Barti, Cybelle was happily busy with the children, Liuma couldn't visit all that often, and Sarogran's Sprinters were forever in rehearsal. Sarogran himself was company in bed, but you *do* have to get up occasionally, if only to restore circulation to the feet. That's when you appreciate someone who can carry on an interesting conversation.

Gods are no good for friendly chats, with the exception of Liuma. When they aren't giving direct orders to their worshipers (™Kill three fatted shoats.™/™Face the setting sun and burn only sandalwood incense.™/™Let's try that one again with you on top™) they only speak in portents, puzzles, and prophecies. Whenever I tried to open up normal conversation with the god, Sarogran would suddenly remember a thunderstorm he'd promised to deliver in the next duchy. I was left alone, lonely and bored.

And what of Stanesinn, the Royal City? What of its manifold delights, its playhouses, its bazaars? They might as well have been on the moon. I couldn't leave the sanctuary. Sarogran did not wish it. The god spoke, the Sprinters heard, and I was grounded.

™A woman's place is on her knees,™ said Sarogran. ™When I come home after a hard day's precipitation I don't want to have to go out looking for you.™

"But it's *boring* here!"

Sarogran shook off a few dismissive drops. ™Take care of the children. Join in a few choruses with Sarogran's Saddle-Burr and the Sprinters. Knit. Start a garden. That's a fine idea! I'll get my sister to come by and help you. Nothing brings a garden along better than the goodwill of the gods.™

"Horse manure," I said. Then I spent the bulk of the afternoon convincing Sarogran that I didn't mean it *that* way.

I got my garden. The acolytes carted in several tons of topsoil which they spread in a ring around the shrine.

Everything I planted grew like mad. It is true, it doesn't hurt to have the goddess of fertility for a friend. Sometimes she would surprise me with a gardenia blooming on a rosebush, but more often she would disguise herself as one of Sarogran's Sprinters and work beside me in the dirt with her own two hands.

™One mustn't lose touch, even if one is divine,™ said

Liuma, gouging out a weed. ™If we gods don't communicate with you mortals on the right level, on a day-to-day basis, soon we shan't be able to communicate at all. And then where will we be? Trapped in a stagnant mythos by a bunch of theologians who'll twist all *sorts* of mistaken meanings into our lives. Just see what they've already done to me and Andraniu.™

I dug some soil out from under my fingernails. "That myth's going to eat at you forever. Would you like me to claim you dreamtouched me with the real story? Sarogran's priests come calling every day, just to see how the Holy Twins are doing. It hasn't been half so much fun since Fair and Chosen were housebroken. I can't stage the Distribution of the Sacred Diapers anymore, and I have to do something to keep their interest. Otherwise I'm just one more canonized concubine."

™Megan, I'd be so grateful! And wouldn't you love to be a fly on the wall of my temple when the truth about Andraniu comes out? Farewell, Liuma's Daughters! No more justifying your behavior in my name, you holy cowards!™ Liuma bounced on her knees, whacking the heads off weeds with little bursts of fireworks. ™Don't blame your passions on your gods!™

"In that case, we'd better wash up and wrestle the Holy Twins into the tub while we're at it. For two-year-olds, they're wonderfully glib with reasons for not washing up. I assume demigods mature faster when it comes to divine double-talk. The priests arrive within the hour. Where are those two wildcats of mine?"

Cybelle emerged from the shrine just in time to hear my question. She wore the robes of a Sprinter, grievously altered. Instead of the high, hands-off neckline Aliska had decreed for the rank-and-file, Cybelle's robe was cut so low that her neckline skimmed an inch above her waistband, leaving her breasts bare.

"They've been consecrated, fool," Barti had informed her some time back, pointing her finger at the exposed titties. "You suckled the rain-god's babies, so now they're a national monument. It'd be a sin not to keep 'em on permanent display for the faithful. If I were you, I'd keep mum. Aliska was only a shrewmouse-dick away from having them tattooed for you. *Fair* for the left, and *Chosen* for the right."

Now Cybelle said, "I don't know where the little dears are, I'm sure. La, they do grow up so fast, milady, may the gods bless their precious hearts." Minar and Nara came up behind her and exchanged a look. They had other opinions of the Holy Twins.

"I saw them, Mama," said Nara, hurrying forward for a hug. "They were in the kitchen."

"Where the knives are," prompted Minar, full of a six-year-old's desire to be of help. "I saw Fair take out a real long, shiny one and then she said, 'Hold still, Chosen, I wanna see if this will work,' and that's when we left."

Cybelle squealed and bolted for the kitchen. Liuma and I decided she could behave hysterically enough for all of us, and so went inside for our baths.

The bathhouse was my idea, one that came to me a week after Sarogran. The shrine was not erected with permanent residents in mind. The only amenities within were for the use of priests keeping all-night vigils. We needed some additions built on around the original structure—a kitchen, a dormitory, a refectory, a larger access to Stanesinn's sewers—but most of all we needed a bathhouse before Aliska Mothtongue decided that Sarogran *wanted* his new temple to smell like a buffalo's armpit. Did you know how much sin you can expiate by stinking? The bathhouse was up, open, and functioning before you could say *sackcloth and ashes*.

Liuma and I were up to our chins in the steaming water when Cybelle hauled the Holy Twins in for judgment. I dislike repeating what she called them. When all's said and done, they were my babies. Suffice it to say, they were no longer *little dears* or *precious hearts*.

They'd cut off each other's hair to the scalp.

"*I'm* not at fault for this, milady, I'm sure," said Cybelle, giving Chosen a shake when he wouldn't stand still. "But what am I to say to the priests, and them due any minute? They always ask for the Holy Twins, they do, and when they see 'em like this don't you just know who'll be blamed!"

Chosen began to wail, his sister joining in on the chorus, and the bathhouse reverberated with their shrill ululations. Nara and Minar plugged their fingers in their ears while Liuma ducked under the water and stayed there.

It was little Minar whose piping voice cut across the uproar. "Why don't you grow their hair back for them, Auntie? You can do magic."

"Of course!" I pulled Liuma's floating hair, and when she surfaced I said, "You're a goddess of growing things. Grow back their hair!"

"Oh, not her, Auntie; you," said Minar. Yes, me.

"That's right, Mama, you can do *anything!*" Nara bobbed her head, a determined woman who was sure of her facts, and no gainsaying allowed.

Liuma got out of the bath and toweled herself dry. ™Well, if the boy thinks you've got any magic that will work the trick, you'd better do it. I know I can't. My specialty is reproduction, not elongation.™

"I've got no magic," I protested, following her out of the water. "A King's Man said so years ago, and the wizard with him, and—many others." A towel around me, I knelt and held Minar tenderly by the shoulders. "Darling, it's very kind of you and Nara to believe in me so much, but there are some things that even a Mama can't—"

"Use that stuff," said Minar. He pointed at the two vials still left me.

"These?" I touched the fragile glass. Urion's keepsakes had grown additionally precious with time—especially so since the seeing-draught had saved our lives—but I still had no idea of what the remaining potions could do. Experimental sniffs told me they weren't seeing-draughts and I was afraid to try more.

"Uh-huh. The blue one makes things grow a whole lot, so that'll work. But if it doesn't, the yellow stuff puts everything back the way it was before. If there's been an accident or something."

"Bless the lad! How can he know that?" exclaimed Cybelle. Minar studied his sandals and turned mute.

I wasn't going to ask how he'd come by his information. I hadn't been without Urion's vials around my neck or had them out of my sight more than twice since the Holy Games. Still, children are quick and preternaturally skilled when it comes to seizing the moment and finding "accidents" suitable for trying out Auntie's funny potions while Auntie is elsewhere. Children always manage.

I'd be happier not asking how.

™May I?™ Liuma held the sealed flacons to her forehead, which the priests teach holds the all-knowing godseye. ™The child is correct. The blue potion is a growth elixir of incredible properties, the yellow is a restorative oil, also exceedingly potent.™

I blessed Urion's memory and beckoned the Holy Twins to come sit on my lap. They sucked their thumbs and looked like sulky hedgehogs. "Which one do you recommend, Liuma?"

™The yellow oil. Such brews are for the repair of unfeeling things. Hair is cut without pain, so a scant drop will leave the twins' heads looking exactly as they were before.™ She held the yellow vial to her godseye once more before returning both to me. ™A *scant* drop, I said. I have never encountered this oil in such concentrated form before. It's like the essence of an essence. We sometimes hear of mortal magicians who labor to find the chrism that restores life itself, but the knowledge needed to decoct such a thing—!™

"And the wisdom needed never to experiment with the results," I murmured. I moistened my fingertip lightly with the oil and applied it to Fair and Chosen.

The priests were pleased to see the Holy Twins looking so sleek and sassy, their hair shining from a hundred strokes of the brush ("And twenty more to be applied at t'other end if you don't behave, I'm sure!" their harried nurse told them before the priests appeared). We received the delegation outside the shrine, amid the thriving vegetation of my garden.

"My lady," said the High Priest of Sarogran, washing his hands in dry air. "Oh, my lady, it does my heart good to see how calm all remains within Sarogran's new temple. Let the world fall to pieces beyond these walls, yet the god's beloved family frolics with the blessed ignorance of newborn lambs!"

I had seen blessed ignorance served up with mint sauce many a time. "Sir, what do you mean, 'Let the world fall to pieces'?"

The priest shooed invisible flies. "Oh, that's all settled now. It wasn't worth troubling you with the news. An upheaval in the royal palace. Rioting in the streets. The former King has been assassinated. Which reminds me, the new King will be along any moment to receive Sarogran's blessing. Is the god at home? No? Well, if the Holy Twins might stand in for their father and bless—"

"My babies will *not* bless an assassin!"

"What a thought unthinkable! Dearest lady, the assassin had no sooner done the evil deed than our new King's own hand cut the villain's throat. Too late to save King D'zent, alas, but a nice gesture. We have assured the people that King D'zent's fate was no better than what he deserved. The gods don't favor fratricides, and we never did find out what King D'zent did with his royal sire after he deposed him." His mouth stretched into a thick-lipped smile. "The gods will be much happier now that His Majesty King Zimrit is on the throne."

Trumpets blared, and a flock of junior priests came hurrying in to arrange themselves into a rank of honor flanking the path His Majesty was even then treading. Preceded by a company of silk-clad lackeys, followed by a troop of King's Guards, King Zimrit strode into the sanctuary.

I tried to swallow, but my throat was dry. At his royal patron's side, in the full livery of a First Thaumaturge, stood Hyu. A creature like a silver weasel with powdery blue wings perched on his shoulder. Only mages of the highest power

could command familiars. Hyu was in deep conferral with his
magical minion and did not notice me right away. I suppose
if I had my choice, I'd sooner chat with a winged weasel than
with Prince—pardon me, *King*—Zimrit.

All that changed as soon as His Majesty declaimed, "Megan!
Ah, Megan, at last!"

The familiar took to the air in a whir of wings, chittering
angrily. It had been knocked from its perch by the rush of
Hyu's leap to the forefront of Zimrit's train. He toppled lackeys
left and right until he ran up against the broad, unmoving back
of the High Priest.

The junior priests had fallen out of their ranks and rearranged
themselves into a semicircle around the King, the Holy Twins,
and me. There was no way for Hyu to push his way through,
and the look on his face told me he wouldn't know what to
say if he did manage to reach me. He jumped in place a few
times, his head bobbing in and out of sight every time he cleared
the High Priest, then uttered a strangled cry and ran off. His
familiar fluttered after.

I was just as taken aback as Hyu by our unexpected meeting,
but I had other fish to fry. Large, smelly fish. A King-fish, no
less, who knelt before my twins and asked their blessing.

"Oh, sure," said Fair. "Bless you."

Chosen snickered. "He's going *bald* on top," he said in a
whisper that carried to Routreal. "Right there inside the crown,
see?"

"Bless him, you jerk," said his sister, giving him a savage
jab in the ribs. The Holy Twins got into a hair-pulling fight
and were carted off by Cybelle, clearly at the end of her rope.

"What adorable children," said King Zimrit as his lackeys
helped him up and brushed the dirt from his knees. "High-
spirited, just like their mother. They'll love it in the palace."

"A ceremonial visit, Your Majesty?" The High Priest sidled
up, oozing benevolence. "A progress to show the Holy Twins
to the people?"

"Hmm. Yes, you might as well cobble together a parade of

sorts." Zimrit adjusted his nose reflectively. "Make it a public event when Megan moves in with me tomorrow, kit and caboodle. We'll have to saddle up a string of horses for the big move anyhow, so we might as well generate some goodwill among the commoners for the same money."

"WHAT BIG MOVE?!"

It was the only time I harmonized with a High Priest.

King Zimrit looked suspicious. "Have you been tippling Sarogran's Nectar again, Eridong? I told you, Megan and I are old friends. She's coming to live in the palace and become my concubine." He grinned at me and added, "Play this right, Megan, and you might even get a crown."

"But—but—she is the beloved of Sarogran! She belongs to the god!" The High Priest was spluttering and sweating, the junior priests milling around like storm-caught chickens. I was too engrossed in observing the priestly panic, but words like *over my dead body* and *when pigs have wings* ran through my mind.

"Sarogran appeared in human flesh to claim her! He performed a miracle *right* here to do it!"

"And we lost a damned nice sports arena as a result. Sarogran's got the biggest temple in Stanesinn now, and he can have his pick of the Sprinters if he's feeling frisky. That should satisfy anyone. I am not an unreasonable monarch, but I can't take a greedy god."

The High Priest groaned and seized handfuls of his own hair. "Sarogran the All-Merciful will smite the land with famine and pestilence! He'll withhold the rain! He will—"

™I will do all that, and more,™ said Sarogran of the Spears. The voice was greatly amplified and echoed from the translucent dome above.

"Daddy's home!" squeaked Fair, who had slithered out of Cybelle's grip and came running out of the shrine to cling to my leg. "Look, Mama, there he is! Up there!"

Up there, the two-year-old demigoddess said. We followed her gesture to the top of the shrine where the huge statue of the god was flushed with life and moving. The marble spear-arm came down as the god levitated from his pedestal and descended to meet us. (A junior priest was later found to have been in the wrong place at the time of the god's descent, but he received martyr's honors and the Sprinters dedicated "The Ballad of Yifni Underfoot" to him.)

™Unwise mortal, your crown is a speck of gold-dust in the eye of a god!™ thundered Sarogran. The head of his spear was nearly the size of King Zimrit's torso. ™Do madmen rule, that you think to take my beloved from me? Beware my wrath, lest you die!™

"The same goes from me," said Zimrit. "With sauce." He snapped his fingers and a waiting lackey slapped a parchment into his hand. Like a glorified market-crier, King Zimrit stood tall and read off his own royal proclamation for the deity's benefit:

"WHEREAS it has pleased the Almighty Powers to manifest themselves as the gods we know and love, and

"WHEREAS it has pleased Our August Majesty, King Zimrit the Avenger, to ever seek the greatest good for his beloved kingdom, and

"WHEREAS the Royal Family (the parlous example of King Wadred the Odd notwithstanding) has always cleaved unto the preeminent worship of Sarogran of the Spears, the rain-god, so that the might of his godhead should favor us and our people in all our enterprises, and

"WHEREAS of late a Miracle has transpired in our very Royal City of Stanesinn which proves beyond the shadow of a doubt and admits no gainsaying that:

"1. Sarogran of the Spears has taken a mortal woman to his bed, disporting himself with her and siring children of her body;

"2. Sarogran of the Spears has distanced himself from his godhead to assume the flesh necessary for such a long-term alliance with a mortal;

"3. Sarogran of the Spears has become enmeshed in the toils of domesticity better suited to a mortal than an immortal;

"4. Sarogran of the Spears has had his godhead unsuitably weakened by his continued fleshly dalliance;

"5. Sarogran of the Spears has shown himself unwilling to listen to reason about ungodlike behavior caused by the aforementioned dalliance with said mortal woman and the lessening of his worshipers' awe, respect, and personal religious satisfaction in transactions with the divinity occasioned thereby:

"THEREFORE we, Our August Majesty, King Zimrit the Avenger, do hereby decree the cessation of all royal patronage of Sarogran of the Spears. This shall include all royal donatives, endowments, supports, stipends, aid, grants, bounties, gifts, subsidies, and any and all signs of royal approval of the abovenamed god, verbal or written, from this day forth and forevermore, in all times and places, without any exceptions whatsoever.

"And to this Proclamation of Intent we do hereby affix our Royal Seal."

"Amen," I mumbled.

Zimrit rolled up the parchment and tossed it to his lackey. "How do you like them apples?"

™Apples? You will fight your own pigs for the few withered apples left after I withdraw my rains, O mortal loon.™

"I don't think so," said Zimrit. He whistled a casual tune and kept an I-know-something-you-don't-know eye on the peeved rain-god. "You can't stop the rain all over the earth. Father Sky did that once, but he promised mankind there'd be no more Great Droughts and he gave us otters as a pledge-sign. You don't outrank Father Sky."

™But I can cause a drought great enough to cover your land, and that is all I need do. Your neighbors will feast under the bounty of my rains while you starve and thirst.™

"Uh-uh," said Zimrit. He snapped his fingers again, and another lackey came forward. This one had a queerly intense look to him. He did not cringe well, an unforgivable lack in a lackey. But all was swiftly clarified when he cast off his livery, the gold and black armor underneath blazing with encrusted rubies.

"Meet Baldrad, High Priest of Imsullah," said King Zimrit pleasantly. "You know, your little brother? The war-god?"

"Kill! Kill! Kill for Imsullah!" shouted Baldrad. "Let the rainless fields drink the blood of our enemies! Let uncounted slaves fill our empty granaries with grain that Imsullah's beloved warriors shall plunder from surrounding lands! Let the widow and the orphan be led in chains to our cities, there to labor and sweat under the righteous conqueror's lash! Rain isn't everything!"

When Baldrad ran out of sanguinary steam, Zimrit spoke. "The choice is yours, O Sarogran. My Proclamation of Intent shall be read to the people within the hour, followed by the announcement that Imsullah is now the Royal Family's patron god. The big mistake my ancestor Wadred made was in switching allegiance to a softy. The goddess of cosmetics? Fiffle. But I doubt anyone will be stupid enough to try harming Imsullah's best friend."

"Let them try," hissed Baldrad, saliva dripping from his chin. "The curse of Imsullah shall rend their bowels to slime. The wrath of Imsullah shall scoop their brains from their skulls. The priesthood of Imsullah shall hunt them down, rip off their eyelids, and make them witness all their families slain by torture before the boon of death is granted them."

Sarogran's spear still hovered near Zimrit's breastbone. ™A dead King makes no proclamations. What priesthood shall avenge your death if it is the work of a god?™

He had to ask. The temple dome roared into a swelter of flames and a wolfish face, gaunt and ravening, glared at the rain-god. ™You touch King Zimrit and I'll tell Father Sky!™ boomed the voice of Imsullah. ™You know the rules: No interfering with mortals' choices! You just try pulling anything and I'll—!™

The younger deity's materialization faded.

"Once I put some meat on Imsullah's altar, he'll be able to stay with us longer, but I think he made his point," said Zimrit. "You see how it is, Sarogran? Once I make the change, there's no going back. Do you want to learn firsthand how many of your priesthood will stand by you in the lean times? Omniscience isn't without a few unpleasant surprises. But you still have a chance. Give up Megan and we tear up the Proclamation. Don't, and Imsullah's the god for me."

I nudged Sarogran's High Priest. "If Sarogran gives in, won't Imsullah be angry and do something?"

"Imsullah's *always* angry. He's the war-god. But his chief myth says he will patiently wait to be made supreme god of this kingdom."

"Patiently? You know, there's something you should know about the reliability of myths. . . ."

A deafening rumble of thunder overwhelmed my words. The living statue of the rain-od was shaking. Hairline cracks manifested themselves at all the joints, spreading rapidly upwards and outwards. Fissures began to appear. The statue's left pinky dropped off. Powdered marble sifted down from between the carved stone teeth.

™TAKE HER!™ howled the god, and disintegrated. The cloud of snowy dust lingered under the dome of the stadium for days.

Everyone present suffered a protracted sneezing bout that left the royal trumpeteers incapable of blowing a recessional for their sovereign. Zimrit didn't care. He'd gotten what he wanted.

He sent the promised parade for us the following day. By tacit agreement with the salvaged priesthood of Sarogran, the Holy Twins would live in Zimrit's palace with me during the week and see their divine father on weekends. They rode in a four-horse litter with Cybelle, Minar, and Nara, making the white steeds stumble in harness with their constant fidgeting and bouncing.

"These are your apartments," said King Zimrit when we were alone. Cybelle was unpacking in the royal nursery, Minar and Nara were making pests of themselves in the royal stables, and Fair and Chosen were learning the best ways to annoy the royal eunuchs.

"Not bad." A broad flight of chalcedony steps spilled into a nine-room suite which included my own private kitchen, banquet hall, and bathing pool. Five doe-eyed maidens slept in alcoves set strategically throughout the suite so that one of them would always be within hearing distance should I call. Five of the rooms faced the palace gardens, and a pillared terrace ran their length. A tub of polished red marble gleamed in the open air in case the whim for a bath alfresco seized me.

"You can have a cat if you want, but otherwise, no pets," said the King. He put his arm around me and leered. "Want to try out the bed?"

"Yes," I said, removing the arm. "Alone. I'm exhausted."

King Zimrit's face clouded. "You were never too tired when you worked for Madam Glister."

"That was years ago, Your Majesty. Nothing's quite the way it used to be." I selected a gilded bench and sat down, sagging my body like a swaybacked mare. "I am more than merely tired. Rest cannot lift this weariness from my bones, woe and alackaday. Sarogran's vigor has ruined me for ordinary wantonness." I rolled my eyes. "After sharing a god's bed, can you blame me for taking a vow of perpetual chastity?"

"Cowflop," said the King, enunciating clearly.

"Nay, nay!" I pressed my wrist to my forehead and fanned myself feverishly with the other hand. "I faint, I die, I perish at the very thought of coupling with anything less than a divinity."

"I'm a King, damn it! My whole Royal Family Tree is riddled with immortals. My mother's grandmother's third cousin was ravished by Kiridar, Lord of the Hunt. My father's great-grandsire took one of Father Sky's rejects as his third wife. My maternal great-great-grandfather's great-great-great-aunt by marriage was best friends with Andraniu. You want something divine in your bed, you've got it!" He started to undress.

I sprang up and yanked his robes closed, tying a double-knot in the sash. "Your peerless wisdom has penetrated the heart of my sham, Your Majesty. I lied. When did I ever turn you from my bed in the good old days? Divinity has nothing to do with my rejection of your royal favor; nothing, and everything. Believe me, my lord, my holy and unbreakable oath of chastity was taken for your sake as much as mine."

"Cowflop," reiterated the King. He was a man of few words; bad ones. "I thought you were dead, Megan. Madam Glister claimed you'd gone swimming in the river and drowned. Then when I saw you dancing on Sarogran's head, I knew the old sow had spun a whopper, though the gods alone know why. Right then and there I swore that if you survived the Holy Games, I'd get you back. And by Netine's nipple-rouge, I did it! I laid my life and my kingdom in the balance for you! I challenged the rain-god himself! I had to deal with Imsullah's mad-dog High Priest and make promises I never wanted to keep, but I'd have kept them to drive Sarogran to the wall! And now . . . after all that . . ." (he was panting, poor man) "you say you can't bed me and it's *for my own good*?"

"The curse," I rumbled, "of Sarogran." I did without the dramatic pause, just in case Zimrit tried to say *cowflop* again. "The gods are jealous. As he departed, Sarogran of the Spears spoke for my ears alone and told me that he had placed an awful curse upon me. 'I dare not act directly against King Zimrit,' he said, 'for fear of Father Sky's decree, but I can exact a sly and subtle vengeance upon him. Megan, be your *si'ir* accursed from this hour, so that the man who ventures to follow in my footsteps shall leave behind therein those parts which make every man a king.'"

Zimrit was not catching on. "You know, your *scepter*?" I prompted. I formed my hands into a clamshell and snapped it shut in his face. "Whap! Like that. And you can kiss the crown good-bye. An imperfect man may not rule. Would one fleeting moment of joy be worth a lifetime spent guarding your successor's harem?"

Zimrit withdrew, saying something about calling in his council of mages to discuss ways and means of lifting divine curses. I summoned one of my handmaidens, had her guide me to the bed, and collapsed on it in relief.

I had forestalled Zimrit for the time being. Now I had to wait and hope that Hyu would come for me. The day waned. No word reached me. I dined alone before retiring. I banished my five handmaidens from the suite first, not wishing to have any witnesses present when my darling should choose to contact me.

For he *would* come, I knew it. Now that he finally knew where I was—that Nara and I were alive!—he would be with us soon. I hugged my knees and cursed the circumstances that had conspired to keep us apart and kept him from knowing what had become of Nara and me. Hyu had not attended those fateful Holy Games. Probably he was closeted in his study, ransacking his grimoires, sending out spells to find us as he'd promised. Would he realize that his seekings could not penetrate the shieldspell covering the arena? For all he knew, I was dead, and his unknown daughter as good as dead since he'd never be able to find her without me.

If only the Sprinters had called me by my real name in their idiot warblings! I thought. *But Aliska Mothtongue decided to keep my identity a Holy Mystery. Who in the Netherplane would ever connect the Virtuous Duskflower with his childhood sweetheart? Or the Thrice-Blessed Doxy? Or the Penitent Courtesan? I'll bet Hyu can hum those tunes in his sleep, but he never knew they were singing about me!*

I wished Aliska Mothtongue and the Sprinters a plague of laryngitis and fell asleep.

"Megan? Megan, I'm here."

"Hyu!" I was fully awake at once, my arms wide for him.

They closed on empty air. I felt a cool wind from the open terrace, but clouds covered the moon. There was only shadow in my bedchamber. I searched the dark for him. "Where are you?"

"Here." The well-loved voice was in my ear, along with a soft thrumming. I groped for the blinded oil-lamp beside the bed and lifted its ceramic cover. The cover's central chimney-hole allowed the lamp to remain burning while its light was kept from a sleeper's eyes. Light bloomed in the bedroom, and a hovering, winged shadow caught in its glow.

I extended my hand and Hyu's silvery familiar alit like a trained falcon. "Thank you." It still spoke with Hyu's voice. "I couldn't come to you any other way, Megan. I don't want to risk saving you from Zimrit's harem until we've got an infallible plan." The winged weasel gazed at me with longing in its godsgift blue eyes. "If you only knew how much I've missed you!"

"Oh, and I've missed you too, my love!" I sleeked the creature's fur. A misgiving struck me. "Hyu . . . you do know about . . . Sarogran? You aren't angry?"

"Did you ever have a choice? Could you really turn down a god?"

"I could have said no."

"And lived?" The weasel chuckled. "You were always wiser than I, and more practical. Losing you has taught me some hard lessons, my love. I'm the King's First Thaumaturge now. I'm the youngest mage ever to come so high so fast. The King and his council of wizardry promoted me directly over the head of the Second Thaumaturge and two other strong candidates. It's not a position they give to a fool. Only a fool wastes anger on something that could not have been otherwise. What happened to you with Sarogran is over; we won't speak of it. I'm not going to lose you again through my own stupid pride. I love you."

I felt reprieved. "Dearest one, I love *you*, and that's something not even Sarogran ever heard me say. How soon can we be together? I can't hug a weasel!"

"How soon can you convince Zimrit to let you keep Nara with you overnight? What I plan is a Midplane-leap—a spell few wizards can master—but I know I can spirit-lift you and the child if you're in the same radius when—"

"The children, don't you mean?"

The familiar's pale blue wings dipped. "What children? You and Nara—"

"And the Holy Twins, Fair and Chosen. Oh, and we can't just vanish like that if it means leaving Cybelle and Minar behind. Zimrit might be mad enough to take it out on them. I'll find a way to have *all* of them spend the night in my suite, and we'll be ready when you—"

The silver weasel spread its wings and flew out the balcony. I couldn't fathom what I'd said to offend it. I was still running over our conversation when I heard the sound of light footfalls on the terrace.

It must be a cat. No nightjack would risk his skin prowling the Royal Palace, least of all the harem wing. The gems you might pick up are nothing next to the jewels you lose if they catch you.

"Megan?" said the cat. It was Hyu in his proper shape, the chill of his Midplane-leap still hanging on him. This time my arms were full, and we banished the Midplane cold together.

As we lay entwined afterwards I whispered, "Why did you come? I thought you wanted to wait until we could escape the palace safely."

Hyu folded his hands behind his head and sighed. "I thought so too. I told myself I'd come to you tonight just to convince you, face to face, that we couldn't take the twins and that wet-nurse of theirs."

"I'm not convinced."

He smiled ruefully. "Neither am I. I was going to get up in a wizardly huff and say I wouldn't do it, I couldn't be responsible for Fair and Chosen. Let Sarogran tend to his own!

Then I saw you, and I knew what you'd say to *that*. I came perilously close to playing the fool again. They're your babes, my sweet Megan, a part of you. That's reason enough for me to love them. And I'll find a way to stretch my powers to rescue every soul you want taken along for the ride: Holy Twins, wetnurse, stray dogs . . ."

"How generous. Are palace guards included?" asked King Zimrit. He made a sign to the men-at-arms behind him on the terrace.

Hyu sprang from my arms, his power a corona of purple fire on his naked body. The flames flowed to his hands, swirling and leaping like two cups of blazing oil. He raised his hands to fling destruction. The Royal Guards cringed and backed off.

Two men detached themselves from the body of Royal Guards attending Zimrit. They moved with unsmiling purpose, in perfect coordination, as if they had been born twins and never learned to act apart from each other. Ribbons of bland yellow light as thick and oily as butter flickered before them, spreading and curving outwards, joining at last into an unbroken sheet that rolled across the floor to wrap itself around Hyu and absorb his fires.

Hyu's mouth opened in a silent yell. He beat on the slick walls of his prison. He was only a blurred shape inside the yellow globe that had formed itself out of the two wizards' joint creation, like a bee trapped deep in the throat of a golden flower.

"Take him away," said the King. The magicians bowed and wafted Hyu's bubble out over the gardens. They followed, walking on the night air. The Royal Guards breathed easier and snapped to parade attention behind their master. "A little late for that, isn't it? You may go."

"But, Your Majesty—" The Captain made significant gestures towards me as if I were likely to turn into a dragon any minute, just for spite.

"Rest assured, Captain, the lady is not the sort to carry concealed weapons in *that* state. I dismissed you. Go. You may attend me beyond the harem entrance, and I'd suggest you don't touch anything on your way out."

The guards marched out in brisk double time, their eyes frozen straight ahead. Don't touch anything in the King's harem? They weren't even going to risk looking!

King Zimrit sat on the edge of the bed. "I must thank my First Thaumaturge, Master Hyu. It would appear that the Curse of Sarogran has been lifted through his efforts. Kind of him to try things out first, to make sure I'd be in no danger."

I pulled the sheets up around my chin, the sick, sour fear-taste in my mouth. "Who were those men?"

"Those, my sweet, were my unpromoted Second Thaumaturge and one of the rejected candidates for First. He was appointed Third instead; hardly what he wanted. I did those gentles a disservice, promoting Master Hyu to First just because he wields such an impressive Destruction weirding. Little did I know he might try wielding it at *me*. Now my new Third Thaumaturge—Master Vorspeel—his specialty is Visions, implanted in the eye of the viewer. Very handy for a monarch who wants to keep constant watch over a troublesome border, or an unguarded treasure-room, or... a certain lovely liar." King Zimrit touched his right eyelid. "That's where you are, Megan, always in my sight; or at least for the time being. I wish Vorspeel could renew the spell indefinitely, but he cautioned me that repeated viewing of the same object would destroy a man's ordinary vision."

"So you've been watching me. For how long?"

"Long enough." He clasped his hands and sighed. "You were enjoying yourself so much, too. You were never like that with me. Oh, a passable counterfeit, but the genuine article shows itself at last. You must love Master Hyu very much."

I nodded. "What will you do to him?"

"That's up to you, isn't it? You love him, Megan. How much do you love him?"

I knew what he was really asking. "Spare his life, Your Majesty, and I swear by all the gods to be yours."

King Zimrit's smile didn't carry to his eyes. "Mine. Like my jewels or my best horse or my pack of hunting dogs? Something purchased, not freely given. I'll have to be satisfied with that much, I suspect. In time I may claim more. Will you give me that much hope, Megan?"

I wouldn't look at him. "I love Hyu. You know it."

"So I do. And I could kill him for it." Seeing my sudden look of panic he quickly added, "But I won't. I give you my royal word that Master Hyu shall live."

"And I give you mine that I won't try to run away with him again. I won't even see him, if that's what you want."

King Zimrit picked up the edge of my silk sheet and peeled it back leisurely, making small sounds of controlled appreciation as he did so. "I take you at your word, Megan. But as for Master Hyu—we shall have to find a means of persuading *him* not to come around bothering you anymore with escape schemes. We must conserve the proprieties of a royal harem, which do *not* include midnight callers other than myself."

I was fully bare now, and shivering. The oil-lamp shed piebald shadows on my skin. King Zimrit stood to remove his clothes, casting the image of a grotesque bat against the wall. As he slipped into bed beside me I had to ask one more time, "But you won't kill him?"

He laughed. "I don't like killing, unless it's a necessity. You have no idea how greatly I repent cutting the throat of the assassin who did in poor old D'zent. But that had to be. Couldn't have him blabbing how much I paid him for the job, could I? A considerate monarch always keeps his eyes on what's best for his people as well as for himself. It would drive prices right through the roof on the open market if that footpad were the garrulous sort, squeeze out the common man entirely when he wants a hired murderer. I always like to think of others." He snuggled up and purred, "And I always get the best of my bargains."

CHAPTER XI
Award of Meretrix

It was King Zimrit's birthday and the harem was in an uproar. My desk was under siege from every side. Eunuchs scooted in and out with piles of record-scrolls in their arms, dropping their loads in front of me and demanding to be seen to first, never mind who was in line ahead of them. Their demands were met with hoots and catcalls from Zimrit's concubines, who were adding their bit to the commotion by pushing and shoving anyone between them and the desk, filling the air with nasal whines for special favors and supplies.

Couple to that their serving-wenches, hairdressers, dwarfs, and duennas—not one without an urgent reason for speaking to me—and you have some idea of why I stood, hooked my fingers under the tabletop, and heaved it over so hard that the priceless malachite and gold inlaid top cracked into a jigsaw.

"OUT!"

No one spoke. It took me a few heartbeats to recognize total silence when I heard it, but I knew it wouldn't last. I balled my fists and set them on my hips. "Did you hear me, you stinking, slinking flock of fluff-brained screebirds? Take your petitions, your scrolls, your pleas, and your butts *out of my office* before I call the Royal Guards!"

The concubines shrugged and motioned for their attendants to depart with them. They left in a tinkle of gold bangles and a massively concerted undulation of hips. The eunuchs bent to gather up the scattered scrolls, bitching under their breath. When the last one had gone (slamming the door as angrily as possible) I folded my legs under me and sank to the floor.

"Long live the King, and I wish he could do it without birthdays."

"You say something, milady?" asked Cybelle. She had retreated to the balcony when the hullabaloo around my now ruined desk had reached its peak. She examined the wreckage, making it clear that she disapproved of my temper tantrum but would sooner die than say one word to me about it, she was sure. Not one *direct* word, not while she was mistress of the oblique word underscored by the meaningful look. And you know who she looked at. An irritating woman.

"I said that maybe there are worse fates than having King Zimrit in your bed."

Cybelle sniffed. "I wouldn't know about that, I'm sure." She spared a moment for an affectionate glance at her belly, which was just beginning to show.

"Feeling well, dear?" I asked.

"As well as can be expected, I'm sure. But it's well worth it, the dearest heart. When the time comes, he'll kick hard, I'm sure. A soldier born, just like his father."

I smirked. Cybelle had continued to wear the spectacular gown wished on her in Sarogran's temple by Aliska Moth-tongue. Even when we settled into the Royal Palace and she might have gone back to more modest attire, she still attended to her duties in the bosomless robe that promised, *If you don't see what you like in the window, ask for it in the store*. The Captain of the Royal Guard saw what he liked, asked for it, and Cybelle became his bride. Their baby would be born with the harvest.

"It could be a girl, you know. Will she be a soldier born too?"

"She'll be what she likes, I'm sure." Cybelle pursed her lips. "Children never listen to sense. And they certainly do have *bad tempers*. If they don't like the way things go, there's naught for it but *destroying* something. All the better if it's something *expensive*. It's not very *civilized*, but that is how *little children* behave."

"Yes." I gave her an innocent smile. "But what *can* you expect from bad-tempered children?"

Cybelle *whoofed* at my deliberate thickness. "I'll get someone to clear this away, milady. And if His Majesty should happen to ask whose fault it was, I'll take the blame for it myself, I'm sure." She made for the door, skirts high, dudgeon higher.

"Oh, Cybelle!" I clambered upright and stayed her from going. "I'm sorry. I know I should be more patient. I've dealt with ructions nearly as bad as this in the past five years, but for some reason the King's birthday always sets me chewing razors."

"I know why." Cybelle bobbed her head and looked sagacious. "You're jealous. No, don't you give me *that* look. I know what I know. How long has it been since His Majesty shared your bed, hey? How many years since you've done no more than rule your own little kingdom inside the harem? A kingdom without a man!"

"The answer is three. Do I get a prize? Three years and eight months, if you're picky. Cybelle, love, I am very happy without King Zimrit in my bed."

"Cowflop," said Cybelle. She had picked up a number of royal affectations. "An accounts scroll won't warm you at night unless you set it afire."

"For your information, the same goes for King Zimrit, and

the priests look down on ladies who kindle their King any way but figuratively speaking."

Cybelle wasn't having any of it. "A one-eyed blind man can see how things are. It's only on the King's birthday that you fly off the handle, and it's only on the King's birthday that new concubines arrive. More competition for His Majesty's favors! You are jealous."

"More competition for the *other* concubines, not me. I've been retired. Now I manage the harem accounts and dispatch His Majesty's nightly bedwarmer on evenings when he can't decide for himself. It's the *old* concubines who drive me mad, especially the ones left over from his princely days, not the new arrivals. They sniff competition for the consort's crown and they're desperate to redo their whole appearance so His Majesty won't set them aside entirely in favor of his new toys. It's his birthday when they come around pestering me for new clothes, new cosmetics, new scents, new slaves. Do they have a sheep's notion of what 'budget' means? Or where the money's to come from? Or the wrangles I have to mount with the eunuchs in Accounting to get a fifth of the things they demand as their right? Meantime I have to enter the names and all pertinent data about the newcomers, get *them* set up in the proper accommodations, supply them with attendants, wardrobes, 'Welcome Aboard' fruit baskets..."

Cybelle shook her head violently. "I still say—"

A broad-beamed harem porter came blustering in, breaching our debate. "His Majesty, King Zimrit the Avenger! All tremble and fall upon your faces!"

"Fall upon your arse," I stated. "Cybelle, you are *not* to grovel in your condition."

"But—but the King—"

I latched on to her arm and held fast, reeling her out of her curtsy. She fought me, determined to lick dust, and it was in the midst of this impromptu tug-o'-war that His Majesty joined us.

"You may rise," he said with a sardonic smile. Cybelle stood up and smoothed her skirts crisply, thoroughly miffed. When the King stared at what was left of my desk, she shot me a killing glare. "Dear me," said Zimrit, two fingers on his cheek. "Is it my birthday again already?"

"Yes, and Cybelle and I were just discussing what to get you. I suggested another concubine." King Zimrit groaned. "That's *just* what Cybelle said, Your Majesty. She said, 'Concubines are like vegetables. You can't have any fresh until you've tucked into what's already on your plate.' Didn't you say that, Cybelle?"

The former wetnurse dropped an abbreviated curtsy. "Will Your Majesty excuse me? I have to look in on the *other* children."

"Run along, run along." King Zimrit waved her out the door. When she was gone, he sighed. "My Captain of the Royal Guards is not a young man, Megan, and your good Cybelle passed her first bloom many years back. Yet they will soon have a child. And I, who am young and vigorous and have only the healthiest virgins of proven stock to share my bed—I am childless."

"'Proven stock'?"

"Oh, you know; fertile mothers. I never accept a girl who doesn't come from a big family. I can't understand it. Well, maybe I'll have better luck with this batch. Here, let's turn this desk right-side up. You must have a lot of paperwork to catch up on before the new ladies can be admitted to the harem wing."

Together we righted the desk. Zimrit pulled up my stool and sat down to concentrate on reinserting the shattered pieces of malachite into their wooden frame.

As he worked on it, I said, "Did it ever cross your mind that you might have more success if you didn't refer to your concubines as a 'batch'? Or 'stock'? They may be gifts, but they're human."

Zimrit rested his chin on his hand and dangled a troublesome green shard over the desktop. "What does it matter what I call them? Ever wonder what they call me? I'm nothing to them but a road to the consort's crown. That's all they think about while they're in my bed. That's what they'll think about the whole time they carry my baby—*if* we should get so lucky— the crown it'll bring them. I may be a lottery prize, but I'm human too."

"Act it, then."

King Zimrit's eyes held a great world-weariness. "I act the way you taught me, Megan. Ever since you came here, my life has been one long tutorial. I've been treated as an inconvenience, an unfortunate necessity, a chore to be tended to as quickly as possible so that it's gotten over with. When I was a child, there wasn't anything I hated more than spinach, but it meant a whipping if I didn't clean my plate, so I ate the spinach first; then I didn't have to look at it. Megan, is it nice to treat an old friend like spinach?"

I perched on the low arm of his bench. "Put that piece there." He did as I directed. "I never said I was going to love you, Your Majesty. You knew that, and you accepted it."

"Let's just say I knew it. What was it about me, Megan? Why couldn't you even *try* to love me?"

I stared at the ceiling. Zimrit had sent me an artist for our first anniversary, a painter who adorned every ceiling in the suite with allegorical pictures of Zimrit and me in the roles of various gods and goddesses in some of the earthier myths. Fair and Chosen had gotten hold of a ladder somewhere and added their own personal touches to the masterworks, notably a dock-strutter's fringed loincloth on every figure of the King.

Zimrit saw where I was looking. "Little demi-bastards," he muttered.

"Your Majesty—"

"Oh, please, Megan, come off that! We go back a long ways, long enough for you to call me Zimrit. Or Nitwit. That *is* what you used to call me, behind my back, not so?"

"Frankly, yes. You always behaved like such a nitwit. Correct me if I'm wrong, but does the royal crown somehow enhance intelligence? You don't seem to be quite so..."

"Asinine?"

"Beefwitted. Chuckleheaded. Numskulled. Choose the one that fits snuggest, but you *have* changed since you became King." (Indeed, I'd never have dreamt the old Prince Nitwit of Routreal days capable of the ambush that had torn Hyu from me five years past.)

Zimrit pulled me onto his lap and traced my cleavage idly as he answered. There was nothing remotely randy in the act, and at least he now had a more eye-pleasing quirk to substitute for playing with his nose.

"My brothers liked to say that they got the brains in the family."

"While you got the good looks?"

"No; just that they got the brains. And then my brainy brothers dined together and got most unfortunate cases of fatal stomach cramps, courtesy of the late King D'zent. Not only did he manage to sweep away all the intervening brothers between himself and our father's throne, but he took care of some of the younger ones as well, just to make sure none of them got any...ideas."

"Younger than you?"

Zimrit sighed deeply. "My royal father did not have such uncooperative concubines as I seem cursed with. Of course he didn't need to keep ordering new ones, so he had fewer to contend with and he often managed to sire more than one child on each lady. D'zent was only my half brother, but K'chel was of my full blood, my baby brother. I wish you could have seen him, Megan! So handsome! So bold! If there ever was a man born to be king..."

He pushed me off his knees and rubbed his eyes. Were those tears? He shoved my hand away roughly when I tried to confirm my suspicions.

"So D'zent poisoned your brother K'chel."

Zimrit's eyes were dry now, and burning with an ancient

hate. "K'chel was too wise to dine with D'zent. Other measures were called for. I begged K'chel to come live with me in Routreal, far from the intrigues of our father's court, but he laughed at me. He was a brave man, Megan, and he actually believed that the gods would protect the innocent. 'I have no desires for the crown, Zimrit,' he told me. 'I've told D'zent so to his face and advised him to save his money at the apothecary.'" Another sigh shook Zimrit's body. "He told him so. He told him so to his face. Two nights later he was found in the Royal Park, stabbed a dozen times or more. He was a long time dying, a painfully long time, but not long enough for me to see his loved face one last time."

He drew a long, ragged breath. "My brother! My poor baby brother K'chel!" This time there was no room to doubt the tears that flowed.

I took him tenderly into my arms and let him cry. I made all the old, reliable, useless gestures: smoothing his hair, wiping his cheeks, telling him it would all be all right. Of course I would have to pretend none of this had happened when he recovered himself.

And he did recover. He escaped my arms, thrust out his chest, and wiped his eyes on a rayed silk sleeve.

"And that, dear Megan, is why it pays to play dumb while you're burdened with a ruthlessly ambitious older brother. Time and opportunity—plus an obliging assassin—can add more to the mind than a Routreal education. Fools live longer in this world than wise men, or else why do we see so many of them in the streets?" He flashed his teeth. "Now that I'm King Zimrit, long may I wave, I can afford the luxury of wisdom. Besides, all kings are wise by common agreement."

"Maybe I should get you a good book for your birthday, in that case."

Zimrit raised his hands. "Let's not get carried away! Well, it *is* my birthday. I'll tell you what: You give me a nice, friendly birthday kiss and I'll grant you a royal boon. Anything you ask—*within reason.*"

I thought it through while I bestowed the requested kiss. "Freedom," I said. I saw his expression—a resounding NO in the making—and explained, "Freedom of the palace only, Zimrit. It gets boring in the harem. Besides, if you give me the freedom of the palace, I can go to the eunuchs' quarters to settle any administrative problems instead of having to wait for them to come to me. They always save the harem accounts for the last minute, even the emergencies, because they know we can't come around nagging them."

King Zimrit licked his lips. "Eunuch-nagging. You're just the woman for the job. By all means, Megan. In recognition of your long and willing years of service to my august and royal person—only a formal term, my dear—I, King Zimrit the Avenger, do hereby grant you the freedom of the palace, to come and go as you wish, at all times and in all places bounded by the outer walls of the royal enclosure, as you shall desire."

"And to this you affix your seal?"

"To that I shall affix my seal as soon as *you* trot around to the Scriptorium and have one of the pen-pushers down there write it up. Tell the Master of Scribes it's a rush order. Make sure you repeat it exactly as dictated, and—oh, yes—take this signet with you as pass and proof of my permission. It is *not*," he added with a sly smile, "the seal needed to legalize the document, so don't get any smart ideas about changing the wording and authorizing it yourself."

I looked artless. "Smart ideas? Me?" I played with my nose.

Zimrit launched me out of the harem with a companionable swat on the rump, the signet ring secure in my fist.

King Zimrit's modest home was the size of a barony—a poverty-stricken one, true, but even so the dimensions of the palace were formidable. I had been carried into the harem wing in a house-litter, which was a junior version of the street-use one that conveyed me from Sarogran's shrine. Intended for indoors only, the house-litter had no roof or side-curtains, so

I'd had a cursory tour of my new home before being confined to the harem.

That was five years ago. Even the best memory and the finest sense of direction can be blunted after five years, especially when in search of one particular cell within the regal hive. There was also the fact that none of my bearers or attendants had thought to point out the functions of the various rooms we passed. I might've gone right through the Scriptorium and never known it. As it was, I got lost almost at once, ended in the Day-Guards' wardroom, and was promptly mistaken for largess.

"Sarogran's spittle! What brings you here, sweetmeat?" A beefy, red-haired man-at-arms dropped the shield he was polishing and came forward to drool on my shoes.

"I beg your pardon. I seem to have made a mistake. This is obviously *not* the Scriptorium."

"The whatsit?"

"Don't you bother repeatin' it, lass!" cried a young sprig of gallows-bait. "Stonker wouldn't know what Scriptorium means if it up and raped his Mum."

"Like summun raped yours, an' her willin'?"

This went back and forth for some time, in similar vein. There were six Guards waiting to go on shift, and nothing to do with themselves but rail at each other, fiddle with their military equipment, or fiddle with their other equipment. I would have excused myself from their society, but the big redhead with the euphonious name of Stonker had barred my way.

"Now what's you want with the scribblers' room, honeypot? If you wants your prices listed pretty, Vardel there was once taught his letters."

"Step aside, please. I'm going to the Scriptorium on an errand for His Majesty, King Zimrit the Avenger." I showed him the signet ring in my hand.

The scholarly Vardel and one other Guard came up to examine my pass-token with Stonker. "That's genuine. Saw it on his finger once. Best let her go."

"Not so fast, there." Stonker held the bauble up to the light. "As one of His Majesty's most trusted Guards, it's my duty to check things out. You can just tell me what sort of errand His Majesty's got that a doxy's got to run for him when he's messengers aplenty. Messengers what *knows where the bloody Scriptorium's at*, what's more."

"Yeah, yeah, Stonker's right," said the third party. "Know what *I* think? It's His Majesty's birthday today, ain't it? And don't he give out treats to those as served him best all year?" The dottle-head nodded furiously. "That's why she's off there, Vardel. She's a thanks-gift from the King!"

"Well, stab my guts, I like *that*!" Vardel looked incredibly put out. "And all we Guards drew was a double measure of wine at mess tonight. What're those quill-ticklers going to do with a piece like this? What'd they do to deserve it, the mangy pack of gall-grinders?"

"Bloody waste." Stonker was sullen, which did nothing to improve his looks. "Half of 'em's eunuchs, an' half's too old, and half'd rather lay hands on her brother. You got a brother, titmouse?"

The stupid bastard chucked me under the chin and I bit him. The other five Guards laughed, which soured Stonker's mood even more.

"Screw the Scriptorium," growled Stonker. "I say she's *here*, and I say we bloody deserve her more'n them blindbats, and I say you don't waste what the gods give you!"

The approving roar from his fellows made my stomach sink. Stonker was already groping for me, and in a leap away from him I landed right in Vardel's grasp. He pinned my arms behind my back neatly as trussing a chicken. The rest of the Day-Guards circled in, smothering my screams and calls for help with their louder taunts and cheers as my flimsy harem garb fluttered away under Stonker's surprisingly deft touch. One of the men bound my gauzy halter on his head and did an extemporary rigadoon.

"What's all this?"

The jigger froze on one foot, the Guards snapped to attention, and Stonker nearly punched a hole in his own chest with the vehemence of his balled-fist salute. My rose-colored panties tangled in his fingers destroyed the smartly military effect he sought. I yanked up the nearest abandoned shield and used it to cover my nakedness before flouncing to the fore.

Dignity and self-assurance are everything to a woman, especially a naked one. I acted as if nothing major was amiss and near-rape a mere inconvenience to a lady of my inner resource. "Thank you, Captain," I said with a pert toss of my head. For the man who had come to my rescue wore the distinctive silver-crested helm of a Palace Captain, just like Cybelle's husband, but with the additional blazon of a battle-chief, and only men with a subsidary link to the royal bloodlines could claim that honor.

"On your way, whore. And don't come mollocking up to my men while they're supposed to be readying themselves for duty." He jerked his thumb at the door.

"Captain, if your dutiful men will return my property, I will show you proof positive that I am no man's whore. *I* am a *concubine*."

The Guards made a hasty pool of my clothes and the King's signet. I dressed behind the shield and explained my mission to the Captain, who was turning the color of a monkey's behind.

"Milady Megan, I'll tender you an apology spelled out prettily in longhand, and I'll use the guts of these motherless fishbuggers for ink." The Guards shook, even big Stonker, and a piercing, unmistakable smell informed me just how much fear the Captain inspired in his men. There would be a few changes of uniform needed before this company of Day-Guards was fit for active duty.

"Dear Captain, you know as well as I that manslaughter causes such a frightful row in the Accounting Department, what with survivors' benefits and all. If you will be kind enough to escort me to the Scriptorium, I'll be happy to forget this ever happened."

The Captain grunted. He seemed disappointed, but he agreed to my terms. Perhaps he'd wanted to practice his longhand. With a seasoned guide to convey me through the roofed labyrinth, I soon arrived at the doors of the Scriptorium.

Light fell in gilded harpstrings from a row of lancet windows closely spaced on the far wall of the Scriptorium. A score of lecterns were set out in five equal rows, each with its own high stool, and a larger, flat-topped desk stood just below the windows. Whoever sat there must be the Master of Scribes, for the desk was placed on a platform that would give any overseer entrenched there a fine view of his underlings' doings.

Someone was seated at the desk when I entered, working with gray head bent over an open ledger. Only six of the lecterns were likewise occupied, and it was tribute to the Master's iron discipline that not one of the young men busily scratching at their scrolls did more than give me a glance, harem flimsies notwithstanding.

Or else Stonker was right about scribes.

A seventh whisper of a man scurried up to intercept me as I started towards the Master's desk. "What are you doing in here, woman?" he demanded. I'd heard rabbits with louder voices.

I showed him the King's signet. The poor clod nearly dropped in his tracks. It was probably his thrill for the day; for the year, more likely. He was in front, in back, and beside me all at once, herding me fleetly through the grove of lecterns with small, ingratiating cheepings.

"Master! Master! Here's a message from His Majesty!" He touched the gray-haired man with all the cautious respect reserved for an aggrieved viper. When the Master of Scribes raised his head, my meek steersman jumped backwards.

So did I.

"Gods above." It was Hyu.

He looked me over once, sharply, soles to crown. "I will take the King's message in my cubicle, Melmut. Get back to work." The timid scribe scooted for safety. I was still standing there, hands pressed to my mouth in shock, when Hyu started away from his desk. The gray hair wasn't the only thing about him that had aged. He walked slowly, painfully, and his back was twisted into an abominable curve. He stepped off the platform and turned. "Well?"

I forced myself to follow him. The cubicle he'd mentioned was a closet right off the main workroom of the Scriptorium. No windows were here to let in air or light, just a tallow candle stuck on a spike above the bed. Even in full day, he had to kindle it or live in darkness. It filled the tiny room with the reek of melting fat.

"Will you sit?" His voice creaked and croaked, old too. Only his face had escaped, its handsome lines looking all the more pathetic in contrast to what the rest of him had become.

I sat on the bed. There was no chair, nor even room for one. Straw crackled in the mattress and stuck up through the thin ticking and thinner blanket. "Oh, Hyu—!"

He leaned his twisted back hard against the door, putting as much space between us as possible. My imploring arms were ignored. Presently I saw how silly I must appear and let them drop.

"This is a surprise, Megan, but hardly a pleasant one for either of us. It will prove even less pleasant if word reaches King Zimrit that you've been in my company. He might think I was trying to seduce you away from him again." He grimaced. "His Majesty's loyal servants would be happy to finish the punishment they started five years ago. Or would they? No. When the victim desires it, it's not punishment anymore."

"They did this to you? Those—wizards?"

"His Majesty's beloved Thaumaturges, First and Co-first. It was the only time in the history of our land that a King made a joint appointment to that position. King Zimrit the Avenger will be well remembered for it. Master Gath and Master Laban haven't acted in concert once since that night—apart from the occasional visit here to see how I'm getting on—but it's good to know they can work together should we need them."

The workings of magic were a mystery to me. My talent was still unknown, but I'd proved to myself that magic had nothing to do with it. Still, I thought I understood somewhat of how spells worked for those able to command them.

"If they haven't worked together since then ... why can't you lift the aging-spell they've put on you?"

Wheezes of laughter made the candle dance. "An aging-spell. Yes, yes, that's good, Megan, that's exactly what it is. Lift it, you say? Nothing easier. I could undo curses like this in my sleep when I was still a first-year pup at the University."

"Then why don't you? And—what are you doing as Master of Scribes? It's—it's humiliating. You could leave the palace, leave Stanesinn, leave the kingdom itself, and serve a worthier lord with your wizardry. Oh, Hyu, if you're lingering here on my account, don't. I gave King Zimrit my word of honor that I would stay his in exchange for your life. Don't waste that life waiting for me!"

He still hugged the wall, but I saw the old tenderness come back into his eyes. He shook his head slowly. "Do you know the first thing they teach us when we come to the University, my love? 'In magic as in life, all answers to Rule, Order, and Underlying Cause. In these you may find the keys to Power.' *Rule!*" One finger shot up. "No imperfect being may command the perfect forces of High Wizardry. *Order!*" A second finger joined the first. "If your foe is powerful enough to undo your weirdings, *first* undo your foe. Underlying Cause..." His voice trailed away and he sagged against the wall as the third finger uncurled. "Would you know? Shall I make clear the Underlying Cause of how you find me here? I must. I must, though I wish I could spare you this."

He undid the knotted cord holding his scribe's gown closed.

No imperfect being may command the perfect forces of High Wizardry.

"So you see, Megan, I am well placed here in the Scriptorium. I can no longer work any magic greater than a village herbwife's brewings. And I get along with my companions in spite of the fact that I was promoted to Master of Scribes over many of their heads. Eunuchs somehow don't seem to harbor as much envy as mages, not when it's one of their own being advanced so rapidly."

I watched without a word as he readjusted his clothes.

"It wouldn't suit to have anyone see me doing this out there, not after being closeted with you alone. All sorts of naughty rumors get started that way. Why, someone might even run to tell Master Gath and Master Laban, and then those worthy men would suffer doubts about the joint spell they used to—neutralize any threat from me. Neat work, isn't it? If they'd've added breasts, I could pass for a woman when I pass water. All done so prettily with their linked powers. Not like a surgeon's clumsy knife and crushers. But my opinion, my admiration of their technique, my testimony to how perfectly unsexed they've made me, mean nothing to them. If they come to doubt the efficacy of their spell, they might decide on more permanent measures. Though the gods know, what they've done is permanent enough."

Hyu finished tying his belt and reached for the door. "Put out the candle, will you? I'm not to request a new one for three more days." When I still didn't move, he finally came near, but only to scoop up a tear from my cheek and use it to pinch out the burning wick. "There. That's all it's good for. Dry your eyes, Megan. I stopped feeling sorry for myself years ago."

Somehow I left that terrible little hole they'd given him and dictated King Zimrit's orders granting me freedom of the palace. Hyu copied them out himself and made a great show of handing me the scroll with hearty congratulations. Only after I was halfway back to my rooms did I realize that he hadn't asked for any word of his daughter.

Zimrit was waiting for me, the tabletop all pieced back together again. "All I'll need is some glue, and—"

I interrupted his proud declaration by upending the desk a second time.

"Why did you do that?"

He made a good target. I lobbed his signet ring right at his face. It caromed off his left cheekbone, making him yelp. "Why did *you* do it?" I wailed. I hurled the scroll too, but rolled parchment has little momentum. Bits of malachite were everywhere, all of them sharp. I gathered up an armload and chucked them at the King. He took refuge behind the overturned desk, using a cushion snatched from the floor to repel the missiles.

"Do what? Put your desktop together? Did I know you wanted to—YOWP!" A lucky shot clipped the royal ear.

"I'm talking about what you did to *Hyu*! What your lousy Thaumaturges did to him! On your damned orders! My word wasn't enough for you, was it? I *promised* not to see Hyu again, but you had to be sure!" I'd been punctuating my accusations with slabs of malachite, but I'd run out. A celadon vase half my height presented itself as a possibility. I dumped out the flowers and flooded the floor with water, then tried hoisting it above my head for the kill.

Children, often he who loses the war is not the man who lacks weapons but the man who chooses arms too big for himself to manage. Just as often these same weapons turn on their wielders and destroy the would-be destroyers.

In brief, I slipped in the spilled water and fell on my back with the monster vase pinning me down. Heavy bastard.

King Zimrit peeked over the top of the table. I kicked my feet like a topsied turtle and cursed him three times through the Netherplane, getting in a lot of specifics about what he'd had done to Hyu and what I was going to do to him to even the score.

"If I take the vase off of you, will you hear me out?" he asked.

"If I *promise* to hear you out, will you believe it? Maybe you should get Master Gath and Master Laban in here to back you up. Maybe their magic can unsex a woman as well as a man! The gods know *you've* got that much power."

"I'm going to pretend I didn't hear that, Megan." Zimrit rolled the vase off and helped me up. Then he picked up the discarded scroll and headed for the door.

"Where are you going? Don't you have a few dozen high-flown lies to try on me?" I railed.

Very calmly Zimrit replied, "I'm going to get your freedom-of-the-palace order authorized. After that, I'll be back. Be prepared to come with me. Select one of your maidens to accompany you." He departed with a very peculiar look on his face.

I summoned my handmaids, but only one of them showed herself. The rest weren't to blame. They'd overheard the row, they picked up on the bloodthirsty note in my voice, and they thought more of their skins than their jobs. The one who did respond was a fawnlike slip called Twilla, and her place as one of my handmaids meant more to her than her life simply because it *was* her life.

When one of my five original attendants turned up pregnant during my first year as Zimrit's concubine and was dismissed (there is no demand for hand*matrons* in King Zimrit's harem), Cybelle brought me Twilla as a replacement. She was the orphaned country cousin of one of Cybelle's new kitchen cronies, and if I hadn't accepted her, she would be scouring pans— *if* the Head Cook didn't put her to work in his bed besides. She was only fourteen at the time, all knobby bones with a miraculously luminous skin stretched over them. The intervening years had done a lot for Twilla and her bones, padding them out in highly interesting ways. Cybelle did a tidy business taking bribes to deliver love-notes to her from her admirers in garrison and pantry and stable, but Twilla ignored them all.

Once I asked her why she was so aloof.

"I'm not," she answered. "I'm happy as I am. If I thought I could be happier than serving you, milady—happier with someone else—then I'd change. But for now, this life is enough for me."

Faithful Twilla ran to answer my summons, her long black braids flying. "How may I serve you, milady?" When I told her we'd be going with the King when he came back, the little bird was thrown into confusion. "*We* are? With His Majesty? Oh no, surely he means just you, milady. And after so long— Ah— What I mean is—"

"What *I* mean is *we* are going, and not for any reason connected with the King's bed. Though I wouldn't put it past the old ox to bundle in bunches. Snakes usually do."

Twilla bit her lip. "Milady, His Majesty is a good man, and he is our lord. It pains me when you speak of him that way."

I was going to speak about him in further terms that would have melted little Twilla's ears, but I didn't get the chance. The harem porter came in and announced that King Zimrit was waiting in the corridor, having a house-litter ready for us. I set my jaw and stalked outside, flung myself into the litter, and locked my arms. Twilla scampered in beside me and the bearers heaved, hoed, and set off after the King's litter, which was in the lead.

A page-boy trotted alongside and thrust a scroll into my lap. It was the freedom-of-the-palace order, duly sealed. A good spirit stayed my hands from shredding it, and another saw to it that Twilla took it into custody.

The two litters, flanked by a token force of Day-Guards, swayed through the palace corridors and joggled down flight after flight of wide steps. I had to unlock my arms and grip the side-strap for dear life or be thrown out headfirst when we made the descents. Twilla looked seasick, her ivory complexion getting yellow-green. I counted seven flights of steps we went down, and a dire thought struck me: The palace did not have seven floors.

Where were we going? Link-boys had joined our train. A musty, damp smell mingled with the smoke of their torches. It was a dungeon smell.

*I knew I shouldn't have thrown that ring at him. Or those
pieces of stone. What would it have taken to play patience and
poison Nitwit some fine day? But no, I had to lose my temper
and now he's going to lock me away. But—why did he tell me
to bring a handmaid along? Dear gods, if I've angered Zimrit,
at least save Twilla from sharing the consequences!*

The King's litter stopped at an arched, open doorway. It
was a strange prison indeed that had no bars on its gateway.
Beyond the arch I saw a smear of fire burning in the gloom
and smelled a variety of aromas—sickly sweet, pungent, acrid,
musky—that overwhelmed all the other subterranean effluvia.

King Zimrit got down from his litter and walked back to
mine. "Now if you can restrain yourself from picking up anything movable and pitching it at my head, there's someone I
want you to meet."

"Your headsman?"

"Megan, Nitwit is *my* title, not yours. I meant what I said
about keeping your hands to yourself down here. This is not
a man to annoy by disarranging his things." The King looked
at Twilla. "Is this the handmaid you selected?"

"This is Twilla." The girl lowered her head modestly.

"Hmmm. I hope she's as honest as she's pretty. She is going
to be sworn as a witness." He looked at her longer, with more
interest. "She should be *very* honest."

Twilla and I walked with the King under the black archway.
None of the link-boys or Day-Guards or pages came with us.
There was only the blur of scarlet flames to lead our steps,
and the farther we went into the chamber where that fire burned,
the more I wanted to turn on my heel and run away. Twilla
grabbed my hand, her fingers icy. Zimrit himself held my other
hand and urged us forward.

The darkness became a friend. I distinguished shapes in the
shadows, long tables and the gleam of burnished metal, the
softer shine of glazed ceramics. The fire outlined the belly of
a cauldron hung above it, the logs beneath crackling and falling

to ash in periodic sprays of crimson embers. Beyond the fire something rustled.

King Zimrit stopped at the edge of the blaze. Heat hammered at our faces, and the heady smells of the room were strong, rising every one from the seething depths of the black iron sea. Twilla crushed my hand, her grip mighty strong for such a willowy creature.

"Milady," she whispered in my ear. "Milady, if His Majesty means you any harm in this terrible place, I—I won't allow it." She removed her hand for a moment, then guided mine to feel the slender dagger she had carried in with her, all unsuspected.

"Where—? Put it away, Twilla," I hissed back. "Zimrit won't hurt me." Saying it aloud somehow confirmed it. Hard to explain how *sure* I felt about that, but I knew what I said was so. Twilla put up her smuggled blade.

The rustling sound became louder. An ancient man in thickly embroidered gold brocade robes sifted out of the shadows. His hair was a white beyond whiteness, the clear white of mountain light, a living torch that let us see plainly where we were. I had seen a similar room before, when I lived with Master Urion, but this wizard's lair was in proportion to Urion's as King Zimrit's palace was to Stepda's hut. Even when the mage called up a dazzling aureole of radiance to enclose us all, its light was insufficient to show the limits of his underground realm.

King Zimrit bowed low to the golden wizard, I did the same, and Twilla sank down on hands and knees to touch her forehead to the floor.

"Is this the petitioner?" The mage indicated Twilla. His voice recalled to me the winds that had soughed through the high vaults of Dragon's cave.

"No, Gracious One. This is the woman." Zimrit made as if to lead me forward, but I sidestepped his touch.

"Come nearer, fair one."

I did as he asked. Power hung on the wizard's being like

unborn thunder in a heavy summer sky. His eyes were nothing human, all glittering black glass, a wisp of violet flame burning deep within them. When we were a palmspan apart, my feet stopped.

"You are Megan," he said. "Megan, the despair of Master Gwyth. Megan, the love of Master Hyu. Megan the comfort of Master Urion. Many dealings with magic, magicless yourself. Ah, yes...yes..." He lifted his hand to my face, but seemed to think better of it and withdrew the touch. "I am S'rad."

My lips felt numb and clumsy when I spoke. "Master S'rad..." It couldn't be. The wizard of wizards, the rumored son of the goddess Esra, the immortal in a mortal's flesh who had guided heroes and wrestled the Midplane darkness before vanishing from the earth, no man knew how or where or why.

The apparition shook his head. "It has been long since any called me Master. I am S'rad no more. I dwell here, in secret, thanks to the honor of kings. I have laid a weirding over myself and my home that reveals our presence only to those who rule justly. Sometimes whole dynasties pass without knowledge of me. But when a worthy king commands, he knows that I am here. Then"—S'rad turned his glowing eyes on Zimrit—"it is his privilege to guard my secret or reveal it to the world."

"While I reign, you are safe from the world, Gracious One," said Zimrit.

S'rad continued as if nothing had been said. "It is also the right of the sovereign to call upon my powers three times in the course of his reign. King Zimrit has ceded the first of these to you. Even shut from the world as I am, with all the Midplane wonders to do my bidding, I was amazed to hear of the woman who could command such a gift from a man."

"A—gift?"

"Megan, my powers have been evoked to send plague-demons against invading armies. I have filled the wombs of queens with demigods and heroes at the behest of kings. I have forged swords that melted into legends and hurled curses that have sunk whole cities into the sea. The rule of my weirding grants a favored king three summonses, but ten years must elapse between each one. If I serve you now, King Zimrit may not call on my help again until the ten years have run."

I was speechless at the enormity of what Zimrit was offering me. I sought his face, but he only smiled encouragement and said, "Go on, Megan. I insist. And it *is* my birthday."

So I told the legendary wizard of wizards all that I could tell of my grief for Hyu. He heard me out and asked, "What is it you want then, Megan? King Zimrit's death? Demons called up to torture Master Gath and Mastern Laban? You could stretch their torments out indefinitely, for I see you wear a necklace any witch would envy." Master Urion's surviving vials trembled between my breasts in response to the mage's words, the swirled glass growing unnaturally warm.

"Yes, you could bring them to the point of death and back again with a touch of that chrism." S'rad pointed at the flacon of restorative oil. "Or strangle them in the growth of their own beards with a drop of that other. Will you have me guide you? Will you have me bring them here and bind them with King Zimrit for our pleasure?"

I started to speak several times, every time without success. Zimrit was staring at me, his look melancholy and resigned to whatever choice I would make. Then I became aware that Twilla was not groveling or hiding her eyes anymore. She was staring at me too, unspoken pleas on her lips. I knew what she would ask, if the awesome presence of the golden wizard hadn't left her as dumb as myself.

Mercy, children. Mercy and the clean heart it leaves.

"Gracious One . . . S'rad . . . if King Zimrit will swear to tell the truth in your presence, I'll hear what he has to say before I make my choice."

The mage shaped a wand out of the light around us. "I am not all-powerful. I cannot guarantee truth. If he speaks, he may lie. Remember that."

"He won't lie." Again I felt certainty in my heart. I addressed the King. "Was Hyu harmed on your orders, my lord?"

"All that I commanded was for Master Gath and Master Laban to tell him of your promise not to see him anymore. I also asked them to try obtaining a matching vow from him not to seek you out by any means, including magic." He made a bitter face. "My palace is large. Not even I know the faces of all those under my roof, apart from my daily attendants. When I didn't see Hyu in the magicians' quarters or haunting the Council table anymore, I assumed that he'd packed up and gone away like a good fellow. When would I ever go into the Scriptorium and see what they'd made of him?"

I closed my eyes. "Thank you, my lord. I believe you."

"Truth is one magic closed to wizardry," said S'rad. He looked amused. "There are others. Mortals must have something that is theirs alone, or they would sink into the dumb despair of cattle, ruled by herdsmen-mages. Knowing the truth, now what would you ask for from me, Megan?"

"Heal my Hyu."

The golden wizard frowned. "I cannot. If it were the casting of one wizard, I could, but spells that come from vinculation of more than one source of power require an equal measure to be undone."

"What? *You* can't undo the rag-ass spell of two hedge-wizards like Gath and Laban? Why *not*?" I folded my arms. "And I want to hear a better excuse than the Vinculation Sidestep!"

"Megan..." I could see the sweat on Zimrit's brow as he laid a cautioning hand on my shoulder. "I beg of you, remember you're speaking to Master S'rad...."

"Well, I might as well be speaking to Cybelle, for all the good it's doing me!"

"Let the woman be, O King." S'rad fanned his wand and filled the air with ghostly nymphs the size of doves. "She has a right to her anger. The rules of High Wizardry are strong and inviolate, but no one said they were just. Megan, although

I live here, alone, I have watched much of what happens above. You saw how the false Gath and Laban left your Hyu? Nothing of man remains. If it were not so, you yourself possess the means to restore him."

The wand aimed at Urion's vials.

"These? Master, tell me how—"

"*If* they had not been so thorough, I say, you might have returned Hyu to what he was. The elixir of growth can only increase the size of something already there. If there is nothing . . . nothing is increased. As for the oil of restoration, it too must have some token of what was there before, to enable the sympathetic magic to work."

"But only a drop—a scant drop made the Holy Twins' hair exactly as it was before they cut it off."

"But their amateur barbering left *some* tuft of hair still on their heads. I know. Master Urion's art was strong, his brewings strong enough to equal any of my own, but even we wizards cannot make matter where there is void, or life where death has come."

For a time there was only the sound of S'rad's cauldron bubbling. Then I said, "Take back the gift, Your Majesty. If it can't be used to help Hyu, I don't want anything else."

"Not even for Master Gath and Master Laban to be killed?" Zimrit couldn't credit his ears. "Take my word for it, Megan, the Gracious Master S'rad has been around long enough to have picked up on some mighty interesting and gradual methods when it comes to the extermination of household pests."

"I don't care. It wouldn't do Hyu any good."

King Zimrit took a deep breath and shrugged. "Gracious One, there is no reasoning with this woman. We won't take up any more of your time. Come along, girls." Twilla rose from her knees and dogged the King's retreat obediently. I would have followed, but a curl of brightness snaked itself around my elbow and detained me.

"Megan." S'rad was somber. "You are rare. Vengeance tempts more souls than gold. Is there nothing I can do for you?

Remember, even if I do nothing, the King has still squandered his summons. He may not return to ask my help again for ten years. Will you make use of what he has given you, or will you throw it away?"

The idea came to me so swiftly that I marveled. I spoke my request aloud, but some trick of S'rad's buried lair kept Zimrit and Twilla from overhearing.

"It's Zimrit's birthday, my lord. Make him happy."

"That's . . . all? When I could fill your lap with gold, or your hands with power? When I could grant you a kingdom of your own? An empire? A *world*? And is that all you desire? Make . . . Zimrit . . . *happy*?" The golden wizard covered his mouth and began to snigger. The snigger swelled to a chortle, the chortle to a chuckle, and the chuckle to a peal of maniacal laughter so hearty that Master S'rad flew apart in a burst of pyrotechnics that whisked me through a corner of the Midplane and dropped me off in my litter before an astonished King Zimrit and Twilla emerged from S'rad's dark gateway.

"How did you do that?" asked my sovereign.

"I've got connections."

"So do I. Move over." He wedged himself in next to me. "Ride in the royal litter, child," he directed Twilla. "It's less bumpity, and Megan and I have a thing or two to discuss."

Our discussion turned out to be a list of Things To Do to the perfidious Thaumaturges, Gath and Laban. The discussion was one-sided, more in the nature of a recitation on Zimrit's part. I never knew the man had such a creative bent.

"Hear anything you like?"

"The one where you flay them alive and roll them in honey before calling in wild bears was . . . tempting. Still . . . I don't know. Why don't we leave them alone? Let the gods decide. The gods have a real talent for screwing mortals."

"You ought to know."

I punched him in the arm. As we cleared the last of the seven flights, a messenger came rushing up to the King's litter.

"Majesty! Majesty! Woe and alas, horror piled on horror!

That ever human eyes should see such a ghastly sight! Master Gath and Master Laban are— Your Majesty . . . you've changed."

"Back here, fellow." Zimrit clicked his fingers while Twilla blushed and giggled over the messenger's mistake. "You were saying . . . ?"

The messenger had lost a lot of his eagerness to serve. It takes the wind out of your sails when you've got a juicy piece of gruesome news for your liege lord and you forfeit the shock value by blabbing it at the wrong person. Miffed and definitely cooler, the messenger said, "Master Gath and Master Laban are dead." His mouth snapped shut like a clam.

"That's it?" The messenger shrugged. "No details? How about that 'Woe and alas' you mentioned? And where do the piled-up horrors figure in this? Not natural causes, surely?"

"Well, I'll tell you if you insist, Your Majesty. Your two First Thaumaturges sort of . . . popped."

King Zimrit leaned on his elbow and gave the messenger a severe look. "Fellow, buds pop in springtime, pods pop in fall, but to my knowledge, Thaumaturges seldom indulge."

"Blood everywhere," the messenger riposted. A dreamy expression stole over his features as he recited the picturesque particulars of their demise. "Little bits of flesh stuck to the ceiling. No bone big enough to be called one—except the skulls, and they were charred black as ravens. The eyes still in 'em, but on fire and dribbling down until . . . eurrrh. Everything sizzling that wasn't already consumed by the flames of the abyss. A really revolting stench. You may have to order a fumigation. Your Council of Wizards suspects they went for each other in an all-out battle of sorcery. They were both the jealous type."

"Go back to my Council and tell them to give my Second and Third Thaumaturges direct promotion, then fill the vacant Third spot. Oh, and by all means commence fumigation." The messenger bowed and sped off. King Zimrit sank back into the pillows."All my pretty plans for nothing. Just like Gath and Laban to play spoilsports. Why did they have to kill each other? I'd have saved them the trouble happily."

I had a different theory on the timely deaths of Gath and Laban, one featuring a wizard who didn't like to leave a favor unfinished. If Master S'rad had decided to terminate Hyu's foes for me, what could I do? His debt to answer the King's first summons was paid in full, and my request for Zimrit's happiness would remain a joke to warm him in the intervening years, or centuries.

So if anyone was going to make him happy (and it *was* his birthday) it would have to be me.

It was time for the noonday meal when the King left Twilla and me within the harem precincts and went off for his lunch. All the debris of my second tantrum had been cleared from sight, including the desk. Zimrit didn't press his luck. The replacement was bolted to the floor and already was topped with a stack of scrolls, all marked NOW!

I browsed through them and said to Twilla, "To come back to this after such a morning! I *still* haven't arranged all the details to welcome the new concubines, and I *still* have to pick out the King's companion for the evening. And don't you think she'd better be something special, today of all days! And I *still* haven't got a proper birthday present for the King either."

"I made him something nice," said Twilla shyly. "I hope he likes it." She reached under her clinging skirts and showed me the dagger I'd only felt when we were in Master S'rad's domain.

I fingered the blade, one of those slim, flexible, deadly beauties that a lady can carry anywhere and still be smartly dressed. "*You* made this, Twilla?"

"Not the blade, milady. I had my cousin buy it for me when he went to market for the Head Cook. But do you see the enameling on the hilt? The King's device done in miniature. That's my work."

Children, to give is an art. King Zimrit had given me more than he knew that day. Hyu was still a eunuch, but at least he might have the satisfaction of knowing he'd been avenged, thanks to the King's generosity. Now it was my care to make a gift of gratitude to Zimrit; a birthday present of happiness.

"Twilla, what do you think of His Majesty?"

"He is . . . our lord, milady."

"Oh good, I was afraid you were going to say that the old goat was a fine figure of a man, well-struck in years, darkly handsome, and all the rest of the nitter-natter one hears."

"Milady! His Majesty isn't *old*!"

"Well, no one that young has the right to be so ugly."

"How can you call him ugly? He's—a very intriguing type."

I snorted. "You're a mere child. What sort of taste in men can you have formed? The young know nothing."

"I certainly know handsome from ugly, and King Zimrit is one of the finest-looking men—"

"Not that he hasn't every right to look like three kinds of gargoyle. After all he's been through—the tragedies in that man's life!"

I continued along the same crooked track and took sweet-natured Twilla for a lovely zigzag ride. Most of what I told her was true—truer than most people knew. The rumors of tavern and marketplace whispered that King Zimrit was behind the slaying of King D'zent, but I told Twilla why. People whispered that he was accursed because only one of the Holy Twins had blessed him, but I pointed out that brats will be brats and evil omens are made of stronger stuff than a brother-sister war. Many folk pointed to his childlessness as proof of the curse on fratriregicides, but I directed Twilla's attention to the fact that the gods were weird.

"With all their celestial battles and terrestrial affairs, you cannot rely on them to schedule every person's life in a way that makes sense, child. Or why else do we find so many babies born at the most embarrassing moments? Uncles a year younger than their nephews! Toddlers able to sit up late for their Mamas' wedding feasts! Crones who are sure they're out of all danger of conception one day, sewing swaddling bands the next! And King Zimrit is still young."

By the time I was done I had her dear, feeling heart abrim with all the tenderest emotions, all of them focused on her King. The gift needed just a pretty bow on top and it would be ready to send.

"Very well, very well, maybe His Majesty *is* as kind and good and generous and handsome as you argue, Twilla. But your gabble isn't going to help me decide who's to share his birthday-bed tonight. Tell me, do you think a blonde? A brunette? I don't think the new girls include any redheads. Come help me go over the list, dear. The gods know, it's not the greatest thrill on earth, but *someone's* got to sleep with the King."

Twilla burst into tears and ran out onto the balcony. I went after her. She took the handkerchief I offered and blew her nose, but she kept right on with the waterworks. Pretending innocence, I asked, "My good girl, why are you crying?"

Twilla snuffled. "I—I'm sorry, milady. But it's so—so *hateful* to think of!"

"What is?"

"They don't care about His Majesty. None of them do! I've heard you say so to Cybelle. They just want to bear his child, because the first to give him a son becomes his queen."

"Ambition is a wise courtesan's friend," I said prissily. "You'd be dreaming of a crown if *you* ever ended up in Zimrit's bed, and don't try telling me otherwise."

"I *would not*! King Zimrit is a good man, and he deserves better than he gets. *I* wouldn't bed him just because he's King! I'd go gladly. I'd be with him because I want him, not his crown. I'd—I'd—" Her face fell. "If I were ever so blessed, I'd ask nothing but to make him happy."

"'Blessed'? *'Blessed'?!*" I brayed. "All right, you silly chit, if *that's* your attitude, we'll soon show you the truth of things. *You* shall go to the King's bed tonight or I'm a marmoset!"

Twilla gasped. "Oh! Oh, milady! But I have no t-training

in—the arts of a courtesan. And I have nothing suitable to wear to come before the King. And I'm one of your handmaids, and handmaids are supposed to be virgins."

My foot tapped impatiently on the balcony tiles. "*I* shall teach you all the amatory arts I've ever learned. Which is *quite* a bit more than any of these so-called courtesans ever knew. As for what to wear, take a bath and that will take care of itself. And as for handmaids being virgins . . . that will also take care of itself."

I took the ring that marked me as Keeper of the King's Pleasure and jammed it onto her finger. "When the porter comes tonight, show him this. He'll know what to do. So will you. Now go into my study and start reading the books on the top shelf, especially the one bound in red calfskin. It is very filthy. Memorize techniques one through fifteen and illustrations twenty-seven through forty-one. Skip number thirty-four. It gives His Majesty a neck-crick. I shall be back to quiz you on this later. Now go!"

A smile of perfect rapture blossomed on Twilla's face. "Oh, *yes*, milady! I'll show you how wrong you are!" She flew to apply herself to the delights of higher education.

"Happy birthday, Nitwit," I breathed. I was on the point of tackling the scrolls atop my new desk when Twilla came swooping back down on me, cheeks flushed.

"Oh, milady, I nearly forgot! Here, this is yours." She dropped another scroll onto the desk and zipped out again, leaving me giddy.

I unrolled the scroll and grinned. It was my gage of freedom, and I'd nearly put its existence from my mind. I didn't really feel like attacking the piled paperwork just then. No, it was noontime, and for once in my life I was going to waltz down to the kitchens and take what I wanted for lunch, the Head Cook's planned menu be damned.

Oh, children, do you ever prize your freedom? Let it be taken from you, even for a short while, and you'll treasure it from then on. I sailed from the harem wing singing, blithesome and begging for a Day-Guard to try challenging me. I whipped the scroll open several times as I swung along, just for practice, so I'd have the proper fillip of the wrist down pat when some luckless armored clod should demand to know by what right I roamed the halls.

No one stopped me. I called it damned lax security and vowed to look up the fire-eating Captain I'd met earlier, just to give him a piece of my mind about proper distribution of Day-Guards. All that scroll-snapping, wasted.

I did get the satisfaction of being challenged when I reached the great kitchen. Although my suite at first boasted its own, there was no substitute for the high quality of goodies issuing from the main cookworks. The Head Cook was a lecher and a sot, but his way with roasts and sauces came from the gods. I converted my private kitchen into a library after one year and had all my meals sent up from the palace kitchens thereafter.

"Hello, my good man," I greeted the Under-Cook, who waved a ladle at me. "What's for lunch?"

"Rabe and radishes, what ill wind brought you? Get yourself back to the harem, courtesan, or I'll whip you to a meringue!"

I flipped open the scroll. "Mutton and mushrooms to you, saucy. *I* have the King's own order for freedom of the palace, besides being head of the Royal Harem. And I don't care for garlic, so what's cooking?"

The Under-Cook lowered his ladle with bad grace. "We've got lamb stewed in cornmeal mush, pickled whole sardines in tomato aspic, boar's head with calf's-foot jelly, and liver-and-lights tart, garnished with kidney pudding. I recommend the sardines. They look honest, but the boar's head's got a shifty look about the eyes today."

"Uh . . . anything else?"

The Under-Cook was nettled. "Cold sliced meats and cheeses in the back pantry. And if our noontime spread—what's good enough for His Majesty's own birthday!—doesn't suit milady's finicky tongue, you can go back there and help yourself."

"Give me a loaf of bread and a pannikin of watered wine

and you've got a deal. His Majesty would eat live mice with cheese sauce so long as they're not garnished with spinach."

The Under-Cook fetched my order and pointed me at the back pantry. This was a small, cold room used to store cooked foods that would keep a day or so and could be fed to the pigs or the apprentices when they went bad. He lit me a candle to dine by, shut the door on me, and wished me a good appetite.

As I sat there dismembering a leftover pheasant with cold lingonberry dressing, I thought I heard him coming back, and not alone. Perhaps the Head Cook had heard about my presence, my scorn for the set lunch, and had decided that freedom of the palace did not equal freedom of the pantry. From the jangling that accompanied the two pairs of footsteps, it sounded like the Head Cook had summoned military backing for my eviction.

I hugged the plundered pheasant to my breast. "Don't worry, my darling, nothing shall ever come between us," I murmured. I ripped off a leg and wolfed it, just to show I cared.

The footsteps stopped outside the pantry door. I braced myself for the assault, clawing off hunks of white meat and stuffing them into my mouth. There was still another pheasant waiting docilely on the shelf. He should not die in vain. I seized him and dragged him into hiding behind a keg of salt herrings after blowing out the candle. To the barricades! We were beseiged! No prisoners! Lingonberry dressing would flow like water when the minstrels sang of the Battle for the Back Pantry someday!

I choked on a gob of pheasant and had to spit it out. So much for heroics. So much for the Battle for the Back Pantry too, for whoever was on the far side of the door was making no move to shout me out of my comfortable nook. I considered emerging from behind the herrings, but just then the knob turned and two men entered, shutting the door fast behind them.

Neither was the Head Cook or his shirty assistant. However, I had been right about calling in the military. One was in the armor of the Guard, polished until it gleamed even in the dark.

"Is this place safe?" asked the soldier. I recognized his voice. It was the horse-crest Captain.

"As safe as any," came the reply. In the windowless back pantry I could only see vague outlines of the speakers' shapes, and this one was warped, twisted, bent, and broken. Even so, he was still my Hyu. "For those who speak murder."

Murder? *My* Hyu? I would have to tell him that Master Gath and Master Laban were dead already, before he spent any coin to have this enterprising Captain slay them. I didn't know the rules of the Palace Guard allowed freelancing.

"You are bold, Master Scribe. We shall need boldness to-night."

"Boldness second, intelligence first. Keep your voice low, Captain Drey. The kitchens may be deserted while all hands run to serve the tyrant his noon meal, but one never knows when a scullery wench or potboy will be sent back to fetch a forgotten dish. If we are discovered, we have simply come here for a snack and a friendly chat. Here. Have a wedge of cheese."

I heard the men chew and swallow. "Not bad," Captain Drey allowed. "A trifle hard and rindy, but better than what we see in the soldiers' mess. The King dines well if this is the quality of his leftovers."

"The King dines for the last time tonight," said Hyu darkly. I felt as if someone had run an icicle through my heart. "We have borne our separate humiliations too long, Captain Drey. Your blood is as good as Zimrit's. Why shouldn't you rule in place of that monster? What I am is all his doing! I've hated him, I've sworn he would pay for my lost manhood, and his lap-dog mages too, but I let the years go by without acting. I know I put off joining your scheme with this excuse or that many times."

"I knew you'd come around, though." Captain Drey sounded confident. "You're the one man in all the palace with reason enough to hate him so deeply and so well. That's what I staked my skin on: your hate. You could've betrayed me a dozen times. It'd mean a fat reward for you, and a confession racked out of my bones. Any one of those times you delayed might've been your chance to turn on me."

"I'm no traitor!" Hyu snapped. "I've wished Zimrit dead from the day he destroyed my life. Yes, I wanted him dead, but I was once a mage, and we do not take life lightly. Then, today, I saw a face so well loved, so dear to me—and so full of nothing but pity where there used to be love. Zimrit dies tonight, Captain Drey. I am your man."

"Well said, Master Scribe." A meaty smack in the dark told me they had clasped hands. "We could not accomplish our goal without you. When the King retires, two Guards are always posted outside his bedchamber. Three additional pair are stationed throughout his suite, but none are permitted beyond those doors."

A glint of whiteness told me that the Captain smirked. "His Majesty craves privacy above security. Let him. Inside, he will be lying abed with his courtesan for the night, but we needn't worry about a girl. I shall arrange things so that the bedchamber Guards tonight are myself and one other trusted conspirator."

"But what about the other six Guards in the King's apartments? Are they your men too?"

"They will be," said Captain Drey grimly. "When this is done, they'll be mine. Until then, a plot with too many conspirators is bound to be discovered. Better to depend on three good men—and you one of them. You must procure an official document from those presently stored in the Scriptorium and come pounding at the outer doors of the royal apartments, demanding to see the King on vital business. I'll make a show of examining the document and escorting you into the King's presence. Otherwise, my man and I wouldn't have a plausible excuse for leaving our posts."

"A show for the other Guards. I see. So you and your man will take me in to the King, and then..."

"Yes, my friend. Then." I heard a hard, slithering rasp. A

dagger was being drawn. "Strap this inside your robes. I'll also make a great display of searching you for weapons, but..."

"But you'll be careless." They laughed. Hyu was the first to stop. "This man of yours... can you truly trust him? It's a great business to kill a King when one is not a close personal relation."

"Don't worry, Master Scribe. My man Stonker's dead loyal to me, and I've filled his head with notions of a better government to come after the King is dead. He reads, does Stonker. Astonishing the amount of claptrap written by folks about ruling themselves, common property, free choice of leaders. Faugh. But if it gives us a faithful arm to serve our purposes, let 'em write! Let 'em read! Pass the cheese."

More chomping followed. Finally Hyu said, "I must return to the Scriptorium. When shall I come to the King's door?"

"Stonker and I take our posts two hours short of midnight. Let's call for midnight, then; a fitting hour."

"Very fitting." Hyu gave his farewell and left the darkened pantry, after first scouting the outer room cautiously. Captain Drey lingered to gulp a third piece of cheese.

"Here's to you, Master Fool." He chuckled and made an end to the cheese before leaving. I hoped he got the leadgut.

Master Fool.

The golden horse's head blazed in my memory. If King Zimrit was slain, and no heir of the direct line left thanks to D'zent's family dinners, war would determine who took the crown. A fine opportunity for a man already in command of seasoned troops like a host of Palace Guards, even better if you had some of the blood royal in your veins.

Stonker, *read*? Stonker could hardly speak. The full scope of Captain Drey's plot was simple to unravel, if you knew the real Stonker; as Hyu did not; as I did. Dead loyal to his Captain, yes, that was true. Dead scared of him. He'd do whatever Drey required. And what would that be?

To kill the faithless eunuch scribe who killed his King. To kill him quickly, before he could blurt any word of whose orders were behind the crime. Hyu would play Drey's cat's-paw, doing all the dirty work of regicide and being slaughtered on the spot. It would give the Captain infinite credit with the people when he came to take the vacant throne. As Zimrit himself discovered, nothing pleases the commoners more than royal murder swiftly and justly avenged.

I untangled my legs from the pheasant bones and gave Captain Drey a good head start before I thought it safe to leave the pantry. Fear makes as good a palace guide as any, and fear took me straight to the Scriptorium with no wanderings along the way. I waggled my pass at the scribe who tried to question me and shoved him aside in my rush to reach Hyu's desk.

"Hyu, I have to speak to you!"

He looked up from his work and glared. "What do you want? I'm busy."

"Busy, and I know what with!" I hissed. "You've still got a crumb of cheese on your chin."

Hyu went pale. He slammed shut the ledger he was working on and took me into his cupboard in silent haste. "All right, Megan." He lit the half-gone candle and waved me towards the bed, checking the doorlatch to make sure we were private. "What do you *think* you know?"

"I *think* I know what you're giving the King for his birthday, and I *think* he won't like it."

Hyu looked edgy. "What do you know of this? Is your talent for visions?"

"Bugger my talent. It's for midwifing sheep, far as I know. Never mind how I know about your plot, I *also* know what Captain Drey's got in store for—"

Hyu's hand darted out like a snake, nabbing a tiny clay pot from a shelf beside the door. He dashed the contents in my face, a fine blue dust that stole my voice and made my head swim. "Sleep, my love," the former wizard said. "I can still concoct a drowse-dust that will keep you quiet until the deed is done."

I coughed and tried to shake off the powder, but it was

already taking hold. My eyes closed against my will, and my body would not respond to any command but the overriding claims of sleep. Hyu's face blurred and I fell over the lip of the world.

I woke up in Hyu's miserable bed, the blanket tucked in around me. The candle was still burning, but it was almost consumed. That much was a hopeful sign that I hadn't been asleep all that long, else I would have woken up in the dark. I opened the closet door by degrees.

Only one of the lecterns in the outer room was occupied. A mirrored oil-lamp burned in a bracket atop the desk, giving the scribe light to work by. There were other, dimmer lamps hung at intervals in the room, but no natural source of light. Night filled the high lancet windows.

I was about to make my presence known when my toe nudged something. It was the guilty clay pot Hyu had used on me, some of the blue dust still clinging to the inside. I slipped it into my sash for future reference. I had the feeling this would be a night for future references.

Yawning loudly and conspicuously, I stepped out of Hyu's closet. The scribbler jumped and whirled. "What are you doing here? Where did you come from?"

"I've just had the most delicious nap," I replied pleasantly, winding up the yawn. "Your Master of Scribes told me I could wait in his closet while he took care of the King's order, but I made myself so comfy that I fell asleep. Do you happen to know the time?"

The scribe climbed down from his stool and went to study the large clepsydra set up in an alcove behind Hyu's desk. "Three and a half hours of midnight."

"Oh dear! That can't be! I came to see the Master right after noon meal. His Majesty will be furious! Look here, he even issued me a freedom-of-the-palace scroll so that I could bring it to him as soon as it was done." I waved my pass in his face, rattling the parchment loudly. "Where is the King's order? I must take it to him at once!"

The scribe caught the germ of my pretended panic. "What order, milady?"

"The order was for a plan of the palace, a copy of the most detailed one on file. His Majesty means to start construction of a new wing tomorrow. *Tomorrow!* He's sending for his architects to meet with him three hours before first light! If he wakes up that early for nothing, he'll have a fit. A royal fit is not a pretty sight, my good man."

"No, I suppose not." The scribe chewed his thumb nervously. "Do you think the Master took the plans to the King himself, while you slept?"

"Gods, how should *I* know? He might have . . . but what if he didn't? Maybe he thought I'd wake up sooner. Maybe he gave them to an underling to pass on to me when I woke, then forgot to wake me. Heavens, if that's so, I won't be the only one to pay for this. Wholesale slaughter of scribes! Quills through your hearts! Mass drownings in the ink-vats! Pyres of parchment! Oh woe! Lackaday! Whatever shall I do! Wherever shall I go?" I commenced pacing up and down, wringing my hands and moaning. If done properly, it aggravates and unnerves most men—even eunuchs—until they will do *anything* to get you to stop.

"Milady, *please*—!" The scribe seized me by the shoulders. "Let me help you."

"You can make me a copy of—?"

"Milady, there's not enough time for that if His Majesty wants it so soon. But I can let you have the original, if you promise to return it safely and *not* to say how you got it."

I kissed his hands, which flustered him, and a flustered scribe moves faster. I had the palace plans in hand before you could blink.

"Now, let's see," I said to myself after finding a secluded niche in the corridor where I could study the map at leisure. "Guards' barracks . . . Day-Guards' wardroom—yes, I remember where *that* is . . . Armory . . . Quartermaster's stores . . . Aha! Night-Guards' wardroom."

This time I gave thanks to the gods that I met no one in the corridors to challenge my presence. At that hour, most of the life in the Royal Palace was tucked away, waiting for first light. Guards did not patrol the halls at night, which was wise when you stopped to think of it. In a palace so rambling and huge, it would take several legions of armed men to patrol it at all efficiently. Instead, the commanders placed what men they had to keep watch over certain strategic doors, gates, and windows. If a nightjack wanted to roam the halls or prowl rooms holding nothing precious—like the Scriptorium or the Petitioners' Heel-Kicking Suite—let him. But venture near important places like the harem, the Treasury, or the wine cellar, and let him beware.

Most of the rooms having to do with the military were grouped in one section of the palace, the exception being the Day-Guards' wardroom. It's only theory, but I surmise it was placed closer to the heart of daytime palace activity so that the men wouldn't have to go so far to reach their posts, thus giving them fewer opportunities to mess up their smart ceremonial appearance. Night duty, being less visible, let them wait closer to their barracks until their shift was summoned.

I found the Night-Guards' wardroom and paused far enough from the door so that if anyone emerged suddenly, I could pretend to be just passing by. Bit by bit I crept nearer, ears sharpened for the sound of voices within. I heard Stonker's growl and two others. A few steps more and I could distinguish their words.

"—glad my shift's done. Where you headed for, Stonker?"

"I pulled the King's crib tonight."

A low whistle. "What you'll hear! The wench they send up for the birthday night's supposed to be a wonder!"

"Lotta good that does me." Stonker spat loud enough for the report to carry. "All I know is, Drey put me on double duty today. By rights I should be abed. I done my work by daylight, but *he* comes round after evening mess and tells me I'm to stand watch with him at the King's door."

"Hard luck."

"Bastard hard. Me an' the boys on second day shift got into a little hoorah with one of the King's women—"

"Bugger my uncle! And you're still *alive*?"

"Nah, nah, we didn't do nothin'. All a big mistake, damn the pox-faced doxy black and blue. How'd we know she wasn't a barracks whore and not a harem wench? Running errands for the King!" Stonker hawked and spat again, this time with a richly phlegmy splat. "So I guess this double shift's my punishment. But it ain't fair for him to fix it on just me, and the others snoring like hogs this minute! Damn."

The third voice laughed. "We'll save you a snore or two when we're abed as well. Come on, Dennic." Metal rattled and booted feet receded. My chart showed a second door to the wardroom that connected directly with the royal barracks, very neat and convenient. When I heard nothing more, I decided it was time to make my entrance.

"Hello, Stonker," I uttered deep in my throat. My hips did figure eights with every step. "Remember m—uh."

Cowflop.

Stonker wasn't alone.

I should have peeked before I pounced. Just because you overhear three voices, never assume there are only three people in a room. Someone may be sulking, or sleeping, or simply sitting there with a finger up his nose. Captain Drey had mentioned three pairs of Guards besides himself and Stonker assigned to the King's apartments, and there they sat, all six.

There they sat until they saw me, that is.

"Name of a northman! A whore!"

"Hold off, hold off," counseled Stonker, stepping between me and his comrades. "Set your pikes easy, men. This is the same bit what got me pulling doubles today."

"What, the King's woman?" The six gentlemen sat down in unison and looked at the ceiling, twiddling their thumbs. Stonker appointed himself spokesman, as having on-the-job experience when it came to dealing (wrongly) with me.

"Milady, how may we serve you?" He bowed awkwardly

and did his best to sound urbane, but it came out servile. "Lost yourself again?"

I looked at the six soldiers. I looked at Stonker, who was equivalent to three more. I looked heavenward to thank the gods for small favors: Only the men who guarded Zimrit's rooms this shift were there, not the whole damned midnight garrison. Finally I looked within myself and took stock of my inner resources before making the ultimate decision.

It was no use.

It had to be.

There was no other way.

I took a deep breath and began to sing:

"Today's a very happy day, and all the kingdom through
We're wishing good King Zimrit, 'A fine birthday to
    you!'
But 'cause you're such good soldiers, and Zimrit's feel-
    ing pleasant,
He's sent me here to be for you a royal thank-you pres-
    ent."

I let the ensuing silence thicken until I couldn't stand it. "Well?" I demanded. Time was running out, and I wanted to get this over with before I lost my nerve. "Who's going to unwrap me?"

"Don't you believe her, men!" shouted Stonker. "She's mad 'cause we had a bit of harmless fun with her today, so now she's gonna wait 'til we do summat bad and then scream the Captain down on us."

"I would not," I said. "Of course, if *you're* the suspicious type, you don't have to have your share of me. No one has to. I won't twist any arms. I do better"—I batted my eyelashes brainlessly—"with other members."

"Bloody balls," snarled one of the six Guards, rising to the occasion. "I'll take my chances!"

"Are you mad?" Stonker was still resolute. "We're on duty

in the King's apartments soon. How can you have the whore—
if what she's saying's true—which it isn't!—and reach your
post on time?"

"I'll tell you this," I said. "You won't do it if you jaw the
time away. Any of you want me, I'm here and I'm ready. But
I'm no barracks whore, and I don't perform for an audience."
I dragged the pads from the wall-benches to the floor for a
mattress. "One at a time, the rest wait their turns, one to a
customer, and you can head for your duty-post as soon as your
turn's through. And you'd better head off when you're done,
because if I catch one of you trying to get second helpings,
that's when I *will* scream. March!"

Stonker folded his arms and took an unmoving stance, but
six more willing Guards surrounded him and mumbled warn-
ings and threats until he shuffled out the door with the rest.
That's democracy.

It wasn't so bad, really. I'd had times far worse than this
while at Madam Glister's in terms of traffic alone, and I'd
learned various skills that speed things along. When the sixth
man came to me, I asked, "Did you mind waiting?"

"Ah, no, sweetheart. You're worth waiting for."

"That's nice to hear. Usually the last man in line feels
cheated."

He chuckled. "That'll be old Stonker, then."

My eyebrows went up. "Changed his mind about me, did
he?" (I thought he might.)

"When he didn't hear you scream with any of the rest of
us, he came around. Give us a kiss and hurry it up. We're due
on post double quick." Double quick was what I gave him.
(And when you've six plus one to service in under an hour,
double quick's your watchword.) He groused about it as he
beat down the hall towards the King's chambers.

It was Stonker's turn.

I curled my legs under me and patted the pads. He sat down,
but he still regarded me askance. Even naked, I made him
nervous. Maybe I made him nervous *because* I was naked?

Men are a mystery. I wound my arms around his neck and drew him down into a long kiss.

"That's more like it." Stonker grinned, finally at ease.

"So's this," I said, and I rammed the clay pot of drowse-dust onto his nose.

Stonker inhaled strongly, ready to roar, but I shall never know what names he intended to call me. He blinked, he sniffled, he yawned, and he keeled over.

I had him undressed in a trice. Funny how all my old training from the House of Prayer came back to me. Stripping unconscious clients was an additional service, no extra charge, all found, that every girl acquired early. When I had him naked, I used his shortsword to gut the bench-pads. Hunks of horsehair were everywhere.

Stonker was a big man, but he rolled easy once you got him going. I mummified him in the pad-ticking and stowed him under the benches, where his sleeping body looked like a roll of canvas some careless workmen had abandoned.

Stonker, as I have already stated, was a big man. So you may imagine what sort of fit his military trews and tunic made on me. The sandals weren't so bad, being of the flat-sole and rawhide-strip variety. I could tie them on tightly enough to pass casual inspection. I slashed off the excess thong and used it to tie Stonker's billowing trews at my ankles, slipped the tunic on, and belted it.

Ugh. There was just too damned much material, belt notwithstanding. Fortunately, the gods provide. I stuffed my new uniform with my old harem clothes, then filled out my torso with the horsehair I'd removed from the bench-pads.

Aaaaaagh. And you may quote me. But it wasn't a night to be thinking of my own comfort. I twisted my hair into a topknot and jammed it under Stonker's helmet, the unadorned nose-guard and cheek-pieces masking everything of my face except my mouth and eyes.

I consulted my palace map before racing for the King's quarters. They weren't far, but when you're wearing prickles next to your skin, ten paces is agony. The Guards standing at the ready at Zimrit's outer doors crossed their pikes to bar my way, but I wasn't having any of it.

"Let me pass, damn you! Captain Drey's waiting!" I hardly recognized my own voice. I meant to deepen it, but the bedevilment I was enduring made me sound like a tavern-tough looking for a knife fight.

"You? But Stonker's the one who's—"

"Stonker's pigging it with a whore in the wardroom, and my Lieutenant caught him at it! He's for a flaying, if Drey don't kill him outright. And if you don't let me through to take his place on duty, you can join him!"

The pikes uncrossed themselves with magical speed. I swaggered into the King's apartments (you have to swagger when you've got a clump of horsehair chafing your thighs) and gave the same spiel to the other four Guards on duty until I was facing Captain Drey himself.

I cut a smart salute. My padded chest absorbed the impact of my balled fist with a muffled *whump*.

"You're in fine shape, for a stripling," said the Captain. He was smiling. "So, Stonker was having his fun after all?"

"Yes, sir. Disgusting sight, sir."

"No worse than what I've been overhearing in there." He indicated the door to the King's inmost room. "The pair on guard before us told me they never heard the like in all their time on bedroom duty. Must be a right little fireball the King's drawn tonight."

"Disgusting, sir, as you say, sir."

Captain Drey's mouth curved higher. "You're young to be a Guard, but old enough to be a prude. I trust your loyalty's as strong as your morals?"

"Loyal, sir, yes, sir." I walloped my chest again.

"With a strong arm to defend your King?"

"The King, sir! May the gods protect him."

"Then you'll do. What's your name and division, lad?"

I thought quickly, recalling all Cybelle had ever let drop

about the section her husband commanded. "Raf, sir, of the Tigers."

"The Tigers, hey? Battle-blooded. You'll do. Take your post there." He thumbed at the left jamb of the King's bedchamber.

As I stood there, sweat trickling down my spine and the backs of my legs, a pikestaff held one precise inch from my nose, I had plenty of time to think. Captain Drey hadn't panicked when Stonker didn't show. That was hardly what I'd expect of a man who had so much riding on tonight's plot, when one of his coplotters was absent.

Which meant that Captain Drey had told Hyu more than one lie in the pantry. Stonker wasn't any more a conspirator than Cybelle's unborn babe. He was just a soldier with a strong arm and an unquestioning mind. That was all Captain Drey needed for his plans, besides a dupe.

A dupe to kill the King, a strong and loyal Guard to kill the dupe, and a blameless Captain Drey to step onto the throne, with no one left to tell that he had been the real hand on the dagger's hilt. You had to admire the man. If his victim had been someone other than Zimrit and his dupe someone other than Hyu, I might have congratulated him on the neatness of his intrigue.

Ho, ho! But wait until I unmask his plot! When Hyu comes in, I'll just step forward and yell for the other six Guards to—

To what? To search Hyu and find a dagger on him? To tear off my disguise and have Captain Drey shout the orders for his men to cut down two traitors? The disgruntled, neglected First Concubine and the vengeful eunuch, in league to slay their lord; a classic situation, told and retold in minstrels' ballads often enough for every Guard there to know it by heart.

They also knew the classic ending: The King's heroic men-at-arms leaped to his defense and trampled the conspirators to mush.

I would have to think again. While I was thinking, a knock

boomed at the outer door. One guard opened it from the hall side and stuck his head in.

"Captain Drey, sir, there's the Master of Scribes here to see His Majesty. Says it can't wait 'til morning."

"Bring him here. We'll soon see what can't wait." Captain Drey gave a fine performance. Hyu was ushered in and subjected to what looked like a brutally thorough search. Drey barked question after question, which my darling fielded smoothly, until the Captain's feigned wrath subsided.

"Very well, Master Scribe. Follow me. Soldier! Lay aside your pike and come behind."

"Sir!" I stamped the pikestaff butt once against the floor and tilted it to the wall. I also made a grandstand play of checking the draw of my shortsword, which pleased Drey mightily, then fell in behind Hyu as we all marched into King Zimrit's bedchamber.

We passed through an anteroom where a pink alabaster lamp glowed like a star caught in a seashell. The King's bed stood high on a serpentine platform borne on the backs of four white jade bears with emerald eyes. Tiers of round steps led up to the silk-hung royal bed, a breeze from the unscreened open balcony stirring the pearl-strewn curtains.

We climbed the steps in silent single file. At the top, Captain Drey stepped aside gallantly to give the supposed messenger the honor of waking the King. Hyu reached his hand into his sleeve, ostensibly to remove the document. The dagger crept into the moonlight with the fearful, unreal slowness of an evil dream. Hyu held it high and ripped the bedcurtains aside.

"Now . . ."

"Zimrit, wake up!" I shouted. At the same time I hooked my arms around Hyu's neck and yanked backwards. He gagged and gurgled, arms flailing, the dagger clattering down the marble steps.

"Help! Help!" yelled Hyu as reflex took over. "Murder!"

"Murder?" A sleepy Zimrit poked his head through the

curtains and saw me wrestling with Hyu. Captain Drey cursed as only a soldier can.

"Save yourself, my lord!" I cried, still fighting Hyu.

"Whuffor?" inquired my King.

"You damned moron!" Hyu twisted his hunched shoulders and threw me off. I leaped back on top of him, but Stonker's helmet soared after the dagger to clong off one of the jade bears and out of the battle. My hair fell into my eyes and I tussled blind.

The door to the royal suite slammed open. Drey's six Guards rumbled through to witness the brawl atop the bed-site. Zimrit was rubbing his eyes, not sure whether this was a very good dream or a very bad awakening. Captain Drey's curses cut off short. As Hyu and I struggled, I used one hand to shove my hair back. That was when I saw the Captain's hawklike eyes whip from the approaching Guards to the King to us and his hand drop to the hilt of his sword.

"Help here! Help ho!" shouted Drey, drawing his blade. "They've murdered the King!"

"But I'm perfectly all ri—"

Zimrit never finished voicing his objection.

Drey's blade lashed down.

They've murdered the King! Shoot your arrow first, then draw the target-circles round it, that was Captain Drey's intent. In all the chaos, who was to say later, when questions were asked and faulty memories probed, that Hyu hadn't stolen the Captain's sword, killed the King, and only then dropped the bloody weapon when I grabbed him from behind?

And doughty Captain Drey had acted boldly to reclaim his honor by wrenching the sword back and killing the murderer with the weapon of his crime.

I screamed to match the victim's death-cry as the silken bedcurtains billowed out, monstrous wings in the semidarkness. Then my scream turned to a startled gasp, for Hyu broke my hold a second time and flung me over the edge of the

marble steps. I rolled to the bottom shrieking. My head struck
the leg of a writing desk and I saw bursts of painful light.

The blow stunned me, but not to unconsciousness. My head
whirled as I sat up and tried to knock my eyes back into focus.
My tumble down the steps hadn't broken anything, thanks to
the padding in my tunic and trews, but by the same token I
was raw as a skinned rabbit from being rolled about in the
thorny stuff.

"Megan?" Warm arms enfolded me. Hyu's gentle hands
smoothed my hair out of my face. "What are you doing here?"

"I don't think I'll have the chance to answer. See there." I
pointed, and a pike-blade pointed back. Two of Captain Drey's
Guards stood over us, their weapons kill-set.

"Get up."

"A minute?" I tore open Stonker's tunic and ripped out the
horsehair pads. I started to give the trews the same treatment
when one of our warders barked:

"That'll do!" His voice cracked oddly. If the fresh air hadn't
felt so good on my bare chest I might have wondered why.

The royal bedchamber was brighter. Extra Guards had been
summoned, and servants bearing torches. There were even one
or two ministers of state, roused from slumber, who were
standing around in their night-caps and shirts, rubbing gummy
eyes. I didn't know it was possible to mobilize so many people
so speedily in the dead of night. The milling crowd parted to
let us pass as the Guards marched us back up the steps to the
King's bed.

A body lay on the platform under a discreetly pulled silk
sheet. But though it concealed the dead man's face, the spreading bloodstain on his breast made it evident that here was one
soul whom the gods had already welcomed home. I felt a huge
lump rising in my throat.

"Alas, poor Zimrit," I said softly to myself. "When shall
we see your like again? How many kings of men could touch
you for kindness, justice, and wearing sandals to bed? . . .
Sandals to bed?!"

"Please don't whinny like that, Megan," said King Zimrit from his couch. "I drank too much at my birthday dinner and now I've got a headache."

Twilla stuck her head out on Zimrit's side, her glossy black hair a mass of tousles, her rosy face all smiles. "Good morning, milady. His Majesty liked my birthday present."

She thrust out the little dagger whose handle she had so carefully enameled by hand. The blade was bloody all the way up to the guard.

"Incredible girl," said Zimrit fondly, pulling her against his side. "I'm lucky she likes me. Those Guards of mine brought her in here after a regulation search, but they never found that knife. How did you manage it, dearest?"

Twilla giggled.

"She does like me, you know," Zimrit continued. "Really like *me*! At least I assume she does, judging from the way she sprang to my defense. You should've seen the look on Drey's face when Twilla came leaping over my head, naked as a bubble, howling like a demon, to knock his sword askew and stab him in the gizzard."

"The heart, my lord," said Twilla modestly. "Up under the breastbone. It's the best way."

"Yes, well, we won't quarrel about it now. As for you, Megan, would you mind answering me two questions?"

"My lord?"

"One: Why don't you cover up your tits? And two: Why shouldn't I have you and your vile-tempered friend Hyu lopped to collops and displayed on the city gates in installments? It's not nice to try killing your King on his birthday."

I jerked the pearl-sewn curtains from their silver rings and swathed myself. "That takes care of number one. As for number two . . ."

By the time I had finished speaking my piece, I had King Zimrit convinced that it was only thanks to Hyu's clever infiltration of Captain Drey's confidence that the plot against the

King's life had been discovered and subverted. Hyu did me a favor by clamming up and keeping his eyes on his toes.

"I owe you thanks, Master Hyu," said Zimrit. Then he gazed with adoration at Twilla. "But Megan . . . I owe you more."

CHAPTER XII
Bawd Rate

We left Stanesinn two months later. We were both declared free of our palace posts the day after the King's birthday, during the sacrifice of thanksgiving at Sarogran's shrine, but the rest of the first month was necessary for settling certain grave, official matters and tidying up the paperwork still on my desk while the leftover concubines fought each other for the vacated title of Harem Head.

Twilla, kept constantly in the King's company, was above the power-squabbles. "You can't be my handmaid anymore, but you'd make a good Harem Head, dear," I said. "At least you know how to read and write. I could put in a good word for you...."

Twilla just shook her head and wore a secret smile. By the time the next month rolled around, we all knew the secret, as confirmed by the King's Thaumaturges, Astrologers, and Council of Wizards whose combined divinations, visions, and second-sight admitted no denials.

"Knocked her up straight off," was the verdict. "It's going to be a boy."

So that took care of any plans we'd had for leaving before Zimrit's marriage and Twilla's coronation. It also gave King Zimrit time to assemble a suitable going-away gift for Hyu and me. Two luxuriously comfortable progress-carts for passengers and three homely freight-carts bearing a rich variety of treasures waited for us at the palace gates when the day of departure finally arrived.

There were many tearful farewells to be said. Cybelle clung to me, saying she didn't know how I'd fare without her wise advice, she was sure. I promised to return and see her baby when it arrived, and judging from the way I saw Nara and Minar gazing at each other, frequent excuses for trips back to Stanesinn would be the norm at our house.

At Sarogran's temple I gave Barti a word of admonition. "All this claptrap about the Holy Twins having to stay here during the growing seasons is Aliska Mothtongue's doing. You make sure *she's* the one who has to keep an eye on them all day. Maybe by next year she'll be the first to announce that the god in his mercy has changed his mind and they can come live with me year-round."

"Pair of conscienceless brats, aren't they?" Barti smirked as Fair and Chosen raced their storm-gray stallions around and around the shrine, churning my former garden to mud. "Still, they've got charm; for demigods. Someone ought to swack their sacred seats for them just once, before they get too big for it. Whoops, here they come again, and *there* goes the kohlrabi crop; Aliska's favorite."

"I always knew she was a pervert."

The Twins reined in their steeds and hit the ground running. They flung themselves into my arms like ordinary children, except that lately an aroma of ozone hung around Fair, and Chosen had discovered he could get anything he wanted so long as he sang his request.

Now he cleared his throat and warbled:

"Oh Mother dear, don't go away.

"We'd be so happy if you'd stay!"

I squeezed him to my chest before I got the second chorus. "You'd be bored in the mountains, love. And you will be coming back with me after harvest. Besides, you and your sister are growing up. You'll have a mythos of your very own soon."

"I'm not sharing my mythos with *him*!" stormed Fair, and a weak jag of leven-light fizzed briefly from her nose.

"Very good, dear. You practice. And—would you mind finding a more aesthetic outlet for your power than the *nose*? Not that it isn't a pretty nose." I kissed it and got shocked.

"Awww, *Ma*ma. . . ." the Twins moaned. It was one of the few things they did together willingly.

I pulled my skirts straight as I sat down beside Hyu in our cart. "I've said good-bye to the Holy Twins. Is there anyone you want to see before we go?"

Hyu said nothing. I didn't trouble myself over that, for in the two months since that fateful night, his conversation had been limited to monosyllables. His responses during our marriage ceremony were the longest string of words I'd gotten out of him.

He's still in shock over how close he came to death, I told myself. *That'd be enough to turn a magpie mute for half a year! He'll get over it soon. Besides, Hyu's not the sort of nattering ninny who jabbers his life away. When he's got something worth saying, he'll say it.*

I was right. We were on the last leg of our journey when he decided to speak.

"I'm going back," said Hyu. For the fifteenth time that day he tried to have the driver stop the regal progress-cart and let him off. For the fifteenth time I hauled him back by his sleeve.

"Is *that* all you can say? What's the matter with you? What's left for you back in Stanesinn? Were you so enamored of the Scriptorium? Would you rather spend your life with a parchment scroll or me?"

Hyu groaned and flung his arms over his eyes, burrowing backwards into the velvet pillows. That was all I could get out of him until the sixteenth time he tried to stop the cart and get down. This time I let him.

"Where are you going, Father?" Nara called from her perch beside the driver of the cart following ours. Hyu put his head down and trudged on, not replying.

"Your daughter asked you a question, Hyu," I said. I wasn't pleased. Hyu's taciturn behavior I could bear, but he'd also chosen to ignore Nara's existence too thoroughly for my liking. Now he even ignored the fact that I'd mentioned he had a daughter. No, I was not pleased, and I yanked the collar of his robe back sharply to show him so.

"What are you doing following me, Megan?" he asked when he got his voice back. "I'm heading for Stanesinn."

"I like to follow you, remember? I followed you to Routreal and got the student-mage good-bye for my troubles. I followed you to the Scriptorium to *try* to make you see reason and got a snootful of drowse-dust for my pains. I followed you into King Zimrit's bedchamber to save your skin and I've *still* got horsehair burns on my bum for my reward. I'm just like a damned sheep's tail, jumping when you jump and always there. Did you ever wonder about that, Hyu? Did you ever stop to think that maybe I'd get tired of tagging after you someday?"

We were standing on the shoulder of the road, the narrow track that would soon bring us back to our home village. Before much longer we would be seeing the fine house King Zimrit had ordered constructed for our use, close enough to the village for company, far enough away for Hyu's desired solitude.

"If that's the case, you couldn't do better than to tire of me now. What use am I, only half a—"

"Hyu. . . ." I put a warning note into my voice and indicated the eager ears of the five cart-drivers in our train, to say nothing of Nara and her four attendants. There were some things I didn't want the child learning about her father's sorry state, although with a child's flexible nature she had accepted Hyu's outward ancientness without a qualm.

Age was one thing, manhood another. By unspoken mutual consent we ambled into the piny grove that flanked the mountain road to speak privily.

In the sweet shadows Hyu said, "It's true, Megan, I'm no use to you. Why did you press Zimrit to host us a marriage ceremony that was a mockery? I can't work magic as I am. I can't be a proper husband to you. I can't even tend sheep all crippled and aged like this. Why would you have me? You'd be wise to let me go."

I held his dear face between my hands. "You're the wise one, with a Routreal education. Don't you know? I loved you before you even dreamed of working wizardry. You hold all the magic I'll ever need just as you are. The day comes when all of us—men and women too—will be old and often good for nothing more in bed than a feeble hug and a toothless kiss. If that day's come a little ahead of its time for us, it changes nothing. I love you. Young or old, bent or straight, a storm between the sheets or only a calm, I love you." I kissed him. "We're together, Hyu. We have our own true home at last, and our dear daughter, Nara, and they're both waiting for us. Let's go."

I thought my words had convinced him. He came along tamely until we reached our new house. As we stepped across our threshold together, I felt something snap at the nape of my neck.

"Oh no!"

Hyu moved with the swiftness of one of Sarogran's spears. He caught Urion's two last vials as they fell from the long-suffering silk cord that had finally given up the ghost. If not for him, they would have smashed to slivers on the fieldstone doorsill.

"It seems I'm still good for something after all." His mouth curved up to one side. "Shall I restring them for you?"

"If you like; but you needn't. They're . . . only souvenirs, now."

"Nevertheless, allow me." He bore them away into the small room behind the kitchen which he marked out as his study and stillroom.

"If I can't work High Wizardry anymore, I can still brew simples." He gave me one of his old smiles as he set the vials down on his worktable. "I do make a wicked drowse-dust. And if I come up with a potion to clear a drunkard's head and stomach, Mistress Shana will buy all I can make for her tavern trade. Do you think Mistress Shana's still alive, Megan?"

She was. We left the house in the care of the attendants Zimrit had wished on us and took Nara up the mountain to see where her parents had grown up. There was Mistress Shana's house, almost unchanged. Mistress Shana was likewise immutable, although she had managed to acquire a husband. And what a husband!

"*Stepda!*" I squealed when I saw him. He was tottering out of Mistress Shana's house with a tray of flagons, serving the customers.

He blinked and squinted. "Megan? But who's—?"

Just then Mistress Shana herself emerged, a sturdy lad toddling beside her. Old wrongs were forgotten, recalled, apologized for, forgiven, and the rest of the day was given over to trying to figure out what Nara was to call her Stepgranda's late-come son. We settled on "Uncle Baby" and only then I noticed that Hyu had slipped away.

He was in his study when we returned home. "I thought I'd go before your Stepda thought to ask who that old man with you was. Megan, don't ask me to go up to the village again. I couldn't suffer it."

"Hyu, you'll have to face it sometime. Folks from the village will be coming down our way to call. It's all good between Stepda and me now. He's bred up my flock well and means to turn it over to us. Mistress Shana's made a new man of him."

"Maybe I should let her try her luck with me." There was only bitterness in the jest.

I hoped that if I did not make too much of his melancholy, it might cure itself. The mountain air was so pure and clear, so full of memories, that I become convinced it could work miracles. Sometimes, too, it's easier to pretend that an unsolvable problem will vanish if you ignore it.

This is not so.

To humor Hyu, who wished to remain unrecognized, I gave out that Nara and I had brought one additional attendant with us from Stanesinn, an herbman.

"He saved my life once," I told Mistress Shana when she and Stepda came to visit a courteous five days after our arrival. I waved at the array of clay pots on Hyu's worktable, the precious manuscripts, the freshly gathered plants hanging in bunches from the rafters as they dried.

Stepda poked at something in Hyu's mortar, then sniffed the pestle's end. "Saved you? With this stuff? Smells awful." He sidled over to the small kettle bubbling over a jerry-built brick hearth, Hyu's own clever improvision for sharing the kitchen chimney. Lifting the lid, Stepda made gagging sounds over the escaping steam.

"You'd be surprised. Please leave that alone. He's off in the woods now, gathering, but he wouldn't like it if he found us trifling with his things."

I tried to herd them into the front room, but something twinkling in the sun among all those dull clay vessels caught Stepda's eye. He picked up a tiny glass flacon in either hand. "What's these, then?"

"Stepda, *please* . . ."

"Not something *wicked*?"

"Oh, for the love of—!"

"Because you're still my kin, girl, even though it's just by marriage, and I owe it to your poor dead Ma to see that you act respectable. Which don't include harboring a cast-eyed old geezer who's cooking up love-potions to slip into your wine when you're not looking, for all you know! It's a tricksy world, Megan, and you can't trust most men in it. You've got a daughter now, and *my* granddaughter she is, and I'm not going to stand for—"

"Essence of rare spices," I said, pointing to first one vial, then the other. "Concentrated distillation of flowers. Very costly. He uses them to sweeten the elixirs he brews, *none* of which are aphrodisiacs."

"Aph—?"

"Love-potions. Tickle-juice. He's presently working on a cure for baldness—almost has it perfected—but it wouldn't do if it tasted so bad that no one could swallow it."

"No." Stepda touched his own peeling pate thoughtfully. "Guess not. I think that's mighty kind of the old—the gentleman."

"Dear, now will you come along?" said Mistress Shana. She linked her arm with mine and dragged me out of Hyu's workroom, whispering, "He'll linger there so long as we pay attention to him, but if we go, he won't tarry." The lady did know her husband. He was with us in the front room in a few minutes.

"Put everything back where it belonged, love?" asked Mistress Shana.

Stepda hemmed and hawed, but before he could answer, Hyu came hobbling in. The withy basket on his arm was full of weird gleanings. His face clouded when he saw we had company, and he rushed past us to the shelter of his study.

"He's—not too sociable," I began making excuses. "A brilliant herbman, but eccentric."

"Then I hope he's brilliant enough to know what he's got in that basket of his, mixed in with the mushrooms," said Mistress Shana. To my inquiring stare she added, "Twistroot."

Children, I can almost see you blanch. Young as you are, you know the deadly power that twistroot holds. It looks like many an edible root, but a nibble can send a man to the gods. It's even said that a piece of meat roasted above a fire where a length of dried twistroot burns will absorb the poisonous vapors and kill whoever eats it.

"Oh my! I'd better tell him." I ran from the front room. "Hyu! Hyu! Be careful, my darling, by accident you've dug up—"

He had removed the kettle from the fire and was stirring it with the twistroot for a paddle. One look at his expression told me that it was no accident—that he knew what it was he held and what its touch would do to the rapidly cooling brew.

"Not very discreet, Megan. Now your Stepda and Mistress Shana will have overheard my name. A closer look at my face and they'll know some part of the truth. Feel free to tell them the rest. It won't matter soon."

"Hyu, you're not—"

He tossed the sodden root aside and lifted the small kettle to his lips. "But I am. The twistroot was only the last ingredient, to make my passage out of the world all the quicker. In this one kettle I've called on death by a dozen different names. Let's see how swiftly he answers."

He drank it down, smiled, and fell.

The empty kettle rang like a bell when it struck the floor. The clangor fetched Mistress Shana and Stepda in time to see me hunched over my poor love, clasping him close, wailing his name.

"Hyu?" Stepda repeated. He stared at the limp body in my arms. "Never'd'a guessed. City life ruins a young man." He picked up the kettle and shook it upside down. "Makes 'em selfish, too. Didn't leave a drop. And him with a fine head of hair. Now I'll never know how it tasted."

His wife gave him a look usually reserved for small boys caught with their hands where they shouldn't be.

"I was going to ask him."

Another look.

"He'd've added 'em himself anyway."

Another, with sharper brow-lines.

"It couldn't have hurt anything."

The look more severe.

"*Megan* said they were only to make it taste good."

"What were?" Mistress Shana was exasperated past the point of mere looks.

"The little bottles. I poured 'em in. He was going to anyhow. I always wanted to play as I was a wizard, and it wasn't like it'd hurt . . . any . . . thing?"

"*Hurt* anything?" shrilled his wife. "*Hurt* anything? The man is *dead!*"

"Oh," said Stepda innocently. "Is he?"

He knelt beside me and tried to comfort me. "There, sweetheart, you mustn't cry so. He wasn't hardly his old self when he died. Still, you might've told me it was our Hyu, and— Well, would you look at that? Maybe city life's not so rough on a young man after all, even if it grays him early. They say if a man dies in *that* state, it's a sign the gods loved him."

He pointed at a certain area of Hyu's anatomy.

It pointed back.

"Oh," I said.

"My," I said.

"Sweet Lady Esra and all the gods above! Look at his *face!*" cried Mistress Shana.

I admit it was hard to tear my eyes from their original target. There was no denying the hard evidence that somehow Master Gath and Master Laban's cruelest spell had been undone. Greatly undone. Now I forced myself to look where Mistress Shana directed, and I saw that their second spell was melting away as we watched. The depredations of unnatural age ebbed from Hyu's body and face until he was the same man I had taken to my bed that terrible night in Zimrit's harem.

The same man plus five years' ordinary aging, to be sure. Plus something more. Indeed, even judging matters through the impeding cover of his robes, I'd say that Hyu's manhood was back in a generously expanded edition.

And he was alive.

Hyu twisted in my arms and opened his eyes.

"Megan . . . what happened?"

I laughed and laughed, laughed until I thought they'd lock me away. My first words when I could speak again were, "Oh, Stepda, you wonderful wizard! I love you!"

"Not fair," grumped Stepda. "He's *still* got all his hair too." He twiddled Urion's empty vials between thumb and fingers, glaring at them with the air of a cheated man. "Hope they blazing well made it taste rotten."

However it tasted, the strange combination of death and growth and restoration worked. Much magic thrills on the slender borderline between life and death. Stepda's brew worked well enough for Hyu to regain all the wizardly powers he'd lost, and then some. It worked well enough for me to bear him four children besides our Nara. It worked. . . . You will have to take my word for it, it worked *very* well indeed.

Ah, wonderfully well.

A shame we haven't been able to duplicate it, but Master Urion's recipes died with him. Maybe someday . . .

As my Stepda himself said, "Megan, you've got a talent for always landing on your feet."

That is only part of it.

The rest of my tale is common gossip that you sucked in with your mothers' milk even if you were born at the other end of King Zimrit's realm. Master Hyu is a famed and feared name hereabouts, with darkling sorcerers and stone-faced King's Men making the tedious pilgrimage from Routreal and Stanesinn to our modest village just to solicit his advice. Mistress Shana's tavern does a coinsome business lodging and feeding them while they're here, and two other homes have been converted to inns besides. Our village thrives on more than sheep, thanks to Hyu.

Likewise thanks to me, as you are all witnesses. You children who now share my story have been sent to my care because King Zimrit's Tenfold Search turned you up as talented, but . . . talented how? How well I know that question! Nothing so solid as sorcery, nothing so high-sounding as war, not even the soft bonds of a minstrel's harpstrings seem to hold your futures. Yet, like me, you have all been found to hold a *certain* talent.

Children, I will teach you to use it.

I will teach you meddling and matchmaking and making love, the mending of quarrels and the joining of lives, the instruction of young brides and old wives, the right words to turn friends into lovers, lovers into husbands, husbands into lovers and friends, and all the proper ways to sweeten the simplest, best, most beautiful part of our time spent living. *Flower to flower, thigh to thigh, moan to moan, sigh to sigh,* let all of you be the thrice-blessed choristers of Liuma's Litany. The tune you choose to set beneath her words is up to you.

You will prosper because you care for others' happiness.

The gentler gods will favor you because, like them, your work will create life.

Above all, I guarantee you, you will always land on your feet.

Your talent is as mine is—and ever was—love. For magic wears a thousand masks, but love is magic of its own and wears a myriad more.

And now it is time to begin our lessons.